AF492159

The Darkest Corners

A Story Collection

Drew Montgomery

Copyright © 2021 Drew Montgomery All rights reserved

The characters and events portrayed in this book are fictitious. Any similarity to real persons, living or dead, is coincidental and not intended by the author.

No part of this book may be reproduced, or stored in a retrieval system, or transmitted in any form or by any means, electronic, mechanical, photocopying, recording, or otherwise, without express written permission of the publisher.

ISBN: 9798754552593

Cover design by: David King
www.kingsizedcreations.com
Printed in the United States of America

CONTENTS

BENEATH THE SURFACE

A while back, I came upon a picture on Reddit of an abandoned underwater conservatory. It was shaped like a dome, dirty, dingy, long abandoned, and you couldn't see through any of the glass, but the image captivated me. I imagined an eccentric millionaire and the party he throws to show off a project of his. A project, of course, that contains secrets of its own.

The story came together quickly and easily, and I hope I've done justice to the image itself. It's such a creepy sight, one that could be creepy even with a well-lit interior and a few dozen partygoers drinking and conversing with the sound of elegant music in the background. And what better place to hide a few secrets than the bottom of a lake?

Music drifted through the hallways, the thick glass walls around him echoing the sound in a way he had never heard before. It was a strange sensation, the way the string quartet's melodies filled the air around him, the sound coming in evenly each way he turned, as though the musicians were right there in the room with him.

He stood in the center, the only one present. It was a dome, the transparent bricks supported by a grid of steel and concrete. Soft light filled the room, powered by electrical wires and large bulbs that lined the base of the wall, creating a ring around the space. His attention, however, was upward, his neck craned back as he stared up through the top of the dome. The water was murky, but at least above the waning light of the sun still penetrated, exposing the floating silt and swimming fish that lurked near the surface.

"You're still here."

His eyes lowered, his neck straightening as he turned his gaze toward the source of the voice. Lila stood in the curved entrance to the hallway, the lights at the base of the dome announcing her presence, bathing her in a glow such that not a single shadow seemed to touch her. Her ash brown hair was braided in an updo, and the makeup painted upon her face mingled with the light to accentuate her features. A scarlet dress clung to her figure, the straps leaving her arms bare and the hem stopping just past the knees.

His gaze returned to the top of the dome. "Do you think this is stable?"

He felt her presence as she approached next to him, her arm wrapped through his, her head tipping upward to follow his gaze. She was close enough that he could smell her floral perfume and the lingering scent of cigarette smoke beneath. "Must you put a damper on the lovely night Gerald has prepared for us?"

"Every gallon of water weighs a bit over eight pounds," he said. "It's a lot of weight for a structure to bear."

She pressed herself closer to him, her body against his, a gesture of support, of comfort. "I am sure Gerald would not have thrown a party if it were not safe," she said. "Come, Edward, let us return. Others are asking after you, they wish to see you. Have a drink, allow yourself to enjoy the night."

"I prefer the solitude here," Edward said. "There is no forced conversation, no pleasantries for people I dislike, and the music, can you hear it? It feels like they're playing right in this room."

"I am sure there is a trick to it," Lila said. "Something with the acoustics. Gerald is always full of little surprises."

"Like this entire place." He lowered his head once more, looking down at her as she stared up at the dome. Maybe it was the light or maybe it was the reflection of the murky water, but her eyes appeared bluer when he looked into them. "Why are we here?"

"Because Clara and Gerald are our friends."

Lila was smirking, but Edward did not return the look. "I mean, why is he having this party? To show off his new underwater palace?"

"This is hardly a palace, dear," Lila said. "And you sound almost jealous."

Just the few spaces they had seen dwarfed their own house, but he did not mention that. "It just seems excessive, that's all." He paused. "And maybe a bit irresponsible."

"Well I think it's wonderful." She released his arm and spun away from him, her dress fluttering around her. "An entire building underwater. Could you imagine this in the ocean? Think of the things you'd see!"

"I can barely see here," he said. "I cannot imagine it would be any better in the ocean."

She stopped spinning and stalked back to him, taking his arm once more. "Oh, stop being such a killjoy. Come, let us return to the party. Perhaps you can occupy your mind with some conversation."

Edward allowed himself to be led from the room, back through the doorway that she had come through. They stepped into a tunnel that ran away from the room, the arched ceiling ten feet high, the structure created from the same transparent bricks and concrete frame as the domed room. The ground was tiled, their steps echoing around them, giving a beat to the string accompaniment. Outside, he saw a fish swim toward the wall, then dart away suddenly, swimming alongside the tunnel for a moment before vanishing into the murky depths.

The tunnel wrapped in a long curve, and as they walked it, he could hear the strings growing in volume, the sound of conversation appearing beneath it. The noise filled his ears, growing to a near roar with each step. The tunnel continued its bend, and then it was gone. They stood once more in a domed room, this one much larger than the last.

The light from the waning sun was more evident here, brightening the room along with an elaborate crystal chandelier and the familiar floor lights. The room was furnished, fit for company with lounge chairs and tables, various finger foods and alcoholic drinks lain out wherever space could be found. All around stood men in black suits and women in colorful dresses, conversing and eating and drinking. A cloud of smoke hung in a haze over the room, the cigars and pipes and cigarettes that burned throughout the space too much for the ventilation system. Off to the side, near another tunnel entrance, the string quartet finished their song and lowered their instruments as they bowed to polite applause.

The conversation seemed to have been subdued by the end of the song, and it was only when Edward saw heads begin to turn toward the center that he turned himself to find that their host had climbed atop a low wooden table. Gerald Teaspring was in his early thirties, a man who had inherited a fortune at a young age and had only built upon it. He still had the glow of youth, dark hair slicked back over sharp features and a sculpted face, a finely tailored suit shaped to his slender body.

More and more guests turned toward him, the remaining conversations silencing without prompting. Gerald only watched, a glass of champagne in his hand, and the rose in his cheeks said that it was not his first.

"Ladies and gentlemen," he said, his voice filling the domed room. "Thank you for joining me tonight. What you see here is the culmination of over two years of planning, designing, and engineering that has resulted in the marvel you now stand within."

Gerald held out his hands, gesturing around him as he turned slowly in place. "Look around you. This truly is a remarkable work of engineering. I wish I could take all the credit for this, but I can only lay claim to the idea. And the funding, of course."

He paused, a smirk on his face as polite laughter rang through the room. Edward looked down to Lila, but her eyes were focused on their host, an eager grin on her face.

"To make this a reality, I needed to find an architect, someone who could share in my vision, who would not scoff in derision or laugh in my face. It took a while, but I found my man. A young man, unproven amongst his peers, but one who would not back down from a challenge. Those widely considered to be the best in the field said it was impossible. But this man, he said it could be done. And here we are."

The crowd began to applaud, and Gerald raised his voice to be heard over the added noise. "Allow me to introduce the man who I now consider the greatest architect in the world. Landon Peters, everyone."

Gerald motioned toward a man who was standing near the wall, arms crossed over his wide chest. He was young, but already balding, tall and broad, sweating in the heat of the room and the suit that he had been stuffed into. He offered up a sheepish smile and a slight wave as attention turned toward him.

It did not linger long; Gerald had never been one to allow the focus to shift away from himself for too long.

"Today is a celebration. A celebration of my vision. A celebration of Landon's genius. And most importantly, the celebration of a beginning. As many of you may know, water has always been a fascination of mine, a personal obsession. Three quarters of our planet is covered in it, but we hardly know anything about what lies beneath the ocean waves, or even the deeper lakes that dot our lands. Those who know me well know that I have studied marine biology extensively, that the mission to understand the life beneath the surface is a passion of mine. This place, this is the first step toward building similar structures in the waters of the world, where we can see, where we can study these magnificent creatures in their natural state."

The room applauded once more. A man in the front raised his glass and called for a toast to Gerald. Other voices chimed in and glasses were lifted into the air. Edward realized he was without a drink. As he looked around for one, he saw that Lila had found one herself and was raising it alongside the others. The toast was held, and everyone around him clinked their glasses and took a drink.

"Enjoy the night," Gerald said. "I promise there will be many more like this, and I hope you have you all join me. But we won't talk business tonight. Walk the grounds, take it all in. See what life is like beneath the surface."

The cue was given, and the lights outside the dome were flipped on, flooding the area beyond the walls with illumination. Clearly visible beyond the clear bricks were the flowing weeds, the darting fish, and the silt floating lazily through the water. There were expressions of awe and wonder as people made their way toward the nearest wall, gazing upon the lake floor for the first time ever.

The room descended into conversation, the chatter filling the air as people crowded around the edges to take a look. Lila moved away from him, her hand lingering on his for a brief moment before floating away, following her body as she trailed after the others. Edward found himself moving, not toward the edge, but instead through the haze of smoke, seeking out a drink, or perhaps just some fresh air.

He wandered through the room, brushing past a few stragglers making their way to the edges, circumventing the furniture. There were plenty of glasses, but not one contained a full drink, though he could have easily formed several from what people had left behind. His steps took him past the gawking partygoers and into one of the four tunnels that extended out from the dome.

Here, there were no dinner guests crowded against the wall, no one pressed up against the translucent surface to stare out at the water that threatened to crush them all. The tunnel curved around, and as he passed the curve, he looked over his shoulder, gazing through the clear bricks and murky water back toward the dome. Beyond the glass walls, he could see through the water to the shapes of the guests in the dome he had left behind, silhouettes, moving shadows against a lit backdrop and a cloud of silt.

"You seemed eager to escape the crowd."

Edward turned toward Gerald's voice, the host and visionary standing a few feet away from him. He looked older this close, or perhaps it was a trick of the light, accentuating the lines on his face and the light colored hairs that mingled within his dark mane. He took a step closer, hands clasped behind his back. "If you wished to leave, the nearest exit is in the other direction."

"I was merely walking around," Edward said. "Taking a look."

"I noticed you and Lila walking around earlier," Gerald said. "It's understandable. This place is certainly one that inspires curiosity, wonder. That's why I built it."

Edward's eyes turned back to the arching wall before him. "But is it safe?"

"Structurally?" Gerald said. "Perfectly."

"It doesn't seem like it," Edward said.

"It's an effect of the location. Your mind is thinking rationally, trying to reconcile it with everything you've ever been taught." Gerald placed a hand against the wall and motioned to Edward. "Feel it, feel the strength of this structure. The walls are solid, nearly unbreakable. There's nothing for you to worry about."

Edward did as he was beckoned, feeling the cold glass and rough concrete beneath his palm. "It's solid, you're right."

Gerald nodded, his eyes seeming to focus on his own hand where it touched the glass brick. "I know the feeling. It takes time to wrap your mind around it. Water gives life, but it also takes it. That feeling of drowning you get when you hold your breath for too long. It's something that sticks with us from the first time we wade in, that feeling of self-preservation. Being down here, beneath the surface, it goes against every instinct in your body."

Gerald lowered his hand and grabbed Edward by the shoulder, guiding him away from the wall. "Come, there's something I want to show you."

Edward allowed himself to be led down the tunnel, further away from the big dome. It curved away, the light fading into the murky water until it was only a dim glow behind them. The conversations had faded, nothing more than a whisper in the still air, drowned out by the soles of their shoes tapping against the tiled floor.

The tunnel straightened and the path widened, the walls to either side gone opaque, the lake no longer visible through the bricks. Edward saw ovular doors to either side, heavy iron ones with thick circular handles in the center. There were a dozen of them, spaced about ten feet apart.

"These are the guest chambers," Gerald said. "A bed fit for a king in each one, and a wonderful view of the lake." He motioned to his right. "On this side, it drops off, a sinkhole of some kind, we think. Soon, we're going to see if we can go deeper." He paused and cocked his ear, as though listening. In the distance, Edward thought he heard a noise, perhaps someone crying? No, he decided, not crying, but something much different. Gerald only grinned. "I think some of my guests have already found their way here. Come, we shouldn't linger."

Gerald led him further down the tunnel. Edward followed, glancing back when the walls could once more be seen through. Through the walls and water, he could see the miniature domes of the bedrooms, lit up just as the big one had been. He turned away, forcing himself to block the knowledge of them from his mind. If he let it slip that these rooms were here, then he knew Lila would not stop until he agreed to stay in one.

"Can you imagine how this will look in clear waters?" Gerald said. He stopped, turning and looking out over where the lake went deeper. As far as Edward could see, it only descended into complete darkness. It could have been bottomless for all he knew. Gerald turned back to him. "Have you ever seen clear waters, Edward? In the ocean?"

"I did not know such existed."

"You and Lila must join me on holiday in the Caribbean," Gerald said. "It's remarkable, wonderful. You can see right to the bottom, to the fish swimming below, the crabs crawling on the sand, the coral. Imagine something like this built in those waters. It would truly be a marvel."

There was silence between them as they both stared out into the abyss. Gerald was no doubt envisioning his behemoth beneath clearer waters while Edward found himself wondering how far beneath the surface now.

Any light from the sun was gone, and though there was no noticeable slope to the tunnel, the guest rooms were clearly higher than where they now stood. To the left, he could see another dome, a large one, one that was sunk even deeper.

"Why are we here?" Edward asked.

Gerald turned to him, a smirk on his lips. "On Earth? In England? What do you mean? Are you getting philosophical on me, Edward?"

Edward did not return the gaze. "I mean this place. This thing you've built. Are you just showing off to us, or is there something more to it? What's the endgame here?"

Gerald chortled. "Do you think I mean you harm? Or that I'm looking to trick you somehow?"

Edward nodded toward the dome below them. "How deep does this go?"

"To the bottom," Gerald said. "Excluding the sinkhole. The lake isn't very deep."

"But it's deep enough. Simple physics states that the pressure grows greater as you go deeper."

"And it's safe enough," Gerald said. "The dome at the bottom was the first one built and the first placed. It is the one that all the other pieces were built from and has stood almost since the beginning of this project. I can assure you, it is perfectly safe from the pressure."

"You haven't answered my question."

Gerald sighed and shook his head. "You've always been a stubborn bastard, you know that? Out of all my acquaintances, you're the one who has always been the most difficult to convince. That is why you're here."

Edward frowned. "Why? What do you mean?"

"Will you trust me long enough to see?"

Edward hesitated. The glow of the dome could be seen below. "I will, but enough with the mysteriousness. Tell me why we're here."

"Let us keep walking," Gerald said. "We're almost there."

He turned once more down the tunnel. Edward followed, the slope more noticeable here, the dome rising before them as they descended. His host spoke as they walked. "You have no doubt seen the people here tonight. They are all like you and I, rich, mostly young, people with more money than we know what to do with."

"I wouldn't say I have..."

Gerald cut him off. "It's not about how much you have, but the fact that you have it. I spent my own money on this place, Edward. It was an investment, but it was a risky investment, the kind that my father would call me an idiot for if he was still alive. I had faith that Landon could do it, but that did not mean that there was no risk. Now that it is complete, I have something to show, but I don't have the funds to do it again. Certainly not in a place where it would truly be used to its potential."

Edward stopped in place. "You need money."

Gerald stopped as well, drawing in a deep breath before turning back to him. "In so many words, yes."

"Then you can stop your pitch now," he said. "I find this whole thing to be absurd and more than a bit ill-conceived."

"I knew you would," Gerald said.

"You say that, but I don't think you understand," Edward said. "This may seem structurally sound, but it's not, not on the long term. Any engineer or architect worth his salt will tell you as much, and I think you know that."

The smirk had returned. "Truth be told, I was unsure whether you would accept the invite at all. I know you have a curious mind, but you're cautious, you always have been. Perhaps overly so at times. I knew that I would not be able to sell you on the concept alone, not like the others. You saw them, the way they behaved in there, even your own wife. They're enamored by whatever awes them, and I can assure you that awing them is a simple task. But the effect never lasts. I've observed it, the way these people will fawn over whatever new wonder is set before them, but no matter what they tell you in person, they will always wait. They wait for people like you, people who keep their emotions in check, to act, and only then will they act as well."

Gerald motioned in the direction they had come from, where the main dome shined a light in the murky distance, where the party continued without the two of them. "Up there are the richest men and women in the country. The politicians may be in control, but these are the ones who truly run things. They made their fortunes in different ways, but none of them did so by being reckless. They have to see the trust shown by someone else, because they won't make the first move. They don't trust me; they don't trust anyone who's looking to take their money. You though, they trust."

"But you're asking me to trust you," Edward said.

"No, my friend. I'm asking you to let me earn your trust."

Edward watched him for a moment, searching out any sign of dishonesty hidden in the man's face. There was none, only a smirk that had sunk into an easy, almost tired smile. "You have my attention," he said. "But I will only listen so long as I feel it is worth my time. The moment I no longer feel that, I will put a stop to it, and I expect you to heed that."

"That is fair," Gerald said. "Come, then, it is not much further."

Edward followed him, the tunnel curving further downward. The dome rose and rose until it towered above them. They reached the end of the hallway, the tunnel connected to the dome with a large steel door, not unlike the ones to the guest rooms.

"Right through here," Gerald said. He grabbed the wheel and turned it, and when he pulled, the heavy door swung open slowly, groaning loudly on its hinges.

The room was large, at least as large as the sitting room, but it was better lit, cast in a bright white light from the fixtures above. There were no luxurious couches here, no smoking chairs, no ashtrays or tables covered in hors d'oeurves and drinks. This was a lab of some kind, and the furniture reflected that, all seemingly crafted from the same stainless steel that reflected the lights, making the room even brighter. There were chairs and beds, and tables covered with beakers and flasks, some labeled and filled, although Edward could not determine with what. In the center was a hole, a portal to the depths below, so calm that it seemed to be glass instead of water.

"You're a man of science," Gerald said, stepped past him into the room. "I thought you of all people would be able to appreciate this. This here, this is the true benefit of my vision. The ocean is unknown to us, especially the deepest depths. This will bring a lab to those depths to allow for the study of the ocean and her creatures."

Edward had turned toward one of the tables, the beakers on this one empty. He ran his fingers over the surface, feeling the cold against his skin. "Everything here is state of the art," he said. "This must have cost a small fortune."

"Almost as much as it cost for the initial dome to be created and placed," Gerald said. "I wanted it to be state of the art because I wanted it to represent the vision as it should be seen." He stopped by one of the tables and flipped through the pages in an open notebook. "We've known each other for what, five years?"

"Seven," Edward said.

"Seven," Gerald said. "The years do fly. As much as we've spoken, I've found that I never knew what really drove you. I knew that you were trusted by others, that you were seen as a cautious man, probably because your father was a cautious man. I knew the person, but I never knew the business side. No one else is so private, so protective. But I knew that I had to make an impression on you if I wanted my vision to catch on."

Edward frowned. "You could have asked."

Gerald returned the expression with a sly grin. "Would you have not grown suspicious? We have been social acquaintances - dare I say, friends - for seven years. For a friend to out of the blue ask you about your investments, about why you choose them? Well, I know I would be at least a bit suspicious."

"Perhaps," Edward said. "Perhaps I would have been more surprised that you did not already know."

"I admit, I should have," Gerald said with a shrug. "But that is in the past now. It was not hard to find, not once I started looking. Grants given to the Cambridge science department, the largest ones in the fields of biochemistry, oceanography, and physics. A surprise, to be sure, certainly from an alumnus with a degree in economics and finance, but I'm sure the provost did not even bat an eye at the source of the gift."

He was focused on Edward now, his eyes seeking confirmation, so Edward gave it with a nod. "Those are my gifts, yes. Going into university, I wished to pursue a career in science, but my father would never allow it. 'A scientist can't run a company,' was how he put it."

"Indeed," Gerald said. "But what can a lowly student do when his father is footing the bill?"

Edward nodded once more and turned away from the table. "I decided that if I could not do the research myself, I would use my means to ensure that others could. Science is the future: steam engines, electricity, medicine. Our society is on the cusp of greatness."

Gerald smacked the table, a grin across his face. "Spoken like a true visionary. That is why I brought you here, you and you alone. Because here our visions align. I could not have said it better myself; we are on the cusp of greatness, and this lab, this building is part of that next step." He motioned Edward closer. "Come, have a look."

Edward approached the center of the room, where Gerald stood at the edge of the hole that led into the depths of the lake. From a distance, the dark water reflected the bright lights, giving the impression of dark glass, but as he approached, he could see beneath the surface. There was a cage of sorts, a wire frame that blocked off the area just beneath the dome from the rest of the lake. He knelt down, watching as small creatures darted around. Tiny creatures sucking in freshwater and using it to propel themselves around the enclosed area, creatures that looked almost like...but that couldn't be.

"What are these?" he asked. "They look like squid."

"They are," Gerald said. "We found them in the depths of the lake. A species that's never before been identified."

Edward watched the creatures, hypnotized by their darting movements. "There are no known cephalopods that live in freshwater."

"Science is only right until proven wrong," Gerald said. "Imagine what else we can find in the depths of the world's bodies of water."

"Incredible." Edward leaned closer to the water, touching his fingers to the smooth surface. The creatures scattered at first, then a few made their way back, slowly creeping up to investigate.

"I wouldn't do that," Gerald said. "One of my assistants did the same early on and they bit his hand something fierce."

Edward quickly withdrew his hand, the tiny creatures reaching the spot and lingering for a moment before returning to their aimless wandering of the caged area. It was mesmerizing, watching them swim around, like being at an aquarium without the inconvenience of a glass barrier.

"Just imagine," Gerald said. "More and more like this. There is so much more to find, so much more to explore, to discover."

Edward watched for a moment more, then stood. He turned toward Gerald. "This is remarkable. Truly, it is. You've accomplished something special here."

Gerald nodded. "Thank you. I knew you would see it that way."

"Truly special," Edward said once more. "But I'm afraid I cannot lend my support to this venture."

Gerald's face darkened, the smile fading as his lips twisted into a frown. "Why not?"

Edward glanced around at the domed lab, the darkness of the lake turning the transparent bricks a deep black. "How long has this place been complete? A month? Two? How long will it last? I can't commit to something unless I'm assured it is safe."

Gerald's voice rose as he spoke. "It is perfectly safe. I can tell you that with absolute certainty."

"Few things have absolute certainty," Edward said, keeping his own voice calm. "A building in a hostile environment is above all uncertain."

Gerald cleared his throat and adjusted his jacket. "I am sorry to hear you say that."

"As remarkable as all of this is, I think it's time we returned to the party," Edward said, finally breaking himself away from the pool in the center of the room. "I must see if Lila is ready to retire for the night."

Gerald didn't seem to hear him. "Very disappointing," he mumbled, snapping his fingers.

Edward had no realization that other people had entered the room. He turned around and saw that there were two burly looking men in suits standing at the door. One of them closed the door, spinning the wheel to lock it in place. They stood there, hands clasped before them, flanking the door to either side.

Edward stood frozen in place. "Gerald, what's going on here?"

Gerald was kneeling beside the water a pair of tongs in his hand. He dipped them into the water and removed them. At the end, held tightly by the tongs, was a single, squirming squid. It seemed even smaller out of the water, less than half an inch in diameter, no more than a few inches long. Gerald held it up before his eyes, watching it.

"These creatures are very unique," he said. "We found them after we build this lab, and we're still learning so much about them." His eyes moved from the creature and focused on Edward. "I want to share with you what we know."

Edward suddenly found himself seized from behind. He had not even heard the servants approach, and now he found himself in their grasp, holding him firmly in place, even as he struggled. "What is the meaning of this?"

His question was ignored, the large men pulling him back and shoving him down roughly onto one of the beds. Their movements were more than strong; they were quick, the practiced movements of those who had done this before. When they stepped back from the bed, he was bound, held firmly in place by leather straps around his wrists, ankles, and torso. He fought, strained, pulled with all his strength, but they did not budge.

"Gerald? What are you doing? Release me this instant!"

Gerald was the one speaking calmly now. "I considered allowing you to find out yourself. The way you were touching the water, they would have found you. But I can tell you from observation that the process there takes longer and is much more painful. We found that assisting makes it easier on everyone."

"Process? Assisting? Gerald, what the hell are you talking about?" Edward continued to tug at his bindings even as he spoke, glancing around the lab for something, anything that could help. He found nothing.

Gerald approached the bed. "It was intriguing, really. They have this strange attraction to humans. It was confusing at first, watching the way they tracked anything that touched the water. It was by accident, really, that we found out what it was, one of my helpers who got a bit too close to one. What's more interesting, however, is the effect it had once it attached to him."

The wriggling creature was closer, and from the corner of his eye, Edward could see its wriggling tentacles stretching out, feeling the air, grasping for him. He squirmed in place, but the straps only seemed to tighten around him, holding him more firmly in place.

"So much depends on you, Edward," Gerald said. "You're important. I told you as much. We talked about caution too, how you don't stay rich for long if you are loose with your money. Well, there's another rule I tend to live by. It's the rule of making sure that you don't allow your fate to be guided by anyone's hands but your own. Leave nothing to chance, don't depend on the risk averse. You have to seize control of your own destiny."

Edward felt the cold slimy touch as the tentacles found the skin of his cheek, sending goosebumps across his flesh all the way down the back of his neck. He could feel it probing at him, searching blindly across the skin of his face. He closed his eyes and gritted his teeth as it crawled over him.

"Don't worry," Gerald said. "I'm told it only feels a bit uncomfortable at first. And you can take solace in the fact that you won't be alone. There are many cautious men here, and cautious men always require just a bit more persuading."

The squid had reached his ear. He moved his head as much as he could, jerking it to the side as he felt the slimy tentacles prod into his earhole, feeling its way in. The creature hardly budged, its grip tight, unrelenting.

"No, no, no," he repeated over and over through gritted teeth, but his words fell on deaf ears. He could feel the creature moving deeper, could feel a burning sensation as it pushed its way into his head.

Gerald's voice seemed different, distant. "Relax, my friend. It'll all be over soon."

Lila checked the clock once again, and once more scanned the room. She hadn't seen Edward wander off, but she knew he wouldn't have left without her. Even with his aversion to the underwater buildings, he wouldn't have just gone, certainly not without at least letting her know.

A few people were glancing in her direction, the woman who had ceased socializing and was searching for her husband. It was hard to be inconspicuous in a setting like this, where just about everyone knew everyone else, knew everyone else's business. Being alone in a place like this made one stick out like a sore thumb, the kind of thing that would get people talking.

She could feel herself flush in the cheeks and quickly removed a pocket mirror from her purse, pretending to check her hair. A thousand thoughts ran through her mind. Had he wandered off and gotten lost? Maybe gone off with a friend? Or with another woman?

She shook her head as the last thought entered in. The looks were making her needlessly paranoid. It was more likely he wanted to get away from the smoke of the main room. He detested the practice, enough that she had stopped smoking herself when their courtship had started. In an enclosed space like this, even she was beginning to get a little lightheaded from it.

The crowd had begun to thin somewhat. Some had drifted off to explore some more, while a few had departed for the night. When Gerald left, which no one seemed to have noticed when that occurred either, some felt that it meant the party was over and used it as an excuse to leave. Many found him to be a bit eccentric, and this setting, wondrous as it was, wasn't doing him any favors in that regard.

"There she is."

The mirror snapped closed in her hand and vanished into her purse as Lila turned toward the sound of Edward's voice. She saw him approaching, Gerald right behind him, a guiding hand on his shoulder. She felt a wave of relief pass over her; it seemed the pair had just been off enjoying a few drinks. The look on her husband's face told her that it might have been one or two too many.

"Where have you two been?" she asked.

"My apologies, dear Lila," Gerald said. "We snuck off because I wanted to show off my whisky collection. I'm afraid we may have had a few more than anticipated, but it was all in good fun, wasn't it, Edward?"

"Of course," Edward said.

Lila eyed him as he spoke, his voice seeming off, distant. She shook it off, though; Edward had always been a strange drunk.

"Thank you for bringing him back to me, Gerald." She looped her arm through Edward's. "I'll make sure he gets home safely."

"I know you will, dear," he said, adding a warm smile. Always the pleasant host.

"Give my regards to Clara," Lila said as she led Edward away. "Tell her I'll call her, and we will get together for tea soon."

"I will," he said, his voice carrying after them as they stepped into the tunnel leading to the exit.

"So, I guess you enjoyed yourself a bit?" she said.

"We did," Edward said. There was something off about his voice, she decided, now that they were in the tunnel away from the noise of the main chamber. It didn't sound like drunkenness, though, no slurring or stumbling.

"What did you speak of?"

"Business," he said, giving an absent wave of his hand. "Nothing you'd be interested in."

"Oh come now," she said, putting her hand on his chest. "Do tell. I want to know what you're involved in. And it is both of our money, after all."

"If you insist, but it's dreadfully boring."

"I insist."

She felt him sigh beneath her hand. "We talked about my investments, my grants with the university."

Lila looked up at him. "He knew about those?"

"He claimed it was easy for him to find. You know he has connections at the university. But that's beside the point. What he was really getting at is that he wants to build more of these, across the world. He showed me the lab he built here, and what he plans to do with it."

"He wanted money," she said.

"He wants investing partners."

She stopped, dropped her hand from his chest, and turned to him. "You said no, right?"

He wasn't quite looking at her, and there was a blankness behind his expression, almost a lifelessness. "I did at first, but he made some very convincing arguments."

She felt her voice rising and did her best to control it, to make sure no one heard them argue. "Edward, I thought we agreed to speak on any investments before we made them. We always said we don't want to rush into anything, not without really thinking it through."

"I know," he said, his tone remaining even. "But this opportunity was much too good to pass up. There's so much we can learn from this, so many advancements to be made. It's the same reason we created the grants."

"That's not the point," she said. "We agreed."

There was the slightest hint of a frown on his face, but it didn't last for long. "You're right," he said. "We did agree." A pause, a breath that came almost like another sigh. "Would it help if we went back and spoke with Gerald some more?"

Lila looked over her shoulder to the end of the tunnel, to the room where the spiral stairs led upward toward the surface. At that moment, it seemed strangely tempting, to leave behind the unwater structure and move on with their lives. There was something strange down there, a feeling she couldn't quite shake. She shivered and ran her hands up and down her arms. Maybe Edward had been right, the way he was acting at the beginning of the night.

"Come on," he said, motioning to her. "Let's just go chat with Gerald, he can even show you the lab. It'll only take a few moments."

She hesitated before stepping toward him, allowing him to take her by the arm, firmly, but not unkindly. He led her, their steps taking them back down the tunnel, back toward the main chamber.

"I'm sure that once you speak with him, you'll see things his way. Gerald is a very convincing man."

THE AQUARIUM

This is another story born from a picture I came across online. This picture is of an aquarium in Australia, where a great white shark was kept. The aquarium is abandoned, decrepit, and the shark is still there, floating in the water, decaying. I imagined someone stepping their way through an abandoned aquarium, maybe one where not everything came from earth, a place where some of the more resilient species may have survived.

And of course, there's always a reason that the aquarium was abandoned.

The ship was deserted.

The assumption had been there beforehand, lingering over the crew as they docked their own shuttle to it, attempts at communication met by empty silence. It was only when Chance Taber stepped through the airlock and into the chilled air, however, that the suspicion was officially confirmed. There were no sounds, barely any light, a thin layer of dust covering every surface as if the spacecraft had been empty for years.

He moved slowly, hindered by the bulky spacesuit he wore, weighed down in the artificial gravity. A high-powered helmet light cut through the darkness in whichever direction he turned his head, exposing nothing but empty walls and dust motes that floated through the air.

"How are we looking?" he asked, his voice carrying through the comm, past the airlock and back to his own ship. He couldn't see his crewmates, but he knew that everything he was looking at was being broadcasted back to them, and after a short delay, down to mission control in Houston.

The voice that responded was from Gretta Tolson, the science officer. "Readings are coming through now. Looks like basic life support is still present. I'd keep the helmet on if I were you, though, no telling what's in the air."

"How basic?"

Darren Jones was the one to answer, the ship's chief engineer. "Basic enough that you won't pass out, but you might feel a bit lightheaded."

"Lovely," Chance muttered.

"Keep your suit on, that's an order." The captain, Miles Scofield. "Your job is to see what's where, not to serve as a potential human petri dish."

"The ship looks pretty sterile," Gretta said. "Better than ours, even. I don't think much could survive on it."

"We'll make that determination when we have all the information," Miles said. "Not a moment before."

Chance tuned out the rest of the conversation, lumbering deeper into the ship. He passed a porthole, catching a glimpse of the Earth far below, moving upward in relation to the stead rotation of the ship. Past the porthole was a sign, simple, arrows pointing the way toward different parts of the ship. He stood there, considering it for a moment while on the other end, his crewmates continued their own conversation.

Finally, he spoke over them. "Well, this makes things easier."

The conversation halted. "What does?" Miles asked.

Chance made sure his helmet was facing the sign, and he could hear the murmurs on the other side. "Looks like our aliens might not be so alien after all."

The words on the sign were in English, written in clear, blocky letters. He read them to himself; *Airlock, Engineering, Lab, Command...Aquarium?* The murmurs in his earpiece grew louder, a mesh of voices on the other end drowning out any clarity until the captain's voice rose above the rest.

"Quiet!"

The voices instantly silenced. "Clearly this is a unique development," the captain said. "But let's keep the speculation to a minimum. We have a job to do, and we're all scientists here, so we're going to make sure we gather all the facts before we draw conclusions. Chance, keep going. If the signs are in English, then maybe we'll be able to find more information about where this ship came from."

"Roger that."

The hall ended in a closed hatch. It took some effort on his part, but with some straining, the wheel turned, and Chance stepped into a room bathed in a bright white light. He blinked at first, his eyes adjusting as he stepped through the hatch, the greenery slowly coming into focus. Plants grew everywhere, creeping from their contained areas to take over the walls, the ceiling, the floor, anywhere they could find purchase.

"I don't think I'd be lightheaded in here," Chance said. "This is...something."

"Wow," Darren said. "Hey Vora, why don't your plants grow like that?"

There was the sound of shuffling, followed by laughing and the captain snapping, "Cut it out."

Chance had moved to one of the plants and gently lifted it with a gloved hand. Beneath, he could see a yellow squash beginning to come in. "They certainly succeeded in something here," he said.

"Keep moving," Miles said. "Once we see what the log looks like, we can come back and admire their gardening skills."

Chance allowed the plant to drop, slow in the lightened gravity. As he moved onward, he wracked his mind around how large the plants could grow in their environment if they hadn't been constrained by the room. Even the ones he could see were larger than anything they had ever been able to grow, larger than anything he had ever seen on Earth.

"This is impressive, guys," he said as he made his way to the next hatch. As he stepped through, he felt his breath taken away.

The space was dark once again, lit only by the light of the nursery behind him and some pale lights shining to either side, their source hidden for the moment. The hallway was narrow and tall, the walls composed of a transparent material that looked like glass. Behind the walls, he could see water, filled to near the top of the space. He couldn't see how far the tanks extended, but judging by the size of the ship, it went on for some distance.

To the left, he saw a beast, the kind he had seen only in pictures. A great white shark floated near the glass, mouth agape, dark eyes staring off into space. It was most certainly dead, starting to decompose in the water, but that did little to take away from the sight of it, the rows of teeth, the blank stare, the ferocious maw of a pure eating machine.

"I guess you found the aquarium," Gretta said.

Darren let out a low whistle. "That is one big ass shark."

"It's dead," Miles said. "Keep going. Control room can't be much farther."

Chance kept his head turned toward the shark as he passed. It floated there, impossibly still, the pale light casting a ghastly glow on its corpse. He could see more signs of decomposition now that he was closer, the light of his helmet passing over spots where the tough skin had begun to be eaten away.

"What do you think happened to it?" he heard Vora ask.

"Judging by the state of the ship, someone probably stopped feeding it," Darren said.

"I think the more important question is, what the hell kind of ship has an aquarium like this?" Chance asked, lingering on the shark's gaping maw.

"No ship that we have," Gretta said.

"Quiet, everyone," Miles said. "Keep going, Chance. The only way we're getting answers is finding the log."

Chance eased his way down the hallway, his eyes still on the dead shark even as he moved past it. He was so focused on it that the movement caught him off guard, and the sound that accompanied it caused him to nearly leap right out of his suit as he turned toward it.

"Holy shit!"

His heart was pounding, his breathing heavy as he watched the creature slowly pull itself from the glass, the suckers of its tentacles sticking to the surface briefly before slipping away. A jet of water shot out from its body, propelling it away into the darkness of the tank.

"What the hell was that?" he said quietly.

The words were lost in laughter from the other end of the comm. He could hear Miles trying to quiet the crew, but Darren's contagious laughter drowned him out.

"You managed to not just scare yourself, but you got Vora too."

"Jones, get out until you get yourself under control."

Chance could still hear the laughter, the sound fading as Darren made his way from the control room. "Did you guys see that? It looked like, I dunno, some kind of octopus or something."

"It wasn't an octopus," Vora said. "It had tentacles, I saw that, but the body was different."

Chance leaned toward the wall, squinting his eyes as he tried to see through the murky darkness of the tank. He thought he saw movement, as though the darkness was shifting in different places, but it may have just been his imagination. It was as if the creatures were toying with him, intentionally granting him a brief glimpse before disappearing.

"Look there," he heard Vora say. "It has more than eight tentacles."

His eyes scanned the tank. "Look where?"

"We rewound the feed," Gretta said.

"And there," Vora said. "That's not a beak. Those are teeth. Sharp teeth."

"Whatever it is, it looks dangerous," Miles said. "Chance, keep going. And keep your distance from that tank."

Chance cast one last glance into the tank, unsure if the shapes he saw moving through the inky darkness belonged to the creature or to the depths of his imagination. "Don't need to worry about that."

The hallway continued on, the aquarium wrapping around the edge of the mammoth ship. There were more tanks beyond the first ones, many dead and decomposing, but not all. There was one filled with a cloud of creatures, perhaps plankton, that moved as one, with purpose. There was one with what looked like flowers, covering the floor and walls, their tendrils floating in the current formed by the tank's circulation. There was a bleached reef, covered in polyps with tendrils that extended out into the water, seeking out microscopic creatures for food.

As he passed by the last one, he saw a polyp that extended out close to the glass, its tendrils seeming to reach directly toward him. He paused, watching as it reached out and touched the glass, as though trying to sense him through the surface. He put his own fingers up against the wall that divided them, and the tendrils stretched toward them. A slight smile reached his face as he moved his fingers and the tendrils followed.

"Friendly," he said.

"Unlikely," Vora said. "Creatures like that are not complex enough for any kind of thinking, at least not as we know it. Probably thinks you're food."

"Still," Chance said, his fingers still on the glass, watching the tendrils reach toward him.

"Keep moving," Miles said. "You can examine the fauna once we find out what happened with this ship."

Chance lowered his hand and moved on, the tendril still reaching even as he stepped away. He knew that the captain was telling a lie, they all did. More likely, they'd set the ship to blow. When it came to foreign objects, nothing came from space into the atmosphere. Even with the suit on, he was probably due a trip to quarantine for several days and some heavy examination by NASA doctors.

The hallway curved with the ship, the walkway ahead slowly revealing itself to him with each step. Up ahead, he could see another hatch, this one lying open. Above, the ceiling was lower, and as he approached, he could see that it was part of a tank, a larger one that was connected above and below the walkway.

Within the tank, the glow was different. It was not the pale backlight that cast the eerie glow in the other tanks. This was a brighter glow, colorful, as though the entire tank was bathed in neon. As he approached, whatever was within the tank began to shift, and with it, the colors. Pinks and purples and blues and whites, mingling with each other as the tiny creatures moved through the waters behind the glass, bathing the hallway in a bright glow.

"You guys seeing this?" Chance asked.

"Yeah," Darren said.

"Wow," Gretta said.

Even Miles' voice was subdued as he urged Chance to continue on.

Chance stepped beyond the next hatch and into the control room. After years spent training and taking flights in cramped quarters, the room that spread out before him was a revelation. Even in the suit, he had space to move between the seats, examining the hardware that lined the walls. Most of it seemed tied to large screens, with some minimal buttons and dials before them. The screens were all powered off, with the exception of a single small one that displayed a series of charts and readings.

He approached the small screen, finding that the words that adorned each item were written in English as well. Oxygen. Air Quality. Filtration.

Rotation. Engines. Fuel.

"I think I found the support system," Chance said, his eyes scanning over the readings. "Definitely running on minimal power."

"See if you can get the rest of it running," Miles said.

Chance moved slowly along the panels and controls, searching for anything he could use, any kind of master switch. None of the buttons were labeled, however, and none of the other screens seemed to have any power switches.

"Any day now," Darren said.

"It would move a lot faster if I weren't in this damn suit," Chance said.

"The suit stays on," the captain said.

"There," Gretta said. "Wait, go back."

Chance turned back toward the panel he had just passed. The screen was emitting a soft glow, nearly imperceptible in the emergency lights. In the bottom corner was a small circle, a touchscreen button."

"Try that button," Gretta said.

Chance did. Nothing happened.

"Your gloves won't work with a touchscreen," Darren said.

Of course they wouldn't.

"No way," the captain said. "That's not happening."

"How are my readings?" Chance asked.

"Stable," Gretta said. "No toxins detected in the atmosphere. Oxygen around you a bit low, but probably not even low enough to make you lightheaded."

"I'm going for it."

"Absolutely not," Miles said.

Chance ignored him, reaching for the depressurization valve on the front of his suit.

"Dammit, Chance, that's an order," the captain said.

"With all due respect, sir, this one's getting overridden for the sake of the mission." Air hissed from the suit as the seal was broken. He twisted the helmet and it detached from the rest, sliding easily over his head.

He placed the helmet down and drew in a deep breath. The air was a bit thin, chilled, almost like being atop a mountain while skiing. There seemed to be nothing in the air that his own senses could detect, not that that meant anything. There could be deadly bacteria, a virus, poisonous gas, any one of a thousand things. But if any of those were the case, it was likely too late already.

"Seems fine," he said as he removed the gloves and set them down on the console. He wriggled his fingers, relishing in the freedom from the heavy gloves. "My eyeballs aren't exploding out of my head."

"Yet," Darren said.

"At least put the damn helmet somewhere we can see," Miles said.

"Copy that." Chance moved the helmet so that the camera was facing the screen, then pressed the button on the screen with a now liberated finger.

The screen came to life instantly, the small circle of the button expanding into an entire interface. He could see the panels in the background, dimmed behind the banner that was welcoming him to the U.S.S. Beyond.

"Well that's interesting," Darren said through the earpiece.

Even the captain's voice had a distant quality to it. "We have any ship with that name in the fleet, Tolson?"

"Not that I'm aware of," she said.

"Get on the comm with mission control and find out for sure."

Chance was pulled from the conversation by a voice. "Welcome back, Captain Hruska. What can I do for you?"

"Uh, what?"

The voice did not respond. The banner had vanished from the screen, revealing numerous images, each clearly labeled in English. At the top left corner was a picture, an unsmiling man with short hair and narrow cheeks, the word next to him reading Jarret Hruska, Captain. The other pictures were all related to the ship's components. Engines. Communications. Life Support. Surveillance. Logs.

"What should I do?" he asked.

"Press something," Darren said. "Like there, Labs. Let's see what they've got in those tanks.

"No," Miles said. "We need to find out about the ship. The logs should give us that."

Chance reached out to touch the screen, then stopped. He glanced around, looking at the system before him. "Show logs," he said.

The voice responded. "I have two hundred and sixty-eight logs available for review."

There was a long, low whistle in his ear, but no commentary. Somewhere in the background, he could still hear the sound of Gretta's voice as she communicated with mission control back on Earth.

"Play the oldest log."

A video popped up over the menu, and Chance found himself face to face with the same man from the image in the corner. "Captain Jarret Hruska here. The date is October 21st, 2135…"

"Did I hear that right?" Vora asked. Someone shushed her.

"I'm standing her on the U.S.S. Beyond as we embark on, to date, the most important mission in the history of mankind."

"Bold of him to say so," Darren said, and he was shushed as well. "What?"

"The warp drive is untested, at least on humans. We know that, and we know that it could mean that none of us are able to come home. But that's not on anyone's mind, not on this ship. We will spend the next two weeks getting clear of Earth, and it is then that we will initiate the test."

Chance could hear more murmurings over the radio. Everything on this ship just kept getting stranger and stranger. An English-speaking ship that was supposedly from over a hundred years in the future, filled with alien creatures. He wasn't sure what else there was to uncover, but the general uneasiness he felt at being aboard was beginning to grow.

"The ship is outfitted with tanks for study of animals, particularly sea creatures, in a low gravity environment. In addition, some of the tanks are sectioned off and left empty for any we encounter…"

Miles' voice came over the comm, drowning out the audio from the log. "Chance, find another one. I want to see how the ship got here."

"Roger." He tapped the screen to back out of the log video and scrolled down through the rest of the entries. The dates were scattered across several weeks after the first, followed by a long break. He tapped the one right after the break and watched as the video popped up and began to play.

Captain Hruska appeared once more on the screen. The shadow of a beard clung to his face, his hair a bit longer, but there was a brightness to his eyes, an almost childlike excitement.

"Well, I suppose you can tell by the fact that I'm standing here, but it was successful. The warp was successful. We arrived at our desired destination with a point oh oh oh one percent error. Medical checks have been run over the past two days, and all aboard have been given clean bills of health. Most importantly…well, let me show you."

Hruska reached forward and the camera moved. Chance watched as it passed through the bridge, catching a brief sight of a couple of the crew members before it finally settled in a spot gazing out the nearest viewport.

Chance felt his own breath leave him. From the comm, he heard Gretta say, "Is that…", followed by a "Yeah" from Darren.

There on the screen, through the viewport, was a planet, a planet with the blues of oceans and lakes, and the greens of foliage. A planet that was most definitely not Earth.

Captain Hruska spoke from off camera. There was an excitement, almost giddiness to it. "We're the first humans to lay eyes on a planet outside our solar system. This is history."

"Damn right," Miles muttered.

The camera shook as it turned back on the captain. "We're preparing our exploration plan. I expect the probe to be launched within the next day or two. We'll see what this planet holds for us."

The video shut off, and there was silence. Finally, Darren said, "Well, don't keep us in suspense."

"Yeah," Vora said. "I want to see what they found."

Chance resisted the urge to continue without orders, to satisfy his own curiosity. "Captain?"

"Keep skipping ahead," Miles said. "We need to see what happened to the ship."

Chance did as he was told, scrolling down the list and selecting one several weeks later. The video popped up, but this time, it wasn't on the bridge. It was dark, and it took Chance a moment to realize that the captain was walking through the aquarium.

"With the probe returned from 18 Scorpii, our collection is now complete." The captain's voice came from behind the camera. He walked slowly, panning the camera between the tanks to either side. "It took a lot of work, particularly on the part of Preston finding the right water conditions for each creature. I know he already has several books worth of notes on his findings."

The camera turned to one of the tanks, and Chance saw the tentacled creatures that had been obscured by the darkness. Here, there were fewer, though they still kept to the rear of the tank. "This is our latest addition, from the planet we took to calling Nix because of the size of the ocean. And these guys…" He paused. "Hey Preston, get over here."

There were approaching footsteps, then the sound of a voice. "Yeah, Captain?"

"Look here," Captain Hruska said, and his finger appeared from off screen, pointing to the glass. "There were two before, weren't there?"

A head entered the frame, a thin man with shaggy hair and wire-rimmed glasses, squinting through the water. "I only see two." He trailed off, tilting his head to the side. "Wait, you're right. There's another one, right there."

"Well I'll be damned," Captain Hruska said. "Didn't think we'd get any reproduction. At least not that quickly."

Preston's head disappeared from view, and his steps could already be heard trailing off down the hallway. "I need to check the feeds. We should have caught it on camera."

"I hope we did," Hruska said. The camera turned, now a closeup of the captain's face. "And there you have it. Science in action. Big discoveries lie ahead, and we're making them right here on the *Beyond*."

The video cut out. Chance scrolled a little further down and selected another video. This one was not on the bridge either, but in a small room, a bedroom as told by the small bunk and lockers that surrounded it, personal pictures pinned to any free wall space available. The camera was facing the captain, and Chance could see that he was not the same. He seemed exhausted, worn out, his hair disheveled and bags forming beneath his eyes.

"This may be the last log entry I make. I hate to be pessimistic, but the problems we've had with the warp drive just might be too much, even with Ray's know-how on the systems. We've been stuck in the 18 Scorpii system for three weeks, and frankly, may have tried to make the jump if Erin hadn't caught the leak. If that had been the case, we'd all have been…" He made a fist and opened it up, miming an explosion.

"Ray thinks he has it. I trust him, would trust my life to him, but the entire system is experimental, more than any of us understand completely. It's so complicated, and the slightest miscalculation could have the most dire effects."

He sighed. "I hope the ship makes it back, even if we don't. What we've found, what we've experienced, that can be told through the data we've recorded, through the creatures we've found. Hell, the one from Nix continues to reproduce. It's incredible what we've discovered, life beyond our wildest imaginations. If the drive malfunctions…"

He shook his head. "No, I'm not going to talk like that. We're going to make it home, and we're going to be able to show our discoveries to those back home. It's happening."

The video blinked out. There was only silence, both in the ship and over the comms. Finally, Darren spoke. "I'm guessing that the entries after that mean they survived the jump."

"That, and the fact that Chance is standing on the ship, you doofus," Gretta said.

"Chance, play another," the captain said. His voice seemed strained. They all did. Chance realized that his breathing had grown heavier, his heart thumping beneath the suit. He wiped a bit of sweat from his forehead and selected the next one.

The captain was there, back in his quarters, but he didn't look much better than before. "As you can see, the jump was a success…kind of. It was a success in that we're still alive, and I think we're in the Sol system, but something went wrong."

"There was a malfunction when we went to warp. I'm not sure I can properly describe it, but I'll do my best. During a normal jump, it feels as though you're being compressed, not unlike the gravitational surge you feel when you lift off from Earth. When we entered warp this time, though, it was…different. Like we were being stretched instead of pushed, almost to the point of being ripped apart. I talked to the others, and it wasn't just me. Everyone had the same experience, and everyone noticed how different it felt."

He sighed, looking away from the camera, rubbing at the back of his head. "There's also another problem, and this one, I haven't really mentioned to anyone other than Ray, and that's only because he's the one who noticed it. Our location tracking instruments are all malfunctioning, just like the warp drive. I mentioned we're in Sol system, but I only say that because our readings say that. By all observation, however, we're not. We're nowhere close to it."

His hand had moved to his forehead, and he looked away from the camera, off to the side. "Wherever we are, I don't know if we can get home, at least not anytime soon. I need to reevaluate and figure out what to do next."

He shook his head. "I'll figure something out."

The video blinked out. Chance didn't wait for confirmation to move on to the next one.

The captain was back on the bridge. His eyes were lighting up as he spoke, his lips almost in a smile. "We've figured out what happened, or at least we think we have. The chronometer was off, which put our heading off. We...we've somehow traveled backwards in time. Or at least, that's the prevailing theory. Ray was the one to notice, the way the stars were aligned, it just wasn't right. We don't know how it happened. Hell, by our understanding of physics, it should be impossible. But the results are right there before us, impossible to argue."

"I can't say what our exact date is, but Ray thinks he can point us toward Earth. It'll take a long time to get there, probably longer than any of us will live, but at least if we can get there, if we can share what we've found, our journey will not have been in vain."

There was a sound, and the captain's head turned. He stood, started to walk off, then paused and turned back to stop the recording.

"Only two left," Chance said.

"Play them both," Miles said.

Chance obeyed, starting the next one.

The captain was close, closer than usual, close enough that Chance could see the sweat that clung to his skin and the way his eyes stood wide open. He ran a hand through his hair, leaving it sticking up in several places.

"I'm at a loss for words," the captain said. "We lost Preston. He was checking the samples, it seems, and I guess he just slipped. He fell into the tank, the one with the creatures from Nix. They...they ripped him apart like he was nothing. We'd been feeding them plant matter. I didn't even realize the damn things had teeth."

Hruska shook his head. "It's my fault, all my fault. I should have been more careful. But Preston was a professional. He had done this dozens, hell, hundreds of times. Nothing like this had ever come close to happening, not with him. Of course, the way the camera feed is, we can't tell exactly what happened, only the aftermath. I just...I don't know."

The video blinked off, as though someone had pulled the plug on the camera. Chance stared at the last entry for a moment, unsure of what it would hold.

"Play it," Miles said.

"Let's hope it tells us what happened to the crew," Vora said quietly as Chance reached out to touch the screen.

At first, the screen was dark, complete blackness. Suddenly, the camera moved, and Chance saw a face, a woman's face lit up in the green of night vision. She was breathing heavily, staring off past the camera, watching for something. Finally, she turned back to the camera.

"This is First Officer Jennifer Stevens. As far as I can tell, I'm the only one left alive. The creatures from Nix, whatever the hell they are, they're dangerous, very dangerous. After Preston died, Captain Hruska went to flush the tank. I was with him, on the scaffold over the tank. One of them was out there, out of the water, and somehow, it *knew*. It knew what we were trying to do, that we were trying to get rid of it. It attacked before either of us could react, latched itself to his face, and I was so stunned that I couldn't move."

There was a sound from off camera, a banging like something getting knocked off a table. Her head jerked toward the noise, watching the darkness for a moment before turning back, her voice lowered. "It knows I'm here. It knows what I'm going to do. I don't have much time. If you're seeing this, if I failed, just know this. *It takes control.* It latched onto the captain's face, but it didn't kill him. Instead, it controlled him, controlled his body. It killed the others, everyone but me, and that was only because I was the fastest, I was able to get away."

A tear slid down her cheek and she quickly wiped it away. "I'm going to flush the ship, tanks, living quarters, everything. It can't be done remotely, but I think I can beat it to the bridge. If you find this, if the creatures are still aboard, do what I was unable to do. And whatever you do, don't let them reach Earth." She drew in a deep breath. "Here it goes."

The video blinked out. Chance realized that he was grasping the collar of his suit so hard that his fingers were hurting. He slowly released it, glancing around, half expecting to see one of the creatures lowering itself from the ceiling behind him. Instead, there was nothing, only the same empty bridge that had been there before. He let loose the breath he hadn't even realized he had been holding, then picked up his helmet and put it back on. Just to be sure.

"That was crazy, wasn't it?" he said aloud. There was no response. He didn't blame them; it was a lot to take in. He reached over to the screen and backed out of the log screen. There was a master control icon, which brought up a diagram of the ship when he touched it.

Everything was neatly labeled, the diagram shifting and turning with a swipe of his fingers. He located the tanks, then found the one labeled *Nix*. A touch, and a menu popped up, a small video display appearing in the corner to provide a live feed of the tank. Even with the camera offering a direct view, the creatures seemed to dance just out of view, almost like they were part of a completely different plane of existence.

"I'm going to finish what she started," he said. He pressed the dump button, and the result was instant. The contents of the tank flushed from the ship, expelling out into space. The camera switch, and he got a brief view of the water and creatures drifting from the ship into space, floating away in the vast, cold vacuum.

"And that's that," he said. "Global crisis averted. Let's get this thing hitched and tow it to the space station."

There was no response. Chance waited, listening, but there was no sound, not even movement around the cabin or whispered chatter.

"Hello?" He tapped the side of his helmet. "Guys? Captain? Darren? Gretta? Anyone?"

The silence was overwhelming, complete. His hands went to the screen, toggling through exterior camera views until he found the one that pointed to the airlock. There seemed to be nothing different, the ship still attached, the green lights around the airlock seal indicating a stable connection. In the cockpit, he could see movement, but even with the clarity of the video feed, he could not make out what was happening.

"Hello?" he said again. "Wonder if my comm went out."

He backed away from the console; comm malfunction or not, it was time for him to return to the ship. He made his way from the bridge, passing the tanks. There was the reef and the plankton, the decaying shark, and of course, the tank that the deadly creatures had once occupied, now empty. He paused before it, taking in the space that now lacked water or life, and he felt a twinge of satisfaction, the knowledge within that he had prevented something terrible.

As he entered the greenhouse, a sound began to play over his comm, distant voices fading in and out amongst a wall of static. He put a hand to his helmet, hailing the ship, then instantly recoiled as a scream ripped through the speaker into his ear, followed by absolute silence, only pierced by the fading ringing.

Chance took off, moving as quickly as he could in the bulky suit. He squeezed his way through the hatch and bounded down the hall to the airlock door. The closed airlock door.

The image on the screen flashed through his mind, the green lights outside of the airlock, the connection that had been made. The connection that meant that people could go between the airlock and the attached ship.

Chance began to pull on the handle, then smashed at the buttons. An automated voice sounded in the hall around him, informing him that the airlock had been locked against entry, that the attached ship was preparing for detachment.

"No!" he yelled. "No!"

He shuffled to the large viewport, the one that gave a clear view of the front of the shuttle, of the windows that looked out from the cockpit. Inside, he could see the movement, the captain, the crew, the creatures that attached to their faces, controlling them.

He banged on the viewport, screamed behind his helmet. The shuttle detached with a spray of air, the lights on the airlock turned a deep red. He banged and banged and screamed, but none of the sound reached the shuttle. The boosters fired, and it moved away from the derelict ship.

He continued banging until his fists were numb, continued screaming until his voice was hoarse, felt but it did him little good, the sound lost in the emptiness of space. In the end, all he could do was watch as the shuttle entered the atmosphere of the planet below.

PER ASPERA AD ASTRA

There are a few stories that play out in similar ways in this collection, and this is one of them. I considered picking and choosing, perhaps only having one of them, but in the end, decided that they were unique enough in their own ways to include. You'll see as you read through them; while the theme is ultimately the same, the approach varies, and I feel really sets them apart individually.

This is one of them, and is the earliest one I wrote, several years ago. This particular one was born from two things. First was the motto that NASA took on long ago, which this story has taken as its title, a Latin phrase that translates to "From hardship, to the stars." The second part was an image I saw a long time ago, a picture taken by Voyager 1 on its flyby of Jupiter (https://apod.nasa.gov/apod/ap160904.html). In the image, you see Io, one of Jupiter's moons that compares in size to our own, transposed across the colorful surface of our solar system's largest planet. What really amazed me, however, was the way that Jupiter filled the screen, that you really get a sense of scale, of just how incredibly large the planet is. It was from that picture that I decided to write this story.

Like with other stories, the theme is the question of what lurks in space, in particular within our own solar system. Here we find a journey to Europa that seems destined to fulfill that very motto.

The size of the planet never ceased to amaze him, the colorful bands formed in the mostly hydrogen atmosphere reflecting the light from the distant sun. At this distance, it completely filled the wide viewport, and even so, nearly half was completely hidden from his view. As though to further emphasize the fact, the moon Io passed by on her short orbit, a satellite comparable in size to Earth's own moon, yet completely dwarfed by the gas giant.

Jupiter, king of the gods, Clive Aston thought. A fitting name for the king of planets.

For all intents and purposes, the first voyage beyond the asteroid belt to the Jovian planets was a success. *Venture*, the, experimental ship that had been built in orbit around Earth in a joint undertaking between the United States, Russia, and the European Union, had performed admirably during the twelve-month journey. With the exception of some minor engine problems that were massive quickly solved by the two engineers in the crew, and a temporary issue with the rotation that generated the artificial gravity, the trip had gone better than anyone ever could have anticipated. Even the expected difficulties of putting people together for such a long period of time were curtailed by the size of the ship and the numerous activities set up to alleviate boredom.

Now the Venture rested above the icy surface of Europa, smallest of the Galilean moons, where a mobile station had been set up. The intent of the trip was to drill through the ice and insert probes into the ocean that rested beneath. Half of the sixteen-person crew was currently down on the surface of the moon, tending to the drill. As of the last status report yesterday, the drill was estimated to be only a half-mile from breaking through the ice in what could be the most important scientific venture ever devised, the possibility of finding life beyond Earth.

Per aspera ad astra. Through hardships to the stars. The motto of NASA, yet a phrase that had not been the case on this expedition.

That was, however, until a few hours ago. The crew on the moon was scheduled to make a status check every four hours. The last one was supposed to have arrived two hours ago, but no message had come through on the comms. Attempts to contact them since had only returned silence.

He stood there now, wracking his mind over the next steps, staring at the swirling patterns of the planet, the hypnotic clouds aiding in his thinking. There was another shuttle that could be sent down, but their staff as is would barely be enough to manage the ship for the return to Earth. If something happened to whomever he sent down, the *Venture* may be stuck in orbit without the means to leave the system until their food ran out, even with the help of the artificial intelligence. On the other hand, there was a very real possibility that they were in some sort of danger and any delay in sending a shuttle would be a death sentence to those below.

Or perhaps they are already dead, he thought, then quickly shook his head, trying to rid the idea from his mind. No, he told himself, it is just some faulty equipment, just a slight malfunction. Yet the thought remained, hiding in the back of his mind like an itch he couldn't scratch.

Clive reluctantly turned away from the sight of the planet, tearing his eyes away. He made his way over to a panel on the wall and pressed a button.

"Laura, you there?" he said through the speaker.

The voice came back, young, yet lacking the normal energy the communications engineer typically displayed. "Yes, Captain?"

"Has there been any word?"

"I'm afraid not, sir," Laura said. "Should I have the shuttle readied?"

"No," he said, the word coming out a little quicker than he intended. "Keep trying. I'm coming up there."

He backed away from the intercom and made his way out of the view deck and into the narrow hallway, moving toward the comm room. His steps moved lightly but deftly, long used to the strange bouncy feeling brought on by the artificial gravity, slightly less than that back home.

There was a ding, and a voice came over the intercom in the hallway, the mechanized voice of Rain, the ship's artificial intelligence. "Captain, you are receiving a transmission from Earth."

"From whom?" he asked without breaking stride.

"Commander Lawson."

"Tell him I'll send back when I get a chance. Have your scans picked up anything?"

"I'm afraid not." Her voice was so calm, without feeling, without emotion. "I have not been able to connect with the life support systems since they went dark."

"Of course not," he said in the midst of a sigh.

"You are not preparing the shuttle," Rain said. "May I ask why?"

"I cannot authorize anything that would put our crew in danger and jeopardize our ability to make a safe return trip."

"I remind you, Captain, that I am capable of running most of the ship's operations with two crew members or less."

"Duly noted," Clive said.

He reached the end of the hallway and the door slid open, granting him access to the comm room. The walls were covered in screens, some with readout displays, different information about the ship and her occupants while others displayed outputs from cameras, covering areas both inside and outside the ship. Laura sat at a console, her slender frame wrapped in a blue jumpsuit. Beside her, a hologram representation of Rain formed, a blue, feminine shape that always made Clive feel a bit uncomfortable, perhaps because it was just a bit too realistic, a bit too human.

"Rain informed me that the scans have been unresponsive," Clive said.

Laura was at the console, running her hands over one of the screens, the digital display shifting with her touch as she responded. "Infrared and X-ray scans have both come back negative. We're sending pings on the channel every five minutes."

"Would you like to view the message from Commander Lawson?" Rain asked.

"Yes, put it through."

The largest screen, which had been trained on the temporary building and shuttle on the moon's surface flickered out and was replaced with the sight of an elderly, uniformed man, his face marred by wrinkles and his hair gone completely white.

"Captain Aston, we received your message about an hour ago and I have spent the time trying to determine what actions to take. The conclusion we reached was this: the mission must be completed at any cost, and that includes the lives of the crewmen down on Europa's surface. I know it may seem harsh, and it pains me to say it, but a failure on this mission will not only mar the face of NASA but will set all we have sought to accomplish back years. Do what you need to make sure that does not happen. My superiors expect to hear back with results in the next twenty-four hours."

The screen blinked out and Clive could only stare in disbelief. *How could they do this? I was tasked with seeing the mission through and protecting my crew.*

"Sir?" The word from Laura's mouth was forceful; she must have tried to get his attention before.

Clive snapped away from his thoughts. "Yes? Sorry. Prepare the shuttle. I'm going down."

A press of the button and the face of a young man appeared on the screen. "Sergeant Ryan, prepare the shuttle, the captain will be going down to the surface."

"Yes ma'am," the sergeant said, and his image was gone from the screen.

Clive turned to leave when Rain's voice stopped him. "Captain, I am picking up readings from the camp."

His heart leapt. *They're alive?* "What is it?" he asked.

"The lift in the drill used to transport the probe has been activated."

"So it was just a comm issue?" Relief flooded through him. It seemed disaster had been averted.

"Not quite, Captain. The lift is coming up."

"Up?"

"Yes, Captain. It seems the lift was already down at the bottom and is now returning."

Clive shook his head. "That's impossible. We would have known if the lift was sent down already." *Wouldn't we?*

"It seems that whatever caused our radio silence also affected our reading of the instruments. I am now reading that the probe was successfully deployed."

"Are you picking up anything else?" he asked, reaching over Laura's shoulder and hitting a few keys to bring up the display of the surface of the moon.

"No, Captain," came the response from the AI.

"Wait," Laura said. "I'm picking up a transmission."

"Why didn't you notice it before?"

"It appears to have been sent on a different channel," she said.

"Why would they use a different channel?" Clive asked.

No one answered, but he was not expecting them to. Clive instantly recognized the face of Frank Peterson, the lead scientist on the surface crew. He looked different, however, his hair disheveled, dark bags under his eyes, a cut on his face dripping blood down his cheek. He was speaking, but all Clive could hear was static.

"What's going on? Where's the audio?"

"I'm not sure," Laura said. "Hold on, looks like it's clearing up."

"...broke through the ice and into the sea. We successfully deployed the probe and immediately began to prepare for our check-in to deliver the good news. That was when the probe began to pick something up, something big. We were bringing up the readings when we lost contact with it." Frank adjusted the screen and began talking again.

"It was when we were trying to restore power that the lift started moving on its own. We were not sure how it was doing that without any power, but we let it go, not sure what to expect. We should have shut it off."

He ran a hand through his hair and glanced over his shoulder to the lift. He turned back, his eyes wide, words tumbling out fast. "There are more coming, I don't have long. Something emerged from there, something horrible. Everyone else is dead. I...I somehow managed to throw it out of the station, into the cold, but not before it sent the lift back down. I hope this transmission gets to you—I...I don't know what else to do. I have no idea if it's the right frequency or whatever, but you need to know that there is something down here, something intelligent, something dangerous. I don't know if it can figure out how to work the shuttle but take no chances. Leave us, it is too late to save me."

Behind him, there was a sliding sound as the door to the lift opened. Frank's eyes widened and he began to shake. "They're here," he muttered, and the screen went blank.

Clive stared in horror, the silence in the comm room overpowering. Slowly the realization began to creep over him, the fact that humankind was not alone in the solar system. And they were not friendly.

"Captain, I'm picking something up from the surface," Rain said. "The shuttle has lifted off."

"Do not allow it access," he said. "Make contact."

"Communications are being blocked," Laura said. "Let me see if I can bypass."

"Rain, do not allow that ship access."

"Shuttle is approaching," Laura said. "It has passed through the atmosphere."

"Rain, block access." His voice was beginning to rise.

"I am unable to do that, Captain." The computerized voice cut through the silence, sending a fresh chill down his spine.

Clive swallowed. "Unacceptable, block access."

"Estimated distance 500 meters."

"Rain, block it!"

"I am sorry, Captain," the computer said, its even tone sounding almost regretful. "The mission's success comes before the safety of the crew."

"What? What are you talking about?"

"My programming does not allow me to do anything to jeopardize the potential success of this mission. If it is required that the crew perish, then so be it."

"You cannot do that!" Clive was yelling now. "I am the captain. You are supposed to obey me!"

"The shuttle has landed in the bay." Laura's words seemed to echo through the room, silencing all others.

Clive stopped yelling at the computer and focused his eyes on the screen. "Laura, give me a video feed of the landing bay."

The view appeared on the screen, and they watched silently as Sergeant Ryan approached the craft slowly. "Captain, you hear me?" he asked.

"I can," Clive said.

"We have a shuttle here, not getting any readings from onboard."

"Ryan, listen to me, get out of there," Clive said.

"There might be someone on board, they might be injured."

"Sergeant, that is a direct order."

"The door's opening, someone's coming out." The view was blocked, but the sergeant was coming around the end of the ship. "What the hell?"

"Sergeant, get out of there!"

There was no response except for the screams coming from the bay as Ryan was suddenly yanked behind the ship, disappearing from view. The screams continued for a couple of seconds before suddenly being cut off. Clive watched in horror as something rolled across the floor in a trail of dark liquid, the distinctive shape that could only be a human head. There was an inhuman cry, and the feed suddenly went dark.

"Rain," he said, his voice somber, disbelieving, "seal the shuttle bay."

"It is too late. The creature has already exited it."

"Where is it?"

"It has entered the living quarters."

The color drained from Clive's face. They had no weapons, and now, no means to seal the creature away. It would finish there, and move on to the engineering sections, and finally, the comm room. He had never felt more helpless than he did now.

The AI spoke, but he didn't hear it. All he could think of was the motto that he had enjoyed so much, *Per aspera ad astra*. He couldn't help but to laugh, a loud, crazed laugh that filled the room. The founders of NASA had never realized the truth in the saying.

Laura was out of her chair, backed against the far wall. Whether to get away from the creature, or away from him, he was no longer sure.

A FIRE FOR THE NIGHT

I started listening to podcasts when I got a job with a longer commute than I had previously had. The first podcast I really latched onto was Lore, which is a long running podcast that explores stories from the past rooted in folklore, usually toeing the line between truth and myth. I have picked up several story ideas from the podcast, including a couple in this collection.

I forget the specific episode this idea came from, but like many of the ideas, it stemmed from a very small part that my mind latched onto, enough that I jotted down a note. As part of the tale, a traveling priest is met on the road, and as I recall, he was asked to help with the particular problem at the time, a changeling, perhaps? Having been raised Catholic, something that's always interested me is the role of religion in dispelling mythical creatures, be they demons or vampires or mythical beasts of the wild. From that, this idea sprang of our protagonists meeting a traveling priest in the wilds, and the uncertainty of whether the tales he spins are true or not.

There was a light between the trees, one that drew them forth like moths to a flame. It flickered and flared, threatening to go out and then coming back as strong as ever. The wind carried the scent of burning wood and roasting meat, and with it, the sound of a low voice singing, the words lost in the wind and the haunting tune remaining.

Tucker felt a hand on his shoulder. He stopped in place, the fire still several paces away, its flames peeking through the gaps between the trees. His head turned slightly, and he heard his companion speak in a quiet voice.

"It could be brigands," Isaiah said.

"More likely it's not."

"We're better off not taking a chance. We should go around."

"I want to at least see."

He tried to take another step, but the hand on his shoulder tightened.

"It's not worth the risk."

They both froze as the tune stopped. A voice called out, the same voice that had just been singing, but the words it spoke were clear. "These lands are blessed in the name of the Lord. If you be demons, begone from here."

Tucker shook off Isaiah's hand and spoke out, even as his companion shushed him. "We are only weary travelers, seeking our path home."

"What are you doing?" Isaiah hissed.

The voice from the fire spoke out before Tucker could respond. "Then come, join a lonely priest around his fire. The night is cold and strange things stalk these woods."

Tucker glanced back at Isaiah, and even in the darkness could see the frown on his companion's face, the look in his eyes. His lips formed the word, "Don't," but Tucker ignored it, turning back toward the fire. "We come as friends," he called out, stepping forward toward the light.

"That's good," the voice said as Tucker stepped past the trees and into the small clearing. A lone figure sat at the fire, a hooded cloak wrapped around his shoulders, the frock of a priest beneath. An aged face looked up at him as he entered and grinned from the shadow of the hood, smiling a crooked grin. "I think we could all use a friendly face in a place like this."

Tucker glanced back at the darkened woods, waiting for Isaiah to emerge. When he finally did, they both stepped toward the fire, taking a seat across from the old priest. "This is Isaiah," he said, nodding toward his friend. "My name is Tucker."

"Father George, at your service," the old priest said. "I wish I had more to share beyond these flames, but I am only a poor priest."

"The fire will be enough, Father," Tucker said. From beside him, Isaiah mumbled an agreement and said no more.

"What brings you out this way, my sons?" the priest asked. He wasn't looking at them, his head lowered as he adjusted the ashes in the fire. "These woods are not the kind of place that you want to find yourself after dark."

"We got lost," Tucker said.

"You got lost," Isaiah grumbled.

Tucker looked over, but Isaiah was looking away, out toward the woods. "We were in town to visit the traveling merchant, but we stayed later than intended, so I thought we could get back home quicker, cutting through the woods."

"You live around here, then?"

Tucker nodded. "Our families have farms next to each other, along the river."

"The river," the priest said, nodding. "A bit off course. I can point you in the right direction."

"You can?" Isaiah straightened where he sat, his eyebrows raising. "Well do so, we're both eager to get home."

"Oh, I wouldn't be so eager to leave, not right now. Dark things live in these woods. Dark things indeed." A slight chuckle followed the words, a low, raspy laugh.

This time, when Tucker glanced over at Isaiah, the look he was giving mirrored on his friend's face. "We've heard the stories," Tucker said. "But those are...just stories."

"Tales meant to scare children," Isaiah said. "No more real than tales of fairies or elves."

"All tales are rooted in the truth," the priest said. "Even your fairies and elves."

The look Tucker exchanged with Isaiah this time was different, a look of doubt. For the first time, he was beginning to grow unsure that he had made the right choice to join the priest. Perhaps a change in subject would ease the air around them. "What is it that brings you these woods, Father?"

"A holy journey, my son," the priest said. He placed the stick down and made the sign of the cross. "I travel these lands seeking those who need my help, who need the help of God."

There was a tugging on his tunic from beside him, but Tucker shook it off. "What kind of help?"

"The kind of help that requires a priest. Baptisms, weddings, funerals." A pause. "Exorcisms."

The tugging on his tunic came a bit harder and he slapped Isaiah's hand away. "Exorcisms. Like demons?"

"Demons, spirits, curses." He had a pipe now and was stuffing it with finely shredded tobacco. "Any and every type of possession."

"Tucker," Isaiah hissed.

"You believe they're real?" Tucker said.

The priest gave another low cackle, the sound piercing through the smoke that drifted from the newly lit pipe. "I know they're real."

Isaiah abandoned any sense of subtlety, standing and exclaiming loudly, "This is absurd. Tucker, are you actually listening to this nonsense?"

"Isaiah..."

"No, I will not sit here and listen to this old...man," he gestured toward their host, "spout nonsense, claiming to be a priest. And I fail to believe that you..."

He was cut off by a piercing cry that seemed to echo through the woods, filling the air around them. Isaiah flinched at the sound, his head snapping toward the dark woods. Tucker only froze, feeling his skin crawl as he listened, his ears stretching out into the silence for any further sign.

"It's just a wolf," Isaiah said, his voice scarcely above a whisper.

"Your tongue voices what your heart wishes to be true." The priest had not moved, though Tucker saw that at some point he had taken up a rosary in his left hand, his right still holding the bowl of the pipe. "Worry yourself not, young man. This place, these flames, they have been blessed by God. So long as you remain within the light, no harm shall come to you."

"This can't be real. This can't be real." The words repeated over and over, even as he returned to a sitting position. Somewhere beyond the trees, Tucker thought he heard a twig snap. Or perhaps it was just the crackling of a log.

"I don't fault good Christian men like yourselves for being skeptical," Father George said. The rosary moved in his hand, each bead pausing between his thumb and forefinger before passing on, the prayer left unsaid. "After all, I am sure neither of you have ever seen a monster or demon or anything of the sort."

"Is that...a monster out there?" Tucker asked.

The priest did not respond, not to his question. "I came from a home not far from here," he said. "The local parish sent for me, wrote me a letter about a witch casting curses on people in the area."

"Old Annie, wasn't it?" Tucker said, his eyes still peering into the darkness between the trees.

"Aye," the priest said. "Annie, her name was."

"Uncle Richard said she's been killing off his crops," Isaiah said. His eyes shifted around when Tucker looked in his direction. "I don't know if it's true, though."

"Perhaps," Father George said. "I can't say what she's done, what she hasn't done. That is between her and God above."

"But you went to her?" Tucker asked.

"I did. I visited with Father Gregory, and he directed me to the old woman's cabin. I'm sure I don't have to tell you that it lies deep within these woods."

"We never knew where she lived," Tucker said. "We only saw her when she'd come to town."

"Ah, well, I can tell you that she resides deep in these trees, deep enough that it seems the sun doesn't shine, that the birds don't even sing."

"Truly?" Isaiah asked. Any uneasiness seemed to have left him, just as it seemed to have left Tucker. They were both drawn into the priest's tale, for better or worse.

"Truly," Father George said. "It was past midday when I arrived, through these woods, across rivers and streams, often without a road to traverse. It is a wonder I did not get lost, and perhaps I would have had it not been for the Lord's guidance."

"But you did get there?" Tucker asked.

"Aye, I did."

"And what did you find?" Isaiah asked.

"A home. A small cabin in a clearing, fed by a stream that had been dammed off. A small garden filled with flowers and vegetables. The kind of place you'd expect to find in an area like this."

"A normal cabin," Tucker said.

The priest nodded. "Aye."

"And the old woman?"

"She was out there watering the garden, pulling the occasional weed."

There was a silence between them. Somewhere in the woods, an owl hooted, but there were no footsteps. Tucker reiterated to himself that it had just been his imagination.

"What did you do?" he asked.

"I greeted her," the priest said. "Must have surprised her a bit because she jumped at the sound of my voice. She turned, hand on her heart, and breathed a sigh of relief when she saw me. I told her who I was and that I had heard a rumor that she was a witch."

Tucker looked over at Isaiah, then said, "What did she say?"

"She laughed at me."

Their voices sounded in unison. "Laughed?"

"Aye, she laughed. An infectious laugh, the kind that could crack a smile on the face of the sternest of men. I'm sure you have seen the kind."

"So she wasn't a witch, then?" Isaiah asked.

"Did I say that, boy?"

Tucker glanced over to see the frown on Isaiah's face, but neither said a word. The old priest took the moment to puff on his pipe, sending the acrid smoke across the flames to mingle with that of the fire.

"She asked how I could believe such a thing. Said that there are no witches, same as you did. Then mentioned that she was an outcast, someone who lived a solitary life, the kind of person who would get these kinds of accusations. The kind of person who just wanted to live her life and be left alone."

"So she was a witch?" Isaiah asked. His voice was rising, the frustration more and more evident with each word.

"I asked her if she knew of a witch in the area. All the while, though, I had my crucifix in my pocket, and I was holding my hand to it. I could feel it growing warm in my hand, like the very presence of God was coursing through the wood. I knew then that the woman was lying to me, that I was dealing with an honest to God witch."

"So what did you do?" Tucker asked.

There was a deep draw on the pipe before he responded, the smoke seeming to fill the air around them. "First, I steadied my heartbeat. I couldn't let her know I was onto her. I gripped the cross harder, hard enough that my palm burned." He turned his palm over, and both of them leaned in, seeing the markings along the inside of his hand, the burns still fresh, the shape of the cross visible. "If you've never seen a cross in the presence of a true witch, it is a sight to behold."

Both of them shook their heads.

"Perhaps one day you'll have the opportunity. Perhaps it is for the better if you never know a true witch, though." He flexed his hand, then continued. "I told her to cast aside her disguise, for the lord sees through her deception. Her smile turned to a glare and the clearing was suddenly filled with a bright light, bright enough that I had to shield my eyes. When I looked again, she had transformed into a twisted, hunched, hideous creature. She was already speaking a curse, and it was all I could do to hold out my crucifix and fend it off. Even then, the force of it sent me flying back.

"As I was trying to regain my senses, the witch was already transforming again, this time into a monstrous beast. Coarse hair grew from her skin and her face stretched into a long snout, her height reaching above the house. She let out a roar that shook me to my very bones, and then she pounced."

"How did you survive?" Tucker asked.

"By the grace of God. She just missed severing my neck. I thrust my crucifix upward, and the creature recoiled from the touch, and it was all I could do to scramble away. At that point, I began to run."

There was silence in the clearing, only the wind blowing. Finally, it was Isaiah who spoke. "So you ran away? You didn't kill the witch."

The priest took a moment to puff on his pipe. "I never said I killed the witch."

"You…" Tucker trailed off.

Isaiah suddenly stood. "This is wrong."

"Isaiah, sit down."

"No, I think this man is a liar. Witches aren't real, and neither are monsters. This man is no more than a drifter who is claiming to be a priest, probably to rob people like us."

"Isaiah…"

Isaiah was standing now. "I'm done listening, and I'm not going to fear these stories that he spins. Come on, Tucker, let's get home."

Isaiah turned toward the edge of the clearing, his foot nearly at the darkness of the tree line, but a sudden crashing of limbs coupled with a loud roar sent him tumbling backwards. Tucker recoiled as well, his eyes locked on the spot, where something large and dark moved behind the trees.

A low cackle emerged from the priest. "A story indeed." He puffed on the pipe. "I hope you boys will stay and help me keep the fire lit. It is the only thing that will keep her away until the morning comes."

BORN UNDER A BAD SIGN

At one of my past jobs, I was part of a writing group that met weekly, first to watch a Master Class, then to discuss writing in general before finally coming together for a group project. After tossing ideas around, we settled on the theme of Tarot cards, setting it around the turn of the century, and exploring the history of Tarot decks and the mysticism that surrounds them.

This was my entry to the project, following something of a con man during the time period in New Orleans, a guy constantly down on his luck, looking for a way to turn it around.

1

The man at the door eyed him over for the fifth time since he had been standing there, glancing between the notebook he held in his hand and at the short, lanky man who stood before him. Or at least, short comparatively; the doorman was the kind of man who could make a giant feel small.

"What did you say your name was again?" The thick creole accent was reminiscent of French, if a Frenchman had lost all semblance of refinement and stuffed his mouth full of cotton, that was.

"Joseph LeClair," the lanky man said as he flashed a smile, a winning smile, the kind of smile that made women melt at the knees and tourists fork over money like it was candy. The smile of a trustworthy man.

He gave the smile a moment to sink in, then tapped the notebook and added, "Mr. Travere is expecting me, and I fail to believe that my name is not on that list." He also failed to believe that the towering man before him could read, but he wasn't about to suggest as much out loud.

The man squinted at the list, staring at it as though doing so would make the words speak to him, then looked back to Joseph. Joseph managed another smile, hoping this one didn't look too nervous. He wasn't sure how long the usual doorkeeper would be on his outhouse break, and he knew he wasn't going to fool that man. His only hope was the illiterate hulk of a man before him.

"Alright," he finally said. "I don't recognize you, but you seem like the type that Mr. Travere would invite, and he don't just give his invite to anyone, you know. He don't recognize you, it'll be taken care of."

"Thank you kindly, my good sir," Joseph said, brushing away the threat and stepping through the door into the dark building.

The door closed behind him and he found himself standing in an empty hallway, lit by dim electric lights that lined the walls. The air was stuffy, both from the heat of the day and from the thick stench of cigar smoke that floated from the room at the end, casting a haze over the entire space. He heard laughter and cursing and the sound of chips clinking together over a soundtrack of cheerful piano playing, and he knew he was in the right place. His kind of place.

A mirror hung from the wall beside him, and Joseph stopped at it, casting a look at his reflection. He removed his hat and smoothed a loose strand of dark hair into place, then adjusted the lapels of his suit, doing his best to hide the ratty stitching and frequent holes. One had to look like they belonged in places like these, but this was the only suit he owned, so it would have to do.

"This is all you," he told his reflection. His mother had been a reader before she had died of the yellow fever during the outbreak of '05, and according to her, he had been born under a bad sign. But men born under bad signs did not get opportunities like these. No, they had bad luck everywhere. A real man made his own luck, and Joseph was about to make his. He knew it.

One last adjustment of the tie, the hat tucked under the crook of his arm, and he strode toward the back room.

There were several tables spread throughout the wide space, each filled with men, most in suits, although some had shed their coats and even their outer shirts against the heat of the room. In one corner was a bar, the walls behind it filled with various liquors, and in the other corner was the piano, a young woman in a red dress belting out a jaunty tune. The air was filled with music and the sounds of conversation and a cloud of smoke as cards were dealt and chips passed, winners celebrating and losers lamenting. Young boys rushed through the narrow spaces between tables, carrying empty glasses and new drinks, emptying ashtrays and lighting cigars, available at every player's beck and call.

Joseph glanced around the room, scanning through several tables before finding an empty spot. He slid easily into the chair and flashed his winning smile at the others. "Good day, boys," he said, placing his hat down. "Hope you don't mind me joining."

His words were met with nothing more than a few grunts, none of the other players bothering to even raise their eyes from their cards to glance at him. Only the dealer in the center of the table stared at him, arms folded across his chest.

Joseph cleared his throat and reached into his suit pocket, pulling out a crumpled twenty, about the most money he had ever carried on his person at one time. It almost hurt to hand it over, but one had to spend money to make money. Joseph turned as the dealer counted out chips, snagging one of the boys rushing past and ordering a bourbon. When he turned back, there was a stack of chips in front of him, and the dealer was already dealing out the next hand.

This was it. Joseph rubbed his hands together and prepared to play.

The dealer used a pair of decks, one with a red back and one blue. Each deck would run for five hands before being swapped out for the other, the unused deck shuffled by a kid behind the dealer. There was no counting, no verification, only a quick cut by the dealer, then another by the man to his right. Perfect.

Joseph played the first few hands straight, watching the table, taking in each player around him, their nuances, their triggers, their tells. It was no different than watching people on the street; you just had to pick the right person, the right time. Conversation rumbled around them filling the air as much as the smoke, but the table was silent, the other players staring at their cards, only speaking when necessary. He had never been one for silence, however, so he simply spoke aloud, directing his words to no one in particular.

"Mighty fine weather we've been having lately. I always like this time of year, you know, before it gets too hot. 'Course, God willing we don't get another hurricane. Last year, I had water in my place clear up to my chest. Good thing the storm passed through before it got any higher, I tell ya. Still, ain't no fun trying to pump water out of your room, let me tell ya. But the flooding is worth it for the view of the river, yessir. Any of you gents live down by the river? Ah, I'm sure you do, y'all look like y'all make some real money."

As he spoke, he continued to glance around the table. Not one person at the table was looking at him, not even the dealer. Typically, his misdirections involved people watching his face instead of his hands, but he supposed that it was good enough.

The hand had ended, and the cards had been tossed onto the felt surface for the dealer to collect. The gentleman to his left, however, had not tossed his, but instead placed them gently down, still fanned out to reveal the pair of aces, meticulously organized with the other three cards.

Joseph spread his hands out, sliding the cards into a pile and pushing them toward the dealer. "Let me help you with that," he said. He covered up the aces with his wrist, and with a well-practiced motion, used his palm to slide them up his sleeve.

The dealer put a firm hand on top of Joseph's, and he felt his heart skip a beat. "Only dealers touch the cards."

"Oh," Joseph said, giving as sheepish a look as he could muster as he pulled his hands back, feeling the cards in his left sleeve. "Apologies. I didn't realize that was a rule. I just got a bit excited, yessir. Just so excited to be playing here with you folks."

The dealer grunted, gathering the rest of the cards into the deck. "You get one warning, then you're outta here."

Joseph continued his conversation with himself, betting conservatively and maintaining a decent stack of chips. The dealer eyed him suspiciously for the next couple of hands, then lost interest. A few hands after that, Joseph saw his chance.

The cards were dealt to him, a pair of aces and three other cards. Joseph carefully rearranged the cards, then shut them together. As he held them close, his fingers maneuvered the extra aces from his sleeve and into his hand, sliding two of the throwaway cards into his sleeve. A simple magician's trick made easier by his table's aversion to his speaking.

"I tell you boys, I've got a winning hand right here. Yessir, I'm plenty confident about it." He slid his entire stack of chips to the center of the table.

There were several folds, but two of the other players called. Joseph fought back a smile; he would have been happy just to have one.

The dealer motioned to the first who called. "Sir."

"Straight, nine to king," the man said, laying his cards out.

The next player showed his hand, a grin widening across his face. "Full house, fives over tens."

Joseph allowed himself a smile of his own. It was only natural when one won big. "Four aces," he said, spreading them on the table before him.

One of the losers cursed loudly, standing and kicking his chair over with a loud bang, while the other simply stared at the cards with his mouth open. Joseph reached over and began to pull the large pile of chips toward himself.

He only stopped when he felt a heavy hand on his wrist. His stomach dropped out as he turned to see a large man to his right, angry eyes glaring down at him. He glanced back down to see the cards slipping out of his sleeve.

Shit.

Joseph gave a slight flick of the wrist, hiding the cards back in his sleeve. "What is the meaning of this?" he demanded.

"We should be asking you the same thing," the man said.

Don't panic, he told himself. Maybe they hadn't seen the cards. His sleeve had been hidden from view, turned inward. Just like on the street. Stay calm, play it off. Most people were too dumb to know they were being tricked, even if they assumed it with every fiber of their being.

The man reached over with his free hand and slid Joseph's sleeve up. The cards slid onto the table, and Joseph heard the gasps around him. "I saw the cards when he reached for the chips," the man said. "He's probably been cheating us this entire time."

"I have not," Joseph protested, stopping just short of saying that it had only been that hand. No matter what, you always deny. Especially in a place owned by someone as infamous as Travere.

For the first time all day, everyone's eyes were trained on Joseph, still held with his arms stretched across the table, his hands on the chips. It wasn't just those at his table, but those around the room. Even the piano had stopped playing.

Joseph cleared his throat. "Gentlemen, I assure you that there's been a mistake. If you will just let me up here, I'm sure we can come to an understanding."

One of the other players at the table stood, slapping the felt with the palm of his hand. "Like hell. The only understanding here is that you're a damned cheater."

"This is a setup," Joseph said, but his words were cut off as his face was shoved down into the felt. All around him was conversation, a combination of anger and excitement as they discussed what to do with him.

Before Joseph could say another word, he felt his face pushed along the surface, scattering the chips around. It caught him by surprise more than anything else, but when they picked his head up and slammed him back down, he did feel pain, a hard, biting pain that reverberated through his jaw and skull.

"What's going on here?" A deep voice echoed through the room, silencing the crowd around him. Joseph tried to angle to find the source of the voice, but a sturdy hand still held his face down to the table.

"We caught ourselves a cheater, boss," one of the men said.

"Yeah," echoed another. "He was sliding cards up his sleeve."

"You can't prove that," Joseph said, but his voice was muffled as he spoke into the felt.

"I see." The voice was closer now, nearly on top of him. Joseph could still not see the man, but he could feel his eyes, boring holes through him. "I know this man. He's a street performer, the kind who will swindle you out of a few bucks by hiding a ball beneath a cup and slipping it out when you're not looking."

"Hand is quicker than the eye," Joseph muttered.

"What was your name again, boy? Johnny?"

"Joseph." He regretted it as soon as he said it. Probably would have been better to lie, but too late for that now.

"Joseph," the man said. "Good Christian name, but a sinner by trade, it seems. I would have expected someone with your skills to be able to outwit some brutes like this."

"Never said I was good at it."

That brought a chuckle at least. Just from the speaker, however; the rest of the men laughed nervously. "I'll tell you what," the man said. "I'm going to give you a break, not because I like you, but because you seem to need one."

Ain't that the truth. This time, Joseph managed to keep the thought in his head.

"Let him go."

Joseph felt the grip release from the back of his head. He pushed away from the table, feeling the chips fall away from his face. He rubbed at his jaw as he turned his eyes on his rescuer and found himself looking right at the broad frame and slicked black hair of Louis Travere. This time, the words caught in his throat, nearly choking him.

"Now Joseph," Travere said, waving a meaty hand as he spoke, "these boys want a piece of you, and rightfully so, but frankly, I don't like fighting in my places of business. Things tend to get broken, blood is difficult to get out of the carpet, and frankly, it just draws the wrong kind of attention. So, in the interest of sport, and for keeping my place clean, I'm going to point you toward the back door, and these gentlemen are going to give you a head start."

Joseph looked back at the men, who were already watching him, their eyes filled with fury. "What if I just remain here?"

"Then, these gentlemen will escort you outside and do with you what they will."

"I think I'll take the first option."

Travere smiled, revealing a shiny gold tooth. "I expected you would." He gestured toward a door at the rear of the room. "Get going. Next time I see you in one of my joints, I'll have you tied down with weights and thrown into the river."

Joseph could only nod as his feet began to move. The entire room watched him, but he avoided eye contact with anyone around him. By the time he reached the door, he was at a slight trot, and as soon as he passed outside, he was at a dead sprint.

The alley behind the building intersected with a larger street. Joseph rounded the corner and ran headlong into what felt like a brick wall, the impact knocking him hard into a sitting position on the sidewalk. He looked up and found himself staring right at the dark blue uniform of a police officer.

The officer looked down at him, hands on his hips, hardly fazed at all by the impact. "Where you off to in such a hurry, son?"

Joseph remained where he was, seated on the ground, his lips attempting to move, but nothing coming out. The cop stared down at him, and from behind, another emerged. Joseph saw the eyes narrow.

"I know this guy," the second cop said. "He runs scams on the corner over by Jackson Square."

"A scammer, huh?" the first officer said.

Joseph suddenly found his voice. "I assure you, you fine gentlemen have me confused for another fellow." He began to stand but felt himself shoved back to the ground. Behind him, he heard footsteps as his pursuers turned the corner and ground to halt when they saw him and the cops.

"You fellas know this man?" the cop asked.

Joseph glanced back at his pursuers and caught the devilish grin of the one in front. "Yeah, we know him," he said. "This guy just tried to rob us."

Before Joseph could protest, he was pulled to his feet, the familiar metal touch of handcuffs sliding around his wrist. "That's good enough for me," the officer said. "We got big things happening in town this week, can't have rabble like you causing trouble."

So much for changing his luck.

2

The cot was even harder than he remembered, but it seemed that way each time they locked him up. It was nothing new; in a few days, they would decide they didn't have a case against him, or perhaps someone worse would come along, and they would have to let him go. If he was rich, he could have a lawyer spring him right away, but then again, if he was rich, he wouldn't be here in the first place. Folks who are rich aren't born under a bad sign.

For now, Joseph lay on his back, smoking a cigarette that the guard had allowed him and staring up at the stained ceiling of his cell. His mind turned, thinking not of where he had gone wrong, of what he could have done better, but of the money he had let go in the process, and of how he would be able to earn it back. There was always the corner, but he was sick of it, sick of scamming people who basically begged to be scammed. Besides, the cops seemed to be a bit keener on cracking down lately; someone with connections must have gotten swindled something fierce.

They had emptied his pockets, but there had been a single card resting on the cot when he had arrived. Joseph had nearly dropped it when he had picked it up and seen the Ten of Swords, but now he twirled it absently in his fingers as he lay there. It couldn't have been a coincidence. If you asked him, nothing was coincidence. It was a reminder of who he was, of what he had been born into.

A voice carried over from one of the other cells. "I heard they were setting up down in Jackson Square."

Another voice answered. "I don't know why you're bothering with that Order of whatsit...Bronze Night?"

Joseph sat up and turned in the direction of the voices. "Golden Dawn?"

He saw the two men in adjacent cells, clad in the ragged clothing they had been brought in. Both turned toward him, one eyeing him suspiciously behind a rugged face, as though he had just noticed that Joseph was there, while the other, a skinny man with scraggly hair and a child-like face, grinned widely. "That's the one. You know about them, mister?"

I only grew up in a household dedicated to their practice. "You hear about them here and there," Joseph said. He swung his feet over the side of the bed and stretched his legs, then stood and made his way to the bars. "They up to something?"

"You could say that," the rugged man said, still giving Joseph a cockeyed look. "Some big to-do over in the French Quarter."

"More than a to-do," the other one said.

"Whatever you want to call it." He nodded toward Joseph. "You got a name, stranger?"

"Joseph. Yourself?"

"Antoine," he said. He nodded toward his companion. "This one is Gilbert. Not the brightest, I'm afraid, but he's alright. What are you in for, Joseph?"

"Got caught swindling some out-of-towners." The lie flowed with ease because it was not far from the truth; Joseph had always been a natural liar, and he was unsure if these guys were connected to Travere at all. "So what kind of hubbub is the Golden Dawn stirring up?"

"Not a hubbub either," Gilbert said. "A big event."

Antoine rolled his eyes. "Some kind of convention, big announcement or something like that. They got a stage and everything, and you can bet the suckers will turn out in droves."

"They aren't suckers, Antoine," Gilbert said, his voice raising. "They're believers."

"I'm a good judge of suckers, if I may say so myself," Joseph said.

"Doubt you are if you're in here," Antoine said.

Joseph ignored the jab. "What kind of announcement?"

"Folks say they're debuting a new deck," Gilbert said.

Joseph felt his eyes widen despite himself. "A new deck?"

"That's what they're saying," Antoine said. "Don't see what difference it makes. Ain't no one but tourists and old ladies and backwoods cajuns who still believe in it around here."

"Antoine, come on, you don't really believe I'm backwoods," Gilbert said.

"Gilbert, you're as backwoods as it gets."

Guess that makes me backwoods too, Joseph thought, though he had never left the city in his life. This man, Antoine, he had clearly never seen the power that lay in the cards, the way a single reading could reveal the truths of a life not yet lived. Joseph had; he was living it.

"You'd be surprised how many people still believe in the cards," Joseph said.

"You saying you're one of those people too?" Antoine asked.

"I'm saying I've seen some things in my day," Joseph said.

"What kinds of things?"

"Things that would make a believer even out of you." Or at least he assumed. Joseph had also met some pretty stubborn men in his day, the kind of men who could look a miracle in the eye and deny its existence with a straight face.

"That isn't very specific." Antoine gripped the bars as though he intended to rip them right apart, a feat Joseph had seen greater men fail at. "You're going to have to detail some real magic to make believers here."

"Antoine, sometimes you just gotta believe," Gilbert said.

Joseph looked down at the card in his hand, then flipped it over, making it disappear and reappear with each flick of the wrist. "Y'all are both local, I'm sure you got a reading at your birth?"

Antoine scoffed, but Gilbert nodded rapidly. "I did."

"It's a tradition," Antoine said. "I'm sure you got baptized too, but it don't mean nothing."

Joseph ignored the latter, focusing on Gilbert. "Do you remember your reading?"

Gilbert shook his head from behind the bars. "My ma never told me the actual reading, just that it said I'd be a screw up. Guess the cards called that one right."

Antoine spat in his direction, the attempt falling well short. "Maybe if you didn't go around thinking you was a screw up, you wouldn't have landed us in here. Or if you wouldn't've stopped and left the jewelry from the last room when I told you we had to go."

"As much as I'd love to listen to you two argue," Joseph said, "I need to know more about the Golden Dawn thing. "Do you know when it's supposed to happen?"

"I dunno," Antoine said. "Sometime tomorrow morning? Or this morning now, I guess."

Joseph glanced over his shoulder at the tiny, barred window. Already, he could see the dark sky outside begin to brighten with the coming dawn. He couldn't depend on being able to see a judge that quickly, much less post bail. Once more, he was going to have to make his own luck.

"I don't know what you're so interested in," Antoine said as Joseph began to pat himself down. "It's just a bunch of superstitious people gathering over superstitious nonsense. Even if there's a new deck, it's not like it'll bring any sort of power to the practice. Anyone who believes as much is a fool."

"Guess I'm a fool then," Joseph said. Him and his mother both for that matter. He found what he was looking for in a seam of his jacket. He felt the small piece of wire, one he had stuck through some threads. He pinched it between his fingers and carefully removed it from his sleeve.

"You're the fool, Antoine," Gilbert said. "You keep putting others down for no reason." He turned to Joseph. "You think you're going to get out of here? Can I come with you? I want to be there."

Joseph considered it for a moment as he leaned forward, trying to gaze through the open door into the office. He saw nothing. No doubt the jail was operating with a skeleton crew this time of night, but you never knew when an officer might bring a new occupant to the jail. He would need to work quickly.

"Joseph?"

"I'll let you out, but you're on your own." He slipped his arm through the bars and navigated the wire into the cell door's lock. The other two watched quietly as he fiddled with the wire, wiggling it until there was a loud click.

He made his way over to the other cells and did the same to Gilbert's. The prisoner emerged, a broad smile on his face. "Thanks."

Antoine scowled from behind his bars. "Go on, then, Gilbert," he said. "Just watch yourself around those believers. They're dangerous."

"I feel sorry for you, Antoine," Gilbert said as they left the cells behind. Joseph was not sure he agreed with him.

Joseph made his way to the front, walking softly while motioning Gilbert to stay back. He could hear the snoring of the officer before he entered the room. He poked his head in and saw the man leaned back in his chair, sleeping.

About time I had some luck, he thought to himself as he stepped past and out the front door of the jail. The sun was beginning to rise on the city as he made his way to the French Quarter.

3

It was still early, but already the heat of the day was causing his shirt to stick to his skin. He would have ditched the suit, but he was not about to fork over the money for a new one, not when he was already trying to replace the money he had lost at the game.

The crowd made things worse. He could feel the heat of those around him, radiating from each body until it felt like he was standing in a sauna. He unbuttoned the top few buttons of his shirt and adjusted it to allow more air in. There was a low murmur of voices, conversation stacking upon each other until there was a dull roar, the timbre of a people eagerly waiting for something to happen.

Joseph could barely see the stage from where he stood, but he could see the large banner with the Order of the Golden Dawn's seal upon it, the rising sun and the cross above it, the same seal that had hung in his mother's reading room, that every single person who had received a reading had gazed upon.

He could feel his hands shaking, his body tense with excitement. There had not been a new deck in...ever. Not since the first cards were printed back in the old world, when the first reading was made, and the first person's destiny tied to the prophecy of the cards. The possibilities of what it could bring ran through his mind. New power, new readings, new beginnings. A fresh slate with the old one wiped clean. A new chance for people like him. A changing of his luck. It had to be. Everything was suddenly going so well.

A figure made its way onto the stage. He heard a few idle claps from around him, but mostly the crowd silenced, watching with intent curiosity. Joseph thought back to the men he had spoken to at the jail, their thoughts on the spectacle that was taking place. To them, this was no more than a curiosity at best and a cult at worst. He almost laughed at that last thought. What would his mother think if she knew that her religion, the one her ancestors had brought from Europe, had fallen so far as to be thought of as a cult?

The man was speaking, Joseph could tell that much, but in the wet air, the words simply died before making it past the crowd in the front. Joseph could see the man holding something up, something that was clearly a deck of cards, but it was much too small for him to see. He made an attempt to move closer, but it felt as though the crowd had closed in more tightly, like water moving to fill a hole being dug too close to the river. Every step he took was impeded, each attempt to push through resulting in a shove backwards, until one sent him to a sitting position in the wet grass.

The crowd threatened to close around him as he pushed himself back to his feet, the others seeking to get closer to the front just as he was. The man on the stage was still speaking, but whatever he was saying was lost to distance and thick, humid air. Joseph knew he was never going to get close from this angle. He needed to find another way.

The crowd fanned out in the square, packing closely near the stage but growing sparse as he moved further away. The rear of the stage, however, was roped off, the area protected from the sun by canopies that provided shade. Beneath sat several tables, and on the tables, he could see several decks, new decks. It also happened to be guarded by a pair of rather burly men.

This close, he could hear the man speaking. "...no longer beholden to the symbology of the old world, nor the whims of those who insisted on hiding the power from the world, who used it only for their own gain..."

Joseph blocked the speaker out. The presentation was no longer important. What mattered was getting his hands on a deck. He had to; his entire life depended on it. He might never have another chance like this.

A pair of men were standing close to the side of the stage, watching the speaker. Joseph moved past one, slipping the wallet from the man's pocket as he did. As he passed the other man, he slipped the wallet into his pocket and continued walking, weaving through the crowd. He listened for a sound, the sound of someone crying out, the sound that told him he'd been caught, but it never came.

Joseph made his way to the guards. They were policemen, by the look of it, out of uniform to be sure. He only hoped that they still felt a duty to preserve order.

"Excuse me," he said.

"What?" one asked in a deep voice.

"I'm sorry to bother you." Joseph turned and indicated the men by the stage. "I believe that man just pickpocketed the gentleman next to him. I would hate to have someone lose their wallet at such an event."

One squinted at him, but the other nudged him that way. "Go take a look."

"Appreciate it." Joseph nodded and stepped to the side.

He watched as the policeman made his way over, approaching the pair and tapping one on the shoulder. The first turned, the motion causing the other to turn as well. Words were exchanged, and the one on the right suddenly realized that his wallet was gone. Even from the distance, Joseph could see it escalating, the crowd gathering as the men shouted at each other, the policeman trying to keep them separated. Without warning, the accused thief leapt at the victim, and fists began to fly.

It was when others began to join the fray that the other policeman left to help. Joseph smiled to himself as he made his way past the rope. No one attempted to stop him, and he did not wait to see if anyone saw him. He stepped in, grabbed a deck from the table, stuck in into his pocket, and made his way from the backstage area, listening to the sound of the ruckus behind him as he passed through the other side and into the French Quarter.

He made his way through, wandering until he finally emerged out the other side. There was a small house in a fenced yard at the edge of the French Quarter, sitting beneath the shade of a towering oak tree. From the eave that hung over the front stoop hung two flags, one displaying a crystal ball and the other the sigil of the Golden Dawn. A reader, a familiar one, and as one that owned a house, a successful one.

A small bell rang as Joseph stepped through the front door. "Just a minute, dear," a voice said. "I'll be right with you." The sound drifted through the scent of tobacco and incense, floating from the rear of the house to fill the room in the front.

"Mother Colette?" Joseph said.

He heard the footsteps approach with the voice, pounding on the wooden floors. "I recognize that voice." The woman that appeared was slightly hunched, white hair tumbling down in curls upon her shoulders. She wore a faded dress and held a cane in a shaking hand to help her walk. When she saw him, she gave him a grin of crooked yellowing teeth. "Well if it ain't Marie LeClair's little boy."

Joseph smiled and gave her a kiss on the cheek. "How are you?"

"Healthy as ever," she said. "Please, sit."

Joseph moved to help her, but she waved a hand, so he obeyed, taking a seat across from her, a small round table between them. Mother Colette leaned her cane against the table and folded her hands in her lap, leaning back in the chair.

"What can I do for you, Joseph?" Her voice scratched like a record on a phonograph, the voice of a lifelong smoker.

"Did you know anything about the Golden Dawn gathering at Jackson Square?"

"I heard rumors dear, something about Mr. Waite. An enthusiastic man, to be sure, a huge believer in the cards."

Joseph reached into his pocket. At the touch, he felt something running through his fingers, almost like a pulse, a power. He removed them and set them on the table.

Mother Colette fumbled with her spectacles and eyed the cards. "Remarkable," she said. "A new deck?"

Joseph nodded. "A new deck. New power. I think it was the man you mentioned who introduced it."

She picked up a card and turned it over, examining the design. "The artwork is certainly impressive. Perhaps putting new cards in circulation will help revitalize the practice."

Joseph frowned. "Revitalize? What about energize? Bring the power back."

Mother Colette put the card down and smiled sweetly at him. "Oh Joseph, dear, power? You couldn't possibly think there is actual power in these cards?"

"But don't they…" He found himself at a loss for words. "What do you mean?"

She placed the cards in front of him. "You can draw a card, but it means nothing, no matter how much you want it to. Didn't your mother ever tell you that?"

"She didn't." Joseph stared at the deck, seventy-eight cards high, each card made of pasteboard, intricate blue design painted on the back. He picked up the top card and found himself gazing upon the Wheel of Fortune, a vividly painted compassed wheel sitting amidst a sky of blue and clouds of white. Atop it sat a sphinx while a snake slithered down the side and a foxlike being slinked beneath.

"It's a fine deck, really," Mother Colette said. "I'm sure it'll bring some attention."

Holding the card, Joseph could almost feel the power coursing through his fingertips. It was like nothing he had ever felt before, certainly not with any card he had ever held. People saw the tricks he turned as magic; this right here was real magic. Mother Colette was wrong, he was certain. Wasn't he?

She lit a cigarette and blew a cloud of smoke into the air. "The power, if it was ever there, disappeared when our ancestors came from the old world. Your mother knew that; I would have thought that she would tell you as well."

"You know, I was wondering if I could have some tea first," he said. "My throat is parched."

"Of course, dear," she said. She placed the cards down on the table and eased herself up. She took her cane and walked into the next room, tapping the wooden floor with each step. "I have sugar, but no cream."

"That's fine." Joseph reached across the table and picked up the entire deck. Almost immediately, he could feel it pulse through his fingers, the power of the cards palpable just through the touch. He stared at the back of the cards, the intricate pattern seeming to move on its own.

Mother Colette's voice snapped him from his trance. "Your mother would have loved those cards. She always appreciated the artwork more than anything."

"Yeah, she did." Did she really not believe? After all she had told him? Why would she have told him all those things, made him think that he was born under a bad sign? He lifted the deck. How could she not feel the power?

From the kitchen, he could hear the sounds of Mother Colette moving around, and the kettle being set on the stove. "She was the best reader I ever knew. She knew how to draw out the best from her customers, put on her best show to those who doubted. I tell you, she almost made me a believer when I watched her."

Joseph turned over the top card and found himself looking at an angel, hovering in a cloud above worshipers, playing a large trumpet. Judgement. The Great Reunion, the freeing of souls. Letting go of the past and opening up. A new beginning.

"I hear you've always had the same showmanship that she did. Yessir, I hear you know how to turn the heads down at Jackson Square."

It was all the sign that Joseph needed. He replaced the card and stood. With the deck in his hand, he walked toward the exit. Mother Colette was still talking when he made his way from the house.

He walked with a purpose, his legs carrying him swiftly through the city, past motor cars and carriages alike, past people walking, their voices talking excitedly. It only took a few words to realize that news of Waite's deck was spreading. He wondered just how far it would spread, how quickly. How much would things change? How many believers brought back into the fold? Or would any?

He reached the train station and bought a one-way ticket. The line ended in Los Angeles. That should be far enough.

Joseph boarded the train and slouched in his seat, placing the cards down on the table before him. He stared at the deck as the train began to move. She had to be wrong, he told himself. There was power in the cards, he had felt it. These cards would bring the power back.

"Excuse me, you aiming to play?"

Joseph looked up at the man who had taken a seat across from him. "Beg pardon?"

The man motioned to the cards. "Play some poker?"

"These aren't…" Joseph stopped himself. A smile crept its way across his face, a winning smile. "Let me tell you, sir, these aren't normal playing cards, no sir, this here is a Tarot deck, one of the first of its kind, the kind with real power. And for a small fee, I could tell your future."

The man cocked an eyebrow. "I haven't had a reading since I was born."

From the corner of his eye, Joseph could see others begin to take notice. Perfect. "Well this here is a brand-new deck, and with a brand-new deck, a new reading. What do you say you give it a whirr?"

The man considered for a moment before laying a shiny new quarter down on the table. "Sounds good to me."

The winning smile widened as the quarter vanished into Joseph's pocket, and he began to shuffle the cards.

"Let's see what your new future has in store for you."

LEFT BEHIND

I wrote this story for an io9 contest, one that was centered on the future of death. It wasn't the first idea I came up with — I initially imagined a business that gave people a glance into the afterlife — but it was the one that I ultimately finished and submitted. It was not selected, but I liked it enough to include it in this collection.

This story takes place in a future of ours, one where death is no longer a fact of life. Of course, not everyone wants to live forever, and some people have a really good reason to want to pass on. Which means having people to take care of such a problem.

The approach was always the most difficult part, the anticipation, the knowledge of what was to come.

The neighborhood was a relic, one of the last like it in the area, the kind of neighborhood built when there was space, when it made sense to waste valuable land giving people their own private lot. The houses were spaced out, wood and brick structures divided by slatted fences and carefully manicured yards. They showed their age but were well kept, the sights of modern living visible everywhere. Driverless cars charging, androids maintaining landscaping, modern additions blended with old construction.

His car pulled to a stop in front of the house, the whirring sound of the electric engine not even present in his mind until it was gone. He stepped from the car, an automated voice thanking him as the door shut, and the car drifted silently away to pick up its next customer, no doubt someone with more joyful needs.

It was in the middle of the city, yet it was quiet. There was sound, yes, but it was not the sound of movement, of crowds, of excitement. It was a lawnmower several houses down. The clicking of a kid's bicycle spokes. Birds chirping, not pigeons, but songbirds, the kind that belonged in a fairy tale. It was strange, different, archaic.

The house itself was as much a relic as the neighborhood around it. It was a single story, with no obvious modifications, as though the house had not been touched in decades. The lawn was overgrown, the exterior missing pieces of brick and shingle. Much of the facade was covered in grime and mold, the windows opaque with dust. He traversed a concrete path shaded by a thick oak tree, uneven and cracked from creeping roots and ground shifted by years of rain and snow and heat and cold. A stained welcome mat greeted him at the door, squishing beneath his feet as he knocked.

The door was slow to open, hinges squeaking loudly in the silence of the day. The first thing he noticed was the smell, of mustiness, of age, of neglect. He could see into the dim hallway beyond the door, stacks of books and newspapers, leaning against peeling wallpaper, their pages yellowed and torn.

The man in the doorway felt out of place, not the wrinkled, hunched man that his mind had imagined, but one who seemed no older than thirty, skinny, face covered in an uneven beard, dark circles for eyes squinting into the sunlight.

"You the guy?" he asked after the two exchanged a moment of silence. "The death guy?"

"Clay. Thomas Barker, I presume?"

The man at the door nodded and stepped aside. "Come in."

Clay stepped through the threshold, and he felt the weight of the air pressing against his skin. It was musty, warm, unwelcoming, the kind of place that welcomed death. It seemed to him what a mausoleum might have felt like, back before the last ones were destroyed, back when people felt there was a reason to have one.

"Is there anything in particular you need?" Thomas pushed past him, stepping through the messy hallway to the living room. There were more stacks there, books and papers filling shelves and tables. A faded couch was piled high with dirty clothes, and beside it, a chair with cushioning poking through tears in the fabric. In here, the smell turned from musty to acrid, like something was rotting in the air.

"A place to sit," Clay said. He glanced around the room as Thomas took a seat in the chair.

"Find yourself one," Thomas said. "I just want to get this damn thing over with."

Clay placed his case down in an empty spot on the floor. There was a wooden chair in the corner, covered in books. He began to remove them from it, setting them carefully aside.

"Just push them off," Thomas said. "It's all going to get burned anyway."

Clay ignored him, finishing the job. The man watched him for a moment, then spoke again. "How is this going to work? You going to shoot me or something?"

"Not quite." Clay pulled the chair next to his case and sat down. He shifted around on the hard seat, then removed a tablet from his case. "Mr. Barker, you are participating in the Reaper Program, a pilot program run by the U.S. government that is exploring the decriminalization of death dealers, a partial reversal of the Mortality Act of 2083. As part of the program, there are several questions that you are required to answer."

Thomas frowned, formerly indiscernible lines emerging on his face. "What kind of questions?"

"Nothing out of the ordinary," Clay said. "The government just wants to ensure there are no accidents."

Thomas sank back into his chair. "Fine. Get on with it."

Clay cleared his throat. "Name?"

"Thomas Earl Barker."

"Age?"

"131."

Clay nodded. "A prior."

"What difference does it make? You could be ten or eighty years younger and neither of us would ever know. Age no longer matters."

"Indeed." The answer was accepted, and the next screen appeared. "Have you had any near-fatal encounters?"

Thomas shook his head. "I don't see what this has to do with anything."

"I understand your hesitancy, but these questions are…"

"Didn't you used to do this illegally? Why can't you just kill me now?"

Clay counted to ten in his head, then responded, his voice calm. "I did. And I was caught. Do you know the penalty for death dealing?"

Thomas shifted in his seat. "In the old days, they put killers to death."

"No, they keep you alive," Clay said. "They deprive you of death and of the ability to live. In perpetuity. If I break protocol, that is my fate. That was my choice." He cleared his throat. "If you choose not to answer the question, then I have no choice but to leave."

Thomas lunged forward before Clay even moved, holding his hand out. "No, please, don't. I'm sorry, I'll answer. I had a wreck when I was in my twenties, was injured and had surgery. I don't remember any of it."

Clay said nothing, watching the screen in his hands, the progress meter filling. As he waited on the answer to register, Thomas asked, "Why do you do this?"

"Do what?"

"This job."

"Because it needs to be done." The next question popped up. "In your estimation, how long have you had your suicidal feelings?"

"Answer my question first. You owe me that much at least."

"Mr. Barker…"

"Please."

"No." Clay stood. "I am done here."

"Wait, please, no." He grabbed Clay's wrist. "I've waited a century for this, that's your answer."

Clay looked down at the man, seated in the messy living room, the relics of the past decaying around him.

"You don't know what it's like," Thomas said, a quiver in his voice. His grip tightened on Clay's wrist. "To want to die and not be able to."

"You were alive before," Clay said. "You had your chance, and you had your chance now."

"No, I didn't. You must believe me. Please. Don't make me continue like this. No one should have to live like this."

Clay remained in place, and he could hear the whisper, the repeated plea, over and over. Thomas was right; he couldn't leave him, couldn't let him continue on. He eased himself back into his seat and pulled the tablet back up.

"One hundred years, that is correct?"

Thomas was still leaning forward, like an attentive listener, and he nodded. "Yes, that's right."

"Was there any one event that triggered your suicidal feelings?"

The man went quiet. He was still leaning forward in his chair, but his eyes were peering off into the distance, focused somewhere on the dirty living room wall. Clay waited a moment, then said, "Mr. Barker?"

"Yes," Thomas said. "Yes, there was something. I can talk about it, if I have to, but I would rather not. Not unless I must."

Clay nodded slowly. "It is required."

"I see." He continued to stare off into the ether. For a moment, Clay was unsure if the man was going to respond, but he did speak, his voice low. "As you said, I was a prior, am a prior. Are you, Clay?"

Clay said nothing. The answer was irrelevant. Thomas must have seen that as well because he continued. "Death was everywhere back then, you know? Old age, disease, trauma. It was accepted, a fact of life that many feared, but all must eventually face. Some sooner than others."

"It's funny to look back, to know what it was then and what it is now. You think of the millions who have died in history and how they could have impacted the world if they only had more time. But that's not how life is. We're meant to die, that is how we're made, by nature or God or whatever."

Clay frowned as he listened. The tablet recorded everything, and he jotted his own thought in the margin. *Depressed?* Nothing that medication couldn't solve. Had this man gone undiagnosed for a century?

"I know what you're writing," Thomas said. Clay paused and raised his eyes to find the man staring right at him. "I'm not depressed. You can check my medical records."

"Based on what you're saying, the government might disagree."

"They're wrong. Do you know what you never hear about the time before? There was death, yes, but there was also loss." Clay could see tears appearing in the man's eyes. "They always talk about what could have been, about what the dead lose, but never what the living lose. Who they lose."

"Mr. Barker…"

"No! You asked me why, and you're going to hear it." He looked down, covering his face in his hands, his voice softer. "They don't talk about the pain people went through when a loved one got sick. The feeling of helplessness as they waste away, until they're little more than a skeleton. How you sit there and talk to them, knowing they will never respond, unsure if they can even hear you. How you must make the choice of pulling the plug or not. And the guilt that you live with, the feeling of being responsible when a month later, the one true cure is revealed to the public. Knowing that death is no longer an option for you, that suicide is illegal. That death is not only illegal, but not even a possibility. That was the point that I knew I wanted to die. And now, a century later, you are here to fulfill that wish, but only if the government deems me worthy."

The room was silent. Thomas was weeping quietly into his hands. Clay looked down at his tablet, watching the spinning circle as the response was processed. A moment later, a green checkmark appeared.

"Mr. Barker, your case has been approved. I will now proceed."

The man did not look up, his weeping the only sound. Clay cleared space on the table and lay his case on its side. He opened it to reveal a series of syringes, each filled with a dark yellow liquid and adorned with a bold warning label. He removed one, holding it carefully.

"I am legally obligated to inform you that this process is final, that death cannot be reversed. You must verbally grant your understanding and consent before I may proceed."

The hands lowered, and Thomas nodded. "I understand."

"Give me your arm."

Thomas complied. Clay gripped him firmly by the wrist and straightened the arm.

"Will it hurt?" Thomas asked.

"You will feel the needle. After that, nothing."

Thomas nodded. "Thank you."

Clay said nothing. The needle pierced the skin and entered the vein. Thomas inhaled sharply as the plunger was depressed, then relaxed.

"How long?"

"Minutes. Not long."

Clay removed the needle and released the wrist. Thomas eased back into his chair and closed his eyes. "I'm coming, Amy."

Thomas was gone by the time Clay closed his case. He checked the vital signs, recorded the death, and made his way to the entrance.

His watch vibrated as he stepped into the daylight. Another. The car was already on the way. He could feel his grip on the case, the tightness in his temple. It was not getting any easier. He breathed in deeply, calming himself.

His heart rate had slowed by the time the car arrived. He stood there, watching the open car door. His ferry for bearing souls across the River Styx. This was not a burden he wished upon any other. This was his, and his alone.

He took another deep breath, then stepped toward the waiting car.

STORMCHASER

I believe this is the oldest story in this collection. I came up with the idea during one of the times I was driving back and forth between college and home. I've always had a thing for rainstorms, especially with the ones we can get here in Texas, and the idea came when I was somewhat mesmerized by the one I was headed towards as I drove. From there, the idea came together quickly.

All was gone but the oncoming storm.

Ian Garner kept his dark hazel eyes fixed straight ahead, focusing on both the storm and the road at the same time. The cruise control was set, just under the speed limit. State troopers liked to post up along this stretch, and he had no desire for them to take notice of him. The last thing he needed was to be noticed.

The storm was hypnotizing, seizing his attention and sucking him in with every mile, seeming to converge with his very path, and without a destination in the very same way he was. He had to force himself to keep attention to the road; he had swerved once already, another sure way to get himself noticed.

The road ahead of him was wet along the edges, evidence that the storm had already left its mark there, although clouds behind him indicated it wasn't finished. The sun still shone where he was, however, sneaking through a hole in the sky and eliminating any indication of previous precipitation, evaporating it into an unbearable humidity in the summer heat.

Lightning flashed in the system ahead of him, beckoning him further, taunting him, insulting him through the twang of guilt that was beginning to creep up the hairs in the small of his neck.

He shuddered, goosebumps running up his spine, across his neck, and on down his arm. He knew that he couldn't have been discovered yet.

Twenty minutes was not enough time, not with the way he had covered his trail. No, this was just his mind playing tricks on him.

The neighbors thought he was leaving for the airport, catching a plane to Boston for a vacation in the Northeast, meeting her there for a nice romantic getaway, weeks as far as they knew. Her family was under the impression that she was too enthralled with her career to even communicate with them. He hadn't spoken with his own family in a decade. Most importantly of all, she had just recently quit her job.

But even the best laid plans could fall apart, which was why he was trying to be careful. And yet there was the storm, something more than the usual Texas summer storm. There was something behind it, something that spoke to him as he continued down the road.

The miles flew past him, bringing nothing, yet he couldn't quite shake that feeling. He shot a glance up to the looming storm, fishing for an explanation, but all he got in reply with was a line from an old black and white movie that stood out somewhere in the back of his mind.

"Murder is never perfect. It always comes apart sooner or later."

And suddenly, it was as if his conscience was riding right there in the passenger seat next to him. He couldn't see it, not the way his eyes remain focused on the point where the storm met the horizon, but he could feel a presence there and was scared to death to look in that direction.

"Go away," he said out loud to the empty car.

And to his surprise, there was a reply. It may have come from his own head, *must* have come from his head, but it was so loud and clear that it may as well have come from right beside him.

"What are you doing?" the voice, one that sounded remarkably like his own, rang out. "I thought you loved her."

"It wasn't love that I lacked. It was hate that overcame."

"What about your vows, where you promised to protect her, to cherish her?"

A single bead of sweat ran from his hair down his neck. "As long as we both shall live. That is not a promise I can keep any longer."

"You will be caught."

"No. My cover may not be airtight, but it will hold until I am safely away." He allowed himself a smile, content with the fact that the crime did not have to be perfect to permit him to get away with it.

"But what happens if they find out before you're gone? There are plenty of cops that can be called to stop you between here and the border."

"They won't."

"Don't be so sure." His conscience lit a cigarette, and he could almost smell the smoke as it floated up from the lit end. Without realizing it, he lowered the passenger window. The apparition next to him continued, "And even if you do get to the border, how will you explain a body in the trunk?"

"I'll be rid of it before we reach the border."

"Hope you don't pick a place that is too obvious."

His hands were beginning to sweat, and he wiped them on the legs of his pants. *What if he's right? What if I can't get rid of the body?* He shook his head violently. "No," he said out loud, "You're not real, you're not here, and everything you say is only an attempt to scare me."

"You say attempt, but you're shaking." The cigarette was flipped out the open window. "You may want to watch your speed."

For the split second it took for him to look down and see the speedometer up to ninety and look back up, the highway patrol car came clearly into view. Panic set in, seizing his chest. When had he even taken it off cruise control? He cursed and slammed down on the brakes, taking his speed down to a modest sixty, but it was too late. The lights had come on and the cop was after him.

Another voice came from the empty car, this time from the back seat. It was a female voice speaking with a slight croak, the sound of someone whose vocal cords had been partially severed. "You should stop, you know. You don't want this to turn into a freeway chase. That could only end badly for you."

He was afraid to glance in the rearview mirror, because even with the disfiguration, he recognized the deliberate tone, the slight drawl, and the impression of smugness that haunted each word spoken by the late Mrs. Ian Gardner, known better as Sandy to those close to her.

His conscience chimed in from the passenger seat. "She's right, you know. A simple traffic stop will probably only result in a ticket, but a chase will end in a search of your car."

"Shut up, just shut up and let me think!" Ian yelled. The siren beeped and the cop's voice came over the bullhorn, urging Ian to pull over.

Ian's hand shook as he moved it slowly to the blinker and put upward pressure on the blinker lever, threatening to move it up to signal a move to the right shoulder. He held there for a moment.

"They're bound to find the body if I pull over," Ian said aloud.

"They'll certainly find the body if you make them suspicious," Sandy said. "And nothing looks more suspicious than running."

The pressure increased and the blinker flipped on, signaling a move to the right. He edged the car into the shoulder and applied the break, slowing the car over the loose gravel and easing further into the shoulder, far enough off so that the officer would have enough room on the side.

The cruiser pulled up behind him, the side of if favoring the left side of his car to give the officer a barrier from oncoming traffic. He sat in the car for a moment, probably running the license plates. Ian exhaled deeply, then rolled down the window and placed his hands at the ten and two positions on the steering wheel like he had always been told.

Red and blue lights continued to flash in his rearview mirror, a fact that was no longer blocked by Sandy's head. The door to the cruiser opened and the policeman, a state trooper, exited and began slowly walking over. He was dressed in the khaki uniforms that were so familiar to any speeder and was a walking cliché, clad in thick leather boots, aviator sunglasses and a cowboy hat.

The officer's boots crunched the gravel and came to a halt, signaling the mountain of a man standing outside of his window. Ian could hear the heavy breathing of a chain smoker and was suddenly stricken by a great annoyance, the same feeling that had absolutely consumed him when Sandy had burned dinner, an act so insignificantly small that snapped something deep inside him and allowed him to pull the knife from the drawer and sneak up behind her...

His hand crept slowly down to the knife that lay between the seat, a kitchen knife that was still freshly sharp and still covered with blood, blood that had dried to a deep maroon now. Instead, he pulled out his wallet, obliging to the officer's request to produce his license.

The officer disappeared for a moment, then returned with his license, insurance card, and a pink slip which he made Ian sign; a warning to decrease his speed.

Ian thanked the officer, then turned the ignition, starting the engine with a roar. As the officer walked back, he stopped and examined the ground behind the car. Ian's eyes widened in horror as he looked in the side mirror and saw a thin red stream emerging from beneath the car.

Ian didn't hesitate. As the officer bent forward for a better look, he shifted into reverse and slammed on the gas pedal. The officer was caught by the bumper and was carried along as the car rode in reverse, still accelerating as it slammed into the front of the cruiser, the officer in between.

Stopped by a jolt, Ian quickly shifted into drive and the wheels spun as the car momentarily stuck on the gravel, then took off down the freeway, cutting off a line of cars as he sped forward toward the storm.

"Now you've gone and done it." Sandy had returned to the backseat, her voice coming off as more nagging than before. Ian reflected on how much he wished he could kill her again.

"Shut up!" he yelled into the rearview mirror. "Shut up, I don't want to hear from you!"

"Now, now," she smiled into the rearview mirror. "Losing that famous temper of yours won't solve anything. I mean, look where it's gotten you now."

"The bitch has a good point," his conscience noted. "You've managed to royally screw yourself here."

"The cops are coming, Dear," Sandy cooed through her harsh rasp. "You're going to pay for what you've done."

Ian grabbed the knife and whirled around, stabbing the spot where Sissy sat, but only piercing air and the cloth and foam that formed the backseat. He turned back quickly, just in time to see the rear of a car approaching quickly. Ian twisted the wheel and narrowly avoided a collision, then swerved to regain control.

Lightning lit up the now dark sky and thunder crashed, a sound that seemed to instantly bring about sirens in the distance. A glance to rearview mirror revealed flashing lights that were quickly blocked by Sandy's head.

"You've already killed me once, Ian," Sandy said. "You'll only succeed in killing yourself."

The speedometer of the car was touching triple digits, but the interceptors were still approaching quickly.

"You can't outrun them," the voice from the front seat chimed in. "They'll go easier on you if you turn yourself in."

"Right, life instead of the death penalty," Ian muttered.

"Better than you deserve," Sandy said cheerfully.

The cops were right on his tail, the lights blinding him in the mirror, the bullhorn trying to be heard over the siren and the storm.

Lightning once again illuminated the sky and with a burst of thunder, the rain began to come down.

It was a little at first, but it quickly turned into a downpour, sheets of rain hindering his visibility. The interceptors backed off, slowing due to the rain, but Ian kept on ahead. The road was straight; he had faith in his driving skills, and he had faith in the storm above.

The storm immersed him now, surrounded him, engulfed him, invited him into its depths and welcomed him with open arms. Suddenly, it was as if he wasn't even driving, but instead floating. His conscience said something, and his wife screamed something in that rasped voice of hers, but he ignored them both.

He could no longer see out any window. The rain came down around him in a roar, as if he was in the midst of a waterfall. A bolt of lighting flared behind the water, followed by a crack of thunder barely audible behind the sound of the rain thumping against his car. If he hadn't seen the speedometer, he wouldn't have even known he was moving.

His worry was suddenly gone, his guilt alleviated, his sin atoned for, washed away by the storm. The voices had disappeared along with their embodied sources. Ian closed his eyes, released the wheel, and gave himself over to it.

Somewhere in the distance, he heard the sirens once again, but he knew they wouldn't find him. No one would ever find him.

CITY OF THE DROWNED

This is the first of several that stemmed from the work I did on /r/WritingPrompts on Reddit. I don't recall the specific prompt, but this is one that ended up going longer than I typically post in response to a writing prompt. I decided to keep it for myself, publishing it on my Patreon before including it in this collection. This is one that combines my love of Lovecraftian horror with that of lost civilizations, and I think it fits well within the lore that I built around my novel <u>Elder Gods</u>, which I think certainly has more tales to tell.

"You may want to take that off, Father."

Jacob touched the cross that hung from his neck. "Is there a safety hazard?"

The captain was a stout man with a hanging gut and wrinkled skin torched by the sun, a permanent scowl on his face. Trent, he had said his name was. He spat a glob of tobacco over the side before speaking again. "Don't want it getting caught on anything. There's enough danger beneath the waters without it."

"I will accept the risk," Jacob said, continuing to don the wetsuit. "God will watch over me, and if He chooses this as my time, then so be it."

The captain shrugged. "No skin off my back," he mumbled. Jacob thought he caught more words, maybe something about superstition? From what he knew of sailors, the man was one to talk.

The boat was anchored over a recent archeological finding, a sunken city in the southwest Pacific, off the coast of Indonesia. He glanced over the edge, peering through the blue water, searching for the site, but he could not even see the bottom, the water darkening somewhere beneath them, obscuring any light that tried to permeate.

Jacob was young for a priest, just past thirty. Though he wore the frock, he was not the kind to say mass. Instead, he had thrown himself into the pursuit of biblical knowledge, which had led him to the Order of Saint Cyprian within the Vatican. It was those studies that had brought him here.

"Are you ready, Father?"

He turned to find the archaeologist, Jamie Kennedy, already hoisting her own air tank onto her back. "Just about," he said. He zipped up the wetsuit and grabbed his tank. He could feel his heart beating, possibly as much from anticipation of what lay below as from the fact that he had yet to actually make a dive beyond his initial certification classes.

One of the crewmen helped him with his tank, then fitted a mask over his head, one the covered his entire face. Air began to flow, and he breathed easily.

"Can you hear me?" Jamie's voice came through a speaker fitted to his ear.

"Loud and clear."

"Good," she said. "Let's do this."

Jamie walked to the edge of the boat and jumped over the edge, disappearing below with a splash. Jacob breathed in deeply, then jumped after her. He broke the surface of the water, feeling it close around him, and fought the urge to kick upward. He breathed in deeply, allowing his body to recognize that he was okay, and put away any potential panic caused by being submerged.

They sank down, Jamie and Jacob and a pair of divers from the boat. The water grew dark around them, and their lights came on. Jacob could see fish meandering in the water, shooting away as the divers passed them.

And God said, "Let the waters bring forth swarms of living creatures, and let birds fly above the earth across the dome of the sky." So God created the great sea monsters and every living creature that moves, of every kind, with which the waters swarm, and every winged bird of every kind. And God saw that it was good.

But was it all good? Theology taught him that it was, but his research had told him otherwise.

The darkness parted beneath them, the lights forming a halo that surrounded them. Up above, he could still see the light of the day, the safety of the surface, but it was quickly fading away.

"You still doing okay there, Padre?" Jamie asked him.

"Just fine," he said. His breathing might have been a bit pronounced, but he chalked that up to nerves.

Below his feet, the ruins slowly materialized into view. Buildings rose from the seafloor, once carefully crafted from stone but now deteriorating away in the salty water. Narrow streets wound between the structures, flat roofs and domes and the occasional tower that still stood.

"This is it," he said.

"This is it," Jamie said to him. "We don't have a name for it yet, so we've been calling it Mu."

"Not Atlantis?"

"Atlantis wasn't in the Pacific."

Jacob gave a slight chuckle at that. They were sinking between the buildings now, making their way to the very bottom. He couldn't believe that he was here, that he was looking at this sunken city. On one of the building walls, he saw writing, faded, but unmistakably Hebrew. This was it, one of the cities that the writings spoke of.

He had found the papers buried deep within the archives, Hebrew on papyrus, origin unknown. They were writings, dated long before Jesus, writings that spoke of Israelites who had ventured eastward seeking out new lands after being freed from Egypt. The papers told of them crossing the deserts and mountains, of the wet forests and strange peoples. And it had told of them occupying an island, an island large enough for three cities: Navah, Yesha, and Chen. He wondered which of the three this was.

And so it was that the wayward Israelites came to an island. And it was this land that they named Berakah, or Blessing, for they knew this was to be their new home.

They were nearly at the bottom when Jamie began to kick her feet, propelling herself between the buildings. Jacob took the cue and made his way after her.

"We believe this city to date to between 1500 and 1000 BCE," she said. "It sank into the sea well before the Romans came to power, likely from the result of an earthquake."

They were lost to the eyes of God, for his people were in the Promised Land, and with it, their problems. So the wayward Israelites, without the guidance of their God, turned away from Him.

"An earthquake?"

"There are fault lines near the edges of the city," she said, " and it would match with the volcanic activity in the area." She paused, floating before him, and pointed to some writing on a building wall. "The interesting part is that this is Hebrew writing. We have no records of Hebrews coming this direction, but this obviously proves otherwise."

They called upon the deep of the sea, a sea that they came to know unlike the seas of their once home. When God created the creatures of Earth, he tried to drown his nightmares by casting them beneath the sea. But instead of dying in the crushing blackness, they thrived in it.

The blackness around them was not crushing, but it was certainly dark enough. At one point, they passed a place where a building had fallen away, collapsed off the edge of a cliff into an even deeper darkness, a place where light did not permeate, and where creatures of the deep lurked beyond the eyes of man.

Jacob found himself moving further away from the lip, keeping close to the archaeologist. At one point, he glanced back to ensure that the two other divers were still there. They were, their lights following behind at a close distance.

"It is the Hebrew, isn't it?"

"Huh?" His thoughts still lay heavy in his mind, the thoughts of the papers from the archives.

"That brought you here. You heard there was Hebrew on the walls."

"Yes," he said. "It...confirmed something in my research."

She came to a stop, turning toward him. "You knew that the Hebrews were here?"

They found their new home, and with it, their new god. A god that was not the God of their people.

"I found writings, in the Vatican archives," he said. "The only ones of their kind, as far as I know."

"Why didn't you say anything?" she asked. "This find would have made so much more sense. We could have already known so much."

And so it was, that when God turned His eyes back to the wayward Israelites, that He saw them worshiping the nightmares He had once tried to drown in the depths.

"There are many books written on many things," he said. "Like all findings, it is important that due diligence is done before the public knows."

Even in the darkness, he could see the look of disappointment behind the mask. "I wish you had trusted me with your findings as much as I trusted you with mine, Father," she said. She turned and continued one.

Jacob sighed and swam after her, kicking hard until he caught up. "I'm sorry, Jamie," he said. "I had to be sure, and now I am. I promise, I'll tell you everything I know once we return to the surface."

The tone in her voice told him that she was ignoring the olive branch he offered. "This is an area we have not yet explored," she said. "It might be dangerous, so be vigilant."

They came around the corner and found themselves in an open space in the midst of several buildings, a plaza of some kind. In the middle was a statue, one that seemed like a person holding something, the finer details lost in the hazy darkness of the sea around them.

"This is strange," Jamie said, swimming up toward it. "This is the first statue we've seen in Mu."

"Have there been other artifacts?"

"We haven't taken the time to pick things out," she said absently, her focus on the statue. "We are still mapping the area."

As Jacob approached, the features became clearer, the shape of the statue, even worn by time, evident. It was human-like, but it was not human. It wore no clothes, and its head had no hair. Much of the detail had been worn smooth, but there was no mistaking the scales that adorned its skin. One hand was stretched out, but there was no space between the fingers, and the other hand was held closer, the palm opened to support some kind of fish, a long one with sharp teeth, its tail wrapped around the forearm. Instead of legs, the thing's body continued on, curling up into a wide tail like a fish.

"This is...fascinating," Jamie said.

God saw the false gods that His people worshiped, and He became enraged, for they had broken the first of His ten commandments. He saw the statues and the temples and the sacrifices, and He knew that his children had become lost beyond recovery.

"Yeah..." Jacob suddenly felt an uneasy feeling rising in his chest, as though a panic attack was setting in. Something felt off about this place, something he could not place. He turned around, seeking the comfort of the lights of their companions, but when he did, all he saw was darkness. "Uh...Jamie?"

"Yes, Father?" Her voice was still distant. She had taken out a camera and was snapping pictures of the statue.

"Where are our companions?"

"They're right behind us, aren't they?" She trailed off when she turned and saw that they were not. "Ryan? Jack? Come in."

Nothing. Only silence greeted the hailing. The silence of the sea around them, of the crushing blackness that surrounded them.

"Ryan? Jack?" She paused. "Trent? Can you hear us?" Still nothing.

The panic was becoming more and more palpable. "Is this normal?" Jacob asked.

"Not at all," she said. "Let's backtrack, maybe they stopped to look at something."

God summoned a great quake, and in the midst of the pleading and repentance and curses that His people threw at Him, He sank them beneath the sea, so that they may join the gods for which they had forsaken Him.

Jacob was shining his light on the buildings that bordered the plaza. He thought he saw something move within one of them, but in the darkness, there was no way to tell if anything had. Jamie was already moving past him, back the way they had come. Jacob quickly followed; the last thing he wanted was to get separated from her.

There was no sign of the other divers, only the stirred-up dust that filtered through the water, obscuring their beams. The city was just as empty as it had been before they had descended upon it.

Jacob had begun a prayer in his mind. It was only when Jamie called his name that he realized that he had been speaking it aloud. "Sorry," he said.

"Don't be," she said.

He turned away from the drop off, inward toward the city. "Is there a meeting place? A landmark or something to meet at?"

"Nothing of the..." She paused, and he turned to see her looking out over the precipice. "Is that them?"

Jacob followed her gaze and saw a light somewhere out in the darkness of the water, a small light. It was bobbing up and down, as though held by a swimming hand. Jamie was already swimming out toward it.

"Ryan? Jack?" she hailed over the radio.

Jacob watched the light, the way it moved. It wasn't getting any closer or further, just moving in place. It seemed strange, not like a flashlight, but like something else, something he couldn't quite place. He reached out and grabbed Jamie by the arm.

She turned toward him. "What are you doing?"

"Something's not right," he said.

"What are you talking about? Look at it."

"I am looking at it," he said. "It's moving in place. It looks like someone swimming, but it's not going anywhere."

"That's ridiculous." She looked again. "It's gotta be one of them. I'm going."

"Jamie, wait."

The light was closer now, close enough that it should have been in the halo of their own lights. They both froze as they saw what did emerge into their light, the dark skin, the flicking tentacles, the razor-sharp teeth.

"Swim, now!" Jacob cried. He felt the water move around him as the tentacles lashed out toward them, all somehow missing their target. It felt as though they moved in slow motion as they made their way back toward the buildings. Jacob glanced behind him, and saw that the light was still there, but he didn't wait around to see if it was pursuing them.

They swam through the deserted alleys of the city, between the buildings, navigating deeper and deeper in. It was only when Jamie grabbed onto him that he stopped. He could feel his chest heaving, his muscles aching from exertion that they had not seen for ages. And they were lost somewhere within the sunken city.

The cities and the land around them disappeared beneath the waves, and God wept, for He had lost His children to the very things that he had cast beneath the waves, the very things that were meant to lay forgotten to time.

They were in another plaza, a smaller one. A fountain rested here, ever filled, and dividers that appeared to be for a garden. They hovered there, both catching their breaths as they waited for any indication that the creature had followed them.

Finally, Jacob broke the silence. "Do you know what that was?"

"I'm an archaeologist, not a biologist," she said. "That light, though, it's just like the angler fish. It was trying to lure us. It meant to lure us. Do you think…"

Jacob did a quick sign of the cross, saying a prayer in his mind for the two lost divers. He glanced around the plaza, then upward, toward the surface and the sky above.

"It…it didn't follow us, did it?" Jamie asked.

"I don't think so. We may just want to chance swimming upward." He paused, waiting for an answer. "Jamie?"

When he looked down at her, he saw that she was looking away, her eyes wide and her mouth agape. "What is it..." He trailed off as he followed her eyes, as he saw what she saw.

As God turned away from His people, the creatures of the deep opened their arms and accepted them. And they were given a new life, a life beneath the sea, with those others whom God had cast aside.

Their skin was a deep green, the surface scaled, their eyes dark, their hands webbed, and their feet given over to fish tails. It was as though the statue had come to life, many times over. They emerged from the doors, through the windows, at least a dozen of them, or maybe more. As far as Jacob could tell, they were still emerging. And they were growing closer.

"Jamie," he whispered, pulling on her arm. "Jamie, we have to go. Now."

They were closer, ever closer. He was certain that one could reach out and grab either of them. There was no time to wait, no more time to hesitate. Jacob grabbed her arm and began to kick.

And in the end, God saw them for what they were, and for what they had become, and so he cursed them to forever lurk beneath the sea, until the final judgement should come forth and call the wicked to light.

He could feel the water rush below them, but he did not look back. From beside him, Jamie began to kick as well. They rose above the building tops, the city growing smaller beneath their feet.

Something grabbed a hold of Jacob, and he jerked backwards, releasing his grip on Jamie's arm. She yelled his name, and he struggled against a powerful grip, fighting as he was pulled downward.

"Keep going," he said as he fought. These things were powerful, much stronger than himself. He could feel them dragging him backwards, the water once more fading into blackness.

For the wayward Israelites, in their sunken home, harbor ill feelings toward their former God, and the people of His who still walk upon the dry land.

Jacob found the latch on his air tank and released it. He felt the straps catch on his shoulders, just as they had when he had put it on. He shimmied beneath them, feeling the burn of friction as it pulled against his wetsuit. It inched down, a bit at a time, until it finally came off in one stroke.

The pull was gone. He was free.

Jacob began to swim upward. He remembered the lesson about waiting to decompress, but he was going to have to take the chance. Already, his lungs were beginning to burn from lack of air.

He kicked and kicked and waved his arms, pulling himself toward the surface. The water around him grew lighter, clearer, yet it seemed to grow darker all the same, as though he had gotten turned around and was swimming downward once again. He fought upward, and he released the air from his lungs, and he closed his eyes.

He broke through the surface with a gasp, ripping off his mask as he did, his lungs filling with air before he sank down once more. Hands gripped him by the suit and pulled him back, and he broke the surface once more to see Jamie leaning over the side of the boat, holding him above water.

She helped him climb aboard, and he sprawled on the deck, breathing heavily. She suddenly embraced him, backing away after a moment. "I thought you were a goner," she said. "I was certain I was going to have to run this boat all by myself."

"What do you mean by yourself?" he gasped.

She turned her head, and he slowly forced himself to sit up, gazing upon the deck. It was completely empty. Empty, that is, except for the wet spots that covered the deck. Some were water, salt water, the kind of puddles one would expect to find. Some were greenish, as though some kind of algae was growing within them. And some were red, puddles of blood that were pooling in between.

"What in God's name has happened here?" Jacob asked, but he knew the answer without her having to say a word. Whatever was down there had not remained down there.

"We're alone," Jamie said.

"God is with us," Jacob said.

"That hasn't done us much good so far." She turned back to him. "What do we do?"

Jacob glanced out over the sea. There was no land for miles, not from where they sat. Could they make a run for it? Would the things even come back for them?

He tried to move but found that he couldn't. His legs had cramped up completely, his body next to worthless. "We have to get going. Give me a moment to rest, and then we'll…"

A sound broke him off, and they both turned their heads toward it.

It is a grudge that time cannot heal, a grudge that will carry forth until the world ceases to exist, a grudge that will one day spill onto dry land, should the wayward Israelites be granted their eternal wish.

The sound seemed innocuous at first, like the sound of a lapping wave. Slowly, it grew louder, as though something was attaching suction cups to the side. Jacob felt Jamie grab his hand. With his other hand, he grabbed the cross around his neck and began to pray.

THE LUNAR WARS

This story is another result of a prompt on /r/WritingPrompts, one that I believe I may have ended up posting. I won't speak too much about it, both because it is a quick story and because doing so would give away the ending, but I always like delving into the mind of a fictional writer, especially one who has a unique way of coming up with ideas.

The office resided in the back of the large house, overlooking a raised deck and the rolling hills of the backyard, as much as that much land could be considered a backyard. From the window, there was not another house to be seen, the land rising and falling in waves of green grass and towering oak trees. It was the land of a rich man, the kind of land that the most successful science fiction author in the world could afford to purchase.

Harold Dipper was seated at his desk, hunched over his keyboard. The house was kept neat by weekly visits from the maid, but the office was one place she was never allowed and as such was never clean, filled with stack of books and loose papers and framed pictures that had yet to be hung and awards that were more useful as paperweights and doorstops than anything else. On the wall was a framed cast poster from the first season of the adaptation of his bestselling series, *The Lunar Wars*, the licensing of which had paid for a new wing of the house.

On his screen now was the conclusion, what was to be the final book in the series. Once he was done with that, he would have to find something new, but he had plenty of material, plenty of ideas for new books, even new series. For now, he consulted the tattered notebook next to him, and the pictures that resided between the pages, scenes from his series that were simply stunning in their realism.

The words filled the page as though the story had already been told and he was just writing it down. He typed almost as quickly as his mind could process, fingers flying over the keyboard, the only sound in the quiet of the cluttered room.

The sound of the doorbell pierced the air, sudden and jarring, startling him from his work. It was an obnoxious sound in the first place, made more so by the fact that his visitor was holding it down, allowing it to drone on for a moment before finally releasing it.

His concentration was broken, his mind pulled from the groove he was in. He considered ignoring it, but he could already tell that his visitor was persistent, much more so than the average delivery man or solicitor. He sighed, removing his glasses and tossing them onto the desk as he stood and began to make his way to the front door.

The door was buzzing again as he entered the foyer. "I'm coming," he grumbled, picking up his pace and nearly slipping on the tiled floor. He tossed a few curses at the empty room as he removed his socks and tossed them aside, then opened the door.

"Can I help you?" His voice was gruffer than he had intended, but nearly slipping on the tile had been the cherry on top of the way he had been pulled from his work.

The young man who stood before him still had his finger pointing to the doorbell, though he had thankfully released it. His mouth was slightly open, his eyes a bit wide, a noise coming from his mouth though he created no words.

Harold dug out one of his grandmother's favorite sayings. "Are you trying to catch flies?"

"I...I'm sorry Mr. Dipper," he said. "I guess I didn't expect you to answer."

He was beginning to think that he shouldn't have. "What do you want? I'm a bit busy right now."

"I'm sorry, my name is Ben. Ben Sanders." He fished around in his satchel and removed a card. "I'm a writer for SciFi Monthly, a new publication, and I was hoping for a moment of your time."

Harold glanced at the card. It was new, the printing seeming like it would leave streaks on his fingers. There was the name, a phone number, and a logo of a star surrounded by a nebula. He had never heard of it, but these magazines seemed to pop up and disappear quicker than anyone could keep up.

He handed the card back and moved to close the door. "I'm sorry, all interview requests need to be made through my agent."

The door stopped before it reached the frame, the man's shoe shoved into the middle to block it from closing. "I did reach out to your agent," he said. "Your manager as well. I tried numerous times, but they wouldn't even take my calls."

"I'm sure they had their reason," Harold said. He pushed harder. "If you would please move your foot..."

"Please, Mr. Dipper." There was a desperation in his voice that matched his face. "I know you're a busy man, but this interview means the world to me. The magazine is already struggling, but a high-profile interview can really drive readership. It could be the boost we need. I promise, I won't take up much of your time."

Harold paused for a moment, watching the young man outside his door. "How quick?"

"No more than thirty minutes, I promise."

Harold once more considered him for a moment. "Very well. Thirty minutes starting now." He opened the door and allowed the man to enter.

Ben's head was craned as he gazed around the foyer. "Wow, what a house."

"And no pictures," Harold added as he closed the door. "This way, into the kitchen."

The kitchen was spotless, the only indication of Harold's residence the pizza box that stuck out of the trashcan. He directed the journalist to a bar chair at the kitchen island and took one himself. "Timer's running," he said.

"Right," Ben said. He pulled a small tape recorder from his bag and put it on the island, pressing the record button, then pulled out a notebook. "Thank you so much for agreeing to this interview. Everyone at the magazine is a huge fan."

Harold only nodded, his arms crossed over his chest, his eyes glancing toward the clock.

Ben paused for a moment before continuing. "So, uh, my first question. What got you into writing?"

Harold managed to stop himself from rolling his eyes. He couldn't even begin to count the number of times he'd answered that very question. "I used to read a lot of old books with my father. Tolkien, Wells, Verne, Boroughs. The classics. From there, I started making up stories using my action figures. Then my father brought home an old typewriter, I started using it to write my own stories, and from there I was hooked."

Ben nodded as he jotted down notes. No doubt he had read the same response in half a dozen prior interviews Harold had done. "You wrote other things before *The Lunar Wars*, but none have had quite the impact. Why do you think your latest series is so much more popular?"

A bit better. He allowed himself a smile. "It's hard to really say. I don't want to pat myself on the back too much, but I do think that compared to my earlier works, it's simply a better work. I wouldn't say that my earlier works were duds, but they don't hold a candle to *The Lunar Wars*. Better plot, better characters, better writing, really, and people are drawn to that."

More nodding, more jotting. "It's true, many people noticed the improvement, even between novels within the series. Did you do anything in particular to make those improvements?"

Harold shrugged. "Just personal growth, I think. Writing is the same as any skill. The more you hone your craft, the better it grows. And I suppose I've been doing this for long enough that I've gotten better at it."

"What's also grown in the minds of a lot of fans is the creativity you've exhibited in your latest series. Whereas many of your early works were loosely rooted in reality, mostly high science fiction that takes place on distant planets, *The Lunar Wars* takes place a hundred years from now in our own solar system, in a world that seems all too real with our current state."

Harold gave the journalist a pleasant smile. "Yes, I am quite proud of the worldbuilding I was able to do for the series. You know, in some ways, worldbuilding within our own timeline is much more difficult, as you're trying to predict macro level trends in global politics, while trying not to upset fans of particular political persuasion."

"Which you are well known for your left-leaning messages."

"In my earlier works, yes," Harold said. "I have become more moderate as the years pass, and I try to present things in a neutral tone."

"True, but in *The Lunar Wars*, you clearly paint the conservative contingent in Congress as the catalyst for the wars."

"While they are the main driver, I also include many from the other side who support the plan. Politics are a complicated beast, in real life and fiction, and I do my best to capture that chaos on the page."

The journalist paused in his writing and removed another small notebook from his bag. He spoke as he leafed through the pages. "Going back to your timeline, I noticed some interesting things."

Harold raised an eyebrow. "Oh?"

"Yes," Ben said, finding the page he was searching for and tapping his finger on it. "I was going through the timeline on the first book, and I noticed that it has Donald Trump winning the 2016 election."

"Well he did, didn't he?"

"Of course," Ben said. "*Sea of Tranquility*, however, was published in 2015."

The smile returned. "Trump had been a player in the 2012 election, which you may have been a bit young to really remember, and at that point, his campaign was picking up steam. It wasn't ridiculous to think that he could win, and it ended up being a lucky guess. It didn't end up having a big effect on the timeline either way."

Ben rubbed his chin, and Harold found himself crossing his legs. "You say that," Ben said, "but here, you specifically point out the tariffs Trump installed on China and the proxy war that developed in Syria during his presidency, both of which led to future tensions."

"I did," Harold said. "The beauty of releasing later editions is that you can make changes like that and tweak the story to more closely match real life. I assume you pulled that timeline from the third edition, which was released sometime last year, and would therefore include those two events."

The journalist frowned. He was doubting himself, despite his notes, Harold could see that much in his eyes. The more he doubted, the better off Harold would be. "I appreciate that you consider me some sort of Nostradamus," Harold continued, "but I assure you I am anything but."

"I cannot speak with certainty to the edition of *Sea of Tranquility* that I pulled the timeline from," Ben said. He removed an image and slid it across the counter to Harold. "That, however, I can speak to."

Harold picked it up and studied it. It was one of his timelines, that was certain, but which one, he was unsure of. He recognized the bullet points and the years, the events over a century that were written in hand in his notebook. He looked over the top items, the ones that had passed, and to the events that had yet to happen, the ones that led to the events of the Lunar War.

"What about it?"

"This is from *Sea of the Edge*, book three, I'm sure you remember it."

"Of course I remember it," Harold said.

"Do you remember the year it came out?"

"No, I..." He trailed off. Was it last year? No, the fourth book had come out.

The journalist nodded, a grin on his face. "Two years ago, not enough time to release a second edition, not when you were so focused on *Sea of Crises*."

"I still don't see why that's important."

"Two years ago, Wade Martin had just been elected as a senator in California," Ben said. "No one foresaw the way he would sweep through the primaries and become elected president. No one, except for a particular science fiction author."

Harold said nothing, only staring at the paper before him. It wasn't possible, he had changed everything he needed to, hadn't he? Changing names was so easy, why had that not been done? How had it been missed?

"Your silence speaks volumes, Mr. Dipper," Ben said.

Harold put on the sternest face he could manage and tossed the picture back onto the table. "This could just as easily be from *Sea of Crises*, or even photoshopped for all I know."

"But it's not," Ben said. "I'm sure you have a copy of *Sea of the Edge* lying around here somewhere around here. A first edition, no less. We can check it right now."

Harold watched the journalist for a moment. "Just what are you trying to accomplish here?"

Ben returned the gaze, then reached over and turned off the recorder. "A lot of science fiction writers like yourself, the ones who deal in speculative fiction, have timelines. They typically focus on big events, high level wars and political events. But yours, it's more detailed. It's still macro, but it focuses on root causes, ones that are taking shape before our very eyes. Some of which have already come true."

"And Star Trek predicted cell phones," Harold said. "I don't understand what you're trying to say."

"I think you know something, Mr. Dipper. There is too much coincidence so far, too much that's been predicted in your timeline. So much that has yet to happen. How can you possibly be doing this?"

"I've gotten lucky," Harold said. "There's nothing more to it." He stood. "This interview is over."

"No, there's more to it than that," Ben said, remaining in place. "How did you know? How have you been doing this?"

"I want you out of my house, now," Harold said.

"Tell me the truth, Mr. Dipper." Ben was standing now, stepping closer to Harold. "I know you're keeping some kind of secret. Tell me how you do it."

"No," Harold said through clenched teeth.

"Tell me!"

"No!"

Harold grabbed the closed thing at hand, a skillet, and he swung. He surprised himself with the swing, and even more so when it connected with the man's head. It made a combination of a clang and a crunch, and Ben dropped to the ground. Harold stood over him for a moment, waiting for him to get up, watching the blood pour from his nose. He swung again, just to be sure.

Harold was breathing heavily, and he took a moment to sit down. His mind was racing as fast as his heart. He closed his eyes, as though to shut away the sight of the body on his kitchen floor, as though it was just a bad dream, but when he opened them, it was still there. He breathed in slowly, waiting for his body to calm.

When his breathing and heartbeat returned to normal, and his mind cleared enough that he could think, he took note of the situation. He had to clean things up, and more importantly, he had to hope that no one knew that the interviewer had come here, but that part was beyond his control. For now, the body needed to be disposed of, and he knew of a place where no one would find it. At least not for a very long time.

Harold took the body by the arms and began to drag it toward the basement door.

The machine whirred, and a bright light flashed, and Harold was no longer in his basement.

The house didn't exist here, not even the foundation. From the looks of it, it had been demolished to make way for more ranch land at some point, or perhaps a game preserve, or maybe no one had use for this kind of land anymore. What mattered was that each time he had come here, there had never been a soul around.

Digging the hole took the better part of the afternoon, and by the time he was done, he was drenched in sweat. He paused to wipe his brow, gazing off to where the sun was sinking in the west. Perhaps next time, he would make sure to come in the spring; that was always a pleasant time in these parts.

Once the hole was dug, he dragged the body to it, and pushed it over the side. After that, he collected the rest of the man's belongings - the notebook, the recorder, the backpack - and tossed them in after. From there, he began the process of filling it back up, a much easier task than digging the hole.

Finally, it was done. Harold tossed the shovel into the machine and took out a bottle of water to have a drink. It seemed strange, that he should feel so numb about having killed someone, but the truth was, there was no other way. No one had ever come so close to figuring him out, and he could never let anyone get close again. He would need to be more careful.

The moon was rising, a bright full moon that lit up the darkening sky. It seemed smudged, as though someone had painted dirt across the white surface, with tiny lights in between. Some of the lights flickered, brightening in a tiny flash before disappearing completely, leaving only the echo etched on his cornea. It was a sight he had watched again and again until he had etched it completely to memory, until he had gotten it completely right, so that the events of the day may adorn the pages of a grand novel.

But tonight was not a night to linger. He had everything committed to memory, every piece of the puzzle, and he needed no more help.

Harold took one last look at the moon above, then stepped into the machine, closing the door behind him. A flick of a switch, and it whirred to life. The light flashed once more, and the machine vanished, taking its passenger with it, leaving the grave in the midst of the peaceful, rolling hills. Up above, the battle continued to rage upon the moon.

WATERS OF THE BOG

This is another idea that came from listening to "Lore", in particular the episodes that talked about bog bodies. If you've never heard of them, it occurs in Ireland, where the conditions beneath the waters of the peat bogs allow for preservation of anything buried within. Because of it, bodies dug up from beneath have been remarkably intact, allowing for study of the people who lived there long ago.

Of course, the story I wrote was anything but academic, delving instead into a more mystical aspect as a village's strongest fighter suddenly dies and a village finds itself in dire need of help.

"Well, what do we do now?"

They stood there, the four of them. Angus Mac Aohda, leader of the clan, old and wiry and tough as leather. His wife, Róise, thin and grey of hair, with an eternal scowl on her face and a tongue like a whip. The druid, Séamus, leaning on his staff and stroking the long white beard that grew all the way down to his waist. And finally, Cian, the youngest of the group, still unsure if his continued presence was expected or if he should make himself scarce.

It seemed like a matter for the elders to tend to, not something for a sheepherder's son not yet twenty, but they had not asked him to leave, and he was not about to volunteer. It had been him who had found the body, after all, and well, it wasn't a normal death. Not by a long shot.

It had been Róise who had said the words, the first to speak as always, while the two older men gazed down over the body. It was a large body, seeming to stretch almost the length of the roundhouse, though Cian knew it was just a trick of the light. Keegan had been big, though, larger than life it had seemed, blessed by the gods with height and strength and the kind of leadership that drew men to him, both in the village and on the battlefield.

He was the best of the village, feared by others for miles around.

And now he was dead. It seemed impossible; from everything Cian had seen of him, always from a distance, it seemed, the man was invincible. He pulled sheep from the bogs, pushed carts from the mud, carried entire logs over long distances. He hunted down wolves that harried the sheep, and when the village had gone to war, he was a terror on the battlefield, striking fear into any who would threaten their way of life.

"We cannot let word of this leave the village," Angus said. "Torin Mac Niall would lead his men here in an instant if he heard Keegan were dead. He knows we have no one else who can stand up to his sons."

Róise shook her head. "We can't keep it a secret forever. We have to bury him at some point." She turned toward Cian. "Did anyone else see him?"

"I was alone," Cian said. "I came straight here."

"That does not mean that no one saw him earlier," she said. "Or that no one did when he was fetching us."

"So there's the four of us, plus Ulick and Ardal," Angus said. "And anyone who may have happened to have seen. But we cannot keep this a secret forever. Sooner or later, word will reach out, and Torin will come. This is a day he has long been awaiting."

Séamus shifted suddenly, the gourds that hung from ropes around his neck rattling loudly as he stepped around the body. "He must be given to the gods," he said, his scratchy voice filling the roundhouse. "The body must be place in the waters and the words said."

"Quiet, old man," Róise said.

Cian felt himself gasp, but Angus spoke over him, drowning out the sound. "Do not speak to him like that. He is your druid."

Róise grumbled, but she shut her mouth, allowing the druid to continue. He held a gnarled staff with crooked fingers, one with more rattling gourds tied to the end, shaking it toward the clan leader and his wife. "The gods speak. A man of violence has taken his final breath, and it is to the gods that we must give him."

"Do what you will with the body," Angus said. "I have much I must prepare for."

"The clan leader must be there," the druid said. "All must be there." He was moving now, walking with quick shuffling steps toward the roundhouse entrance. His free hand reached out and snagged Cian's sleeve as he passed. "You too. Come along now."

Cian found himself following trailing the druid out of the roundhouse and into the cool night. The old man was barking out orders as he moved. "You two," he said to the two men who had brought the body, still waiting by their cart. "Bring the body. Quickly now."

The commotion drew attention, people stepping from their homes into the night. The druid called them out as he passed, using no names, only providing orders. One was told to gather herbs, another to bring a sheep, another to bring torches. The rest, he only told to follow.

None hesitated. All sprung to action without question as the orders were given. There were mumblings, a question as to what was happening, but there was no hesitation.

The orders stopped when they passed the edge of the village, but the speaking did not. "An offering to the gods, yes. We have upset them, it is clear. Dangerous magic at work tonight, dangerous for us all should it continue. They worry about the neighboring town when they should be worrying about something much greater. The eyes of man are too narrow, too focused on what lies before him to see the greater world, like a child playing in the mud while great treasures are laid before him."

They passed the pens, the sheep huddled in one corner, baaing lowly. Past the edge of that were the bogs, the waters and shifting lands and quicksand, an ever-changing terrain that could not be mapped, could not be learned.

The druid, however, continued right on without the slightest hesitation.

He was still speaking, at least until he realized that Cian had stopped following. He stopped and turned toward him. "Well, are you coming?"

Cian looked down at the wet ground. To the right, he could see the outline of a pool, recently formed, at least by his memory. There was no telling how else the bogs had changed. It had always been a point of emphasis to never go out alone, and to absolutely never go out at night.

"What are you waiting for?" Séamus said. "It's perfectly safe. The gods watch over us tonight."

"I thought you said the gods are angry with us," Cian said.

"The fog lifts," Séamus said. "You will see things as they are. Now come, there's not a moment to delay."

Cian still hesitated, watching as the druid began to fade in the dark. He took a deep breath and followed. The mud squelched at his steps, his feet sinking part of the way into the ground, pulling out with heavy plops. There was no such sound where the druid stepped, and Cian was not certain the old man even left footsteps. He did his best to walk where Séamus walked, keeping his steps to those that the old man made. A prayer touched his lips, carried away by the wind, and he could only hope that it would reach the ears of the gods.

A lone tree rose out of the bog, settled on a raised patch of land, its roots poking out of the packed dirt on the sides. Séamus used those roots to climb up to the dry land, and Cian followed, breathing out deeply as he once more set foot on solid land. The druid was already making his way toward the tree, a massive oak whose roots extended deep into the soil of the island, its branches spreading out above, blocking out the sky.

Séamus stuck his staff into the ground, leaving it standing there. Amidst the roots was a circle of stones, and in it, a pile of twigs and branches, already stacked up. Séamus knelt over it, reaching into his robe and pulling out a small pouch. He chanted some words low on his breath, the old language, Cian thought, and sprinkled something over the wood. Nearly immediately, flames began to lick at the branches, soon engulfing them and casting light across the spot that the tree grew from.

"Since as long as anyone can remember, we have given our dead to the bogs," Séamus said. "The gods give us the gift of life, and we return the gift to them when it has passed its usefulness."

Cian stood watching, unsure of what to do. Was he supposed to help? Watch? What role was he to play?

There was the squelching of footsteps approaching, seeming to appear out of nowhere. Cian turned quickly, a gasp escaping his lips, but the druid only said, "Worry not, the rest approach."

There were no lights, only the dark figures emerging from the darkness, figures of many shapes and sizes. Cian's mind flashed to the stories he had been told as a child, of the bog people who came out of the darkness to steal children and livestock to take them back to their underwater abodes. But when the figures approached the light, the air of mystery faded, and he only saw the townsfolk, coming at the druid's beckoning.

The body came first, carried by Ulick and Ardal, and then the sheep, bleating loudly as it was carried by Fintan. Torin arrived with his arms wrapped around several torches, and he proceeded to light them in the flames and hand them to others as they arrived. Angus and Róise were the last ones, taking a single torch between them and standing on the edge with the rest. In the flickering light, Cian could see the scowl on Róise's face and the furrowed brow on Angus's.

All were silent, yet the druid still raised his voice to project his words. "Tonight, we give our brother Keegan back to the gods." There were murmurs at the mention of his name, but Séamus continued. "Life is a gift from the gods, and it is the gods who take it back. It is from the bogs that our people came, and it is to the bogs that we return to when our lives are no more."

The body had been lain out on the grass in the middle of the island. Séamus removed a small pouch from his robes and dipped his fingers into it. When he drew them out, they were covered in a fine reddish powder. He drew on Keegan's bare chest, writing out a prayer in runes, then nodded to the men, who picked the body up once more.

"We give the body to the gods, that they may ferry his soul into the beyond and bring him the peace and happiness that we all so desire."

The men brought the body over the edge of the land, the spectators parting ways to allow them to pass. They lay his body on the water, and as soon as they released it, it began to sink, slowly vanishing beneath the dark surface. They stepped back, and Séamus stepped forward, pulling a knife from somewhere in his robes.

He motioned toward the man who held the bleating sheep. "Bring it here," he said. The sheep was brought forward, and Séamus maneuvered it so that it was being held over the water. Without warning, he drew the blade across its throat, silencing it with one final cry as its blood spilled into the bog waters.

"We give the gods this gift of our flock," he said, smearing the blood covered hand across his face and beard, and then the rest onto the sheep's wool. "We ask them to bless this soul, to guide him, and to guide our people, that we may continue on even without our brother and all he brought to our lives."

The murmurs started up again, and Cian found himself glancing around, looking at the people of his village, the folks he had known his entire life. They had been pulled from the comfort of their beds, brought out into the bogs to watch the man who was known throughout the land as their protector, as their greatest warrior, be placed beneath the waters of the bog.

"Go now," Séamus said. "The gods will watch over us."

The townsfolk moved away from the land, back toward the lights of the village, until only Angus, his wife, the druid, and Cian remained.

"What now, druid?" Angus asked.

"Prepare your people," the druid said. "Set your defenses and sharpen your weapons. The gods will provide for us, but we must still protect ourselves."

Word reached them that Mac Niall's men were approaching two days later. In that time, Angus ordered the walls repaired and strengthened, the spiked stakes running in a semicircle around the village and sheep pens, ending at the edges of the bog. What harvest could be managed of the crops outside the walls was made, but the rest was at the whim of the invaders.

By the end of the third day, the Mac Nialls were camped within sight of the village, their torches visible at the top of a low hill when Cian peered through a gap in the stakes. It wasn't long before three large men approached, mere shadows, like spirits emerging from the falling mists.

Angus and Séamus stood at the gates to greet them, a quartet of fighting men flanking them for protection, Cian only able to watch from a distance. The Mac Niall men became clearer as they entered the light of the torches that lined the walls, and Cian could see that they carried no weapons, at least none that were visible. The thick leathers and furs they wore certainly could have concealed weapons, but Cian's father had always said that a parlay never came to violence, that any who broke it would be forever cursed by the gods. Even the Mac Nialls would obey the gods.

The one in the center was the one who spoke, a broad man with a braided red beard and long red hair to match. "Angus Mac Aohda," he said as he stopped several feet from the gate, his voice booming in the night. "Didn't expect you to be the one to show."

"You can tell your father that a real man speaks for himself, Daley," Angus said, spitting at the ground before the man's feet.

"We heard from a little bird that your man Keegan has gone to the gods," Daley said. "That true?"

"No truth to the rumor," Angus said.

Daley examined the men standing with the clan leader. "Don't see him with you. You'd think a clan's best warrior would be front and center."

"Didn't want to bother him with such a trivial manner," Angus said. "Like to let him deal with real trouble."

Daley gave a wide grin. "Father always said you were a joker. Never saw it myself."

"What do you want, Daley?"

Daley raised his voice, ensuring that all who listened could hear. "Our demands are simple. Throw down your arms and submit yourself to Mac Niall rule. Your clan leader will be given to the gods, but the rest will continue to live peacefully. Only thing that changes is who you pay your tribute to."

There was silence, though Cian could almost feel the anger in Angus's sneer. "You have one day. Then your village will burn."

They turned away, leaving Angus and the rest standing there, watching their backs. Finally, Angus turned away. "Close the gates, gather around," he barked.

Cian made his way close, feeling the others gather in behind him. Angus waited for the gates to be closed and for those around him to be silent before he spoke. "You heard what the man said. They've come here to burn your homes."

A voice sounds from behind Cian. "He said if we surrender, they will spare us."

"Do you believe him?" Angus said. "Those men are thirsty for blood."

"For your blood," another voice said. "Not ours."

Angus began to speak, but the old man took his arm and urged him back. "If you do not believe him, then heed me," he said. "They will not kill me, whether they torch the village or not. My place is secure, and to kill me would be to be cursed."

There were murmurs, but they all knew the truth, as much as Cian did. Druids were to be spared, no matter what. Only a druid could strike down another.

"The Mac Niall clan has spread like a sickness across the land," Séamus said. "You have heard of the other villages they have taken, the people they have killed. Rumors you may say, but I have seen it myself, in my travels. They promise mercy and deliver pain, and then they move their own people onto the lands."

There were more murmurings, but Cian could feel the crowd's tone begin to shift. They may not believe Angus, but the druid spoke for the gods. He was above reproach.

"I can promise you, whatever happens tomorrow, they will not spare you, not the men, and likely not the children. If you want to continue your freedom, you will fight. And the gods will protect us."

"How can we stand without Keegan?" someone asked, and the message was met with agreement from amongst the crowd.

"Keegan was not the only one who fought," Angus said.

"Aye, but he was the best," someone said.

"The gods watch over us," Séamus said.

"Will the gods fight our war?" a new voice called out. "Seems by taking Keegan, they show that they are not on our side."

"The gods work in mysterious way," Séamus said. "And they bless those who have faith, not those who doubt."

There were more murmurs, but none spoke out. Angus scanned the crowd for a moment, waiting for another word, then finally spoke. "Those with the watch tonight, take your places. The rest of you, get some sleep. We need everyone fresh tomorrow."

When Cian awoke, his senses were dulled. The room around him was dark, the ground hard, the air cold, and in the distance, he could hear shouting.

Cian lifted his head, blinking away the sleep, but his eyes shot straight open when he heard the scream, just on the other side of the wall, and the shouting that followed. Iron rang on iron. They were under attack.

He threw off the blanket and stood, snatching up the sword and wooden shield that lay by him. The shield was just attached to his left arm by the time he reached the doorway, and he immediately threw it up to block the blinding light that greeted him. The town was aflame, even with the rain that fell, and there was chaos, fighting all around him, men engaged with their blades, a man holding off blows from an axe with a splintered wooden shield, a woman being dragged kicking and screaming to the side.

There was no time to take any of the sights in. He was barely out of the roundhouse when he saw the blade of an axe flying toward his head. He gave a startled cry and fell backwards, bringing up his shield as he fell. The axe blade missed the shield and his head both, but Cian was flat on the ground, pieces of dirt from the house dropping onto his head.

The warrior already had the axe out of the wall and pulled back over his head, ready to bring it down. Cian dropped his sword and braced the shield with both hands as the axe descended. The blow shook his body to its very core, but he felt the struggle as the man tried to unwedge the axe from the wood. He felt pressure as a heavy boot planted itself on the shield, but he managed to free his hand, feeling around for the dropped sword.

The axe came free and raised again, but Cian felt the grip of his sword. He grabbed it and thrust upwards, driving it upward. There was blood, lots of blood. So much that he was almost sick right there. The blade slid out as the man stumbled away, screaming, gripping himself as he fell to the ground to die.

As Cian climbed to his feet, he forced himself to look away from the man he had just doomed, just in time to see another Mac Niall warrior bury his axe into Ardal's head, scattering bits of bone and brain and blood across the ground. This time, he was sick.

He was trying to gather himself as the warrior turned his direction. Cian didn't recognize him, didn't know this man's name, but he knew that this man wanted to kill him. It was clear in his eyes, in his gritted teeth, in the mud and blood that stained his beard and skin. He gripped the axe with both hands and stomped through the mud toward Cian.

Cian backpedaled quickly, but found himself out of room quickly, bumping roughly into the wall of the roundhouse. He lifted his shield, trying to move along the side, but the approaching warrior was moving much more quickly than he was.

The first blow came from the side, but instead of striking him, it knocked the shield aside. The move startled him, the strength of the blow knocking one of the leather straps from his arm so that the shield hung loosely. The next blow came from the handle of the axe, striking him in the side of his head, jarring his vision, the sword once more slipping from his hand.

It was almost like a dream, the way everything moved so slow. The sword was at his feet somewhere, but he was standing, and the axe was rising. He reached out a hand, slow, clumsy, and gripped the axe handle. The warrior should have been able to pull it free easily, to shove his feeble attempt aside and smash his brains. Instead, he seemed put off by the maneuver, and instead, he pushed the handle into Cian's throat.

Cian could not even mount a resistance. The man was a half foot taller than him and outweighed him by at least three stone, a man grown if he'd ever seen one. The handle was pushed in and up, pressuring the spot where the jaw met the throat and lifting Cian up so that his feet left the ground.

Pain coursed through his throat, through his jaw. His lungs burned as he gasped for air, his feet kicking, his arms straining as he pushed back against the axe's handle. Below, he could see the man with his gritted teeth, the skin stretched over his cheeks and forehead and the tendons of his neck.

The night around him seemed to get darker, even the torches seeming to burn less brightly. His entire body was burning now, and he could feel himself struggling for air, even as his body seemed to weaken by the moment.

The axe handle was suddenly gone, and Cian fell to the ground. He landed hard, falling flat on his face in the mud. He coughed, over and over through a burning throat, struggling to suck in breath as quickly as he could. He tried moving his body, trying to get up, but it would not cooperate, would not obey his brain. He waited for the axe to descend, to end it for him completely.

Except it never did. Instead, something struck the mud in front of his face. He froze, the only movement the rising and falling of his chest as he struggled to see what the black mass was before his eyes. It was only when something larger hit the ground behind it, jarring it so that it wasn't as much in shadow, that he saw that it was a head. Not just any head, but the head of the man who had been holding him up. The thing that had jarred it was the rest of his body.

Cian managed to push himself back, pressing up against the wall of the roundhouse. He was still sucking in air, staring down at the severed head and body. The head hadn't been cut, but had been pulled off, the edges jagged, a chunk of spine still attached.

What had done it? What could have done it? Even wolves didn't do this kind of damage to sheep that they caught.

Cian did not have time to think on it any further. Something grabbed him by the collar, and he turned quickly, half expecting to have to fight, but unsure of how he would ever be able to.

When he turned, however, he found himself staring right into the aged face of the druid. He could smell the herbs wrapped within Séamus's beard, hear the rattling of the gourds, so loud that he couldn't believe he didn't hear the man approach, even with the chaos of the battle and the pounding rain.

"What's happening?" Cian asked, raising his voice above the ruckus. "Was that you that saved me?"

The druid shook his head and held a single finger up to a beard covered mouth, his blue eyes wide open as they staring into Cian's. A scream pierced the night, and Cian's head snapped toward it, just in time to see a figure vanish through the gates, and beyond, the sight of men fleeing toward the Mac Niall camp.

"Come, boy," the druid said, his voice calm. "The gods do their work. It is better that we were not here to witness it."

"Why not?" Cian asked. More of the torches had been extinguished by the increasing rain, but he swore he could see a figure slowly pursuing the fleeing men. A tall, broad figure carrying a large axe in his hand. "Don't they fight for us?"

"They do," the druid said, pulling on his arm. "But that does not mean that we are safe from their works. Come."

Cian took a few steps, then followed, the old man leading him to his own roundhouse. Inside, Cian found a fire going in the middle of the floor, and surrounding it, many of his fellow men, the ones who still lived.

There was an eerie silence in the roundhouse, the men who were still upright looking on with little more than blank stares while the ones with worse injuries were being tended to. The room was silent except for the low moans, the sounds of pain from those fortunate enough to survive, but not enough to escape injury.

A figure stood, a man with blood pouring down his face, his cheek mangled, his hand holding a cloth to his face. It took Cian a moment to realize that it was Angus, nearly unrecognizable with his wounds. "What now, old man?" he asked. "Are we supposed to be safe in here?"

"The gods provide," Séamus said.

"Provide what?" Angus said, waving a hand over the room. "Death? Maiming? We may as well line ourselves up to be sacrificed in here."

"They're fleeing," Cian said. The words felt strange on his tongue, his throat still aching from the attack. All eyes turned toward him, and he felt his own eyes gazing over the room. "I saw them."

Róise stood from her spot near Angus. "You saw them, boy?"

"With my own eyes," Cian said.

"You're certain?" Angus asked. Cian nodded, setting off a fresh set of murmurs throughout the room. "What could cause them to flee?"

"The work of the gods," Séamus said. He held up a finger, shushing the room. "Quiet. Listen."

They obeyed, and Cian found himself straining his ears. In the distance, there were shouts, screams, the sounds of horror and death.

"Those are the sounds of our enemies being destroyed."

A man stood, one of the uninjured ones. "We should help," he said. "This is our time of victory."

Angus was nodding his head, lowering the cloth to display the true horror of the wound that covered his face, a slash that ran from forehead to cheek, right through one of his eyes. "I would love to stick my blade through some more Mac Niall throats."

The druid held up his hand. "This is not your victory," he said. Over the protests, he spoke further. "This is the victory of the gods. To claim otherwise is to deny them what is theirs, and to join in the carnage is to put yourself in the way of their retribution."

"So we can't even join in the killing of those Mac Niall bastards," a voice sounded out.

"You can," Séamus said. "But I cannot guarantee your safety. Only those who remain within these walls will be certain to be safe."

The druid's words were met with grumbles, but nothing more. Angus returned to his seat, and the battle's survivors settled in around the fire, sitting quietly.

Cian found his own spot in the rear, laying down and closing his eyes. Sleep never came, however. All he saw was the gritted teeth as the man lifted him by the throat, the memory accompanied by the distant screams from the Mac Niall camp.

"What could have possibly done this?"

There was a group of ten of them, those from the village well enough to walk and who had not been relegated to start the cleanup. The ones here were all armed; they wanted to make sure there were no survivors. They were quiet as they walked, the only sounds their feet squelching in the mud and the jingling of the druid's gourds with each step.

The camp somehow looked worse than the village. Items the Mac Nialls had brought were strewn about, and so were the bodies. Or rather, what was left of them.

The Mac Niall warriors had been ripped apart, like a monster of some kind had gone on a rampage through their camp. Heads, limbs, even torsos lay scattered about, the mud running red from the blood. Cian felt his stomach turn as he walked through the site, threatening to expel whatever meager breakfast he had managed. He thought he might succeed in keeping it until another one of the other men threw up. Once that happened, any hope of holding it in himself was one, and he was sick for the second time in as many days.

He was still bent over, spitting on the ground, when he heard one of the men calling out. "Come here, found a survivor."

Cian took a moment, collected himself, then managed to stand upright and amble over to where the men gathered. There, resting against a tree, was the same man who had come to parlay. The braids from his beard had loosened, his hair matted against his head, his face stained dark from a gash that ran across his head. His breathing was labored, his eyes part closed, and as Cian got closer, he saw the real cause of his distress. Part of his chest was caved inward, his lower ribs broken, and one of his legs had been ripped clean off below the knee, a leather belt tied tightly around his leg to slow the bleeding.

They all watched him for a moment, then the druid stepped forward and nudged him with the butt of his staff. The man opened up his eyes, ever so slightly. "I suppose you're here to finish the job the monster started. Well, get on with it.”

Angus stepped forward, his face washed, a poultice applied over the wound and his eye to give it a particularly grotesque appearance. “What monster?”

“You know damn well what monster,” he said. The words were slow, labored, as though every ounce of energy was going into speaking them.

Angus glanced at the druid. “This your doing?”

“The gods work their will in their own ways,” Séamus said.

“I should have known a man like you would stoop to such magicks, Séamus,” the dying man said. “Finnén always said you were never above the darker arts.”

“What dark arts do you speak of?” Séamus said. “I only entreat the gods on our behalf.”

“To do your dirty work.”

Séamus hawked and spat. “Finnén is a hack who couldn’t conjure a spirit if his own life depended on it. He knows nothing of the gods or their works, nor of what I do.”

The man drew in a deep breath. “Do what you will. I’ll die knowing my people never stopped to such depths. And that your village will be cursed by the gods for your druid’s arrogance.”

He leaned back and closed his eyes, his chest still slowly heaving and falling with his breathing. Angus gave the druid a long look, then slowly slid the sword into the man’s chest. He body shuddered, and then he lay still.

“Gather the bodies,” he said, wiping the blood from his blade. “We will give them to the gods before the sun is down.”

“No,” Séamus said. All eyes turned on him, the lone word hanging in the air.

Angus was the last to turn, the movement slow, his head not lifting until the last moment, his eyes burning even as he spoke calmly. “Even our enemies deserve to be given to the gods.”

“The gods have no use for these men,” Séamus said.

“The gods have use for all,” Angus said. “It is our duty to deliver blood and flesh for their blessings.”

“And I say to you that you will receive no blessings for these bodies. Burn them; their sins leave them no place in the eyes of the gods.”

The druid turned away, but the clan leader called after him. “And what of your sins? What is it that you did? What killed them?”

The druid hardly turned, his voice sounding older even than his advanced years. “It is not for us to guess how the gods choose to work. We can only say our words and make our sacrifices and hope that they may heap their blessings upon us.”

The men said nothing, neither Angus not the rest. Cian felt a chill run down his spine. The druid only started on his way, his gourds rattling with each step, fading as he made his way back to the village.

They all stood there for some time, and it was finally Cian who worked up the courage to speak. "What do we do?" he asked, unsure if his voice even carried far enough in the still air to be heard. "Do we take them to the bogs?"

"No," Angus said. "We do as the druid said. Gather wood and stack it with the bodies. They need to be burning by sundown. And I do not think we should be out here when night comes."

The men began to move to obey, and Cian followed. As he left, he heard the clan leader draw in a breath and speak, nearly lost in the sound of movement. "May the gods forgive us for what we do."

RED WINTER

Long available on its own, I decided to include an updated version of "Red Winter" in this collection. I tried to keep much of the structure and story the same, including the era, allowing it to still lead into my novel <u>The Plague</u>, but as an artist, it's impossible not to look back on something done a decade ago and think about what you could have done better. I do think it still holds up in a lot of ways, especially as we go through COVID, but of course, we also learned a lot about humans in general in this time. And at the base of all my works, including this one in particular, is a human story.

Thursday, November 15, 2012

Overblown?

So I know you all usually come to my blog for less serious topics, but I had to get this one off my chest because it's everywhere now.

This flu panic is starting to get out of hand. Walking home from work today (ah, the wonders of living three blocks from the office), I saw several people wearing those masks, as if that will save them from the disease. The emergency rooms are filled with anyone who has so much as a sniffly nose.

The worst part is the people coming into work. Bastard only two cubes over was sneezing and sniffling so much it was distracting. Go figure it would be the one day I forget my headphones. Seriously, people, if there's any indication of being sick, freaking stay home and rest, don't get the rest of us sick. I swear if I get sick, I'm going to track that guy down and kick his ass.

I'm glad that the news is all over this, I'm not sure where I'd be without the daily reports showing people getting their shots and seeing doctors. Of course, the shots are in short supply. I'm glad the government has stated they're working on getting more shots available, they're so efficient at everything they do (sarcasm, in case you can't tell through reading).

I can't wait for this to blow over so we can get back to our normally scheduled programming. News is only worthwhile when it's something you can laugh at, like that whole balloon boy mess.

For something on the lighter side, I got a slight promotion. Nothing more than a title change, but at least I get an assistant now. Guy who had the job before me got the flu, but he had had numerous "sick" days prior, so this was the final straw. Feel bad for him but guess those are the breaks. This job is finally shaping into something worthwhile, can't wait to get out of that cramped little cube.

With any luck, this will be the last you hear me talking about this, but guess we'll see.

Tuesday, November 20, 2012

Still going strong

This flu strain really seems to be picking up steam. Half the office was out sick today, although I luckily haven't had any symptoms (thank God). Kind of annoying really, means a bunch more work I have to pick up.

News reports are as sensationalist as ever, but when you can tell it's getting ridiculous is when they mentioned something about a guy being dead and coming back to life. I mean, come on, this is the real world. When did all the supposedly "reputable" outlets turn into the equivalent of the National Enquirer? Isn't there already enough panic out there?

Just look at those stupid surgical masks. Just walking to and from work today, there were hardly any people I passed who were not wearing one. I tell you, I'm in the wrong business. Somewhere in the world, there's someone making a crapload of money selling cheap masks at inflated prices. I guess there's nothing more profitable than a panic.

As for myself, I've been holding out fine, which is unusual, because any time there's a flu going around, if I get so much as a wrong glance from a sick person, I'm spending the next several days moving between the bed and toilet (I'm pretty sure I'm the only person who throws up every time he gets the flu).

Vaccines are finally starting to hit the streets, not government sponsored, which is perfectly fine by me. I honestly don't trust any medicine administered by the government, that which isn't driven by money results in an inferior product. Of course, supply is short, so I should probably jump on it while I have a chance.

Well, it's getting late, going in early to take on another mountainload of work. With any luck, I can make some sort of dent in it. Can't wait for this thing to blow over.

Wednesday, December 5, 2012

What's going on?

I...I'm in complete shock right now. I...Jesus Christ, I can't even type, I'm just...shaking all over. Hold on, I need a drink.

...

Okay. Okay, that's better. Thank God I keep plenty of liquor around. It only took half a bottle of Jack, but my hands are finally steady enough to type. But my nerves are still on end. Just a few hours ago, I watched my friend and coworker Ben bleed to death.

In my last post, I discarded the rumor circling around about flu victims awakening, rising from the dead, but I saw one myself and...oh Jesus, my mind is racing. I need another drink.

!!!!!

The room is spinning now, but I've got a good buzz going and I am a lot calmer now. Here goes.

Ben and I had ducked out for a quick lunch. We've both been worked stupid over the past few days, trying to keep up with almost an entire department's work. We had both put in vacation for the next two days, planning on an impromptu trip somewhere, Vegas probably, or even just Louisiana to gamble and relax some. It had taken a lot of coaxing, but we got it out of Linda (our boss for those not keeping score).

I'm getting off track, though. As those of you in the area know, it was a nice day today, lower 60s, clear, although there was a decent breeze. Living here my entire life, anything below 70 is painful, so I was wrapped up in a jacket over my usual polo, which probably saved my life. Ben, of course, is a Yankee, so he was in short sleeves, enjoying the weather.

We were walking to a small deli down the street from our building, a local joint owned by an irritable Italian man named Gino, who knows us by name and still treats us like crap, although in a seemingly affectionate way.

Agh, getting off topic again. The sidewalks were unusually empty, maybe a person or two on the other side of the street, but the flu has really depleted the pedestrian population, people just want to stay indoors, I guess. Ahead of us was someone in a hospital gown. St. Mark's isn't far from our building and every once in a while, someone manages to escape, but this one was different, he seemed really sick, and was wandering aimlessly, his head twitching and his right foot dragging along the ground, chaffed from the concrete against his bare skin and leaving a trail of blood with each step.

I don't remember what we were talking about, but Ben stopped me in mid-sentence.

"What's that guy doing?" he asked.

"Huh?" I hadn't noticed him until Ben said something. "Oh, just a runaway, don't worry, the police will probably pick him up soon."

"I don't know, he looks pretty sick. We might want to call and stay with him."

"I'd rather not get sick right now," I said. Honestly, I wanted nothing to do with the guy.

"I thought you Southerners were supposed to be nice," he said with a smirk, as we approached the patient.

"We are," I muttered, then without him hearing, said, "Just not me."

We approached the patient, who was looking down at the ground. Ben put his hand on the patient's left shoulder and leaned in slightly, saying, "Hey, you okay? Anything we can help you with?"

The patient continued looking down and Ben looked at me. "Call the police, Chase, we need to get him back."

As he said this, I noticed the man looking up, his eyes empty and his teeth stained with blood. I tried to speak, to warn Ben, but it was as if my throat closed up, letting no noise escaped.

Ben must have seen my face change because he looked up and tried to fight the man off with his free hand. But the man was too fast or too strong or too something because in a flash, his teeth were wrapped around Ben's neck, tearing through the skin and his jugular. With a disgusting rip, a chunk of Ben's neck was gone, and blood was leaking down, staining his clean, neatly pressed white shirt.

The man then turned to me, his empty gaze focused on my eyes, freezing me in horror. Ben lay bleeding to death on the ground, a rabid man was about to attack me, and I couldn't move to save my life.

When his hands grasped my left arm in an iron grip, I was suddenly broken out of my trance and began to fight. I couldn't break his grip and began to panic. With my free arm, I was pushing off his face, keeping his snapping jaws away from me.

What saved my life was the combination of a cheap jacket and the typically uneven Houston sidewalk. In my struggles, I shifted over an uneven crack and slipped, turning my ankle. But what directed my attention from the pain that would inevitably come was a ripping noise. A quick glance revealed the seam along the zipper beginning to burst. I pulled again and the seam ripped further.

With one final pull, the jacket was completely torn, and the man fell, landing square on his ass, holding my jacket in his hands while I still stood. As I backed away, I saw him rise to his feet, his bloody mouth forming a gruesome sneer. I backed away further, preparing to run when I heard a deafening bang and saw the man's head explode.

As the body collapsed to the ground, I saw Gino standing there, smoking shotgun in hand. I don't think I've ever been more relieved to see the old bastard in my life.

"Chase, are you alright?" he asked in that thick accent, but I ignored him and rushed to Ben. It was too late for him, though. The blood was already congealing in a pool beneath him, his eyes gazing lifelessly into the sky, but I wouldn't believe it.

"Gino, call the police, quickly!" I said.

Gino rushed away as I grabbed up the remains of my jacket and tried in vain to stop the remaining blood from leaving Ben's body, a fool's errand.

So here I am not, and if you're reading this, STAY INDOORS. Something's happening, something awful. I haven't turned on the news, I'm afraid to, so maybe I'm out of the loop, but...Jesus Christ. I don't know how I'll survive this.

Tuesday, December 11, 2012

Gone to Hell

I'm fine.

It took almost a week, but I've finally collected myself. A week of left-over pain pills from the car accident last year (past the expiration date, but I don't care) and booze, but last night I finally had a restful sleep. I still dreamed of Ben dying on the ground in front of me, but it didn't seem as bad for some reason.

I also finally gained the courage to turn on the news this morning. Seeing as work didn't even bother calling me on Monday, I could only assume the worst.

And of course, the worst has come. The emergency broadcast system is running with that god-awful tone, but no one comes on. I have the TV set up right by my computer and on mute, but after several hours, there is still nothing. Maybe someone can clue me in, or maybe there's no one left to.

I still haven't looked out my window, but I guess I should. I need to get out to get supplies at some point.

But...what if this is all in my mind? What if the attacker was simply a mental patient who couldn't be controlled? What if everything is really okay, that this is just a bad flu season?

No. No, no matter what I tell myself, that's not true. There was something I left out of my last post, something about Ben's death that made it worse. I had felt his neck, felt for a pulse and found none. None on his wrist or beneath the bicep either. No heartbeat, nothing.

But when the authorities came and zipped him up in that body bag, I saw him move. I told myself at the time that it was just grief, just my mind playing tricks on me, expecting him to jump up, laugh at the joke and continue on with our lives, but that's not the case. I saw him move and deep down, I know that ambulance did not make it to the morgue.

There hasn't been much noise outside my apartment. Even on the ninth floor, there is always the noise of people, of cars, of sirens. But the past few days have been silent. It's unsettling. I never thought I'd miss all the racket of downtown, but right now, I'd give anything for noise, even that stupid dog that the owner has no control over.

And yet, I still cannot bring myself to look out the window. Not yet. Maybe I'll write again when I do, but for now, I'll leave with this: be careful, anyone who may be reading this. There's something going on out there, something big.

Wednesday, December 12, 2012

Safety?

There! On the TV! Finally the authorities give me something of substance.

I almost missed it, having gone to the restroom for a moment, but I was able to quickly spot the change in the screen and with some difficulty, grab the remote and turn up the volume.

The report went something like this (I'm obviously paraphrasing, don't remember it exactly):

"...no exact reasoning for this phenomenon, although it seemed to be brought on by the flu.

"We repeat for all those still alive out there. If you are in a safe place, remain there. Barricade the doors and arm yourself with whatever means available. The authorities will arrive shortly. Do not, repeat, DO NOT approach anyone on the street unless they can give a verbal confirmation of being of sound mind.

"Safe zones are currently being organized by the United States Military, but it is not advised to attempt to travel. The army will be conducting organized sweeps of major cities to rescue any survivors. If you are, however, close to one of the safe zones marked on this map, attempt to devise a signal and help will come.

"We ask that you do not panic. If any of your party is bitten or contracts flu-like symptoms, they should be quarantined immediately. If a person begins to turn, they should be put down quickly with a blow to the brain."

I tuned out the rest, it was very obvious that it was quickly contrived and given by someone with little experience addressing people. Of course, me giving the gist of it didn't help. The map was most important to me, showing that the nearest safe zone was miles away, by the Galleria, it looked like. Well, guess that means I'm stuck here.

I'm already beginning to run low on food. Sooner or later, I'll have to leave my apartment to search for some. Not sure how I'll be able to do it, but hey, maybe the army will have its act together and I'll be able to get out before I run out.

Friday, December 14, 2012

Venturing Out

I left my apartment today for the first time since Ben's death.

I guess you could say it went well. Or, well as in I'm not dead, and didn't get bitten. I did run into one of them, but I'll get to that.

I used up my last can of food this morning, some canned cherries that were more meant for a pie and not terribly appetizing without being baked in one, but at least they were somewhat filling. Luckily the water and electricity are both still working for the moment.

It took a while for me to get up the courage to leave my apartment. That all started with looking for some kind of weapon. I finally decided that the best I could do was an aluminum baseball bat I had from playing in high school. Not quite sure why I've kept it for so long, but I wasn't about to complain.

The next hour or so was me standing by my thick wooden door, splitting the time between my ear pressed against it and my eye looking through the peep hole, hearing and seeing nothing. I probably would have been able to go sooner, except I had made the mistake of looking out my window to the outside world.

Yes, I finally gained enough courage to look outside and what I saw scared me shitless. The streets were covered with people aimlessly walking around, or well, shuffling I guess. They made no noise, at least none that was discernible from the ninth floor, but they were there. I backed away from the window slowly, shutting the blinds and turning away.

When I finally found the strength to leave my apartment, I did so slowly. It seemed to take hours to turn each deadbolt, but in reality, it only took seconds. Each one emitted a deafening click as it slid away from the wall. I stared at the knob for a moment before finally reaching out and turning it slowly. The door creaked as it opened and I cringed, hoping no one heard it.

There I was, the door finally open, holding the bat in my hand loosely and staring into the empty hallway, a bare, cold concrete monstrosity, the cheap carpet the only semblance of decoration other than a few doormats. I inhaled deeply to keep myself calm and leaned out, looking both ways.

Nothing.

I ventured out into the hall and shivered, remembering that the hallways were never temperature controlled. Hot as hell in the summer and (sometimes) freezing cold in the winter. I almost returned to grab a jacket, but refused, knowing that if I returned to the safety of my apartment, I might not have to get up the courage to leave again.

It was slow moving down the hall, the only noise being the sound of my shoes against the floor and my heavy breathing. I came to the first door and tried it. Locked. I knocked twice, waited, and moved on when there was no answer.

This went on for a few more doors before I came upon one that was partially opened. I approached it and then stopped, staring down at what could only be smeared blood on the floor right inside. My heart was pounding as I eased the door open slowly.

For the first time, I noticed the noise, that grotesque sound of something feeding, gorging itself. I wasn't able to put an image to the noise until the door was fully open and I had a view of the sunlit apartment.

The smeared blood drew a path from the door to a large rug in the middle of the apartment, where one of my neighbors, another 20-something who I had only seen in passing, was being fed on by an infected. His stomach had been ripped open and the thing had buried its face into his organs, chomping greedily. The worst part, however, was his eyes, staring right at me with a glassy look, as though he was still alive, as though he could see me.

I gagged and turned away slightly, overcome with sickness. The noise alerted the infected, who stopped and turned toward me, her face smeared with blood. She hissed at me and I froze, overcome with panic.

She moved faster than I would have expected, and I barely got my hands on her in time to hold her off. She was stronger than I expected, and her teeth snapped mere inches from my neck.

We struggled briefly, but I was finally able to knock her against the door, causing her to release her grip on me. In the excitement, I had dropped my bat and now searched frantically for it as she regained her feet.

I finally found it and wrapped my hands around it, bringing it up into a batter's stance as she charged again. I swung as hard as I could and connected, feeling her skull crack as vibrations shot up my arm, numbing it briefly. She collapsed at my feet, bleeding out her nose and ears as I stepped back.

Just to be safe, I delivered another blow and another and another until I couldn't do it anymore. I backed away, dropping the bat and turning as I fell to my knees and vomited.

Once I regained myself, I quickly exited the apartment, pushing the body inside and closing the door, making a mental note to not return to it.

From there, I decided to return to a locked one, where I beat at the deadbolt with my bat until it finally came loose, allowing me entry.

There wasn't much in the way of food, but it should last me a week at least.

I don't want to run into another one of those things, but I fear I won't be able to make it without a run to the corner market or something. Maybe I'll get lucky and get rescued.

Right now, all I can do is wait.

Sunday, December 23, 2012

At the Bottom

It's been a while since I've been able to post. I've been busy since my last one, and food is starting to run low. Not that I care that much, there's only so much you can do with canned food.

But the reason for the lull is the power finally went down. My apartment is usually pretty well insulated from noise, but there was a big enough bang that I could hear it even through the thick walls. Not sure if the two are related. Hell, maybe the army is starting to firebomb the bastards.

It took a while for me to leave my apartment again after the food run. It was just that...well, killing that girl disturbed me. I know she would have infected me, but I've never killed someone before. I mean, I can't even remember the last time I was in a fight. Middle school, maybe?

It makes me wonder about people who try to blame video games for violence. I've played video games for my entire life, and uber-violent ones since my parents would allow it, but killing a person, even an infected person, is a completely different thing. I keep seeing her in my dreams, her blood covered mouth, her tangled hair, her ear-piercing cries.

But that fight is in a different time, a different world. None of that matters now, only survival.

Once I finally got up the courage to leave again, I explored the building pretty thoroughly. I only ran into a couple of infected, but instead of fighting, I locked them in their rooms. They seem to have trouble with doors.

For the most part, the building is deserted. I'm not sure if everyone evacuated or was just somewhere else or if they're all dead and shuffling around with the rest, or what, but a lot was left behind. Unfortunately, most of the food was spoiled when the power went out, but I was able to salvage a little bit. More importantly, I found a 3G wireless card that worked and a gas generator in the garage beneath the building and a few cans of gas, enough to power my computer and run a space heater when the weather turns, which it has lately.

The only problem is that the noise attracts them.

I've been keeping it on the balcony to keep the exhaust out of my apartment, but just over the noise of the motor, I can hear the collective moan of the horde standing beneath me, shuffling around aimlessly as they search for their next meal. During the day, I sit and watch them beneath me, massed together like a lynch mob that has cornered their victim and is only biding their time to take him to the gallows.

I can only hope that they don't figure out a way into the building. There's no way I can fight that many off.

I have never been much on religion, but I have taken up praying, hoping against all else that someone is out there reading this, that there are other survivors clinging to the hope of rescue like I am, that the army is still active, still doing their best to control the situation, and that they haven't given up on finding those left uninfected.

If you are somehow reading this, know you are not alone.

Tuesday, December 25, 2012

Oh Holy Night

It seems fitting that I'd be spending Christmas alone. The past few years, I've found myself spending less and less time with my family. My parents divorced when I was in college and I took my mom's side, alienating myself from my father. I eventually forgave him, but any time we are together, it's very awkward, such to the point where Christmas and Father's Day are the only times we see each other. My mother married a new guy and I absolutely despise him. Last time we were together, the arguing escalated until I broke his nose.

And yet, on this day, what would normally be a joyous day, I'm stuck here, feeding myself off canned food and a hot plate plugged into a gas generator. I would give anything to see someone: my cheating father, my pushover mother, even my asshole stepfather and his spoiled kids.

I treated myself to a little extra tonight, even though it's a waste of gas. I hooked up some Christmas lights, giving my apartment the first artificial light other than my computer screen since the power went out. It's surprisingly beautiful, the flashing colors against the dark backdrop of the dead city. I even played some Christmas music on my computer to lighten the mood and drown out the cries of the infected.

Maybe this night will help me, maybe this glimpse of civilization, though brief, can get me through. It gives me hope, and however artificial, it is still hope.

Right now, that is all I have left.

Merry Christmas, everyone. Maybe for just tonight, the survivors can forget their struggles and remember for just a moment what it was like to live in a normal world.

Saturday, December 29, 2012

Survivors

I got an e-mail today. The first in months, hell, even the spam had stopped. I never thought I'd miss junk mail from porno sites and Nigerian princes, but I did.

There is no describing the feeling I got when the pop-up notification appeared. My heart leapt, my stomach turned, and my mind raced. I clicked on it, and there, just a simple message from a woman named Jenny:

Chase,

The three of us found your blog a short time ago. We don't have much internet access outside of a blackberry we found, but your blog gives us hope. It lets us know that there is still someone else out there, someone trying to survive just like us. Keep writing as long as you can, it's making a difference.

Jenny

I was speechless, unable to move for a while. I can't believe I'm making a difference. Maybe there's a reason I'm still able to get a signal, still able to get the word out...

Good feelings are short lived, however. I'm running low on gasoline. I took a trip down to storage this morning, but the apartment building is all out. I've shut it down for now, but my battery is already running low. The real question is whether it would be worth it to risk going to a gas station. Of course, even if I could get there, with no electricity, I'd never be able to work the pumps. Perhaps a gas truck?

I guess I'll cross that bridge when I get there.

Tuesday, January 1, 2013

New Start...

The battery-operated digital clock is counting down the moments, the end of another year. But this time, there are no parties, no dancing, no kissing, no champagne, no one to share it with.

As I type this, there are just a few minutes of 2012 left. It was hardly a month ago that life was normal, that I was just a normal guy working a steady job. This...disease was nothing but a seasonal flu scare, nothing more than anything you hear about any other year.

But now I'm here, freezing in my small apartment, typing on a laptop powered by a dying gas generator and only able to see by the light of candles stolen from another apartment. But there's still hope, and therefore, still a chance. I've made it this long.

What's your resolution? Mine is to stop waiting for this thing to blow over, because it won't. I need to make something happen, because waiting for help will not get the job done. It may be too late, but at least I'll have tried.

It's midnight. 2013 is here.

Here's hoping it's better than the last.

Sunday, January 6, 2013

Once Bitten...

I can feel my heart pounding in my chest, as if it is threatening to crack the very ribs that contain it. My lungs expand and contract, taking in air and squeezing it back out. Slow and deliberate.

It eases the pain somewhat with each exhale, but each time I inhale, the pain heightens, leaving me dizzy, my consciousness threatening to leave me. The wound on my side is deep, torn from the love handle I could never quite get rid of. It's just fat, just a flesh wound, except mixed in with the blood is the poison from one of those...things.

I remove the towel I've been holding to the wound. It's grown heavy with blood, and drips onto the carpet. Oh well, it's not like the deposit on this place matters much anymore.

I've cleaned the bite and applied pressure, but something in the saliva is preventing it from clotting, preventing any sort of healing. It's turning a strange color, and I'm starting to feel hot.

I guess I shouldn't be on here. I need...I need to find something to stop this. There has to be something around here, maybe some kind of anti-viral medicine or something...

Countdown to the End

I finally managed to stop the bleeding, and some Vicodin from one of my neighbors has eased the pain, but definitely not eliminated it.

This is my doing, my own fault. I got too bold, thought I was smart, thought I could protect myself. I was wrong.

The generator ran out of fuel yesterday, which is what started this whole mess. The blog wasn't important, but I somehow convinced myself that it was. Besides, who wants to be without electricity? It was something I could hold onto, that reminded me of a normal life.

I loaded myself up. Long-sleeve shirts, jeans, worker's gloves. Anything that could protect me from them. I grabbed my bat and a backpack with a gas can inside and departed the safety of my apartment.

My plan was flawless. There's a fire escape on the side of my building, one that runs along the side and stops on the second story. Adjacent to the building is a gas station, a new Shell that was built last year and parked right alongside the pumps was a large gas truck. A quick jump across a narrow alley and I'm on the roof, easily able to get into the store via a convenient trap door on the roof.

I had it all scouted out and perfectly planned. All I had to do was execute.

The first part went off without a hitch. Or well, sort of. It was easy enough to get onto the fire escape and move down, but it sure as hell made a lot of noise. And noise is a sure way to attract our hungry friends. By the time I was down on the third story, the alley below was packed.

It's one thing to look at them from several stories up. It's another thing to be right above a crowd of them. They moved around as if in a mosh pit at a concert, fighting against each other, raising their arms to the sky and staring through with their empty eyes, knowing only one thing: hunger.

I sat there, watching, mesmerized by the chaotic mass. They stared and I stared back.

Finally, I stood and looked across the alley at the gas station roof, sitting slightly higher than the second floor of the apartment. I climbed to the railing, crouching and hanging onto the ladder beside me to keep my balance. I primed myself and leaped, flying above their reaching arms, grasping at air.

The landing was awkward, thanks to a misjudgment on my part. I attempted to tuck, but was too late and instead turned my ankle, feeling pain shoot up as I rolled over, finally coming to a stop with a painful collision with a vent.

I don't think I was knocked out, but I was definitely dazed, and when I snapped out of it, my hair was matted down with still-wet blood. I stood up but doubled back over with pain. My ankle throbbed, not broken, but definitely sprained. It took some time before I was able to walk again, but I won't bore you with the details of that.

I was extra cautious as I slid open the trap door that led down into the back area of the gas station. I shone the light from my flashlight down into the area, scanning thoroughly to make sure there were no unwanted guests. Satisfied that it was empty, I gingerly made my way down the ladder.

It wasn't until I made my way into the store that I realized what I should have before I got down there: the gas was outside...with them. I collapsed down against a shelf of candy, staring out through the glass windows at the mass of people moving through the streets, aimlessly searching for food.

I must have stared at the display case for ten minutes before it hit me. I struggled to my feet and hobbled over to the formerly refrigerated cases still filled with various drinks. I pulled open the glass door and removed a twelve pack of Budweiser bottles (I figured if I was going to waste beer, it may as well be crappy beer) and brought it to the front of the store.

One by one, I popped the cap off each bottle and poured the beer on the floor. I then pulled a bottle of lighter fluid and began filling each bottle with it. Once that was finished, I used some rags from the office as fuses and grabbed a couple of lighters from the counter.

A quick glance out the front showed me that the sun was sinking, meaning that time was short. I didn't want to be caught after dark. The lighters were all filled with fluid, but I still held my breath as I flicked it, my hand shaking. It took a few tries, but I finally got it, lighting the first one.

The door was unlocked (pure luck, would have figured that I would set myself on fire because the damn door was locked), and I heaved the first one out to the street. It smashed against the cement and shattered, spraying the flammable liquid everywhere and setting off a blaze, catching many of the creatures on fire.

Before the first had landed, I was already lighting the next one. My luck was holding out, none of the ones not on fire had noticed me yet and I tossed the second one out toward another large group.

The cover seemed sufficient, and I decided to take the chance. I grabbed another one without lighting it along with two gas cans and sprinted out, holding my hand up to ward off the heat from the flames. I blocked out their screams of pain, not wanting to feel any empathy toward the mindless creatures.

I passed the pumps and reached the truck. I pulled the hose from the hole in the ground that led to the tank and prayed that the truck hadn't been emptied. I held it over one of the canisters, not knowing how well it would work, and turned toward the valves on the side. I reached out with my hand and turned it and felt my heart leap as I felt the liquid pouring through.

It shot out and I struggled to control it at first. Luckily, the fire from my molotovs hadn't spread this far and the gas wasn't reaching it. More importantly, the first can was almost full.

I was almost done with the second one when I heard the moan, much too close to me. I turned quickly, moving the hose with me, which probably saved my life right then. I sprayed the zombie right behind me, which caused it to pause, giving me enough time to hurl the hose at it. It fell backwards and I heard the sickening crack as its skull collided with the tank and cracked open.

I quickly screwed on the caps and looked up in time to see more heading over from the back of the truck. I tossed both gas cans toward the store and picked up the molotov, flicking the lighter quickly as I backed away. They moved quickly toward me, and I nearly panicked, unable to light the fuse.

I may have had time, but it certainly didn't feel like it. Finally, the lighter sparked and lit, taking to the cloth that had been dowsed in lighter fluid. I looked up quickly enough to see a zombie reaching out for me and then chunked the molotov right at its feet, engulfing it in flames.

I briefly celebrated, but then saw that in its panic, it was moving toward the spilled gasoline. I turned and sprinted toward the store, scooping up the gas cans and moving toward the ladder to the roof as quickly as my crippled leg could carry me.

By the time I reached the roof, the gasoline on the ground had been lit up and was spreading quickly. I watched in horror as it spread toward the truck. I didn't have a second to waste. A fire spreading to a contained area like that would only lead to an explosion and I didn't want to be around for that.

I tossed the cans onto the fire escape and tried to gauge the distance. It seemed too far, but I had to try. I stepped back and dashed to the edge, planting my good foot on the ledge and leaping as far as I could, extending my hands to the railing. I hit it hard, jarring myself and biting my tongue, drawing blood as I hit my chin, but somehow managed to grab hold and hang on as gravity fought against me.

It was as I hung that I felt hands grabbing at me. I violently kicked my feet, trying to fend them off as I struggled to pull myself up onto the fire escape. I strained with every muscle in my body before I finally managed to pull myself up.

My body said rest, but my mind said go and luckily, it won out. I grabbed the gas cans and scrambled up as quickly as I could.

When the explosion came, the sound was deafening (my ears are still ringing from it) and the force sent me flying, knocking my head against the wall and causing me to go unconscious.

It may have been hours or only a few minutes before I awoke, but the fire was still burning. My head pounded and I could feel blood running down the side of my face, but I collected myself enough to slide into the window of whatever floor I was on. I pushed open the first door that would open and locked it behind me before collapsing onto a made bed and falling into a deep sleep.

I was awakened by a scratching at the door. My head was pounding, and I could hardly see straight. Still half asleep, I made the worse mistake I could have made. I walked over to the door and before I knew what I was doing, pulled it open.

In the dark, the zombie was just a dark figure, reaching out to me like a monster from a child's nightmare. It snapped me awake and I reached out, pushing it away from me as I stumbled backward. I stepped down on my bad ankle and it rolled again, unable to hold the weight of my body as it sent me sprawling to the ground, the zombie falling right with me, snapping its jaws loudly in the silence of the apartment.

I wrestled with the creature, grabbing it by its short hair and holding it back as its arms flailed wildly. I was so focused on keeping the head away that I never saw the arm as it clocked me in the side of the head. It didn't so much hurt as it startled me, causing me to loosen my grip and give it the window of opportunity it needed.

Time ran in slow motion as its teeth tore through my shirt and sank into my side. It tore its head aside, ripping out a chunk of flesh and sending pain radiating through my entire body, dampening my shirt in warm blood.

I managed to push it off and roll away, leaving a streak of blood on the floor. I could feel the pain like white hot fire, but I couldn't afford to linger. Adrenaline pumped through my veins as I scrambled away, searching for something to use against the zombie. I felt around, keeping my eyes on it at all times. My fingers wrapped around something heavy and without looking, swung at it as it charged toward me.

It felt like I was moving in slow motion, allowing me to see that I was swinging a dumbbell, a five pounder. It connected with the jaw of the creature. It recoiled and turned back, its jaw hanging loosely, grotesquely disfigured. I used to opportunity to deliver a quick kick to the face, knocking it onto its back. Faster that I even knew I could move, I slammed down the weight, caving in its skull and ending its life for the second time.

Backing away, the rush fading, the pain returned. I held my hand to the wound and felt only wetness. I wiped it off on my pants and picked up the gas cans, eager to get out of that apartment.

So here I am, writing this and already starting to feel feverish. I don't know how long I have. There's nothing that can be done now.

I've never felt so alone in my life.

Tuesday, January 8, 2013

Watch It Burn

I've never been more glad to live in a gun-friendly state as I am right now. The building is loaded with rifles and pistols left behind by their former owners. I have a nice little arsenal built up now, but I only concern myself with the hunting rifles.

The skin around the wound has begun to turn a greenish color. I can only imagine how little time I have, the countdown to the end of my life.

There's no point in going out quietly. There's no one to say goodbye to except you, dear reader. No one to watch me go, no one to give me my last rights, to read my eulogy, to bury me.

So here I am, atop my apartment building. To my left is a case of Shiner bottles I chilled by hooking up a mini fridge to the generator. To my right is the unused gas can and all the rifles I could find.

I sip my beer, feeling the calming effect take over me. I raise a rifle to my shoulder, take aim, and fire. On the ground below, a head explodes as a zombie drops dead.

Wave, eject cartridge, repeat.

I have to say, it's rather fun. It's almost like a video game, taking out things that almost seem unreal, not living.

A clip empties and I toss the rifle over the edge. It's easier to just pick up another one than to reload.

It doesn't take long doing it like this. I'm soon out of ammo and have no rifles left. There's only one thing left to do.

I begin to fill up the beer bottles. The gasoline should burn better than the lighter fluid did. Or at least I can aim better, hit something wooden, or maybe make it through a window, catch something flammable. With any luck, and obviously without any firefighters, the city can burn for days.

I scan the area for my first target. An old, wooden house, one of several scattered through downtown, sits a block over. That will be perfect. I light the molotov and hurl it out, watching with a strange fascination as it twirls through the air, landing just short and breaking, sending the fire scattering. The house catches fire quickly, and it begins.

By the time the sun has gone beneath the horizon, there is no difference. I can see as if the sun was high in the sky. The house was a good start, and some fell short, but the fire has begun to burn, and the best is yet to come.

For now, I simply stand there, watching the flames build as the zombies below are consumed. I can feel the heat from here, basking in the glow as their screams of pain fill the night.

A smile crosses my face as I gloat in their suffering.

This is where I end it. I hope that anyone reading this will learn from my mistakes, that my downfall will help others survive. There is no hope left for me, but I won't go down alone. And maybe from the ashes, something new will rise, something better. Or maybe there is nothing left, and all is for naught.

The gas should have built up sufficiently by now, after all, I did leave the valve open all the way. An old building like this, the vents are all interconnected, and it vents through the roof. I kick off the cover and glance down, quickly looking away and gagging on the stench of natural gas.

Perfect.

The last molotov is now lit. In a moment, I will drop it down the vent. If I'm right, there's enough pressure built up and it will be over quickly.

Even if I'm wrong, I know I won't have to know what it's like to be one of them.

BEFORE THE STAKE

This is the first of two de-facto prequels to my most recent completed novel from Nanowrimo, the first in a planned trilogy that takes place in a version of our world where supernatural creatures are real. The inspiration for this story came from another episode of "Lore", this one talking about an island off the coast of Chile that legend says is the home of powerful sorcerers amongst its native peoples. There is a story told of a priest who had a book composed of spells he had collected from around the world, and that he challenged these sorcerers to a competition to see who had the more powerful magic. As the story goes, the priest lost, and as part of the wager, gave up his book of spells to these sorcerers.

It was the priest's spellbook that I latched onto in that tale, and an idea began to form for an order of priests who deal with the supernatural on behalf of the church. The idea is just beginning to form in this story, and it is in the future novel that it will be further fleshed out.

The padding on the kneelers was thin, almost nonexistent, causing the ache to carry through the arthritic joints in Father Rodrigo Torres's knees and up his legs to his hips. He ignored it as much as he could, put it away as he had for so many years, for the many decades he had spent as a member of the cloth.

Everything in this life was nothing before the glory of God.

The church around him was small, empty, the kind that hardly registered to the local bishop, much less to the Papacy, but it was on behalf of the Grand Pontiff that Rodrigo was there. It was the only kind of business he dealt in, and it took something truly special to draw his attention.

Above him was a crude crucifix, the cross itself misshapen, the body of Christ whittled from wood. A far cry from the elegance that adorned the walls of Saint Peter's Basilica, but still the work of an honest craftsman and still stationed in a holy place. It was what the community could afford, which made it blessed.

His prayers were spoken silently, little more than whispers, lost in the arch of the ceiling, in the stone walls, in the wooden pews. He was alone; he always prayed alone. The larger churches, the cathedrals in places like Paris and Cologne and Rome and Seville had private prayer rooms, but a town like this had no use for a grand temple. Nor the means to build one.

The last words were uttered, and with them an "Amen". He gave the sign of the cross and stood, slowly, feeling his bones creak as he did. He turned from the crucifix, then turned back and said a quick blessing over it.

At the far end of the building were a pair of wooden doors, thick doors, the best craftsmanship the church offered. He walked toward them, his hand clutching a leatherbound book with worn pages, pages stained by water and ink and time. He clutched it close to him, as though the book held a power in itself. In a way it did; words always held power, and he was a collector of words, of a sort.

There was a limp to his walk, a nagging ache that slowed him, borne by age and strain, supporting a body with a growing gut and greying hair. He kept his back as straight as he could, though at times, it felt as though the weight of the world was on his shoulders. In a way, it was, the burden that he carried as a man of God. As a voice for God.

Rodrigo reached the door, pushed them open, and the shouts of an angry mob immediately filled the air. They had to have been angry, riled up enough to be willing to bear the cold, dreary day. Rodrigo had been many places, to China and India and Africa and all across the kingdoms of Europe. Cold and hot and wet and dry. But none depressed him like the eastern part of Europe, where the skies seemed eternally overcast and the snows refused to melt well into the month of April.

The shouts of the townsfolk filled his ears, threatening to block out his own thoughts, but they were not angry with him. And that was why he was here.

None faced him, but they still moved aside for him. There were some sidelong glances, a few hushed whispers, but nothing more. They knew why he was there, and as far as they were concerned, he was far from the main event. That manifested itself in the tall stake that had been stuck into the ground, stacks of wood piled around the base, visible even above the heads of the tallest spectators.

The crowd was out for blood, and blood would be given to them, but not before Rodrigo did his own work. He crossed the small town square, his shoes sinking into the cold mud that had been stirred up by the crowd. On the other side rose another stone structure, similar in size to the church, but different in all other respects. The lord's manor was a small keep, bordered by a wall scarcely wide enough for a grown man to walk along, a meager protection against any real army, but should the town be attacked, it would be all the townsfolk would have.

Rodrigo stepped through the open gate, past thick, reinforced wooden doors and a raised portcullis. In the courtyard stood a small building, the lord's home, and a single tower that rose above the walls. He stepped toward the latter.

The climb was no more pleasant than the kneeling had been, his legs screaming at him for relief as he took each stone step, climbing his way to the top floor. When he reached it, there was no landing, only a guard standing on the final step in front of a wooden door with a round handle in the center, held closed by an iron latch.

The guard nodded as Rodrigo approached. "Ksiądz," he said, giving the title in his own language. Without waiting for a response, he turned and pulled back on the latch, releasing it and allowing the door to open inward. Rodrigo nodded and stepped through.

The woman was seated on the stone floor, dressed in grey rags, hardly fit clothing for the cold that seeped through the walls and holes that served as windows. One leg rested beneath her, the other pulled to her chest, her face buried in it, hidden behind the leg and a mess of brown hair. The door closed behind him, the latch sliding back into place, leaving the two of them alone.

Rodrigo watched the woman for a moment, but she hardly moved. Down below, he could still hear the yelling from the crowd, though somewhat dampened. It seemed so absurd, that this crowd, this town would be so afraid of this meager creature that they would be driven to such anger.

He shook his head, in turn shaking the thought away. He had seen enough to know that it was never the exterior that gave it away. The worst ones came in all different shapes, even the meek. Especially the meek. He silently made the sign of the cross.

The woman spoke, the voice matching the appearance. Quiet, defeated, meager. "I guess it's time."

"That is not my purpose," he said.

At his voice, she looked up, revealing the pale, young face, the bright eyes ringed in red, narrow cheeks and thin lips. When she finally gazed upon him, she frowned. "Oh. A priest."

"Yes, I am a priest."

"What did they send you here for? To investigate? To proclaim my guilt? Or to ensure my body burns properly?"

Rodrigo folded his hands over the book, resting it at his waist. "I am here because it is my duty. Because the church must be certain."

She nodded her head toward the window. "They are all certain."

"I am not them," he said. "May I pray?"

She frowned. "No skin off my back."

There was a chair against the wall by the door. Rodrigo picked it up and moved it to the center of the room, then sat down in it, placing the book in his lap. "What is your name, child?"

The girl refused to make eye contact with him. "Elżbieta."

"Elżbieta," he said. "A beautiful name."

She didn't react. He continued. "Let us pray. In the name of the Father, the Son, and the Holy Spirit." Still no movement. Not damning, but certainly not in her favor. "We ask your guidance as we judge this woman, that the truth may come to light. Grant us your spirit, and let the truth be brought to the light."

There was a guffaw from the girl. "The truth. Like that would stop them from burning me."

"Amen," he said, making the sign of the cross once more. "I may be able to save you, but only if you are truthful with me."

"My fate has been decided," she said. "My guilt determined. Nothing can stop it."

"Still we must try, for all souls may be saved."

"You should speak with the priest here. Bastard has a different view of things."

Rodrigo slowly nodded. "I read what your priest wrote. He is the one who called me here, to investigate the allegations against you."

She shifted in place, looking at him now. "I'm here. Go on and get your investigation over with."

Rodrigo studied her for a moment. "Are you guilty?"

Another guffaw erupted from her mouth. "Straight to the point, eh? No, I'm not."

"But you must know that one in the grips of Satan can spin a lie even more easily than a truth."

"Then why did you ask?"

"To gauge a response."

"And you got one. I see this will be no different from my trial. Just a different audience."

"Were you allowed to face your accusers?"

A sly smile crossed her face. "Of course. I was in chains, but each one was marched forward to describe the terrible things I did to them."

Rodrigo opened the book and removed a folded sheet of paper. He opened it up, eyes gazing upon the words on the page. "Jakub, a farmer, claimed you cast a curse on his livestock."

"He cursed them with his own incompetence. One grew ill and he refused to separate it from the rest."

"The blacksmith's wife said you gave her sores around the mouth."

"Probably got them from what she's been doing with the merchant who passes through town every few weeks. That's no secret, except perhaps to her husband."

Rodrigo raised an eyebrow, but said nothing, choosing to continue. "There was a claim that you paralyzed a man, confining him to bed."

Elżbieta shrugged. "If I knew I had that power, I probably would have made much more use of it."

"A woman claimed you gave her scratches and burns while she slept."

"Does it mention I tried to scratch her during the trial? Probably left that out."

"Several claims to have seen you dancing naked around large bonfires in the woods, chanting in strange languages."

Another laugh. "That was my favorite. I don't know any other languages, nor any spells."

"And finally, there were reports of strange creatures lurking the town at night."

"Probably wolves. There are many in these parts."

The priest folded the sheet and put it back into the book. "Is there anything else you wish to confess?"

"If I had a broom, I would have flown it out of this place already," she said.

"I mean spells, incantations, potions."

"I have none. Just like I have no powers."

Rodrigo removed another piece of paper from the book and unfolded it. On it were not words but drawings, pentagrams and skulls and untold beasts. He turned it toward her. "Your priest said these were drawn on the floor of your home. Do you deny it?"

She shook her head. "Anything they found they drew themselves."

"You deny drawing these?"

"Of course. I don't even know what those drawings are. But you won't believe me. Just as they didn't."

"I believe what I see with my own eyes."

"And did you see my home or just what they told you?"

"I saw the evidence presented."

She shook her head and pressed it against her knees. "Let them burn me then. You are not here for anything but to condemn me, just as they did."

Rodrigo put the sheet back into the book. "I am here to seek the truth."

Elżbieta looked up, and he could see the red in her eyes. "It doesn't seem like you are."

"Did the images I show you mean anything to you?"

"Nothing beyond what they showed me at my trial."

"I see." He opened the book and pulled out another paper.

"What is in that book?" she asked.

"It is not important to this conversation."

"It is to me."

Rodrigo's grasp on the book's spine tightened, an involuntary response. He could see the girl look upon his fingers, then she glanced up to meet his gaze with wide eyes.

"Years of research," he said.

"What kind of research?"

"Research for the church."

"Into witches?"

"Yes." He made the sign of the cross.

"Real ones?"

"Real ones."

"Can I...can I see?"

"I'm afraid not," he said.

"That's unfortunate." Her head lowered again. "I was hoping I could at least see the kinds of things I was being accused of. That I could at least know what I was missing out on before I die."

"Evil," he said, making the sign of the cross over her. "The work of Satan through those who sell their soul to him, who forsake God Almighty."

"I would still wish to see."

Rodrigo watched the girl, his face calm but his mind racing. Was she being truthful? Or was she full of deceit? The girl proclaimed her innocence, but a witch would have no qualms about lying to a priest, to anyone. Of course, few could lie with the ease in which the girl made her denials.

God, guide me through this. Show me the way.

"Will you let me see?"

"Why do you wish to see it?"

The girl had lowered her legs and was now sitting with them crossed before her. "I told you. Curiosity. I'm about to be put to death, as a witch no less. I feel I should be allowed to see what a real witch would be like."

"You should be spending your time trying to repent for your sins."

Elżbieta frowned at him, gesturing with her hands as she spoke. "For what sins? For the sins that my village projects upon me because they fear me?"

Rodrigo said nothing. She stood, pacing the room as far as the chain around her ankle would allow. "Do you know why they fear me, Father? Because I am independent. Because I refused to marry the man my parents marched before me. Because I survive on the wages I receive from making and repairing clothing for others. I don't need a man, and that scares them."

Rodrigo remained silent for a moment. When he spoke, he kept his voice calm. "Did you tell them that at your trial?"

"What good would it have done?"

"Someone might have listened."

Elżbieta shook her head. "Not here. Not at my trial. They were convinced of my guilt from the moment I stepped into the court, from the moment they began the testimonies, from the moment they brought those drawings, the pentagrams…"

"The what?" Had she not denied knowing what the drawings were? Had he heard her correctly?

"The drawings. They showed them before the court, and their minds were made up." She shook her head. "I cannot believe they waited for you. I expected to be dragged out there and burned right there and then."

"The church must always investigate such matters," he said. His finger twitched on the spine of the book, and he drew it in, acting like he was stretching his fingers. "There must be other sins. None but Jesus are without sin."

She shrugged, her eyes looking off to the side. "I have lied. I have felt wrath. I have found myself envious of my friend's husband." She shrugged. "Maybe more."

"But no witchcraft?"

"No witchcraft."

"Are you willing to swear on the bible, before the eyes of God and His Son, that you participated in no witchcraft?"

"That and more," she said. She stopped pacing. "But would you believe me?"

"If the signs are there," he said. "If God points me in the right direction."

"Show me the bible and I will swear upon it," she said. "Just as I did during the trial."

Rodrigo turned and rapped on the door behind him. It opened, and the guard stuck his head in. "A bible, a crucifix, and a vial of holy water. Bring them to me."

The woman stopped in place. "That is more than just a bible," she said.

"If you are innocent, then you have nothing to worry about," Rodrigo said.

"I worry about being doused in water and freezing to death."

"It will only be for a moment," he said. "Once we prove your innocence, you will be able to dry off."

The girl resumed pacing, going back and forth in the small space, each time stopping just before the length of chain ran out. Rodrigo only watched her, tracing her in his mind as he thought of the girl's reaction. It meant nothing, he knew. Many reacted that way, many who were innocent. It was a hard blow to the psyche to be found guilty, to hear the accusations of those one had known for their entire life, and many began to believe it themselves, almost in the way a captive may start to empathize with their captor. The girl was not in the right mind, and the proof must be irrefutable.

The door opened and three items were handed through. Rodrigo set each of them on the floor before him. He then picked up the bible and handed it to Elżbieta. She took it, holding it gingerly in her hands. There was no screaming, no cursing, no physical pain to be seen.

Rodrigo nodded toward her. "Go on. Proclaim your innocence."

Elżbieta held the bible close to her chest, trembling as she spoke. "I swear on the word of God Almighty that I am not a witch."

Rodrigo watched, waited for a moment, then reached out. "Very good."

She handed him the bible back, and he held out the crucifix in turn. The girl hesitated this time, staring at the cross as though it were aflame. She slowly reached out, her hand shaking as she moved toward it. She suddenly lashed out, bridging the last few inches and grasping the cross as though she expected it to sear her flesh. Once more, however, there was nothing, no reaction of any kind.

Elżbieta let out a deep breath and said, "I swear on the body and cross of Jesus Christ that I am no witch."

Once more, Rodrigo nodded. "Very good," he said again as he took the crucifix back.

"Is that all?" she asked.

Rodrigo stood. "You have sworn on the Word of God and on the Body of Christ. All that is left is to absolve you of your sins."

A tear rolled down the girl's cheek, and she nodded quickly. "I...I don't know how to thank you."

"By dedicating your life to praising God," he said. "Kneel, my child."

She quickly knelt, her knees pressed against the stone floor. Rodrigo extended one hand over her, gripping the vial in his other. "May our Lord Jesus Christ absolve you; and by His authority I absolve you from every bond of excommunication and interdict, so far as my power allows and your needs require."

With his free hand, he made the sign of the cross, while he dusted her with the holy water from his other. "Thereupon, I absolve you from your sins in the name of the Father, and of the Son, and of the Holy Spirit."

He trailed off as he said the final words. The water had fallen upon her, mostly upon her hair and clothing, but it was a drop that fell upon the bare skin of her shoulder, where the thin dress had slid down. The tiniest tendril of smoke drifted up from it.

Elżbieta frowned when she saw his face, and she followed his gaze to the spot where her skin burned. Neither said anything as her gaze returned to him. All that could be heard was their breathing, hers light and fluttering, his deep and full.

Finally, it was her that spoke. "You have said the words. My sins are forgiven."

The words she spoke were not Polish, but Latin, the tone of her voice changed, husky, as though having spent a night breathing smoke. He responded in kind. "Some sins cannot be forgiven."

"I only wished to live my life," she said. "It was true when I said that I did none of those things."

"You are still an abomination."

"And you carry the words of others of my kind in that book." When Rodrigo said nothing, she motioned toward his book. "I had heard of your kind, of the order you are a part of, of how you collect spells from witches and sorcerers you come across. Do you deny it?"

"I do not," he said. "I study their words so that I may understand them. So that I may fight them."

"Does that make you any better?"

"I walk in the footsteps of God, just as Saint Cyprian did. I did not give my soul to Satan."

The frown remained, but she looked away. "You will not let me walk free, will you? Not even to live my life in solitude."

"That I cannot do."

"Then you know what I must do."

Rodrigo took a step back as Elżbieta stood, seeming to grow even taller. Her eyes were closed as she began to chant something in a language he did not recognize. When she opened her eyes, they glowed, and there was something in the air, something evil. He tried to recoil, and he felt it strike him, nearly knocking him over, clapping the air like thunder as the invisible force met an invisible wall.

The priest grabbed the chair for support, working to catch his breath. The chanting had stopped, and he heard her speak. "What...how?"

The door flung open, the guard rushing in with another behind him. "What happened?" the first one demanded.

"There was a flash of light," the new one said. "Everyone saw it."

"She is a witch," Rodrigo said through heavy breaths. "She should be weakened for now, but the burning must happen now."

The guards did not waste a moment. The shackle was unlocked, and between them, they led Elżbieta out of the tower cell. As she passed Rodrigo, all he could hear was the muttered question.

"How did you stop that?"

"Be careful with her," he said. "She is powerful."

They were gone, the tower cell empty except for him. He eased himself down into the chair, his breath returning to him slowly. One thing was certain; he was getting too old for this kind of work. The time to pass the torch was rapidly approaching.

There was a cheer from below, the people greeting the arrival of the witch to her pyre. He had seen it enough times, enough that he could see it in his mind. It never changed, no matter where it occurred, no matter the people who bore witness.

There was a burning in his chest, and he slowly undid the top buttons of his frock, exposing his skin to the cold air. In the center rested the medallion, burning to the touch, more so than he had ever felt before. She was powerful, more powerful than just about any he had encountered, almost too powerful, even for the spells that the medallion held within.

The cheers grew louder. The pyre must have been lit, the first flames licking at the kindling as the wood at the base of the stake caught.

He touched the medallion. It burned to the touch, but he did not draw back. He embraced the heat, as he always did. A reminder of the power that existed in the world. He still remembered the way the African woman had smiled when she had given it to him, when she had told him in that pidgin language of hers that it would protect him. He didn't believe her at the time, but he had seen it many times since.

He could see the light of the flames against the stones, the smoke beginning to rise. They would grow higher and higher until they burned out, no different from any other power. Like the gods of old, like the gods who had fallen before the might of Jesus.

The African woman had burned at the stake as well. He had been a young priest then, and he had tried to stop it. It had been his own teacher who had ordered it, who had explained that it must be done. There was evil in the world, and to make room for the good, it must be destroyed. Rodrigo had cried that night, and for that, he had been given a long penance, one that outlasted his teacher's remaining years. But he had completed it. There was a duty to, a duty to God, to Jesus, to the Pope and the Church. It was why he had sent the young woman to her death. It wasn't because she deserved to die, but because she needed to.

Rodrigo slid the medallion back into his frock and buttoned it back up. Tonight, he would not sleep. There were prayers to be said, forgiveness to be asked, and notes to be made. He wasn't sure he could recreate the words in the pages of his book, but he would try. They needed to be recorded, to preserve the power, to know that it existed so that it could be fought, to perhaps even learn it to one day use it against the forces of evil. Because the evil needed to be cleared to make way for the good.

From outside, the woman began to scream. Rodrigo knelt down on the cold, hard floor and began to pray.

THE BIOSPHERE

Another /r/WritingPrompts entry that ended up being too long to post there, as well as also fitting into the "space is scary" category I alluded to before an earlier story. The prompt in question here was actually an image prompt, a beautiful piece of digital art that showed a lush biosphere with an astronaut floating in the middle of it. Looking at the picture, it just screamed "alien presence" to me, and the story came together from there.

As I mentioned earlier, there are definitely similarities between this and the other space stories. I do feel they are each unique enough to stand on their own, but as a reader, you of course may feel differently. The only way to find out, however, is to read them all yourself.

The distress signal had appeared as soon as they had dropped out of warp into the system. Delta Pavonis loomed in the distance, a star similar in size to Earth's sun, and her planets were visible in orbit, none yet explored or settled. The only expeditions thus far had been to establish the biosphere to set up base in the system and explore the surrounding stars, meaning the signal could only be coming from one place.

Captain Errol Sanders watched from the bridge of the USS Horizon, listening to the chatter of his crew as they went about their jobs. Their mission was to bring relief to the current crew of the Delta Pavonis Biosphere with the passengers they shuttled, but it seemed that the mission's parameters were changing by the moment. Then again, missions to deep space were never simple. It could never be simple when you are that far from home.

"Captain, we will be at the biosphere in half an hour," came the voice of his head pilot, Mara Trent. "Your orders?"

"Continue on," he said. "If something went wrong, there may still be survivors. If there are, they'll need our help."

"Acknowledged." A hush had fallen over the bridge, a terse silence as the ship continued on its trajectory toward the biosphere. Sanders knew the feeling, the inherent dread of drifting into the unknown. Any traveler would be lying if they said it didn't occur the first time they made the warp jump. Or any time they did for that matter.

The ship maneuvered through the empty space of the system, none of the planets close enough to appear like more than a large star through the viewport. It was humbling, the vastness of space. Them, their ship, even their planet little more than specs of dust in the vastness of the universe. Up ahead, he could see another spec, one that grew and grew as they approached until it dwarfed the ship, a structure the size of a small moon.

The biosphere grew in the viewport, a massive orb that was soon all they could see. The outer shell was transparent, double layered and tinted to offer extra protection from solar radiation while still allowing enough light to permeate through for the plants within to be able to grow.

They were close enough that the communications officer, Annie Berstad, began to hail. He could hear the repeated phrase. "Delta Pavonis Biosphere, this is the USS Horizon responding to your distress signal. Come in, over." Each call was met with only static, the ambient radiation of the star feeding into the comm signal. Finally, she turned to him and shook her head.

Mara had taken the controls and brought the ship around toward the station. He could hear her on the comm, seeking permission to dock, but there was no response. Not that anyone expected a response, not when there was a distress signal like that. She eased the ship toward the station, lining up the airlocks so that the ship's met with the biosphere. There was a vibration through the ship as the airlocks met, and he could hear the hissing as the airlocks met, establishing the connection that would allow them to pass between the ship and the biosphere.

"Prepare the suits," Sanders said. "I'm going in."

"Yes sir," came the answer, and people began to move around the bridge. Sanders made his way through the middle of the chaos toward the door. He needed to prepare.

There were three others; Jason Bridges, Anton Elsin, and Elia Ruiz. Three astronauts who he knew had gone through numerous spacewalks into the unknown. They were preparing their spacesuits, going through the through the arduous process of getting their suits on. Sanders opened the panel hiding his own and began to get dressed, putting on the spacesuit one piece at a time. A part of his mind wondered at the need for such precautions, but he knew that if there was a problem, the biosphere may be compromised. They had to be ready, had to ensure that they were not walking into an environment where they could not survive without help.

Finally, they were ready, all of them. Captain Sanders stepped through first, using his own code to open the entrance to the airlock. He waited for the door to open, then stepped through, leading the way into the cylindrical space than now connected the ship and the biosphere. A moment's waiting, a hissing of air, and the opposite door opened, allowing them entry. The others followed him, and he heard the doors close behind them, cutting them off from the ship. They were alone.

The sensors told him that the oxygen level was fine, even a bit high due to the abundance of plant life, but he made no order for removing the suits, not when there was still a risk of contamination. He made his way forward, stepping into the biosphere's station, and he found his breath taken away at what he saw.

The station had been conquered, not by some kind of alien lifeform, but by the plants themselves. It looked as though the station had been abandoned for decades, judging by the way the plant life seemed to intertwine itself with the machinery. It did not take long for him to find the panel sending out the distress signal, the screen flashing over and over with the message. Sanders stepped forward and disabled it.

"Let's spread out," he said. "Look for survivors."

The team moved through the station and into the large space beyond, floating through the foliage in different directions, spreading out as they searched the interior of the biosphere for any sign of survivors. Sanders was the last to leap out, propelling himself into the low gravity. All around him grew plants and trees of all types, no longer constrained by gravity as they grew in all different directions.

The light from the star peered through, deadened by the tinted glass, the towering trees casting much of the sphere in shadow. Here, the plants grew in all directions, stretching in bizarre shapes, longer than their counterparts on Earth ever grew tall. It was strange, being inside the biosphere - Errol had made many trips to the system but had never actually passed through the airlock. Even in the silence, with the crew vanished, there was a beauty to it, a surreal reminder of the forests that grew back home.

The rest of his crew were chattering over the comm, calling out the positions they were taking. They headed to the edges, so it was on the captain to move upward. He touched the side of his helmet, changing the comm channel. "Talk to me, Annie," he said.

"What can I do for you, Captain?" came the voice at the other end.

"Get me the schematics of the biosphere," he said.

"Just a second." He could hear movement on the other end as she tapped away at her screen. "Sending your way."

There was a blinking on the inside of his helmet, and the schematics popped up, displaying the biosphere outlined in blue. "Much appreciated," he said. He began to talk quietly to himself. "Jason went to the bottom, Elia starside, Anton far end." He scanned over the schematic. Where to go?

"Captain." Mara's voice came over the comm. "The crew's quarters are straight ahead from your position. There should be a log in there that your credentials will unlock. Might give us an idea of what happened."

"Copy that." He looked upward to gain his bearings, then activated the jetpack, propelling himself forwards.

Errol could see the structure ahead, attached to the hexagonal panels by thick beams. It had the same appearance of the airlock, the plants grown over the structure. The door hung open, and the flora had grown over the edges, snaking its way in and across the floors, walls, ceilings. He eased his way in, using a hand to navigate along the wall.

"Okay, I'm here," he said. "What am I looking for?"

"There should be a panel on the wall in the rec room," she said. "It's integrated as part of the system."

It did not take him long to find the rec room, marked by the screens that lined the walls and the table in the center, a chessboard with a partially played game sitting untouched. He moved past it to the screen, the screensaver playing beneath the overgrowth. He used his hand to clear the growth away. As he touched the screen, the login panel popped up. He entered his name and password and was granted entry into the system.

"You ready, Mara?" he asked.

"Ready, Captain."

"Coming your way." A progress bar appeared and began to move steadily across the screen.

"Receiving," Mara said.

There was a beeping in his earpiece. "One sec," he said, then switched channels. "Talk to me."

"I think I found something, Captain," Anton said.

"What is it?"

"There's...some kind of movement."

"Movement? There shouldn't be any lifeforms aboard the sphere."

"I'm seeing it, Captain," Anton said.

"Describe it."

"Like some kind of...I don't know, goo? It's not moving very fast. I'd say it was sap if it wasn't so deliberate."

"Don't touch it," Errol said. "Elia, get over to him and take a look."

There was another beeping. "Switching," he said. "Mara?"

"Captain, we've received the log. The last entry is only a few days ago."

"A few days? Growth like this would take years."

He could hear the log playing in the background. Most of it was indistinguishable, but he could make out words here and there. One in particular caught his ear - "accelerated growth".

"What's it saying?" he asked.

"They found something in the bushes..."

The beeping cut her off. He switched. "Captain, you might want to come see this," Elia said. "It's definitely something that's alive."

"It's coming off the tree," Anton said. "Like it's sniffing at us or something."

"Don't touch it," he ordered. The ship beeped him, and he switched.

Mara's voice was frantic. "Captain, you need to get everyone out of there."

"Wait, what? Why?"

"There's something aboard, something deadly. It killed the crew."

He froze, silent. "Captain? Captain?"

"I copy," he said, hearing the comm beep once more. "Giving the order. Whatever you do, make sure it doesn't get onto the ship."

Without waiting for a response, he switched back, only to recoil at the piercing screams that filled the comm. "What is it? Anton! Elia! Report!"

"It's eating him!" Elia said, her voice a high-pitched wail. "It's eating Anton!" Anton was still screaming, his voice given to the pain that was engulfing him.

"Elia, get out of there!"

"Captain," Jason said. "I see them, I can help."

"No," Errol said. "Everyone to the ship. We need to get off this thing."

He turned in place and found himself staring at something rising from the ground. It stood as tall as him, a solid that seemed to move like a liquid, an ever-changing shape that moved as if it was considering him, like a curious animal with none of the features. The stuff of nightmares.

He glanced around, looking for something, but there was only organic matter, the plants covering every surface around him. The thing moved closer, slowly approaching him, reaching for him, its movements sluggish in the low gravity. He had no weapons, but he did have mobility. He hit his booster and tore through the room.

The creature seemed to be surprised by the movement, recoiling, or perhaps simply moving in place as Errol rocketed past it. His aim was less than true, and he struck the wall by the door, sending a jolt of pain through his body. He grunted, shaken by the impact, but he didn't look back. He propelled himself into the hallway and out the door into the weightless forest.

He hit his jetpack once more, using it to push him toward the entrance. "Elia, Jason, someone report."

"It's just me." Jason's voice was labored, his words coming between heavy breaths. "Another one popped out at Elia. I...I had to leave her. She called after me, but I left her."

Errol closed his eyes. "You did the right thing, son."

"It doesn't feel like it."

"I'm somewhere behind you. You focus on getting to the ship. And make sure one of those damn things doesn't touch you."

"Roger, Captain."

Errol passed through a wave of foliage and up ahead, he could see the airlock. His booster was beginning to run low on fuel, but it should be enough to get there. Up ahead, he could see Jason, a tiny white figure amongst the herculean trees, heading toward the airlock. Except there was something off, something he could not quite see.

He was moving faster than the other man, gaining ground on him as they both zoomed through the zero gravity toward the airlock. As he grew closer, Jason came into further focus. So did the dark patch on his back, the patch that looked like a puddle that could not sit still.

"Jason, there's…" He was cut off when something appeared over his helmet, something that completely blocked his entire field of view. His momentum was halted, his legs swinging out as he was pulled backward by his head. He felt a fresh jolt of pain from where he had struck the wall, but his mind was on the mass that covered his helmet.

There was panic in his mind, but he would not let himself get lost in it. Jason was calling for him in the comm, but he ignored it. He needed to focus his mind, or he would be just as lost as the others. Whatever this creature was, it was corrosive. Already, cracks had formed in the helmet's screen forming holes that it could squeak through. He saw the tendrils poking through, reaching toward him.

Errol reached up, fumbling at the clasp at the base of his helmet. He missed once, then again, unable to gain purchase with the thick gloves. He thought he heard a report of being in the airlock, but he might have imagined it. The tendrils were growing closer, so close that he could smell the stench of rotting vegetation that accompanied it.

He fumbled at the clasp once more, and this time, it caught. He twisted the helmet and pushed, propelling himself away. As he spun, he caught glimpses of the thing, larger than the one in the crew quarters, a great shifting mass that knew no true shape. His helmet vanished into it, but he was moving safely away from it.

Years of zero gravity training kicked in. He grabbed hold of a branch as he passed, using it to stabilize himself, though he lost his grip quickly. The next one he was able to keep hold of. He stopped only quickly enough to gain his bearings, then pushed away from it, toward the airlock. Once he was on his way, he activated his booster, the rest of his fuel going into the final blast toward the airlock.

His aim was less than perfect. He went wide to the right, and unable to slow his momentum, he struck the wall hard. Pain coursed through his body, in particular the wrist he had used to stop himself. He felt the compression of the suit; if he still had his helmet, it would probably be telling him that the bones were broken.

Through the panels, he could see the outer portion of the airlock. And the ship. Except it was not right. It was further away than it should be. And there was no sign of Jason. His mind flashed to the darkness that had attached itself to Jason's suit and his stomach dropped.

Errol pounded on the surface with his good hand, screaming, yelling until he was hoarse, not stopping even when the ship had moved completely from his view. When he finally gave up, he simply allowed himself to float there. He knew the protocol; after a mission like this, the ship was to return directly to Earth.

Time seemed to slow. It was just him; him and the creature that had made its home in the biosphere, that had already taken two of his people. He closed his eyes; there was not much more he could do. From behind, he heard a noise that sounded like someone walking through mud.

CURSE OF THE TOMB

I've always had a soft spot for Egyptian-based horror and adventure. There's something magical about the setting: the sand, the tombs, the mummies, the tales of curses that have been spun over the years. It's hard not to be fascinated, and with that fascination, I decided to write a tale of my own.

This one originally started out pretty straightforward but ended up morphing into something a bit more on the eldritch side. There's always been a connection between the two, so it made sense to go that direction as the story developed. I don't make any direct connection to my other eldritch type works, but I like to think that they exist in a shared universe. Maybe something for a future project to bring it all together.

The sand had been cleared away, taken out a bit at a time by the workers, and what was left was a narrow tunnel, the stone walls covered in faded carvings, writings in the pictorial alphabet of the ancient Egyptians. It was clear from the way his head turned that Allan was eager to decipher the writings, but Peter Cummings only had eyes for what lay at the end.

The doors were stone, covered in more of the same carvings that lined the walls. Where the doors met, he could see a binding, holding the doors together. A binding that was unbroken.

Peter drew in a deep breath, then turned and grinned at the rest of the team. "We're the first."

Carter Belling, the beneficiary of the expedition, stood there with his arms crossed over his wide chest, dressed in a fine shirt and slacks despite the heat and sand, the clothes stretching against his heavyset frame. "You're certain?"

His wife, Rita, pushed past him, ignoring the rip that came from scraping her dress against the rough wall. She flipped dark hair from her face, speaking in her Spanish accent. "He said so, did he not, dear?" She stopped just short of where Peter stood, close enough that he could smell the perfume she wore. She grinned widely, showing a mouth filled with pearly white teeth. "Do not keep us in suspense, Peter. Open it up. Show us that all the money we've spent has been worth it."

Peter turned back to the doors, taking in a deep sigh and suppressing the cough that threatened from the dust he breathed in. "Ladies and gentlemen, this is history in the making. The tomb of…." He drew a blank as his eyes fell upon the hieroglyphics. "Allan?"

The scholar leaned in, adjusting his spectacles as he took in the symbols etched into the wall. "Amun-Djehey."

"A pharaoh?" Carter asked.

"No," Peter said. He could read that much, at least. "He's a seer."

"A sorcerer," Allan said.

"Not a pharaoh?" Carter's voice raised, the pitch increasing.

"Dear…" Rita said.

"He's important enough to have been buried amongst kings," Peter said. "That means he was as esteemed as one. It's time to go in."

The seal broke easily, the aged, dried wood and rope wrapped around it snapping at the slightest pressure. The stone doors were heavy, refusing to move at first. Peter tried to pry it with his fingers, joined by Allan and Carter, but it was only when the workers brought the crowbars in and used them to pry the doors apart that light finally flooded into the tomb.

Peter was the first through the threshold, but Carter quickly pushed past him, holding his lantern up high. Immediately, there was a glint of gold as the treasure in the chamber beyond caught the light, and Peter couldn't help the smile that cross his face.

Carter turned back, his own smile matching Peter's. "We did it."

Peter said nothing, stepping past, holding his own lantern up. He heard Allan muttering to himself as he began to examine the writings on the wall, while Rita audibly gasped, the heels of her boot thumping on the stone ground.

The tomb was untouched by all but age. Everything lay just as it had when the doors had been sealed so many centuries ago. There were statues, furniture, jars that once held food and drink. As he moved to the next room, he saw armor and arms, a wide chariot pulled by a pair of golden horses, an army of tiny statues, standing ready for battle. Beyond was a chamber with a long boat, nearly collapsed in on itself, and within, corpses, the mummified remains of Amun-Djehey's slaves. And beyond that, the sorcerer himself.

The sarcophagus stood from floor to ceiling, taking up much of the room. The walls were depressed on each side, colorful scenes depicted on each one. The corners were rounded, crafted from gold, or at least layered in it. There was nothing else in the room, only the dirt of the floor and the bricks of the outer wall.

"Hello there, Amun," Peter said quietly.

Another lantern appeared behind him, scattering the shadows in different directions. "Will you look at the size of that thing?"

Peter cringed at the sound of his benefactor's voice, so loud that it seemed an affront on the sanctity of the chamber. He said nothing though; there was still a need for the money. Instead, he spoke in a quieter tone, hoping the man would follow. "We'll need to catalog all this before we try to open it up. Preserve as much as we can."

The technique didn't work, the rich man stepping forward and running his hand over one of the scenes. "What's all this mean?"

"Allan will be here soon," Peter said. "He should be able to tell us."

"Dear?" Rita asked, entering the chamber. Peter turned and nearly felt his heart give out when he saw that she now wore several golden bangles on her wrists, holding them out before her. "How do these look on me?"

"Marvelous," Carter said without turning to look.

"Mrs. Belling," Peter said.

"Rita, please," she said idly. "You didn't even look, dear."

Another entered the room, out of breath. Peter's assistant, Gloria Jennings, had her long brown hair tucked under a brimmed hat, khakis hanging loosely on her frame. "I'm sorry, Mr. Cummings, she picked them up and stepped away before I even knew what was happening."

Rita was still admiring the bangles on her hand. Carter still had not looked over, and a darkness had grown over the woman's face. "Look, dear," she said, more forcefully.

Carter glanced over. "Looks nice," he said, then returned to examining the surface of the sarcophagus.

"Mrs. Belling," Peter said, more forcefully.

She turned to him. "Yes, Peter?"

"If you could please not touch anything, we're trying to catalogue the findings."

Rita flashed the bangles once more, the gold catching the lamplight. "What's the point in digging up old tombs if you can't enjoy the spoils."

Peter managed to catch both of her hands and draw them down. "Mrs. Belling, everything here will be sold into museum collections. That is where the money will come from, not from the riches."

She frowned, almost pouting, turning toward her husband. "Dear, are you listening to this? Tell him that this is our expedition, and that these are our treasures."

Carter turned his attention toward her. "Listen to what he's saying, Rita. We're only here to ensure the money is spent well. Peter and his team are handling the rest."

The woman's face turned dark, and she said something in rapid Spanish as she slid the bangles from her wrists, allowing them to fall to the ground before storming out of the chamber. Gloria gave an exasperated look, while Peter only shrugged.

"I told you it was a bad idea to have them along," Gloria said as she took up the bangles and left them alone.

Peter turned away slowly, locking back toward the massive sarcophagus and the benefactor. "Apologies for that," Carter called out. "I think she fails to understand the reasoning behind us supporting this."

"It's no problem," Peter said. He approached the sarcophagus, the scene facing the door showing the sorcerer in a place of honor, at a height with the pharaoh on his throne.

"It is a problem," Carter said. "Unfortunately, you know how those Spaniards have blood that runs hot. There's no controlling her. Had I been able to leave her at home, I would have."

Peter moved around, making his way to the opposite side from the rich man, gazing upon further depictions in the surface. Feats of the sorcerer were displayed here: bringing forth the floods to stem a drought, what looked like a vast battle that the sorcerer was overseeing, a foiled assassination. The kind of superstition that may follow a person with extraordinary luck.

"So all this," Carter said, drawing Peter from his examination of the images. "You think it's cursed?"

Cursed? Peter fought against audibly reacting, only shaking his head. What kind of pulp magazines had this man been reading? "Silly superstitions," he said. "Their gods were long ago proven to be nothing more than fabrications. A good Christian man like yourself should know as much."

"Still," he said, poking his head around the corner. "You see these carvings. This man must have done something remarkable to garner this degree of respect."

"Maybe so," Peter said.

"Like this," Carter said, gesturing to the sarcophagus wall before him. "What do you make of this?"

Peter made his way around to where Carter stood, holding his lantern up as he stepped before the wall. It was a shorter wall, home to a single scene. There were people in a prone position, bowing before something. Peter noticed that the pharaoh was one of these, and that only the sorcerer stood, staff in one hand while the other pointed upward. Above him was a lone eye, hanging above them in the sky, and what seemed like beams floating down to the people below.

"I…" He took a moment to examine it. "I'm not sure."

"Not sure?" Carter said. "Aren't you supposed to be an expert on this kind of thing?"

"I am," Peter said. "I've never seen anything like this before." He leaned around and called out Allan's name.

The portly researcher appeared after a moment, using a handkerchief to wipe the sweat from his brow. "What is it?" he asked. "I was just translating the writings in the outer chamber."

"Come here," Peter said, stepping back and holding up his lantern as Allan approached. "Have you ever seen anything like this?"

Allan stepped up, adjusting his spectacles. He examined the carvings, running the tips of his fingers over them. "This is odd."

"What is?" Carter asked.

"It's not the Eye of Horus," Allan said.

"The eye of what?"

"Horus," Peter said. "The god of the sky. It represents dreams. But it looks different than this."

Allan nodded. "This is just...an eye." He pulled out a notebook and began to sketch. "I'll need time to study this."

"What about the mummy?" Carter asked. "Aren't we going to open this thing up?"

"Not until he's done," Peter said.

Carter motioned toward the carvings. "Can't we just, I don't know, cut them out?"

"We can't risk damaging them," Allan said, still sketching.

Carter sighed and grumbled something under his breath as he stomped loudly from the room. Peter followed it with his own sigh.

"Remember why he is here, boss," Allan said.

"I do," Peter said. "I dream of a day when we can make these treks without the need for a benefactor."

"If this tomb draws as much as I think it will, we won't ever need one again," Allan said.

"I hope you're right." The man usually was, which was why Peter always asked for him specifically. But there would be a lot of hoops to jump through. He wondered how long it would be once everything was shipped away before they'd be able to come back and resume digging in the sand without a benefactor gazing over their shoulders.

"Have you seen how they got the body in there?" Allan asked. He had moved around and was making sketches and notes on the next side.

"Not that I've seen." His eyes fell once more upon the carved scene, the bits of color that had survived the years of erosion, the way the eye gazed down upon the prostrating worshipers, the way the sorcerer stood proudly declaring his worship. The whole thing seemed off, unlike anything he had ever seen. He reached out and brushed his fingers across it, just as Allan had, then quickly drew them back, shaking off the chill that coursed through his hand. It was as though he had just touched ice on a frozen mountaintop, a sensation so cold it burned.

From around the corner, he heard Allan speak. "Come here, boss, I found something."

Peter made his way around the sarcophagus, stepping to where Allan crouched, pushing at something beneath the carving on this side. There were hinges and a latch, and when Allan tripped the latch, a small door swung open, revealing a long, golden staff with a gem at the end. A staff just like the one the sorcerer held in the carving.

"Incredible," Allan said.

Peter reached for it, and it was like there was electricity running through his skin as his hand approached it. He almost expected to receive a shock when he finally did wrap a hand around it, but there was nothing, the feeling faded. He lifted it from the stand that held it, feeling the weight of it in his hand.

"What do you think it was used for?" Allan asked.

"The library might have information about it," Peter said. "For now, we should get it catalogued with the rest."

Allan jotted down a note in his notebook. "I wonder if there's anything else hidden here."

"We'll have plenty of time to find out," Peter said, stepping around, examining the base of the sarcophagus.

There was the sound of running footsteps, and Peter looked up to see Gloria entering the chamber, out of breath. He frowned. "What is it?"

"You'd better come quick," she said. "The workers are refusing to work."

"Refusing to work?"

"Yes," she said. "And Mr. Belling is trying to talk them into it."

"Oh God," he said. He shoved the staff into Allan's hands and hurried after her.

When he finally found them, they weren't even in the tunnel anymore. All the workers had moved several yards away, standing in a group beneath the hot sun, watching as a rich white man argued with their leader through a translator.

"We're paying top dollar to have you out here," Carter said. "The job isn't supposed to stop when you dig out the entrance. There's a whole damn tomb to excavate."

The leader spoke rapidly, and the translator spoke his words in English. "He says that the tomb was not part of the deal. They are not going to do any more work here."

"Is it a money problem?" Carter asked. "Because they're going to get paid for their work. I can guarantee that."

"It's not a money problem," the translator said in his thick accent. "The workers will not go back into the tomb."

"Why not?" Peter asked, frowning.

The translator turned his dark eyes on Peter. "They say that the tomb is cursed."

Carter scoffed, putting his hands on his hips as he spoke. "So you're telling me that they refuse to do the agreed upon work because of some Arab superstition mumbo jumbo?"

Peter held out a hand to silence him. "What do you mean cursed?"

Carter turned to him. "I thought you didn't believe in curses."

Peter shushed him as the translator looked at the leader and translated for him. The leader looked between the translator and Peter, his breathing heavy. He began to speak, his words coming quickly, quietly. His eyes continued to move, sometimes darting to the tomb entrance, then always back.

All were quiet, even the translator, until he finished. When he did, the air lay heavy, like the sun itself was weighing down the world around them. The translator spoke. "This is an evil place, built for an evil person. The other tombs they've excavated, there have been curses, but not like this one. This one has an actual feel of evil, built right into the stones. This was a place that was meant to remain hidden, and they want no part of it."

Despite the heat, Peter felt his skin tighten into goosebumps. Carter, however, seemed completely unaffected. "Is there anyone in this damn country that will, then?"

The words were translated, and the leader said, "You will have to bring your own people. No one here will empty this one for you."

Carter cursed loudly while Peter remained stoic. "What will happen if we continue with this?"

The leader looked him in the eye, and spoke without the translator, the words nearly bleeding into his accent. "You will die. You will all die."

Outside, night had fallen, but inside, the work continued, guided beneath the light of oil lanterns hanging from the ceiling, the walls, or sitting in any place where the light was needed. The workers were long gone, leaving behind a cursing Carter kicking at dirt before retiring with his wife to their spacious tent. Peter was relieved at the silence on that front, both of them out of the picture for the time being.

Gloria was in the first chamber, going through the painstaking process of cataloguing and marking each item, while Peter and Allan were in the burial chamber. Allan continued his work on the carvings, while Peter excavated the rest.

The first thing he found were the canopic jars, the home to the late sorcerer's organs, limestone containers topped with the painted heads of the sons of Horus. From there, he found another compartment, this one with a lever. He pulled it, and immediately drew back as the sarcophagus began to move, slowly opening with a loud grinding sound.

Allan poked his head around the corner. "What did you do?"

"I don't know," he said.

They stood together and watched as the side panel began to lower, the scene before them vanishing behind the wall of the sarcophagus, revealing the space within. Both men stared at it for several moments.

"Well, at least we won't have to destroy it," Peter said, stepping forward.

Allan approached behind him, holding up a lantern to light the interior. A musty smell greeted them, the smell of dust, of decay that has gone beyond rot and into something more akin to the sand that surrounded them. The light slowly entered the dark space, and they gazed upon the body of Amun-Djehey.

Or at least, what was left of it.

The sorcerer's body was far from whole, his limbs and head and torso separated from each other and in some cases chopped to pieces. It was a mess of limbs, placed in a jumbled pile of blackened skin and rotting wrappings.

"Guess someone wasn't fond of him," Peter said.

Allan's face was turned in amazement. "I've never seen anything like this. What do you think it is? Why did they do this?" He turned toward Peter. "I've never read about anything like this."

"A punishment, I guess?" Peter said. He felt his own breath caught in his throat. What could something like this mean? A discovery like this, something never before seen in an Egyptian burial. He leaned in, lifting the lantern up. "Is there writing? A warning?"

Allan was focused on the mummy, picking up a forearm with the hand still attached by the leathery skin. "They did him the service of a burial, but they took him apart, like Osiris."

"But unlike Osiris, they didn't put him back together," Peter said.

Allan stepped past him, still holding the hand, moving around to the end of the sarcophagus. Peter followed slowly, stepping around until he was once more gazing upon the carving of the sorcerer and the worshipers, gazing up at the eye.

"Look," Allan said. "They feared what he could do." He held up the hand and attached forearm. "Even in death."

"Even in death," Peter repeated.

Allan turned toward him. "Maybe the natives were right. Maybe we should stop now."

Peter scoffed and turned away. "Like our benefactor said to the workers, it's a bunch of superstitious nonsense." His own words to Carter earlier. He believed them, didn't he?

"I don't know," Allan said, stepping past him and quickly putting the hand back. "I don't feel right about this."

"I think you've been here too long," Peter said, stifling a yawn. "Let's call it a night and pick it up again tomorrow."

"I think we should reconsider this," Allan said.

Peter patted him on the shoulder. "Sleep on it and let me know if you still feel that way in the morning." He led Allan away from the sarcophagus and to the tents outside.

It was strange being in the camp without the sound of the workers, the chatter in their language, the laughter, the smell of their spiced food as it cooked over an open flame. Instead, there was just emptiness, the places where their camp had been made reduced to trampled sand and refuse they had left behind.

Peter settled into his tent, resting on the pad that had been laid out on the ground to serve as his bed, lantern providing light as he reviewed the notes and sketches the team his team had put together. There were layouts of the tomb, itemized lists of the treasures, writings that had been carved in the wall, and rough copies of the images in the sarcophagus.

It was the scene that he kept coming back to, even when his mind went elsewhere. There was something about it, something odd, different. Maybe it was the way the eye was depicted, unlike any hieroglyphic he'd ever seen. Maybe it was the way the sorcerer worshiped it, staff held high in the air. Or maybe it was the way that all others bowed, even the mighty pharaoh, who had been considered a god on Earth to his people.

The night drew on, and he could feel his eyes grow heavy. He closed them, falling into a deep sleep with the image of the scene etched into his mind.

His mind was active as he slept, the world of dreams appearing before him, but it was not the scene that he saw, not like he expected. Instead, he found himself in the tomb, amongst the golden relics that had been laid out, the treasures to accompany Amun-Djehey to the afterlife.

Peter found himself looking around, the layout just as it had been that day, yet everything was different. The rooms were lit by braziers, fires burning brightly, giving off the fragrance of incense. There was a certain sheen to everything, the look of newness, of freshness. The tomb before the doors were sealed.

The sound of footsteps sounded behind him, and Peter turned, stepping backwards as he watched the figures approached from the dark corridor. He backed up until he was against a wall, nestled between the treasures that lined the room.

The men who entered were cloaked, dressed in dark linens from head to toe, every bit of skin covered but for that around their eyes. They walked with purpose, their steps together as they made their way past him, never glancing his direction.

Peter watched as they passed, taking note of their demeanor, their posture, the items they carried. Two led while bearing torches, walking before one who carried the staff, held straight up and down, like a priest holding a crucifix to lead a procession. Four behind him carried the canopic jars, each carrying one in his hands. Two behind them carried a sagging bundle, and behind them, a lone man with nothing, his palms pressed together before him.

They made their way through the chamber, and Peter followed, stepping quietly, as though any sound might turn their attention toward him. But there was a determination to their movements, a purpose, and they continued to the final chamber without hesitation.

It was at the threshold to the burial chamber that Peter stopped, standing at the edge watching. Even with the braziers and torches burning, it felt impossibly dark in there, as if the light was being swallowed by the blackness as it left the edges of the flames.

The canopic jars were placed first, into the same chamber where Peter had found them earlier that day. Next came the bundle, the two men lifting it into the empty space that formed the side of the sarcophagus. They stepped back, allowing the man with the staff to step forward.

Peter could hear them speak, the words familiar, the same words that he had heard Allan speak as he translated hieroglyphs, yet they were different. Maybe it was the accent, or maybe the way they pronounced the words, but it seemed more alien than what he knew, more ancient, enough that he could not understand it.

There did seem to be some doubt, at least on the part of some, those doubts expressed to the man holding the staff. He responded, his voice low, calm, solemn, pleading his case, and when he was finished, the others conceded. He held up the staff, and whatever ceremony he had planned began.

The staff was held up, over the ceiling, and as the man spoke, the gem at the end began to glow. It was a blue, subtle at first, subtle enough that Peter wondered if it was a trick of the mind, an idle reflection of the flames from the torches. Soon, however, it grew brighter than even the fires that lit the room, a glow that pierced through the darkness and illuminated the space in a way nothing else could.

And then, it was done. The staff was lowered, and the room grew dark again as the sarcophagus was closed. The darkness crept back in, seeming to come on stronger with the absence of the staff's light. It seemed to spill from the chamber into the next, licking at the light, and Peter found himself taking a step back as it seemed to consume his feet.

The men were speaking again, and he could see a bit of movement, but they had almost vanished completely in the darkness. Their voices seemed muffled, reduced to little more than whispers. But he was no longer focused on them.

The darkness was creeping upward, making its way up the legs of his pants. He took more steps, trying to shake it off, but it stuck to him, like sap from a tree. It was creeping up his legs, reaching like tentacles to his waist, clinging its way upward.

Peter began to struggle, feeling it pull on him, constricting against him. It passed his waist, pulling his arms in close, and no matter how hard he struggled, he could not shake it off. It pressed harder, and he could feel his breathing began to labor, each breath feeling harder and harder to take in. As the darkness reached his neck and moved toward his mouth, he could feel himself begin to choke.

And then he was awake, sitting up, breathing heavily. The blanket was wrapped tightly around him, enough that he struggled to break free of it. His skin was covered in sweat, the heat of the desert still lingering even without the sun above.

He finally managed to shake off the covers, tossing them aside, scattering the notes in the process. He sat there for a moment, gazing upon the mess he had created in his tent. It had all felt so real, more real than any dream he'd ever had. He wiped the sweat from his face and shook his head, trying to shake the image from his mind.

"Just a dream," he said out loud. "Just a dream."

That was when he heard the scream.

Peter pushed through the flaps of his tent, standing up and gazing around in the moonlit night. He heard movement and saw both Gloria and Allan emerging from their respective tents. "You hear that?" Peter asked them.

"It came from the Belling tent, I think," Gloria said.

Peter turned toward their benefactor's tent and made his way toward it, walking swiftly. There were no further sounds coming from it, no movement. Nothing. He could see light through the canvas of the tent, their lanterns still burning.

"Carter?" he called out. "Rita?"

There was no response. Allan took up the call. "Mr. Belling?"

Peter approached the flap that formed the entrance, his hand reaching out to grab the edge, to peel it back. He took a breath, licked his lips, and peered into the tent.

It seemed as though the couple had brought the luxury of their home with them. The ground was covered in fine Persian rugs, and there was a full bedroom set, including a wardrobe and a vanity, along with a small table for taking their meals and a wet bar for their alcohol. And there, in the middle of their large, four post bed, the couple lay.

At first, it looked as though nothing were wrong, but only at first glance. There was no movement when he entered, despite the fact that they were dressed for bed, he in his underwear and her in a slip. They both lay there, eyes focused forward, staring into nothingness.

"Carter?" Peter said. "Rita?"

He heard a shriek behind him and turned to find Gloria right behind him, Allan behind her. "Get her out of here," he snapped, and Allan obliged, casting a glance past as he led Gloria from the tent.

Peter turned back and approached the bed, getting a closer look at the bodies. The heads lulled a bit inward, the eyes wide open. Rita's lips were stretched open, no doubt the source of the scream, while Carter seemed more peaceful, almost surprised.

As he got closer, something caught his eye. He snatched up one of the lit lanterns and held it up, getting it closer and throwing light upon the bodies. It was subtle, almost imperceptible in the dim light he had entered to find, but with the closer light, it was clear. Around the eyes and around the lips there was some sort of substance, a black liquid that had the look of tar to it, as though it would stick to his finger if he touched it. He had no desire to do so.

Allan had started up the fire by the time Peter departed the tent. Gloria was huddled next to it, a blanket on her shoulders and a cup in her hands, while Allan stood near, smoking a cigarette. As he drew the cigarette down, Peter could see that his hand was shaking.

"What did it?" Allan asked.

Peter shook his head. "No idea."

"Well did you see anything?" He took another long drag, blowing the smoke out quickly.

"There was something in their mouths," he said. "Around their eyes. But I don't know what it was. Didn't see anything else."

"Maybe the workers were right," Gloria said, looking up at them. "Maybe this tomb is cursed."

"That's what I was saying," Allan said. "I was told it was ridiculous."

"This means nothing," Peter said, crossing his arms. "It's a coincidence."

Allan nodded toward Gloria. "Tell him."

Gloria shook her head, and Peter looked toward Allan. "Tell me what."

"About the dream."

"You tell him," she said. "You had the same dream."

Peter felt his stomach turn. "Dream?"

"We had the same dream," Allan said. "She told me about it while we were waiting on you."

Gloria nodded, sipping from her cup, and the scent of whiskey drifted up from it. "The same one," she said.

"Is that a coincidence too? Huh?"

Peter kept his voice as calm as he could manage. "What was the dream?"

"We saw him getting buried," Gloria said. "Amun-Djehey."

"In the tomb," Peter said.

She nodded. "There was a procession, and they had the staff. It was so dark."

"You saw it too, didn't you?" Allan said. He was staring right at Peter, who slowly nodded. "I thought so. But you can't understand them, can you, Peter? You've never had a good grasp on the language."

"I couldn't," Peter said.

Allan poked at his own chest. "I could. I understood every word. Want to know what they said?"

"Tell me," Peter said.

"They didn't want to bury him, not like this. Not the way they did. They wanted to burn the corpse, use it for kindling. But the one who carried the staff, he said it was the only way. That he would never be at rest as long as he remained unmummified."

Peter didn't look at either of them, staring off into the darkness. It couldn't be real, could it? It had to be a coincidence.

"Peter," Allan said. Peter turned his head. "We have to seal the tomb."

Gloria nodded. "We do. It's the only way."

"You guys are insane," Peter said.

"What?" Allan exclaimed as Gloria stood.

Peter began to pace. "This is ridiculous. We have a few setbacks, and you want to give up."

"Setbacks?" Allan said. "Peter, our workers are gone, we are having the same nightmares, and our benefactors are suddenly dead. What more do you want? Do you want God to spell it out in fire in the skies?"

"This is all superstition," Peter said. "It's in your head. Some bad things happen and you're attributing it to a nonexistent curse."

Gloria was glaring at him now. "How can you say such a thing, Peter? Don't you trust us?"

"Clearly not," Allan said, squishing out the cigarette. "And I don't think he's going to change his mind. But that doesn't mean we have to stick around."

Peter frowned. "Where are you going?"

"To find a hotel," Allan said, trudging away toward the tent. "I'm not spending another moment by this God-forsaken tomb."

Peter took a step toward him, but didn't follow, raising his voice instead. "Just like that? Years of work thrown away?"

"Even that work is not worth this," Allan yelled back.

"Well, I hope you know you're getting none of the credit. None of it!"

He could hear the engine of their lone car fire up, and just like that, it was gone, faded into the desert night. Peter was alone, left by himself amongst the dead.

"Fine," he said aloud. "If you want to be like that, fine. There's plenty I can do by myself. I know the cataloguing system. I can get it all accounted for and then go back for more men." He was walking now, trudging toward the tomb entrance. "Yeah, that's what I'll do."

He thought he heard someone speak his name, and he paused, listening to the stillness around him. All he could hear was the wind breathing through the dunes.

"I don't think I'm getting anymore sleep tonight," he said. "I can get a jump on things."

He made his way to his tent, grabbing his lantern and lighting it. When he did, he noticed the staff laying there. "Strange," he said. "I don't remember bringing this from the tomb." He stared at it for a moment. "No matter. I'll just take it back."

Peter picked up the staff, feeling the weight in his hand. It felt strangely warm, as though it had been sitting in the sun all day, and there seemed to be a slight glow in the crystal, but it vanished when he moved it out of the light. He shrugged it off and made his way toward the tomb. As he approached, he was certain he heard his name called again, right as the wind blew, whistling past his ears. Just a mirage, he figured, no different from the way the desert warped one's sight during the day.

Gloria had been working in the first chamber, and Peter had every intention of continuing her work there. When he arrived, however, something drew him further in. The tomb was dark, the lanterns from the day all extinguished. As he grew deeper, the darkness seemed to deepen with it, seeming to consume the flame in the lantern.

He was in the second chamber when he heard his name again. This time, there was no mistaking it. "Hello?" he called out, his voice echoing off the stones of the tomb. "Is someone there?"

No one responded. In the back of his mind, something was telling him that he should listen to the others, that he should go join them, find a hotel in the city. He could be relaxing with a drink in a hotel bar, spend the rest of the night in a real bed, apologize to Allan and Gloria and return to the tomb in daylight with more workers. The idea was tempting, but he shook it off. He was here, and he above all remembered why.

The staff was still gripped in his hand as he entered the third chamber. As he did, his name was sounded again, and he stopped in place. It was clear now, still the tone of a whisper, but there was no doubt in his mind now. It was his name, and it was coming from the next room.

Peter could feel his heart beating faster in his chest, the hair on his neck standing on end. He stood still, the lantern in one hand, the staff in the other. The flame in the lantern game the impression of fading, even if when he looked at the flame itself, it didn't seem that way. The voice in the back of his mind was no longer speaking, but instead screaming at him to return, to leave this place.

The voice in the chamber spoke once more. "Peter. Come here." A pause. "Bring that to me."

Peter began to walk, making his way toward the burial chamber. The air around him grew darker, seeming to swallow both himself and the flame as he entered it, until the flame was no longer even casting light. He was in total darkness. At least, that was, until the staff began to glow.

He lifted the staff up and found that it lit the chamber. The room behind him was still dark, but he could see the sarcophagus itself, cast in a shade of blue, the open space within still dark, still hidden from view.

The voice spoke again, clearer here, coming from within the sarcophagus. "I have waited a long time for this, for someone to free me. There is so much left undone."

Peter was silent, only able to watch. He could not run, could not even walk from the room, as though his feet were cemented to the ground. Something moved, and he watched as a hand emerged from the sarcophagus, a browned, dried hand, with some of the faded wrappings still clinging to it.

"Bring me the staff."

Peter watched the hand, waiting patiently. In his mind, he could see the carved image, the way all, even the pharaoh, bowed to the priest, the eye in the sky, the power of the staff. What was going to happen? What could this man do?

What he failed to consider, however, was what he could have done. The answer seemed to be nothing, as though his body was no longer under his own control. His feet were already walking toward the sarcophagus, his hand already holding the staff up. He fought against it in his mind, struggled to resist, but nothing worked.

The last thought that ran through his mind as the mummified hand gripped the staff was how Allan had been right all along.

WASH AWAY

This story is a bit of a shift from the other stories. I wrote this one as a submission for a story collection with a local press in Galveston. It was initially selected, but due to some unfortunate circumstances, the collection ended up being canceled, so I decided to include it here. I do think it still fits the overall theme, just in a different way than many of the other stories. Besides, I've always enjoyed a good western.

The sound was persistent, the water constantly churning, beating against the coarse sand and stirring up white foam before retreating back to the sea. There was something peaceful in sitting there, watching the waters of the gulf encroach and retreat, a peace that he had never been able to find anywhere else.

It had been several weeks since he first came here, perhaps months at this point. It was about the longest he had stayed in any one spot, at least in the past decade. Maybe it was the isolation, that few would venture through the marshes to reach the beach. Maybe it was that no one expected that he would be in a place like this. Or maybe they had simply given up searching for him. It's not like it had always been his choice to move on.

Not that he would expect them to have stopped looking. The last town he'd passed through, the posters had the reward set at five thousand, more than enough to incentivize any man to turn him in given half a chance. The man at the station had tried, and it had earned him a bullet in the head.

Here, though, there were no bounty hunters, no amateurs thinking they can make a quick buck, no lawmen who seem to take a sadistic pleasure in the dirtier parts of their jobs. Just him, the sand and water and small camp he had made, and the occasional fishing boat, never closer than the edge of the horizon. He was alone, just him and his thoughts.

On some days, he'd strip down and wade out into the water, allowing the waves to pass over him. He would close his eyes, feeling the crash against a body that had already begun to be broken down by years. He liked to imagine that each wave washed away some of the blood, the blood from those he had killed throughout the years, but it seemed that when the waters receded, there was still a redness there, a stain on his skin that would never quite wash away.

The sun was low in the sky, but the light lingered, the last vestiges of a hot summer evening, cut just a bit by the warm breeze that came off the gulf. The water was warm too that evening, warm like a bathtub left to sit too long in the sun. It dripped from him as he walked back toward the beach, the waves lapping at his ankles, the water splashing with each step.

"Stop right there."

He hadn't seen anyone approach, and even at the sound of the voice, he didn't initially look up. Maybe it was the fact that he hadn't heard a human voice in weeks. Maybe it was the way the waves crashed around him and the wind blew past his ears, drowning out nearly everything. Or maybe he just wasn't ready to face someone who had come so far out of his way. Such a person could only want one thing.

"I said, stop right there."

His voice spoke, deep and scratchy, the first words he'd spoken aloud in weeks. "I heard you the first time."

"Then you should listen. There's a gun pointed at you right now."

He leaned down and picked up a shirt, pulling it over his wet skin. He heard the clicking of a revolver hammer. "Don't make another move, or I'll shoot you where I stand."

"If you were really worried about me doing something, you would have already shot me."

The shirt pulled over his head, and he shook off the water from his thickening hair and beard, both showing traces of white. For the first time, he turned toward the source of the voice and found a young man standing there. He couldn't have been older than seventeen, scarcely past boyhood, his face still bare and smooth, dark hair cut short. True to his word, he held a revolver in his hand, though the grip was hardly steady.

"I'm unarmed," he said. "Why don't you put that away before you hurt someone?"

"No." The boy motioned with the revolver. "I've heard you're a dangerous man, and my pa said to never take your eye off a dangerous man."

"Your pa must be a smart man," he said, casting a quick gaze out toward the gulf.

"My pa is dead."

"That's too bad."

"It was you who killed him."

He kept his expression even, searching the kid's face for any kind of resemblance to any of those that had stuck around in his mind. He found none. "Wasn't nothing personal, kid. It never is."

The kid's voice rose. "Well it was personal to me. But I guess you don't care about that, do you? You don't care about who you kill or who it affects."

He turned his eyes back toward the gulf, to the clouds forming to the south. "Can't say I do."

"Well let me tell you."

"Put the gun down first, and you can tell me all you want."

The kid shook his head. "No, I won't. Because I'm going to kill you."

"No you're not."

"Yes I am."

"You ever shot a gun like that before, kid?" The kid opened his mouth, but he cut him off. "I bet you haven't. It's got a kick to it, and your hand's shaking like you drank a full bottle of whiskey last night and still haven't worked out the kinks."

"I can still hit you."

"You're more likely to hit yourself."

"Shut up," the kid said. "Just shut up."

He took a step toward the kid, and the kid thrust the gun in his direction. "Stop. Stop right there."

He took another step. His voice was calm, even. "What about killing? You ever killed a man?"

The kid took a step back, still holding the gun out. "I'm warning you."

"You ever looked into someone's eyes and pulled a trigger? You ever watched the life bleed out of them? You'd know if you had. It changes you."

The kid took another step back, his hand shaking.

"It's the kind of thing that sticks with you, that haunts your dreams."

"Stop," the kid said. "I'll do it."

"I bet you will," he said. "You'll fire that gun, but your hand is shaking so much you wouldn't hit me, much less kill me. And you don't want to miss with a killer like me, do you?"

The kid shook his head and took another step back.

"I'm giving you a chance to run, kid. Take it. Your pa didn't and look where it got him."

"Don't talk about him. You didn't know him."

The sudden outburst was surprising, but he had long ago learned to hide surprise. You didn't live long in times like these when you allowed yourself to be surprised.

"I didn't," he said. "But I know enough now. You learn something about a person when you kill them."

"I'm going to kill you."

He was close now, his steps steady, though still able to approach, to gain ground on the kid. The kid was stumbling now in the sand.

"Are you? Pull the trigger then. Stop talking and take action."

"I will." The kid's hand was still shaking. It was a wonder he could still hold the revolver like that.

"Do it." He put more strength behind his voice. "Do it!"

He could almost reach out and grab the gun from where he stood. He took another step toward the kid, and that's when the gun went off, the shot echoing through the air, reverberating across the empty expanse until it was lost in the sound of the crashing waves.

His ears were still ringing when he stepped forward again. His left hand swiped the gun aside, knocking it from the kid's hand. His right hand reached out and grabbed the handle of the knife that was holstered on the kid's belt. In a single motion, he brought it upward, driving the blade upward through the kid's jaw.

The kid was shaking, his eyes wide as he stared out, blood pouring from the wound. The eyes were no different from all the ones he'd seen before. It was always the same look, a look of fear, of pleading, as if he had the power to take back what had been done if they wished hard enough. Maybe on some level, he wished he could too.

He stared into the kid's eyes, hearing the choking sounds as the kid tried to speak through a mouth that was forced shut, as his life drained from him. He said nothing, only gently lowered him, laying him down on the sand. It was only when the kid stopped breathing that he released the knife handle, standing up straight and gazing down at the kid's body lying there in the sand.

"You should have listened," he said quietly. "You should have gone."

He turned away from the body. He would bury it later, somewhere down the shore. He wondered if the kid had told anyone. Maybe not; kids that age were reckless, and this one sure as hell wasn't thinking about reason or precautions. Emotion drives people to do reckless things; it was something he'd seen more than once. It was something he'd certainly done more than once, back when he was younger, dumber. Maybe he still did.

Of course, the kid could've told someone. Maybe he had told everyone he knew, bragging about how he was going to avenge his father, collect the reward. Maybe in a few days, someone would come looking for him. Maybe it would be better if he moved along. He didn't want to, of course. Maybe it would be better if he didn't, if he just let them come. Maybe it would be better for everyone.

He was back at the water's edge. The waves washed over his feet, and when the next wave came in, he dipped his hands in it, watching the blood run off into the salty water. When he lifted them out, he could still see the stain on his hands, the shade of red that was left behind. He stared at it for a moment, wondering if it would ever come off. Maybe not; maybe it was meant to be that way. Time would tell.

He turned away from the water, making his way back to the camp. Tomorrow, he would deal with the body. Tonight, as with all nights, he would let the sound of the waves drift him away to sleep. Maybe tonight would be the one time he slept well.

But probably not.

IN THE EYES OF THE SAINTS

This one is another story submission that ended up not being taken. I drew inspiration on this one from a piece of art I found online, a pretty standard medieval plague depiction. From it, I imagined a massive city-state facing an unseen threat within its walls, and the story came together from there.

I do think I want to revisit this setting at some point. It has a decent amount of worldbuilding for a short story, and as with any world I build, I never want it to just be a one and done kind of thing. Whether that ever happens is a different story, of course, but you never know.

In the history of the city of Minas Afon, Saint Branwen's Day had only failed to be celebrated once. It had been during one of the many skirmishes that followed the revolution, when the Crens had laid siege to the city, parking their massive army outside the wall for nearly sixteen months in hopes of starving the people out. Or well, the annals referred to them as skirmishes; Delwyn had always considered them acts of war.

This year was different, though. The siege was not of the kind from their once rulers and constant adversaries to the east. No, the attack was from some other force, one that could not be seen but in the suffering of those afflicted.

A bonfire still burned in the square in front of the church, just as it always did on Saint Branwen's Day. Just like always, he could see the tips of the flames from the windows of his tower, a joy he often took amongst his books and scrolls, far from the drunken revelry that came with celebrating the city's freedom a century past. But this fire was not built for the straw effigies of the late King Richard and his tyrannous lords. No, this one had a much more tragic purpose.

The door creaked open as Cerys entered. From the corner of his eye, he could see her standing tall, leatherbound ledger book held at her waist with both hands, waiting to be acknowledged. Her hair was cut short above the ears, to avoid maintenance, she always said, and she wore the simple robes of a scholar apprentice, the first of her ropes to mark mastery of knowledge hanging from her belt. A new one had appeared in the last week, the crimson one to signal that her knowledge in anatomy had been tested and found adequate. It joined the rapidly growing collection that she had already attained; horticulture, history, theology, philosophy, civics, and the Cren language.

This was not a time to celebrate such matters of hubris, however. Delwyn turned to her, clasping his hands behind his back. "How many today?"

Cerys lifted the ledger book and opened to a marked page. "Collectors reported three hundred and seventy-one."

By the saints, over three hundred. Delwyn shook his head, turning back to the smoke that was billowing out of Saint Gareth's Square. Yesterday, it had been two hundred thirty-one, the day before just over one hundred fifty. It was multiplying, spreading faster, and at this rate, there would soon be no one left in the city.

"You met with the advisory council?"

"I did," she said. "Your absence was noticed."

I'm sure it was. "Give me the notes."

He heard the page turn in the ledger. "The mayors…"

"Not them, not yet. Their complaints are the same by the day. You can come back to them."

"As you say, Master. Captain Ifan has restricted access to the barracks and the wall. There is concern of unrest due to the gates being closed. There have been crowds forming at both the north and the south gates."

"Not the east?"

"Captain Ifan says the east is quiet."

"Perhaps because it has been the least hit. Continue."

"He mentioned patrols have had problems enforcing the curfew, but they are managing. His Holiness has sent his priests out to bless the marked places."

Delwyn whirled around. "Is he mad? Priests are not approved to break the curfew."

"Captain Ifan pointed that out, and His Holiness produced an order from His Majesty granting it."

"The king? I was not aware of this."

"Based on the wording, the king feels that the clergy is an important tool in fighting this blight and felt that their presence would be beneficial to the ill."

He sends them to their graves. "I will speak to him on the matter. Continue."

Cerys turned another page. "Lord Doctor Padrig informed us that his efforts at finding a cure are not yielding the results he hoped for."

"Last time, he mentioned he was seeing promising things from a concoction of herbs and a particular type of wine."

"All patients showed initial signs of improvement before turning for the worse," she said. "He has indicated that he will have to try something new."

Delwyn was pacing now, trying to ignore the smoke billowing up in his periphery each time he passed the window. "Was there any good news to report?"

"Mayor Price feels that he's contained the disease in his sector. Mayor Rhys, however, disputes that claim. Mayor Maxen…"

"Still feels it's some sort of attack from the Cren," he said. "I've heard this song and dance before. Anything new?"

She cleared her throat and flipped another page, giving a bit of a huff before continuing. "Mayor Lew is now openly accusing Mayor Elain of sending her sick to infect his own."

Delwyn gave a sigh of his own. "Does he have proof?"

"He claims isolated outbreaks were caused by strategic placement of the ill that are spreading quickly. He also…" She squinted to confirm what she had written. "…claims to have seen her dancing naked on the rooftop of her manor beneath the full moon."

Delwyn squeezed the bridge of his nose. "Send summons to him. I want to speak to him myself."

"At once, sir."

"Anything else I should know before I meet with His Majesty?"

Cerys closed the book and looked him in the eye. "I passed Alis in the hall on my way here. The way she was acting, it seems His Majesty is in one of his moods today."

"Good to know," he said. He adjusted his robes, the brocade material a mark of his station, then folded his hands within the large sleeves and made his way to the door. His apprentice followed, her short steps falling rapidly on the stone steps, two for each one he took.

"Do you have any further instructions, Master?" she asked. Her words came between breaths; he wondered how long she had waited outside his door before entering. Perhaps he could suggest physical prowess as her next pursuit.

"No," he said. "Once you have delivered word to Mayor Lew, you should return to your chambers. I don't need you spending any more time than necessary in the city, breathing in those putrid airs."

"Of course, Master."

She was still following him as he reached the bottom of the tower and turned down the hall. He got about a dozen paces before turning and facing her. She skidded to a stop, nearly colliding with him. "Is there something else, Cerys?"

"I...uh…" She looked away, clutching her ledger close to her chest.

"Spit it out," he said. "You know my time is valuable. If you are to be in a prestigious role one day, you cannot hope to get by with dancing around your words."

"I was hoping to attend to His Majesty with you."

"My conversations with His Majesty on this matter have been private, consistent with Lord Doctor Padrig's instructions to keep the king isolated to prevent illness. Is there a particular reason you wish to be present?"

"I feel it would be pertinent to my training to attend," she said. "If only to observe the way you present yourself to His Majesty."

Delwyn considered it for a brief moment, then turned away from her once more, continuing his brisk place down the hallway. "You're silent the entire time," he called back. "Not one word."

It was a moment before he heard her hurrying after him, scurrying in his footsteps in an effort to catch up. The hallway was long, just as all the hallways were in the Castle of Saint Traherne, made longer by the walk being to the king's private chambers instead of the throne room. He passed windows that looked over one of the courtyards, this one given over to the horses while the more spacious stables had been relegated to Lord Doctor Padrig's work. He did not envy the smaller space the stablehands had to deal with, nor the work they were having to do to keep the horses warm in this weather. At least it was not raining today.

The guards at the king's door offered no resistance to his entry, both standing tall in their matching armor, the golden lightning of the king's sigil emblazoned on their chests. Delwyn pushed the door open, holding it as Cerys stepped in after him, then allowing it to close.

King Folant sat slouched in his chair, papers spread on the desk before him, many Delwyn recognized from his own hand and that of his apprentice. The king had one letter in his good right hand, his crippled left hand resting on the desk, the two functioning fingers tapping the thick wood. He wore no crown at the moment, though the imprint was visible in his thick blonde hair, and he did wear the silken tunic and violet fur-lined overcoat that he would have worn had court been in session, though his posture here accentuated the growing gut beneath.

The king's eyes raised at them, but he made no effort to sit up or even turn in their direction when they entered. Delwyn gave a low bow. "Your majesty."

"I don't know who she is, but she's staring," the king said in a droning tone.

Delwyn turned to see Cerys standing slightly behind him, ledger still clutched to her chest, her mouth slightly agape. He motioned frantically with his hand, finally snapping her out of her gaze. "Oh," she said, quickly matching his bow.

"Apologies, Your Majesty," he said. "My apprentice."

The king raised an eyebrow. "A girl?"

"Best marks in the bunch, Majesty."

"Must be a pathetic bunch." The king tapped several times, as if sending a code. "I'd be inclined to accuse you of fucking her."

Cerys drew in a breath but said nothing. Delwyn kept his own face as stone. "We are here for today's update, Majesty. I was unable to attend the council, so Cerys has accompanied me in case further information is required. She will not need to speak…"

"No, no," the king said, lifting his left hand slightly. "I would like to see if this apprentice of yours is sharp enough to take over for you. You are growing quite old, are you not, Delwyn?"

"Indeed, Majesty." No need to mention that his predecessor had been nearly two decades older before stepping down. He turned and nodded toward Cerys. "Go ahead."

Cerys looked at him for a moment, then stepped forward, clearing her throat. "Go on," the king said. "You surely cannot bring any worse news than old Delwyn does. Or make it sound any duller."

She cleared her throat again, then said, "The death count today is…"

"No." The outburst caused her to jump as the king slammed the paper onto the desk and sat forward. "No, I can get the report of numbers of dead from these papers here that are delivered to me with my breakfast. I will tell you what I've told your master a hundred times. I don't want numbers, I want a solution. I want to know where this plague has come from and what is being done to stop it."

He leaned back once more. When Cerys did not immediately speak, he turned toward Delwyn. "If this is the quality I can expect from your apprentice, I shudder to think what it says about the rest of our scholars her age. I swear by the saints it would look better for you if you were fucking her."

"We have no information on its source." The girl's even tone was gone, the words coming out like wine from a broken spout. "And our efforts to curtail it have been limited to shutting down each of the sectors. Lord Doctor Padrig is attempting to find a cure, but he…"

"The good Lord Doctor wouldn't know a cure from his own ass." The king stood. "I applaud your report, girl, but that will be all from you for now. It is no different than Master Scholar Delwyn has given me these past weeks."

Delwyn bowed again. "It is as much as I can provide, Majesty."

"And wholly inadequate."

He rapped the knuckles of his good hand on the wood of his desk. A side door opened and Delwyn turned to see a woman emerge, seeming little older than Cerys. She wore a flowing black and purple dress that matched her dark hair in both tone and texture. She walked with grace, her hands held before her, coming to a stop near the king's desk as he once more took a seat, reclining back. She turned her eyes on Delwyn, an icy blue that seemed to chill his very blood.

"Before you ask, I'm not fucking her," King Folant said. "But she seems to be much more useful than yours."

"I have heard much about you, Master Scholar Delwyn," she said. Her accent was foreign, but familiar. He searched his mind for the source, even as he replied.

"I am afraid you have me at a disadvantage."

"My name is Catalan," she said. "Where I come from is of no importance. Just know that I am here to help the king." She raised a hand to brush a strand of hair away, and his eyes caught sight of the large sapphire ring she wore, a stone that seemed to glow with a blue nearly the same as her eyes, the setting intricately woven strands of white gold that wrapped around her finger like a tiny snake.

Delwyn felt the breath sucked from his lungs, the bottom fallen from his gut. There was only one place where a stone like existed, only one type of person who knew how to make use of one. He turned to the king. "Your Majesty, this woman is a...a..."

"A what, Master Scholar?" she asked, her voice friendly, innocent, naive.

"A witch!" He stepped toward the king's desk, making sure to distance himself from her, though the woman made no movement. Not that distance mattered; there was no telling what manner of spells she could speak just with him standing there. "Your Majesty," he said, keeping one of his eyes on her. "You must get rid of this woman immediately. She is immensely dangerous."

"Is she?" the king asked. "She seems quite innocuous to me. Are you dangerous, Catalan?"

"Only to the king's enemies," she said. Her eyes remained focused on Delwyn. "Are you the king's enemy, Master Scholar?"

The word yes seemed to dance on his tongue, and he nearly bit it. There was some magic at work here, without a doubt. "Your Majesty, may we speak on this matter in private?"

The king stood once more, making his way over to a place where a bottle of wine and two glasses had been set. He picked up the bottle and began to pour. "You see it fit to discuss your business in front of your apprentice. I see no reason we cannot speak with Catalan in the room as well. Say your piece and be done with it."

Delwyn's voice came out in something near a whisper, though it was no doubt heard by all in the room. "Majesty, your great great grandfather rid this city of the last of the magic users and fortified the walls against their kind, and he was absolutely right to do so. They are dangerous, deceitful, unable to be trusted."

"Such hurtful words, Master Scholar," Catalan said. "Such hatred for one you do not know."

"I know more than enough about you, witch," he said. "If King Colwyn had listened to his advisors, your kind would have been wiped out." He turned back to the king. "Have you nothing to say about this?"

The king was mid sip, and he took the time to finish. "Catalan is perfectly capable of speaking for herself."

"You betray this city…"

The king held up a hand. "I will hear no such talk in my presence."

"Are you a religious man, Master Scholar?"

"Of course I am," he said, turning to face her for the first time. Her gaze made his hands shake, but he stood tall, hiding them in his sleeves. "I worship the saints as much as any man in this city."

"The saints, of course," she said. "Miracle workers, healers of the sick and infirm, vanquishers of longtime foes. But one has not been here since the reign of King Colwyn, correct?"

"I don't know what you're getting at…"

"They were no different, and your king ran them out."

"This is absurd. Majesty, I don't know why you're even entertaining this witch's ideas and superstitions. She is an enemy of our city, as her people always were."

"There is one foe here, Master Scholar. That is the blight that sweeps through this city, that kills her people and threatens the very sovereignty of Minas Afon. I am not your enemy, Master Scholar, but I know who is."

"And who would that be."

"Our oldest enemy, Delwyn." The king finished another sip and stepped back to his desk. "Catalan has brought proof that the Cren have employed their own…"

"Toare," Catalan said. "A word from the old country."

"A word for witch," Delwyn said.

"More nuanced than that, but if you prefer it."

"Toare," the king repeated.

"The Cren king has brought many of them from my lands," Catalan said. "He has used them to place a curse, here and in the other cities."

"He means to slay us all and take the cities back without a fight." The king's voice was growing fiercer. "We won our freedom, and he wants to take it from us, to beat us down until our people are begging him to rescue us. And then he will provide the cure, and with it, place our people back in chains." His fist struck the desk. "I will not let that happen. I will not let it be said that I am the king who lost Minas Afon back to the Cren."

Delwyn's gaze turned between the two of them, his mouth agape. "Surely you do not believe this madness, Majesty?"

"Is it so hard to believe?" the king asked. "Is it so much less believable than the dozens of theories your scholars and the Lord Doctor's lackeys can put forth." He swept his good hand across the desk, sending many of the papers flying across the floor.

"We are making progress," Delwyn said. "We just need time."

"You are making no progress that I can see," the king said. "All I hear from your reports are more deaths, of the doctors failing to contain it. The fires in Saint Gareth's Square have burned for two weeks straight without rest. Do not tell me that we are making progress."

Delwyn turned away from the desk, throwing up his hands and taking a couple of steps before turning back. "This is absurd. Even if the annals speak truly, no torey or whatever they're called was ever powerful enough to send a blight upon a city, much less many cities at once."

"Are you so familiar with our ways, Master Scholar? Do you truly know so much about what we are capable of?"

"I know what has been written," he said. "And I find that the written word is often exaggerated."

"There's a bit of truth to any legend," she said. "But I can assure you that this one is quite true."

"And what proof do you have."

She spread her hands, glancing around the room with them held out. "It lies all around you, in the death of your city. One must only look to the streets to see."

"Your claims mean nothing, witch."

"Enough," the king said. "My mind has been made up."

Delwyn turned back to the king. "But Majesty..."

"I said enough," the king said. "Catalan has come to me with a solution to the blight, which is more than my own trusted people have presented to me. This evening, she will work her magic, and rid this city of its blight."

The room was silent, the king's good hand formed into a fist pressing down on his desk, the witch only giving him a mysterious smile. "What solution is that?"

"A blight this strong required human life to be wrought in such a way," Catalan said. "It is life that we must return to break their curse and throw their magic back at them."

It was Delwyn who was gaping now, looking between the woman and the king. Cerys gave no indication of what she was thinking, but the way she looked at her feet said she had no intention of getting involved.

"Majesty, you cannot possibly think to do this," he said. "This is madness."

"I will not hear another word about this."

"Majesty..."

His fist slammed into the desk. "I said not another word. I have made my decision, and I will make it again a thousand times. If I can save the rest of the city for the death of a few, then I will make it in a heartbeat."

"And when it doesn't work?"

"Oh, it will work, Master Scholar." The woman moved toward him, and Delwyn stumbled as he backed away. "It only takes a bit of faith. I can end the blight and ensure Minas Afon is prosperous for ages to come."

"Majesty, she lies through her teeth."

"I have already shown the king what is possible," Catalan said. "Allow me to show you as well, Master Scholar."

Delwyn was still backing away. "No, I want nothing to do with your magic."

"Leave us, then, Delwyn," the king said, even as Delwyn was already making for the door, his eyes never leaving the witch. "We have much to discuss, and I'd rather do so without you making a muck of it."

"What is he thinking?" The words only began to spill out when they were in the solitude of his tower, the door closed and the latch down. Delwyn immediately began to pace again, picking up a small bottle of whiskey and choosing to forego the glass.

"It's madness. Sacrificing people, our people, to that witch, to whatever gods she worships."

"I could tell you if you need to know," Cerys said. "I am studying it for my mystics rope."

Delwyn waved his hand as he took another swig. The whiskey burned, more than he remembered. Had it really been that long since he had drunk anything this strong?

"It is a betrayal to our very city. To everything His Majesty's forefathers stood for. To the memory and worship of all the saints. To everything we swear to protect when we take our oaths in Saint Gareth's Square."

He stopped pacing and turned to her. "This is the first you heard of it, is it not?"

Cerys nodded quickly. Perhaps a bit too quickly, or perhaps his mind was simply reeling from what he had just heard.

Delwyn pulled out his pipe and snuff box, his hand shaking as he filled the bowl. "We need to find out what he plans to do. Where it's happening. What it entails. Who is to be involved. How long that woman has been around. How we can stop it."

"Master, is that wise?"

He stopped, turning to look at her over his shoulder. "What was that?"

She was avoiding eye contact. "I don't know," she said. "The king had a good point. We're no closer to a solution than we were when the first cases were discovered."

"How can you say this, Cerys? What has gotten into you?"

She took a step forward, speaking quickly. "But Master, Scholar Grigor always says that to find a solution, we must approach each problem with an open mind."

"Bah! Grigor is an old fool, always has been. There's a reason he is not Master Scholar."

"He says you let the title affect your judgement."

"An open mind is one thing, accepting the solution of a witch is something else entirely!" Delwyn turned from her, snatching a piece of paper and a pen to write a message.

"You don't even know that it won't work. And we can't know unless we try."

"That will be enough on the subject. I have heard your thoughts and I deny them." He finished writing, signing his name and then applying the seal of his office to his signature. He gave it a moment to dry, then folded the paper and handed it to her. "Assemble the council. This message should be read by each of them and only them. Discretion is key. We must meet within the hour. Is that clear?"

"Yes, Master." The phrase sounded meek, defeated.

"They will come here, not to the council chamber. I will be waiting."

"Yes, Master."

"Hurry, now. No time to lose."

She vanished through the door without another word. Delwyn finished the bottle, then got to work.

By the time the first of them began to arrive, Delwyn had gathered several books from the tower's private collection, whatever he could find on magic, and for good measure, the saints. They filed in, Lord Doctor Padrig leading the way with his ample belly and dark robes, followed by several of the mayors, men and women of various shapes and sizes representing each of the districts. Bishop Meuric appeared next, hobbled over, using his scepter to support his frail body, and with him came Captain Ifan. The last two mayors, Lew and Elaine, entered at the same time, the looks on their faces telling him that they had been arguing on their way up. The spymaster, Morgan, was the last to enter, standing out from the rest in a fine dress, her bright red hair tied into braids and pulled into a tight bun.

"Thank you all for coming on such short notice," Delwyn said.

Mayor Maxen stood by one of the shelves, arms crossed over his barreled chest. "You can't be bothered to attend a meeting, but you have no qualms about calling us all up to your tower at a whim. Explain yourself, Delwyn."

"Master Scholar," Captain Ifan said. "You may be upset at him, but we still carry respect in this circle."

"I will show respect when I am shown respect," Mayor Maxen said, standing upright from where he leaned. "My inquiries into this disease and its sources are mocked in this very circle. Where is the respect there? Why should I show respect to any of you?"

"We are not here to discuss respect," Delwyn said. "There are more pressing matters at hand than anyone's feelings."

"Which brings us to his original question," Mayor Elaine said. Her grey hair fell in a straight line down the back of her dress, her expression and voice giving a presence much larger than her tiny frame. "For what reason have you brought us here?"

"Indeed," Mayor Lew said. "Our time is not so ample that we can afford to be away from our districts. There is a plague that is spreading like wildfire in this city."

"Perhaps in your district," Mayor Price said, leaning on his cane, the lips beneath his thin moustache twisted into a smirk. "The Lowyards are officially clean."

"Did you have them all killed yourself?" Mayor Rhys asked.

"Silence," Delwyn said. "This concerns the blight, and much more, in a way that will affect us all. Our city is in grave danger."

Their voices filled the air, and Delwyn slapped his hand on the table to silence them once more. It was Mayor Elaine's voice that rose above the rest. "What danger could be as bad as the blight?"

"The Cren," Mayor Maxen said. "I have been trying to say…"

"There is a witch within these walls." It was as if the air had been drained from the room, all eyes turning to Delwyn as the words left his mouth.

"A witch?" Bishop Meuric said, his mouth hanging open like a fish. "Are you certain?"

"I don't know how she could have gotten past my guards," Captain Ifan said. "There is no man that would let a witch through these gates."

"It is not so hard to get something past the guards," Morgan said from her spot in the corner, examining her brightly painted fingernails. "Especially a person."

"You doubt the competency of my men?" Captain Ifan asked.

"I speak from experience alone."

Mayor Rhys moved to block the captain as he stepped toward the spymaster, the bishop giving a cry and ducking to the side. "Order!" Delwyn yelled. "All of you, get a hold of yourselves. We cannot afford to bicker amongst ourselves while this witch makes her plans."

"And what plans are those?" Mayor Elaine asked.

"She plans to make a sacrifice to her gods."

Once more, the room filled with chatter, the actual words lost in the overlap of voices. The only one who didn't seem to be speaking was the bishop, who had turned a shade nearly as pale as his robes.

It was Mayor Elaine whose voice finally broke above the noise once more. "His Majesty is allowing this to happen?"

Morgan spoke before Delwyn could get the words out. "The witch would not be here if His Majesty did not approve of her being here. I can assure you the king is well aware."

The quivering bishop finally found his words. "How could he do such a thing? He forsakes our very city, our church, all the saints by allowing this woman to conduct her...her...rituals right here in our very city. It's an outrage."

"What does he hope to accomplish?" Mayor Rhys asked. "Does he truly believe that this...ceremony can stop this blight?"

"It seems to me he does," Delwyn said. Morgan nodded her agreement.

Mayor Maxen turned toward the spymaster. "You knew about this and you said nothing? Why are you even here?"

"My job as spymaster is to provide information to the king," Morgan said. "My work with the council is to answer questions about threats to this city, not to spy on His Majesty."

"And when it is the king himself whose actions threaten our city?" Mayor Elaine asked.

Morgan gave a long shrug. "If I thought it was worth the council knowing, I would have said something."

"This is something that we cannot allow to happen," the bishop said. "Our very souls are at stake here. If we allow a witch to be welcomed into the city, to sacrifice our own people to her heathen gods, then we forsake everything our forefathers built."

Mayor Rhys shook his head. "How can we hope to stop her if His Majesty himself stands behind her actions?"

"That is why I called you all here," Delwyn said. "Alone, none of us could hope to accomplish what we must to stop her, but together we can."

"What do you intend on doing?" Mayor Maxen asked. "How can we hope to stand against a witch's power?"

Delwyn ran his fingers over one of the open books on the desk before him. "While Cerys has been gathering you all here, I took to my private collection. Many of these books date back to the days before our freedom, before witches were driven from our city. One of the books talks about how King Colwyn and Saint Branwen rid the city of the witches. Unfortunately, a large part of their success was based in Saint Branwen's ability to neutralize a witch's power."

"Seeing as we don't have a saint, that doesn't help us much," Mayor Elaine said. There were murmurs of agreement around her.

"You are right that we don't have a saint. But there is more to it than that. Saint Branwen could not of course be everywhere; he mostly attended to the more powerful ones. The king's guard took care of the rest. I think we can do the same with Captain Ifan's men."

"My men are here to protect," Captain Ifan said. "But do you feel they can stand against this witch?"

"With the blessing of the church, I believe they can," Delwyn said.

"And what then?" Mayor Rhys asked. "What do we do with her when we have her in custody?"

"Any execution must be done with proper blessings from the church, or we risk a curse," Delwyn said. "In the days of the revolution, they were kept in the church under guard until it was time for their execution." He turned to the bishop. "Your Holiness, do you know where that might be?"

"I know of no place within the church to imprison anyone." He paused for a moment. "Wait, there are some areas in the catacombs that have been locked away, where no one goes. I can have those opened and checked."

"Do so, and get word to me," Delwyn said.

"What should the rest of us do?" Mayor Elaine asked.

"Be ready to be called," Delwyn said. "If the king protests, we need to show a united front against him."

"The king will see this as treason," Morgan said.

"Which is why we need you to ensure it remains a secret," Delwyn said. "The king must not know what we plan to do."

"Do you truly expect her to be silent?" Mayor Lew asked, nodding toward the spymaster. "A woman who deals only in secrets has no trust."

"I will keep the secret well enough," Morgan said. "It would not be the first I kept about any of you."

The murmurings began again, and Delwyn called for order. "We must act quickly. Captain Ifen, bring your men and wait for word from the bishop. Morgan, I'm depending on you to bring the captain and his men to the witch. Once we have her in custody, I will send for the rest of you to have the trial."

"And what happens if this is found out?" Mayor Elaine asked. "What do we do then?"

"Ensure your affairs are in order," Mayor Rhys said. "The king will see this as nothing but treason."

"Which means we must not fail," Delwyn said. "It is our duty to succeed, regardless of the risk to ourselves."

The bishop nodded his agreement. "Saint Branwen wrote after the revolution that no king should ever come before the city and her people, or God above. It is that which we all have sworn to protect."

The murmurings this time seemed to agree with the sentiment. Delwyn cast his eyes over the room, searching for any signs of dissidence, but if there was any, the opposing council members were good at hiding it. "It is decided then. We must move quickly and with discretion. You all know your roles in this."

Side conversations carried on as the council members filed out of the room. Two members remained back, however, Mayor Elaine and Mayor Lew. Delwyn glanced between the two of them, finally speaking when the door closed. "Is there something more you two wish to discuss?" he asked.

"We want to know what you plan to do, Master Scholar," Mayor Elaine said.

"Right or not, this is still treason," Mayor Lew said. "If the king truly backs this woman, he will not be made to see reason."

Mayor Elaine nodded. "King Folant, unlike his father or grandfather, is not one I'd ever describe as open to new ideas."

"I understand," Delwyn said.

"The way we see it, this ends one of two ways," Mayor Lew said. "Either the king is unseated and replaced, which could cause a succession crisis, or our heads end up on stakes."

"I'm not keen on either," Mayor Elaine said. "It may not be enough to just take the witch."

Delwyn glanced between the two of them. "All this time we've been meeting as a council, months and months of constant bickering, accusations, even threats, and this is what brings the two of you together?"

"The sovereignty of our city is not something we take lightly," Mayor Lew said. "We have our disagreements, yes, but we know when it is time to put our squabbles aside."

Delwyn's mind went to a recent meeting where they had threatened to send their personal guard forces after each other. "What are you suggesting?"

"When Captain Ifan sends his men against the witch tonight, we send our own to take the king into custody," Mayor Elaine said. "Our combined forces will be enough to take on whatever guards are there."

"And what then?" Delwyn asked. "One of you takes the throne?"

"We are not even secure in our own positions," Mayor Elaine said. "Neither of us, as I'm sure you are aware. I have no children, no living relatives, and Lew has enough bastards and natural born sons that his district will be fought over for years to come. No, it cannot be either of us."

"We don't have a name in mind, but we do have a council who can rule until someone is chosen," Mayor Lew said. "A new dynasty can rise, one who understands what it takes to keep our city safe."

Delwyn considered them both for a moment. "Many called it treason when we met just now. That was merely going against the king's will. This is truly treason."

"We approach you because you hold the power in the council," Mayor Elaine said. "We would not be here if we did not feel it was for the city's best interests." Mayor Lew nodded his agreement.

"How long have you two been planning this?"

For the first time, they looked at each other, and it was Mayor Lew who spoke. "The king has been...unpredictable lately. Even before this blight."

"It was never anything beyond a contingency," Mayor Elaine said. "A plan should there ever need to be a plan. With what you tell us, it is clear that the time is now."

Delwyn chewed on the inside of his lip. Did he dare take part in an open coup? Could it work?

"If you accompany us, we think the king's guards will stand down," Mayor Lew said. "Without you, there will be bloodshed. With you, it can be done without blood being spilled."

"We know you care about this city, Master Scholar," Mayor Elaine said. "It's time for you to show it."

Delwyn's hand fell to his belt, subconsciously grabbing one of the ropes that hung there. When he turned his eyes down, he saw that it was colored a stone grey, the same color of the bricks that had built the city. It had been granted to him for proving his knowledge of the city's politics and history, upon which he had pledged his oath to protect Minas Afon against all enemies, both outside and within.

"I'll do it," he said.

Mayor Elaine gave a brief nod. "We will meet you in the Founder's Courtyard at midnight. Do not be late."

With the clouds brought by the late season, there was no moon or stars to guide his way. Delwyn dared not carry a torch or lantern, so all he had to go by was the scant light filtering through the windows above.

He stood back beneath the covered walkway, watching the open space in the middle and the edges for any sign of movement. Short bushes ran along the edge, not tall enough for anyone to hide, but in this darkness, one could sneak an entire army through. Of course, the courtyard was only accessible through the castle, but it still seemed strange to him that it would be so unwatched.

Delwyn pulled his robe close and shivered, the cold more direct here than up in his tower. He had been a bit early, but they should have been there by now. It was long enough that his mind was beginning to race, running through every possible scenario. Maybe they had been caught on their way, and there were king's men on their way to capture him. Maybe the whole thing had been a ruse to remove him from his own position. Maybe they just wanted him to sweat, to think something bad was going to happen, perhaps as a warning. Or as blackmail.

The thought of returning to his tower occurred to him more than once and was creeping its way back into his mind when he heard a whisper.

"Master Scholar."

He turned toward it, squinting in the darkness, trying to find the source. When it was spoken again, he saw a shadow move, closer to the scant light from the windows. The shadow motioned to him, and before his mind could think of any possible danger, he approached.

"You're here. This way."

He didn't recognize the voice, but he followed anyway. There was the sound of scraping on stone, and a dark space opened up in the wall, somehow darker than the surrounding space. When he stepped through, the door behind him was closed and there was a striking as a lantern was lit. It was held up by a gauntleted hand belonging to an older soldier, nearly as old as himself, an eye missing, his armor bearing the telltale marks of Mayor Elaine's house.

"This way," he said.

Delwyn didn't recognize the hallway they were in. It felt claustrophobic, the ceiling just above his head and the walls not quite wide enough for two men to walk abreast. The guard led him through a couple of turns, then arrived at a set of stairs that wound upward into the castle. Delwyn followed him up, the walls around him seeming to absorb every sound, leaving only that of their boots striking the stone floor.

The curve of the stairs prevented him from seeing far ahead, so he received a bit of a shock when he turned the corner and found himself at a landing, staring at a fully lit hallway filled with soldiers. His first instinct was panic, the idea that the king had found out and his guard was waiting to arrest him, but that was quickly relieved when he recognized the respective sigils from both mayors.

The pair themselves stood at the far end, conversing. He was led straight to them, past the watching eyes of their men. Their conversation stopped as he approached, and they both turned to greet him.

"Where are we?" he asked. "I've never been to this part of the castle."

"The castle holds many secrets, Master Scholar," Mayor Elaine said. "Morgan is not the only one who has knowledge of them."

"This will take us right to the king's chambers," Mayor Lew said.

"Is the spymaster here?" Delwyn asked.

Mayor Elaine shook her head. "She's with Captain Ifan, leading him to where the witch is. We know the way, though."

"No sense in waiting," Delwyn said. "The sooner we move, the sooner we can be done with this unpleasant business."

"Very well," Mayor Elaine said. She nodded to the guard who had met Delwyn in the courtyard, and the signal was given. The men began to move, making their way down the hall. Delwyn tried to count them but lost it as they moved about. It was at least twenty, which should be more than enough. He hoped.

The hallway led into a larger, more elegant one, the guards spilling out and taking position on either side as he and the mayors emerged. Delwyn took a moment to gain his bearings, then turned in the direction of the king's chambers.

There was a quartet of guards outside the king's bedroom door, and when they saw the group coming, they immediately formed up into a defensive position, their halberds held out at the approaching force. The mayors' combined forces stopped short, and Delwyn approached the guards, stopping several paces short.

"Master Scholar," the one in the middle said, his armor marked with the sign of a captain. "What is the meaning of this?"

"Step aside, Captain," Delwyn said. "We wish for no bloodshed."

"No bloodshed? What other reason is there to have so many armed men accompany you?"

"Our business does not concern you," Delwyn said, holding his hands up, showing his palms. "We're here for the king."

"If it concerns the king, it concerns us."

"We outnumber you at least five to one."

"And we have the hallway to help us. The only way you pass us is over our dead bodies."

The door opened behind the guards, and a voice called out, the king's voice. "Let him pass."

"But Majesty…"

"At once."

The captain watched Delwyn for a moment, then motioned to the others and stepped aside. "I'm not alone," Delwyn called out.

"I know," the king said. "You don't need to worry about them."

A sudden scream cut through the hallway, sending chills down Delwyn's spine. It was joined by another and another and another until a chorus of cries filled the space, drowning out any other sound that might have occurred. As he turned, the first thing he noticed was how the mayors had separated, pressing against the walls on either side of the hallway. Mayor Elaine held a hand to her mouth, her face twisted in horror, while Mayor Lew only gaped. Between them, the one-eyed guard was lying on his face, blood pooling beneath him, while beyond, the rest of the men were still in various states of dying. Delwyn tried to focus on any one person, but all he saw was a mess of bodies twisting about, their bones breaking without being touched, blood leaking from their eyes and noses and mouths as they died in agonizing pain.

Even with the screams, he heard the voice, this time not from the king, but the eastern accent of the witch. "Come, Delwyn. There's nothing you can do to help them."

The chill grew even deeper. The witch was there with the king, which meant that the plan had already failed. What had happened to Captain Ifan and his men? Were they dead, like the ones behind him? Or were they staring at an empty room, where they expected the witch to be? Or perhaps it had been the captain who had turned them in.

Delwyn didn't remember starting forward, but he found himself walking toward the room. The dying had ceased behind him, leaving Mayor Elaine's sobs as the only sounds in the hallway. Even his footsteps fell quietly on thick carpet. He passed the guards, trying to ignore their curious eyes, and stepped into the king's chambers.

The last time he had been in this room was when King Ofydd had fallen ill, before his son had taken the throne. The decor had changed little, and truth be told, looked like it could use some cleaning. Of course, that was before he saw the floor.

The witch drew his eye first, sitting in a chair, wearing a robe with what seemed like little underneath. The king himself stood behind her, cup of wine in hand, making no such attempt at modesty. On the ground was another naked figure, a young man, perhaps in his twenties, his wrists both cut, his skin paled in death. A strange symbol had been drawn in chalk beneath him, and the blood seemed to stay within that symbol, as if held put by an invisible wall.

"Welcome, Master Scholar," Catalan said.

Delwyn managed to swallow. "You did that? All that out there?"

"A taste of my power," Catalan said. "And a small taste of the power that lies in blood. Tomorrow, this blight ends, and your city's enemies pay."

"I am disappointed in you, Delwyn," the king said. "I know you disagree with the toare being here, but I never thought you would be so bold to attempt a full coup."

"You cannot blame him," Catalan said. "He thinks he does the right thing for the city. I have never found ignorance something that should be punished."

"But actions should," the king said. "Who did you intend to put on the throne? Yourself?"

"Who told?" Delwyn asked.

"Does it matter?" the king said.

"Of course it matters," the witch said. "It's a natural desire to know who betrayed you. Except it was no one, Master Scholar. I saw your plot unfold, and I set the wheels in motion to stop it. As we speak, the rest of your council is being gathered up and put in the dungeon."

"The entire council," the king said. "I don't know how you did it, but you somehow turned them all against me."

"Fear stabs deeply," the witch said. "It drives people to follow paths they would not otherwise. Your council felt the fear of what they saw as an ancient evil, and they saw no choice but to act."

"What's going to happen to me?" Delwyn asked.

"You'll spend the rest of the night in the dungeon," the king said. "I'll deal with you come morning." He whistled to the men outside the door. "Take him away."

Delwyn turned away, doing his best to maintain dignity as he was led away.

"Reflect on your transgressions, Master Scholar," the witch called after him. "Pray to your saints for deliverance. Perhaps they will provide the righteous path for you."

Delwyn might have slept in the damp, cold cell he was placed in, but with how dark it was, there seemed to be little difference between sleeping and wakefulness. Time passed, the speed at which it did also unknown, and his mind worked, not on a plan or a way to escape, but at all the possibilities that lay before him. Would the king have mercy? Would the witch convince him to spare the former council? Or would it be a long painful death, the death of a traitor?

At some point, in a moment that felt no different from the rest of the moments since he had been locked in the cell, the door creaked open, and a guard stood there holding a lit torch. Delwyn held up a hand, blocking out the blinding light that seemed to be engulfed by the darkness.

"Get up," the guard said. "You've been summoned."

This was it. The walk he had seen so many take to stand before the king, to receive his judgement. Some made the walk with defiance, showing no remorse, but most approached with defeat, dejection, heads hanging as they received their sentence. He wasn't entirely sure, but the latter felt more appropriate here. He had failed; he had failed to protect his city from a danger thought long extinct.

Another guard clamped some shackles on him, attached to a long chain that they used to lead him onward. He followed without giving any trouble, stepping through the damp tunnel, past the doors to other cells. His eyes lazily traced to either side of the hall, trying to see into the tiny windows, but the darkness was complete, hiding whatever condemned lay within.

A spiral staircase led up and into a courtyard, one Delwyn was unfamiliar with, not an uncommon occurrence in the expansive castle. He blinked at the light of the morning, bright to him even with the heavy clouds that hung above. A damp wind blew, and with it a mist-like rain that made the cold day seem even colder.

"This way," one of the guards grunted, pulling on the chain.

They walked across the courtyard, empty except for a squire dashing across with a breastplate in his hands. At the far end, through the same door the squire had run through, Delwyn stepped into the stables, immediately greeted by a warmth and the smell of horse manure.

His eyes darted around. "Are we not going to judgement before the king?" he asked.

"The king requested you," the one holding the chain said. "But he's not in the castle."

Not in the castle? What was happening? Why would the king not pass judgement from his throne?

Delwyn was led to a cart that was already fitted with a pair of horses, a driver in the seat. The guard waited while he climbed in and took a seat, then attached his shackles to an iron loop embedded in the wooden side. The driver gave a word, and the cart set off.

Delwyn had traveled through the castle gates countless times, but never like this. The city felt dead around him, empty, and perhaps it was because much of it was. Shops and homes passed on either side, some boarded up, some with the windows broken out, many with the sign of the curse, the sign that the blight had been within. The road between the castle and Saint Gareth's Square was amongst the richest in the city, but even it had not been untouched. All the money in the world could not help one escape death.

There was a crowd of some kind up ahead, gathering around the square. More interesting to him was that the fires that had burned for so many weeks, visible from his tower, the fires where the bodies had gone, were not present. In their place was some kind of wooden structure, though he couldn't quite make out what it was.

The cart drew nearer, and the crowd parted to let it pass. He gazed out over the faces, dozens and dozens of the city's people looking up at him, a man so quickly fallen from such a prominent post. Or perhaps to them, those who had never seen him, only a prisoner, carted out to a public space for a spectacle.

His stomach dropped when he got a good look at the structure. It was not so much an organized build, but instead a pile of wood, stacked in place with several poles sticking out from the top. From each pole hung shackles, and almost all of them held someone in place. It was only when he grew nearer that he began to recognize the faces. He saw Captain Ifan, the bishop, Morgan, Mayor Elaine, and the rest of the mayors. The entire council was present, each and every one of them, attached to a pole. And there, in the middle, an empty one. His.

Delwyn did not resist when he was led up the stack and shackled to the pole. Ahead of him, he could see the king atop the balcony that spanned the front of the church, dressed in full regalia, speaking to the crowd below. Delwyn could not hear, but there was no doubt he was condemning his former council, listing their crimes before they were to be executed.

The smell of oil drifted up to him, and he glanced down to see guards drenching the lower portions of the pyre. The king had ceased speaking, and all eyes had turned to the center of the square.

On the balcony, the witch stepped forward, her pale skin shining like a ghost in the morning drizzle. Her voice rose up, no doubt boosted through magic, and he could hear every word clearly.

"People of Minas Afon. You may not know me, but I know you. More importantly, I know your suffering, of this blight that has plagued your city for so many weeks, that has killed your friends and family."

Beneath her voice came another, the same voice, but one he heard not with his ears, but with his mind. *Can you see, Master Scholar? See how they look to me?*

He looked around, glancing not at the crowd but at those around him, the council members, his fellow condemned. None seemed to be hearing what he heard, with some hanging their heads, dejected, some watching the witch as she spoke out loud, and the bishop weeping.

You hear me, Master Scholar, only you.

His eyes traced upward toward her spot on the balcony, and he saw her icy blue eyes focused on him. "Why do you torture me like this?" he said quietly. "Let me die in peace."

A smile seemed to grace her lips, even as they continued with her speech to the crowd. *No, you're not seeing, Master Scholar. They hate me, just as you did. They know who I am, and what I intend to do here. The king may be blind, but you never were, and neither are your people.*

"Then why go forth with this? They will come for you, eventually, when this fails to work."

It will work. But you're not wrong. They will welcome me when it does, at first. They will accept me as their savior with reluctance, watching me from the corner of their eyes. Sooner or later, something will happen, something I can't fix, and they will come for me then.

"Just leave me be."

I know you're the mind behind the throne.

"You drove the king to this. You can live with it.

They'll never trust me, but they will trust one of their own.

"I want no part..."

They will trust a saint.

Delwyn was silent for a moment. "I'm no saint."

No. There are no saints.

"But you said..."

Behind every good saint, there was one of my kind. A person feared projecting power to a person of faith. A true partnership, until one went back on his word, until jealousy and prejudice led to our expulsion.

"Saint Branwen?"

And the woman he refused, the power he rejected. A choice that cost my kind dearly.

The story was different, at least from the one he had always known.

"His wife, wasn't it? Siani."

Saint Siani, she should have been. But that could never have been accepted. The true power behind his sainthood, and he slayed her with his own hands.

"How can I know what is true? How can you?"

It matters not. The fires will soon be lit. I will save you regardless of whether you choose to cooperate or not. The only question is whether you see yourself as a martyr, or as someone who truly wants to make a difference.

Above on the balcony, he saw her step back. The king gave a signal, and several guards stepped forward with torches. They touched the ends to the base of the pile, and the oil caught, spreading quickly around the structure in blue flames that quickly engulfed them all. From the audience came gasps while the screams grew around him, cries of agony from his fellow conspirators as they burned alive.

For Delwyn, though, he hardly felt a thing. He certainly saw the flames, closing his eyes when it grew too bright, the imprint lingering behind his eyelids. Around him, he felt no heat, even as those nearest to him burnt alive. At most, it was a distant feeling, like a fire at the far end of a room, giving off just enough heat to make its presence known.

He kept his eyes closed until the flames vanished, and it was only when he began to hear the gasps from the crowd that he slowly opened them. The eyes were all turned on him, from everywhere. He gazed around, first at the crowd, trying to avoid looking at the charred corpses that were on the pyre beside him. He then turned his eyes up toward the balcony. The king stood there, leaning on the railing with his mouth gaping open. Beside him, the witch just smiled.

"Decades, it's been," someone said, making the sign of blessing on himself. "He's touched."

The person who spoke knelt, then those beside him, then more, the motion spreading like a wave through the crowd. Above, even the king and his entourage knelt, all but the witch herself.

"This man stands before you once condemned, and once baptized by the flames. Only a saint can hold such power."

Beside her, the king stood. "Blessed be the saints," he bellowed. "Blessed be Saint Delwyn."

The crowd around him echoed the latter words, shouting them in unison over and over again. Above, the witch's smile widened ever so slightly.

A HERO'S RECKONING

I've sat down to write a superhero story many times, formulating the origin, the powers, the enemies in my mind so much that they've become as familiar to me as any other character. But for whatever reason, the story could never quite come together.

I forget the context, but one day, a thought occurred to me, and I sat down to write a story, one that did come together. Here, we see the hero not at the height of his fame and power, but at the end, when life had beaten and broken him down, when the ghosts of his past and a lifetime of decisions continue to haunt him.

I still hope to write his story one day. It may seem like you know the ending with this, but maybe that will make the story better. Even if I don't, I'm glad that at least a piece of it was able to come together in a complete way.

The room was dark, but Jake Ender could still see. It may have been the streetlamps seeping through the blinds, or the years he had spent working in the dark, or perhaps it was just that he knew the room so well that he could see it even when he could not.

He sat in a thick, cushioned chair, the padding good for his aching muscles and joints. He leaned forward, his elbows resting on his knees, a glass of whiskey and ice in his hand. He was drunk, but he hardly felt it, the alcohol these days as much a part of him as his own blood.

Even with the cushions, his body pained him. Not in the satisfying way, like after an intense gym session, but in an annoying way, as though he had slept on every part of his body in a wrong way. It was the result of years of taking blows, of deep bruises and broken bones, of giving himself to the protection of the city.

Forty years. Forty years had he donned the mask. He had cleaned up the city as best he could, but it was never enough. Instead, the threats only seemed to grow. He cut off a head, and three more sprouted up. His persona had come to strike fear into the hearts of criminals, yet that had not been a deterrent. Instead, it had only seemed to bring out worse criminals.

The liquor dulled his senses, dampened the aches, made things just a bit better. No, that was wrong. Not better. Just a little less bad.

"This is not a business where you grow old." The voice was so familiar, one he had heard many times. "If the villains don't get you, the people will. They always fear that which is powerful enough to protect them."

Jake did not look up from his glass, watching the ice swirl as he turned it in his hand. "It's fitting that you would show up. You always had a knack for appearing at the worst possible times."

The man chuckled, the sound coming from the direction of the couch. "You're not still bitter about the whole wedding incident are you? I told you at the time, it was nothing personal. Besides, I could never resist a good party."

This time, Jake did look up. Peter Briston sat on his couch, looking just as he had the day he had shown up at Jake's wedding. The suit was expensive, Italian cut, custom tailored to fit his slender frame. It was immaculately clean, except for the single splash of blood on the collar of his shirt, the red stain continuing up his neck and to the cleanly shaven cheek. Peter was sitting comfortably with his legs crossed, smiling widely at Jake, the same smile he had that day as he stood there in the church.

"So you're here to ask the same question you do each time?"

He noticed for the first time that Peter had his own drink, which he now raised toward Jake. "Will your answer change?"

"No."

"Then I must ask. Did killing me give you satisfaction?"

"No kill I've made has ever given me satisfaction."

"Is that so?" The voice was different from Peter's, rougher, less educated, and coming from the direction of the kitchen. "You did not seem to have the same opinion when you threw me from that roof."

"Come now, Jordan," Peter said. "We're all friends here."

The source of the second voice emerged from the kitchen, his hair grown to his shoulders, his head nearly brushing the ceiling. He was dressed only in a pair of pants, the thick muscles making him look akin to the Incredible Hulk, minus the green skin. Where Peter had just a glass, Jordan had an entire bottle.

"I would prefer if you called me by the name the newspapers gave me," he growled, taking a swig and wiping his mouth with the back of his hand. "It did me a lot better than the one my parents did."

"If I recall correctly, it was while you were still going by the Titan moniker that our friend here threw you from the top of the Chase Tower," Peter observed.

"Yeah," Jordan remarked as he took a swig from the bottle, "you're right. But things were going mighty fine until then. Better than they ever had."

"It is not about how things start, but how they end," Peter said. He smiled and raised his glass toward Jake. "Isn't that right, Jacob?"

"I would prefer if you did not use that name," Jake grunted.

"Oh?" Peter remarked. "You would prefer I went by *your* media name? Very well then, *Executioner*. Not my preference, to be honest. The press is rather unoriginal. Though I guess you can't blame them, not when all the good names are taken by comic books. Our friend here would have made a good Colossus, and I would have loved to have been Dr. Strange."

Someone out of Arkham Asylum would have been more fitting. "Why can't you just leave me alone?"

"Don't you know?" There was a third voice, coming from above his head. Jake glanced up, watching as the man crawled along the ceiling. His skin was a strange color, his eyes almost glowing in the dim light. He crawled past where Jake sat before continuing. "We are here because you want us to be."

"That's a lie," Jake said.

The man dropped from the ceiling and landed elegantly in a crouch. He glanced up at Jake. "Yet here we are."

"Who knew someone the press referred to as *The Animal* could be so eloquent," Peter observed, raising his glass. "Perhaps there is a bit of chimpanzee mixed in with the others."

The Animal hissed at him before slinking away from the light. Peter chuckled at him, taking another sip. "You know, Jacob, you really had an interesting effect on this city. Everything was so...mundane before you showed up."

"Before I showed up and began to do what the police could not?"

"Oh yes," Peter said, waving his free hand through the air. "You are the reason any of us exist. After all, where's the fun if there's no challenge? God knows the police do not pose one."

Jordan gave a chortle. "I would get more resistance robbing Halloween candy from a five-year old."

Jake ignored him. "So you're saying that I am the reason for you being here?"

"Not me," Peter said. "I would have been there regardless of what you did. But him," he nodded toward Jordan. "And him," he motioned toward The Animal. "They may not realize it, but they came to this city because you were here. You gave them a purpose, and their existence justified yours."

Jake frowned. "They would have been here regardless."

"If you insist," Peter said with a shrug. "I suppose we will never truly know."

"Oh leave him alone," a light, feminine voice said from behind him. A chill ran down his spine as Lydia Saunders ran her fingers lightly over his shoulder, the cold present even through the fabric of his shirt. "He does not deserve this torment."

Jake moved his shoulder ever so slightly, and her fingers slid from him. He watched her through the mirror above the wet bar, and she smiled as she met his gaze. An icy glow seemed to emanate from her pale skin, her snow-white hair, the wintery dress that clung to her; even her smile was cold. Her drink of choice was a cosmopolitan, the conical glass held high, frosted from her touch, the drink so cold that the air condensed around it.

"Indeed." A snap and a light flashed as Lynn Saunders lit a long cigarette, the flame hovering above her fingers. A spitting image of her sister, except her bright red hair seemed to illuminate the room, her crimson dress a torch in the darkness, her voice husky, burning. "He stood up to all of us when none other dared do so."

She crossed in front of him and leaned down, exposing the low cut of her dress to him. He reached up with her hand and took him gently by the chin, gazing into his eyes, the red in her irises swirling around before him, the effect mesmerizing.

"We have every right," Animal said with a hiss.

Warmth pulsed through her fingers and his skin tingled beneath. Smoke floated past her lips, but it lacked the strong cigarette smell he was expecting. Instead, he was greeted with a pleasant aroma, of burning spices and perfume.

"No," she said as she released his chin and stood straight up, the fiery dress every bit as clingy as Lydia's. "He beat us. Each of us"

"He got lucky against me," Jordan said, pointing a thick thumb against his beefy chest. "I broke his legs and was about to break his neck."

"Yet you're here," Peter said.

"You're all here," Jake said. *And I just wish they would leave me alone.*

They were all silent. Finally, Peter stood. "We are," he said simply. He walked over to the wet bar and began to pour himself a refill before he continued. "We are all here because of you. If it were not for you, we would all still be alive, albeit likely still committing crimes, or perhaps even rotting in prison."

"No prison would hold me," Jordan said.

"No, they would execute you after dealing with your shit for five minutes," Animal said.

"Shut your mouth before I break your neck," he growled.

"Good luck with that," was the mumbled reply.

"Why you?" Jake asked. "Why not any of your lieutenants, Peter?" He turned to Animal. "Or Jack Maren? He was more responsible for you than you were for anything you did." Jake looked up to the sisters. "Did you not have another sister?"

"Two," Lydia said. "One who was not as special to you."

"And one who met a different fate than us," Lynn finished.

"Exactly," he said. "Where are they?" Jake shifted in his seat back to Peter. "And that's not all. What about the Illusionist, or Hydro? Did they have something better to do?"

"There's little better to do when you're dead," Peter said.

"Then where are they?"

"You tell us, Jacob," Peter said. "We're here because you brought us here."

"I didn't bring any of you here."

"Did you not?" This time it was not Peter, nor any of the others. The voice was soft, but then again, Cal Xander had always been soft spoken. He walked into the room as though he had just appeared from the darkness, just as they all had, but he commanded it. Jordan turned away, pretending to look at something on the wall. Animal slinked away on all fours to a corner, bringing his legs to his chest as he tried to make himself inconspicuous. The sisters stepped away to a different corner, standing near each other as they watched. Even Peter turned away, making his way back to his spot on the couch.

Cal had always worn the thick body armor, covered by a trench coat to conceal his weapons, but he did not here. He simply wore a t-shirt and jeans, though it made him no less imposing. His hair was cut short, the beginnings of a beard growing in on a face marred by a pair of thick, uneven scars that started at the corners of his eyes and ran down the sides of his cheeks. He should have been of an age with Jake, yet he looked not a day over thirty.

Jake frowned at him. *Anything but this.* "I did not," he said.

Cal nodded to the glass in Jake's hand. "It's always when you drink."

"No, it's just when you feel like appearing."

"We do not have that ability, Jake," Cal said. "We are only here at your bidding, whether you realize it or not."

"Fine," Jake said, draining the rest of his glass. He stood, the rapid motion enough to make him stagger, almost enough to make him fall. He regained his balance and stormed over to the wet bar, each step deliberate. "So what if that's the case? It doesn't explain why it's only you. I killed plenty in my career."

A glass eased its way through the air, lifted by an unseen force. There was only one other person besides himself who could do such a thing, and Jake was not the one doing it. The glass landed gently in Cal's hand.

"Because none of the others meant to you what we did."

The bottle removed itself from Jordan's hand. A look of anger crossed his face, and he took a step toward Cal, but suddenly thought better of it and stepped back, empty handed.

"One whose help you refused and turned into a blind hatred."

The bottle reached his hand and Cal began to pour.

"One who could not help what he was."

He released the bottle and Jake watched it as it floated gently to the wet bar.

"One who loved you..."

Where is he going with this?

"...and one who lusted for you."

Cal took a step toward him without sipping.

"One who could have been your twin."

He is trying to faze you. Cal was always playing head games.

"One who made you turn away from your ideals."

Worst of all, it was working. *No, please don't,* but the words did not pass his lips.

"And the one you couldn't save."

"No!" This time, the word did pass his lips. He stood and heaved the glass at Cal, a perfect strike. But the glass only passed through air until it shattered against the mirror, sending cracks through the surface. Cal was gone. Peter was gone. They were all gone.

Jake stood in his living room alone, his chest rising and falling in deep breaths. The words echoed through his mind, the way Cal had spoken of each of the people in the room, and the words he hadn't said.

They all come back to her.

Thirty-five years. Thirty-five years and the day was still as fresh in his mind as if it had happened yesterday. The blood, the screams, and worst of all, the laughter. Before then, the moniker had only been symbolism, a metaphor. That was the day it had become his life.

He was looking down at his hands, hands that shook with age and fatigue, hands that had been broken and bruised, hands that were soaked with the blood of many. All had deserved it, or at least he thought they did. But the blood that he truly cared about was hers, and it was on his hands as much as it was on Peter's.

There was a touch around his waist, the feeling of arms sliding around him, and a body pressed close to his back, just the way she had always approached from behind when he was too deep in thought. Or when something was wrong.

"It's okay, baby, I'm here now."

He did not move, did not look up into the fractured mirror, did not return the touch. "No, no you're not," he replied. "You haven't been for decades now."

"But I am now."

Jake shook his head. "They were right. It all started with the wedding, and it's come to this."

"That is just one event. You do not live your life based on a single event."

"But one event can shape the rest of your life," he said. "And it was my fault."

"It wasn't."

"Yes it was." His voice was firm as he stepped forward, breaking away from her grasp, though he still did not turn to look at her. "Peter would never have been there had I never taken up the moniker."

"You cannot blame yourself for the actions of others," she said.

"Yet I could have saved you." His voice was quiet, shaking. "I could have saved you, and I was unable to."

"I was meant to die that day. Nothing you could have done would have ever saved me."

"You don't know that."

"I do."

Jake closed his eyes and turned his head away. He felt her hands on his shoulders and wanted to break away from her, but something in the back of his mind would not allow it.

"Why do you torture me like the rest of them?"

"Because we have to be reminded."

"Reminded of what?"

"Of the things that make us into who we are."

Jake was silent. He could not bring himself to turn to her, to look her in the eyes. Her hand was warm against his back. "You know I still love you," she said.

"And you know I never stopped."

"One day we'll be reunited."

And suddenly she was gone, her touch, her scent, her presence vanished like the wind. *One day we'll be reunited.* The words continued through his mind, as they did each and every night. Well, as he saw it, it needed to be sooner rather than later.

Jake closed his eyes, feeling the weight of the pistol in his hand. He didn't remember picking it up, but the weight felt so familiar, so right. It was a gun he had carried since the early days, a gun that had killed many by him pulling the trigger.

Now it's time for one more.

The bottle Cal had been holding was sitting on the table before him. Jake took it up and took a drink directly from it.

"We're waiting for you." Peter had resumed his customary spot on the couch, but it was only him. The blood was gone, and there was a look on his face that spelled relief. "We've always been waiting for you."

"In hell, I presume."

"It's what you make of it."

"Then I suppose I will have to make the best." Jake took one more drink. For courage, he told himself. *I'm coming to you, Kelly.*

With a deep breath, he pulled the trigger.

The sound of the gunshot filled the room. He had heard it said that when you die, everything moved in slow motion, but for as long as he remembered, everything moved in slow motion. He watched as the hammer clicked, could see the small burst of energy as the gunpowder ignited, and his eyes traced the bullet as it made its way toward the center of his forehead.

The bullet seemed to slow even further, until it came to a stop, several inches from his face. It hung there in midair, as though hovering, right where he could reach up and touch it. He did and it immediately lost whatever it was that held it, falling to the ground with a clink. Jake gritted his teeth and brought the gun all the way against his temple. He fired once, twice, again and again until hammer clicked over and over again, nothing left to fire. Not one reached its target, and when he lowered the gun, he could feel the impacts as several bullets dropped to the ground.

It had long ago ceased to be a reaction, not that it ever really had been. If it had, he would have died long ago. He had never, however, thought it would include bullets he fired on his own. Perhaps he had just assumed that if he didn't try to stop the bullets, his power wouldn't do so. As it turned out, he was wrong.

The gun slipped from his hand and fell to the ground with a clatter. Jake slouched in the chair, staring off into the dark room. It was his gift, his curse, but whatever it was, it would not allow him to escape so easily.

From somewhere out in the darkness, he could hear Peter begin to chuckle.

THE GWYLLION

Earlier this year, I released <u>The Last Dragonkeeper</u>, the first in a planned fantasy series that follows a mercenary who has befriended the last known dragon. I've written several stories that take place in the world, which to this point have mostly only been used as worldbuilding, exploring other areas and people, always coming back to Joven's story in some way. This is one of those stories, taking place in an area known as the Disputed Lands, claimed by several of the Free Kingdoms, but it is a claim that is hard to enforce due to the mountainous terrain and the people who live within.

While the Dragonkeeper himself does not appear in person, this is a setting and people who will become central to the overall narrative.

The man had been dead for several hours, at the very least overnight. Long enough to freeze at any rate, frost forming in his thick beard, his skin a grotesque shade of blue.

It wasn't the body that troubled him; Rove had been there when they had buried his father after he had died of the plague and that had been much worse than this. At least the winter air had frozen the blood to the wound so that it was no longer running.

"Rove?" Tomos's voice carried through the thin mountain air and Rove turned in that direction, trying to spot his friend through the trees.

"Over here," he called back.

There was a rustling behind him as Tomos made his way through the undergrowth of the thick forest to the edge of the brook. He didn't have to turn to visualize his best friend's skinny frame, shaggy hair, and pale cheeks that were flushed from the crisp winter air.

"What are you doing over here..." Tomos trailed off as he saw past Rove down to where the body lay washed up on the slope, the slow-moving water lapping below.

"You recognize him?" Rove asked.

Tomos shook his head. "Never seen him in my life. Any idea what happened to him?"

"No," Rove replied, "but I can tell you it wasn't natural." He reached down and pulled back the cloak, revealing a wide slash across the man's belly, his now frozen entrails spilling out of the wound. Whatever had killed him had done so quickly, and it had gone right through the thick mail that the man wore.

"A lot of good that armor did him," Tomos said. "Does he have anything on him?"

"He had a sword at some point," Rove said, nodding toward the empty scabbard on the man's belt. "It's probably lying in the bottom of the river somewhere."

"Shame," Tomos said. He craned his neck to try for a better view, but he would come no closer. "I think we should probably tell someone."

"Yes," Rove said. "Go and fetch your father, he'll know what to do."

"Why don't you?"

Rove turned his head and looked up the bank at his friend. "Would you like to stay with the body and make sure it doesn't float away?"

The color seemed to drain from Tomos's face. "I'll be right back." He turned and scurried through the underbrush, disappearing into the thick forest.

Rove turned back toward the body, studying the man's features. Everything about him seemed strange, different from the rest of the people of his village or of the people from the tribes that surrounded him or of the other villages in the area. His hair was dark, his skin tanned, his armor hammered from some kind of strong, shiny metal. There was no doubt that this man was a stranger, an alien to these lands.

A cold wind came off the mountains and swept through the trees, causing Rove to pull the furs draped across his shoulders closer. The body had not bothered him, but the thought of what could rip through armor like that did. He found himself wishing that Tomos would hurry.

The room was smoky from the fire in the middle, the air thick despite the hole in the roof for ventilation. Rove stood to the side, staying out of the way as the elders examined the body, which now sat atop a table usually reserved for slaughtering animals. The only reason he was there was because he would have to answer questions about the body; at sixteen, he was rarely welcome in the company of the elders when they met like this.

It was Tomos's father, Uriah, who commanded the attention of the room, a large, imposing man with a thick red beard and completely bare head. Even though the air was cold, his furs were set aside, his arms bared to reveal thick, powerful muscles covered in runes tattooed into the skin with black ink. It was a custom of the village, a means to represent significant events in a man's life, the first of which being a passage into manhood. Rove himself was still awaiting his first, whereas the man who stood before him had more than any other man in the village.

"Rove, come here." His voice was quiet, not needing to be imposing as his body did more than enough talking. It continuously amazed him that Tomos was this man's son with his skinny frame and fearful demeanor, as well as the fact that his older brothers all seemed cut from the same cloth. Or rather, stone in Uriah's case.

"Yes?" Rove asked.

"You were out in the forest when you found this body?"

"I was," he said.

"I needn't tell you what you already know?"

Rove kept his gaze neutral, staring right at the towering man before him, drawing in a deep breath. "No, you needn't," he said after a moment.

"What were you boys doing in the forest?"

The young man was not about to lie to the leader of the village elders. "Hunting."

"You know full well that you boys are forbidden from entering the forest."

I thought we agreed you needn't tell me what I already know. "Aye."

Uriah nodded, his gaze firm. "I'll allow your mother to deal with you."

A chortle came from beside Uriah and all eyes turned toward Oren Rafferty. He was the opposite of Uriah in form and manner, but his body indicated that he was no less of a fighter, perhaps more so. A pair of parallel scars ran up a skinny arm, a glass ball stood where his left eye once was, and one of his legs was angled oddly from an old fracture. He brushed a strand of wispy white hair away from his good eye and looked directly at Rove.

"You ought to deal with him yourself, Uriah," he said, his voice as rough as the bark of an oak tree. "The boy hasn't had a proper man to punish him in years. Made him soft, rebellious."

"Aye, that hasn't stopped your daughter from taking to him." Rove could not see who said the words, but he could see the reaction in Oren's face. The old man had a sneer that would make even the hardest man shiver in fear. Of course, Rove felt his own blood beginning to boil when he saw Oren's reaction.

"Enough," Uriah said. "We are not here to speak of Rove's family, nor of village gossip. We are here because of this man." He motioned toward the body. "There are strange men in our forests."

"We had to know this day would come," one of the men said.

"Not in our lifetimes," said another.

"Perhaps he was alone, and just got lost."

"One does not simply get lost into our woods," Oren said. "You men have yourselves seen what it takes to get into our valley, and that is a trek that is hard even for the Roans."

They had seemed to have forgotten that Rove was in the room, and he was glad to take advantage of it. The lands outside the valley had long been referenced, but no one was ever quick to speak of them, and details were few and far between for any who had not been accepted into the fraternity of manhood, and Rove was more than eager to hear anything he could.

"So you are suggesting there are more?" Uriah asked, his voice refusing to rise in the way others spoke. It was not the first time Rove had watched the man lead the elders, but it was the first time in a situation like this. It struck him how much power the man held, even speaking so softly. It was evident to all in the room, and none dared question it.

"I am," Oren said.

"And what do you suggest we do about it?"

"There is nothing needed to be done." Everyone turned at once at the feminine voice, one that all knew. Uriah may lead the elders, but it was his wife who truly commanded respect amidst the village. Faye Ruden still maintained a look of youth, even in middle age, her thick, curly red hair grown down to her waist, her slim figure wrapped in a cloak sewn from rabbit hides, her bright green eyes betraying her serene expression. *The most powerful men in the village stand in this room and they are all terrified of her.*

An outsider would probably call her a witch, but the people of the village called her Màthair, and Uriah was as much her protector as he was her husband.

What interested him more, however, was the young woman who trailed her. Catrin Rafferty was Oren's youngest child, but she was the most important by far. After all, only one girl was chosen to be the successor to the Màthair, and Catrin had proven herself very willing to learn. She was dressed more simply than the Màthair herself, wearing a simple woolen dress, her light red hair tied back in a braid away from a pale face dotted with occasional freckles. Even so, she carried the same aura of power as she trailed behind.

Faye continued as she reached the body and gingerly pulled back the cloak to reveal the gap in the man's mail that continued into his gut. "The spirits have protected us for generations, and this here is proof that they continue to protect us."

Rove watched the elders and saw that they were uncomfortable. The tales of spirits protecting the village were told since all of them were young, and even before, but there was never much credence given to the tales. The valley was secluded, difficult to access and just as difficult to leave. Fairies and spirits were stories used to alleviate fears in the young ones, not ideas to lean on when the prospect of danger lurked in the forests outside the village.

"This looks like the work of a blade," one of the men said, carefully choosing his words. Insulting the Màthair was not a favorable prospect, even for one of the elders.

"Do you know of a blade that would cut through this armor?" she asked, running her finger along the edge of the mail. "Our own iron would simply bounce off this as though it were made of stone."

Rove found himself glancing toward the swords that hung from the earthen walls of the roundhouse, neatly placed in even increments the length of the room. It was hard to believe that anything could withstand the heavy blades, but he knew she was right. That cut was not made by one of their blades.

"Perhaps one of his own slaughtered him," another said.

"Why would this man wear armor that would not protect him from the very weapons his own kind wield?" Faye shook her head. "You men doubt the stories your mothers told you because you have not seen it with your own eyes."

Rove caught Catrin's eye and managed a weary smile, but her face did not return the gesture. She appeared worried, uneasy. *Does she believe what the Màthair is saying?*

Faye turned toward him. "Rove, come with me. It is too late for these boneheads, but you are perhaps not beyond help."

The women turned and walked toward the exit. As Rove followed, he felt an iron grasp on his arm. He turned to see Oren's face right in his, so close he could smell the rank breath that came from the man's mouth. "This boy must serve his punishment before we can allow him to leave, Màthair."

Faye stopped and turned back toward them. "Punishing a boy for being curious is like punishing the wind for blowing."

Oren sneered. "We make these rules to keep them safe. If we do not teach them caution, then they will wind up dead like that man there."

"I assure you that our boys are just as well-equipped to deal with the wilderness as you men are. You simply fail to see it."

The grip only tightened as Oren took a step toward the Màthair. He was stopped by a thick, muscled hand on his chest. Rove had not even seen Uriah move toward them, but there he stood, towering over the two of them. "Release the boy," he said.

The words did not need to be repeated. The grip released and Rove moved toward the women, avoiding the urge to run his hand over the spot in his arm where Oren had gripped him, the muscle throbbing as though he had just been hit one of the wooden practice swords in the ring.

Content that none of the other men would try to stop them, the Màthair led him out of the building.

The Màthair's home was more comfortable than the roundhouse the elders had met in, though not by much. The scent of incense filled the room, burning from a small bowl that sat atop an altar against the far wall. A fire burned, like in the other one, but the room seemed to be better ventilated, and at the same time warmer. Faded wool blankets covered the dirt floor around the fire to provide a place to sit, and behind them, the walls held shelves filled with all manner of potions and powders that the Màthair used in her work. Through an opening partially covered with a curtain, he could see the beds belonging to Uriah and Faye and to their children who had not yet left to start their own families.

"Have a seat." Her tone was inviting, but there was something in her words that told him it was not a suggestion. He picked a spot on one of the blankets, lowering down to the ground and crossing his legs beneath him. As he did, Faye walked over and placed a fresh coal on the incense. "Catrin, would you put some water on the fire for tea?"

Catrin did not say a word, though she slipped Rove a slight smile as she fetched a kettle from the cupboard and disappeared outside to pull water from the well. Rove was silent, watching the Màthair move about on the other side of the flickering fire. Through the hole in the roof, he was able to see the thick, heavy clouds that rested over the valley, threatening snow. It was still early in the winter season, and it was already promising to be a bad one. There had already been two heavy snows, more than there should be at this time of year.

"Your mother was looking for you," Faye said, content with the coal and now watching the smoke that curled up toward the ceiling. "You know she needs help with your brother and sister. Children are handfuls at any age, but it is truly difficult when they are at that age of development."

Rove nodded, not wanting to avert his eyes. He would not let her try to shame him into a disadvantage; he was at enough of a disadvantage as it was dealing with the Màthair. "She would have told me this morning if she had really needed my help."

"The men may have been upset because you intruded on their territory," she said, turning toward him, "but you should know that you are protected in this valley. Morrigan watches over us, as that man's body proves."

Rove had indeed heard the stories for years, of the hidden protectors that watched over the village, that protected them from outsiders. At his age, it seemed more like fairy tales than anything else, but there was something about the way Faye spoke of them, the way she sounded so sure.

"You are unsure," she said.

He hesitated. "The stories seem so extraordinary," he said. "I mean, we've never seen these protectors, nor have we proof of their protecting us."

"What of the body that you found?" She settled into a spot across the fire from him as Catrin returned with the kettle and placed it over the fire before stepping away to the side. "You know that no blade could have pierced that armor."

Rove admittedly did not have a response to that. He had honestly never spent much time thinking about Morrigan or any of the other gods and goddesses or even the protectors that the Màthair spoke of. There was too much to worry about; tending to the livestock, chopping firewood, helping with the village gardens. The fact that he had been able to get away from his mother long enough to get out of the village was a wonder, really, when he thought about it.

The water had begun to boil, so Faye picked up a cloth and wrapped it around the handle in order to move it off the fire. "It's incredible how the faith has deteriorated as the years go on," she mused, spooning the sweet bark into the water. "Your grandfather never would have put up with what my husband has put up with. He was a hard man who stuck true to the faith and stuck by the Màthair through thick and thin. My husband, unfortunately, has met resistance at every turn, regardless of whether the topic is religious in nature or not."

"Why do you think the faith has faded?" Rove asked.

Faye poured the tea into a mug, skillfully avoiding any bits of bark attempting to slip in. She handed the mug to Rove, who took it, holding it close to his chest with both hands, feeling the warmth. The fire was nice, but even with it, the roundhouse was colder than he would have liked.

"I'm not sure," she said, pouring another cup and handing it to Catrin. "Perhaps it is my fault for not trying harder to ensure the children were being taught the ways of our ancestors. Or perhaps it was those who came before us for not making us realize the importance of those who protect us."

Faye handed a mug to Rove, then picked up her own, pursing her lips and blowing the steam away. "What matters is that the belief must return to our people. If our people fail to make tribute to our gods, then they will eventually stop protecting us. If they stop protecting us, then who will we be able to turn to? These men are more advanced than us, more powerful than us."

Rove focused in on the woman across from him. She had always appeared young, but in the past few moments, it was though she had aged a decade. "Why are you telling me this? Why not your husband? Or the rest of the elders?"

The Màthair looked over to where Catrin sat, sipping on her own drink. "The older ones are already set in their ways. I realized long ago that I need to start with my own children, and with the ones who are important for our village's future."

"How do you know I am that important?"

"Because our future Màthair needs a husband and protector." She was still looking at Catrin, who seemed to be completely ignoring either of them. She turned back to Rove. "There are important things happening outside of our borders, that body is more than proof of that. Those old men in that building may be hesitant to admit it, or possibly even flat out ignoring it, but more men will come. We will not be able to remain isolated forever, and we need our people to be strong in their faith if we are to survive."

Rove held his still untouched cup in his hands, the warmth radiating from it. "If the gods continue to protect us, how is it that we will not be able to remain isolated?"

"There is a limit to what the gods can do," Faye said. "If more come, if they march an army into our valley to find their missing people, if they destroy the trees and trample the land, then our gods will lose their power and we will be left to our own devices."

"Perhaps we can learn from them," Rove said. "Their weapons and armor are stronger than our own, and maybe they have more that we can take."

"Men so advanced in tools of war are such because of necessity, and such men would not be quick to trust people strange to them." She turned toward her apprentice. "Catrin, fetch me my powders, the fire is ripe for a reading."

Catrin stood, her eyes looking from Faye to Rove. "Is it proper for us to do this with Rove present, Màthair?" she asked.

"A man in his position must witness a reading eventually," Faye said with a wave of her hand. "He needs to start sooner or later."

Catrin gave no further argument, instead making her way once again to the shelves and fetching a small container. Rove watched her with interest. *The Màthair sounds so sure of herself. How could she possibly know?*

The Màthair took the container from Catrin and removed the lid, putting it aside. She reached into the container and removed a handful of powder. "Guide us in your light, oh blessed lady of the woods," she said in a low voice. "Reveal to us the truth of your ways that we may live in your grace and commit ourselves to your will."

Rove bowed his head in reverence, more out of habit than anything else. When the Màthair prayed, you were expected to pray with her, or at least pretend you were. Outside of that, he rarely found himself praying; few seemed to practice anymore, though all claimed the faith.

She threw the powder in her hand over the flames and the fire flared up suddenly, filling the room with a green light. Rove threw up his hands to shield his face, watching the flames maintain their new height and color. A strange, acrid smoke drifted through the hole in the ceiling, an unpleasant aroma associated with it.

Catrin and Faye both appeared unfazed, staring deeply into the flames as if hypnotized, oblivious to himself and anything else in the room around them. "The flames speak to us, reveal that which the gods wish us to know," Faye said. She waved her hand over the fire, passing through the flames, yet untouched by the heat.

She turned toward Catrin. "What do the flames say to you, my child?"

Catrin's eyes were empty, staring directly into the flames. "I see..." she trailed off, her eyes rolling back into her head, yet still seeming to see the fire before her. "I see fire. Not like the flames of our own fires, but from the skies, falling upon us, spreading over the valley."

"Like a fire coming from the trees?" Rove asked, but he was quickly shushed by the Màthair.

Catrin responded regardless, though her voice was absent, as though she didn't realize he was there even though she answered him. "No, it settles upon the trees like rain. It doesn't spread quickly because it has rained, but it does spread, crawling its way to the village. And everyone is there. But not me. And not you, Rove."

Rove frowned. "Why not?"

"It is not for the flames to tell us why," Faye said, her own gaze focused on Catrin. "No more talk. Listen."

"They're asking after us. They think we've abandoned them, though my father is insisting we haven't, that we are coming back."

That's a new one, Oren standing up for me, Rove thought.

"But we're not coming back. Something is holding us back, I'm not sure. We're not coming. There is no hope for them."

Catrin suddenly blinked her eyes and Rove found himself doing the same. The odor was gone, the smoke, even the brightly colored green flames. Before them was just a normal fire, the rest gone as though it was just a hallucination, the only remnants the slight echo of a flare in Rove's sight.

"What does it all mean?" Rove finally asked, breaking the silence.

"I know not," Faye said. "The gods often speak in riddles, leaving it for us to decipher."

Catrin sat silently, still gazing into the fire, but now with what seemed to be a bit of shame, or perhaps worry, instead of the intensity she had during the reading. Rove fought the urge to go over to her.

"I won't leave the village," he said.

"None of us truly know what the future holds. But the flames rarely lie."

"I won't," he repeated softly, not sure whom he was trying to convince.

She stood. "You had best get back to your mother. We will speak on this again."

Rove was lying awake on the feathered pad that made up his bed, covered in multiple layers of fur. Insomnia set upon him, brought about by the combination of the dead body and of Catrin describing the village burning. He sighed and turned onto his side, pulling the covers tighter.

"Rove?"

The voice came from outside, soft and welcoming. He sat up in bed and smiled. It could only belong to one person. "Shouldn't you be sleeping, Catrin?"

In the dark, he could make out the outline of her head and shoulders as she leaned on the sill. "I couldn't sleep," she said. "I was thinking about our meeting with the Màthair today. About people coming into our valley. About how we won't be isolated anymore. About how the gods wouldn't be able to protect us. About our village burning and us not being able to stop it."

Rove allowed the furs to slip from his body as he stood and leaned against the wall. "She may be wrong, the flames may be wrong. Maybe this guy just got lost and stumbled into our valley and we'll grow up and live our lives in the valley like our parents and grandparents before us."

"But the flames never lie," she said.

"There's a first time for everything."

"And what about the body you found? What if there are more?"

"I'm more afraid of what was able to kill him," Rove said. "Something cut through his armor as if it were butter."

"That's no mystery, you heard what the Màthair said."

"Do you really think some magical creature slew him?"

"I don't think it's out of the question."

"How could you know? You've never seen one."

"But I have seen the sort of things that are possible through the gods." Rove thought he could detect a bit of annoyance in her voice, though she hid it well.

"Like what?"

"Like when you fell through the ice and was under for several minutes before we could pull you out."

Rove smirked. "Stranger things have happened without help from the gods."

"How do you know there was no help from the gods?"

"How do you know there was?"

"Maybe in time I will share with you."

"What's that supposed to mean?"

"Nothing." She stepped back from the sill. "Come out here, let's go for a walk. The full moon is out, and the forest looks beautiful."

"A bit late, don't you think?"

"Come on, you said you couldn't sleep. Besides, you wouldn't want me going for a walk all by myself, what with a mysterious killer lurking in the woods." She smiled over her shoulder at him as she started away. The moonlight only served to enhance her beauty.

"I'm not sure I want to be out with a mysterious killer lurking in the woods."

"Well, I'm going for a walk, with or without my protector."

She turned her head away, heading toward the edge of the village. Rove sighed and pulled his cloak around his shoulders before jumping out of the window. He landed softly and then jogged after Catrin.

She gave him a knowing smile as he caught up to her. "I knew you'd come."

"I'm sure it was such a difficult prediction to make," he said.

"You do have a tendency to surprise everyone from time to time." She smiled, wrapping her arm through his own.

They made it to the edge of the village and entered the woods. Everything darkened around them, yet the bright moonlight still permeated through the canopy of leaves, lighting their path as they made their way down the game trail. Despite the cold air, it had not snowed for over a week, leaving the ground dry beneath their boots. Leaves and pine needles crunched as they strode deeper and deeper into the forest.

The sound of trickling water reached his ears, the same stream that he had found the body beside. He shivered, partly from the cold and partly from the thought of the body as he had found it. He found himself picking up the pace to get away from the area more quickly.

Rove only slowed when he felt a tug on his arm. He came to a stop and turned to look at Catrin, a concerned look spread across her face. "What's wrong?" he asked.

"Did you hear that?" Her voice was quiet, concerned.

Rove craned his neck, listening. The only sound to him was the rustling of leaves as the wind blew through the trees. *Is she getting as spooked as I am by this whole thing?*

"There it was again."

Maybe more spooked. "I still don't hear anything."

"There's someone out there, we need to get back to the village." She turned and stopped suddenly, the sound of a soft thud as she ran into a man standing right behind them, followed by a quick shriek as she tried to back away. A dark hand grabbed her by the wrist, preventing her from backing up any further.

"Well, well, what have we here?" The accent was strange, alien. Rove had never heard anyone speak like that before, so differently from the people of the village, from his own accent. "Seems a young filly has gotten herself lost in the woods."

"Get your hands off of her," Rove found himself growling, suddenly wishing he had a weapon, any weapon.

The man grinned at him, his teeth rotten, yet retaining enough white to reflect the moonlight. In his features, Rove could see the same dark hair, thick beard, and heavy build that the dead man had. *They could have been brothers.* Worst of all, he had something the dead man did not: life and an aura of pure malice, just the kind of man the Màthair feared.

"Seems the filly has herself a little mate," he said. Catrin struggled against his grasp to no avail. Rove quickly scanned the area for something, anything he could use as a weapon. He froze when he heard a noise from behind him and the man spoke again, "What do you say we do with 'em, Corl?"

"I reckon we slit this boy's throat and take the girl back to camp." Rove felt a steel grip on his shoulder and tried to move away, but felt the hand hold him steadily in place.

"Best take him back to camp first," the one that held Catrin said. "We don't want to leave the body where the villagers could find it."

"You're forgetting about Arun, aren't you, Yurin?" Corl replied. "They probably found him and killed him themselves. That be the case, then they already know we're here." Rove felt the grip tighten. "Maybe we send them a message."

"Arun probably just got drunk and lost himself in the woods." Yurin snorted loudly and spat off to the side. "Besides, maybe he can tell us a thing or two about the land. Steffan would be right pissed at us if we didn't seize such an opportunity."

"Aye, you're probably right," Corl said. The hand suddenly released as the man shoved Rove forward. "Get a move on. And no funny business."

Rove moved forward without a word, following Yurin, who maintained his own grip on Catrin. His mind raced, a dozen different ideas running through his head, each one sure to fail. He was unarmed, and at a severe disadvantage both in terms of size and no doubt fighting experience. He was at a loss about what to do.

A light emerged through the trees after a few moments, a flickering that sent shadows careening across the forest, a haunting dance against a stage of leaves. Three more men sat amidst the fire, watching as Corl and Yurin emerged into the clearing with their prisoners.

"Well, it looks like our boys caught 'emselves something," the one nearest them said, standing. He was shorter than either of Rove's current companions, but he had the look of one who had seen many a battle in his time. Maybe it was the patchy beard or the battered armor or the scars up his arms, but he was not one to be messed with.

"Couple of locals we found nosing around in the forest." Rove turned and finally got a good look at Yurin, his stringy hair, his crooked teeth, the sinewy muscles beneath the thick wool, the painted wooden ball that stood in for one of his eyes. "Couldn't have 'em running back and talking 'bout us, could we?"

The one in the middle looked up quietly. "Did you find any trace of Arun?" he asked, his voice carrying even though it seemed like it shouldn't be heard over the fire.

"No, not the slightest," Yurin said. "Probably slaughtered by their people." He nodded toward Catrin and Rove as he spoke, emphasizing the word "their".

"Let them go," the man said. Rove could only assume he was the Steffan that Yurin had referred to.

"I'd advise against that," Corl said.

"'Tis madness," Yurin said. "They'll only run back and tell them we're here."

"No doubt they already know we're here," Steffan said, maintaining his calmness. "Either they found Arun's body, or they took care of him themselves."

"Right, but they don't know our camp is here," the first man said. He had drifted over to Catrin and held a strand of her hair, sniffing at it between his dirty fingers. He turned back toward Steffan. "Can't we keep her, Steffan? It's so lonely up in these mountains."

"Back away, Marl," Steffan said. Marl threw up his hands and obeyed. "We're withdrawing from this valley. Something feels...strange about it." He ran a hand over his thick beard, the experienced eyes beneath the receding hairline dashing across the edges of the clearing. "We were sent to scout, nothing more." He spat. "There is little here to speak of. I'm not sure why the king desires this land so much."

Yurin was quite evidently still not pleased. "Might be they know of something that can help us," he suggested, glaring toward the leader.

"Might be you listen and do as you're told."

"I really don't think we should be letting them go." His hand was resting on the hilt of his sword, though as of yet he made no indication of drawing it. Perhaps just a habit. Rove glanced over toward Catrin, but she appeared calm, her eyes closed and her lips moving subtly. *Is she praying?*

"Well, you weren't brought along to think," Steffan said. "Now are you done?"

Yurin said nothing, only maintaining his gaze. The wind kicked up around them, rustling the trees and flicking at the flames in the middle of the clearing. The two men were staring each other down, the silence overpowering, the tension thick. No one moved a muscle, no one spoke a word. All eyes were on Yurin and Steffan.

Another gust of wind pushed through the clearing and suddenly the fire was gone, the woods plunged into darkness. There was rustling and cries from the men as they stumbled around. The grip loosened from his arm, and he felt a touch on his other arm, much gentler.

"Quickly, we have to leave," he heard Catrin say from beside him.

He was having trouble seeing after looking into the fire, even with the full moon. He allowed her to lead him away, stumbling through the night. "What is it?" he said, his voice a whisper.

"The Gwyllion come," she said.

"The..." he trailed off and looked back. His eyes were still adjusting, but he could make out the shapes of the men around the remains of the fire, fumbling around in the dark. One was huddled over the fire, attempting to get it to start back up, while the others moved around, with one just standing there, watching.

That was when he realized that there was more than the five that should be there. The others did not seem to see the one standing there, oblivious in their confusion. Rove came to a stop and stood there watching, ignoring Catrin pulling on his arm.

"Rove, we can't stay, we have to go," she said.

"What's happening?" he asked quietly.

"Rove..."

One of the men stumbled, his momentum taking him toward the dark figure. There was a sudden movement, so quick that Rove almost missed it as the figure lashed out with a blade, ripping through the man's armor and into his gut, spilling his innards onto the forest floor.

Catrin pulled on him again, more insistent this time. He moved a few steps, still watching even as they began to pick up the pace. He stumbled and looked forward to catch himself, finally breaking the spell. He followed Catrin through the forest, no longer having any desire to look back.

"We need to tell her." Catrin had her arms crossed over her chest, her face scrunched in disapproval. Rove fought the urge to laugh; he had learned from experience that she was very serious whenever she made that face.

"I didn't say we shouldn't ever tell her," he said. "I just think maybe we should sleep on it first, think about what happened."

Catrin shook her head. "No, we tell her now."

Rove sighed. Catrin had the same stubbornness that the current Màthair had, and he was well aware that she was not going to let this go. *That must be a required attribute for the role.*

Catrin was already walking into the village, making her way through the dark avenue to the Màthair's house. She was already calling Faye's name loudly on the wooden door when he caught up to her. *It's like she's trying to awaken the entire village,* he thought, gazing over his shoulder back toward the dark woods. The wind picked up momentarily and he shivered, though he was positive it was not from the cold this time.

There were footsteps and Uriah stepped past the curtain, his wide frame filling the doorway, dressed only in a pair of short pants. He was an intimidating sight in the best of times, but standing before them right there, Rove was finally able to grasp just how immense he really was. Even in his forties, there was not an ounce of fat on him, his broad shoulders about double the width of Rove's own. The tattoos that covered his arms, the mosaic of accomplishments that cover his rippling forearms and biceps continued down his chest, all the way down his abs, surrounding the rune of manhood that stood proudly right over his heart.

More intimidating than his size was the look he had plastered across his face, the look of a man who had been pulled from a pleasant sleep and was not too pleased with it. His eyes flickered between the two of them. "This had better be important," he said.

Rove found his own tongue filling his mouth, unable to speak, but Catrin maintained the steady confidence she had displayed all night. "We need to speak to the Màthair."

"The Màthair is asleep," he said, folding his arms across his chest, the runes moving as he flexed the muscles in his arms. "You will tell me, and I'll decide if the matter is worth waking her."

"There were men in the forest." It was Rove who spoke, not Catrin, finally finding his own voice, surprising himself that it didn't come out in a squeak.

Uriah's eyes widened. "That is not a matter for the Màthair, that is a matter for the elders." He was already turning back into the house, no doubt to fetch his sword and armor.

"Were," Catrin called after him.

Uriah stopped and looked over his shoulder. "What do you mean, were?"

"They were killed," she said.

"By whom?"

"That's why we're here for the Màthair."

Uriah stood there, rubbing his beard. Finally, he sighed. "I'll wake her. Come on in out of the cold. Catrin, light the fire, she'll be in shortly."

Catrin entered immediately and set to work stacking logs, setting kindling beneath. Rove took a seat and watched as she grabbed two stones and started to flick them together. It was only then that she started to show the first sign of weakness, her hands shaking as they moved. She groaned in frustration and began to flick them harder, trying desperately to make the sparks catch. Without warning, she threw them down hard and ran her hands through her hair.

Rove stood and walked over to where she sat, calmly picking up the stones and leaning over the fire pit. It took him a few tries, but the sparks finally caught the kindling and smoke began to emerge as the wood slowly caught fire. He sat back and turned toward Catrin. "Are you okay?" he asked softly.

"I...I think so," she said.

He put a hand on her shoulder and rubbed it gently. "It's okay, we're okay."

"I don't know what came over me," she said. "I was fine until now. It's just...I don't know, now that we're here, I think you were right, we should have waited."

"No, you were right, we needed to tell her."

They were interrupted by the Màthair entering the room, a fur robe draped around her shoulders. She did not say a word, but immediately came over to the two of them, both standing in greeting. Instead of her normal greeting, she wrapped her arms around both of them, embracing them closely. Rove felt an immense feeling of relief, as though her very touch had a healing effect. Beside him, Catrin had lost her composure and allowed the silent tears to flow.

"Are the two of you alright?" Faye asked, releasing them and stepping back. Past the fire, Uriah stood by, watching without expression.

Catrin ran a sleeve over her eyes and nodded. "We're fine."

"Tell me what happened." Her voice was that of a mother, caring and sympathetic, a welcome change from the growl Uriah had greeted them with.

"We went for a walk in the woods..." Catrin began, but she was quickly interrupted by Uriah.

"What were you doing out there?"

The Màthair turned back toward him. "We can deal with the why later. For now, we should be thanking the gods they are safe."

Uriah kept his stone gaze, but it was evident that he would not bring it up again. Catrin continued. "We were set upon by a pair of men, foreigners. They took us back to their camp."

"And you were unharmed?" Catrin nodded in response. "What happened then?"

"Their leader wanted to release us, said they were just there to scout. He sounded like he wanted to leave."

Uriah grunted. "Sounds like he at least had a bit of intelligence."

Catrin did not acknowledge him. "They started arguing amongst themselves. Some of them wanted to kill us. Then, the Gwyllion came."

Uriah's eyes went wide, but the Màthair maintained her calm demeanor. "You saw the Gwyllion?"

"The fire went out, it was dark. I was just trying to get us away from there."

"I saw one," Rove said. All eyes turned toward him, and he averted his own. "Or at least, the silhouette of one."

Catrin was looking at him in disbelief. "Why didn't you say so?"

Rove shrugged. "I didn't think it was important. I looked back and saw that there was more than just them. I...saw it kill one of them."

The Màthair nodded thoughtfully. "Morrigan was watching over you tonight. Uriah, you may wish to take some men there in the morning and rid us of the bodies."

Uriah nodded. "Rove, do you think you can lead us there?"

"It was dark, and I do not know the woods terribly well, but I think I can."

"Then I'll be by to get you in the morning." He stepped up and planted a kiss on the top of Faye's head. "I'm returning to bed. Don't think I will forget, you two. You'll still be held accountable for disobeying our laws."

Uriah disappeared into the bedroom and the Màthair took a seat, prompting the two of them to follow suit. "Don't you worry about him," she said with a slight smile, using a wooden stick to move the burning logs around. "He may seem mean, but he really does care about you, about the village."

"Why was it so important that I saw one?" Rove asked.

Faye looked at him across the flames. "The Gwyllion do not show themselves to anyone, not to those they kill, not to the villagers, not even to me. There was more to that than just saving the two of you. Morrigan is watching over you. You're important, perhaps more so that even I have seen."

"Important how?"

"Every Màthair needs a protector, a man to be her husband and to be the one who stands beside her no matter what. It's been assumed for some time that you and Catrin would be together, it's plain to anyone who watches. But you seeing the Gwyllion is something more, something that the flames could never show. The gods have chosen you, for what, I cannot tell, but Catrin's reading today and you seeing the Gwyllion mean that something large is in store for you."

Rove felt Catrin's hand on his, squeezing gently. "What am I to do? How will I know what to do?"

"Trust in Morrigan and she will guide you. Until then, there is nothing you can do but live your life until the time is right." The Màthair stood. "You two should be getting to bed. Uriah will be coming for Rove, and we have much to speak of on the morrow, Catrin. Dawn will come sooner than you could know."

Faye showed them to the door and closed it quietly behind them. Rove walked with Catrin through the silent village, both silent until they reached her home. She turned to him at her door, staring up with her big blue eyes. "Rove, I..." she trailed off.

He shushed her. "We can talk more tomorrow."

"I don't know if the Màthair will let me out of her sight," she said with a half-smile.

"And we still have to face whatever punishment Uriah can dream up," he added, returning the smile.

"I'm sorry I made you go into the forest with me."

Rove shrugged. "Hard to say no to a pretty face." He brushed a loose strand of hair from her face. "Are you going to be okay?"

She nodded. "I think so. Slight moment of weakness. Not very becoming of a future Màthair, is it?"

"Everyone has their moments," he said. "I'm sure even our Màthair does. What matters is who you allow to see it."

"I was hoping no one would ever see it."

Rove reached out and pulled her close to him. "I promise I won't tell anyone," he whispered into her ear.

"Thank you," she said, then leaned up and kissed him. It was brief, but more than enough to leave Rove walking on air as she broke away, her hand lingering on his cheek for just a moment. She gave him one last fleeting smile and disappeared into her home.

The party had consisted of five other men besides Uriah and Rove. The men were in high spirits as they returned to the village, all dirty from digging the graves in the hard ground. Perhaps there was something in the air, or perhaps it was just the knowledge that the village was once again safe, but the men were laughing and joking as they went their separate ways.

"Rove, a minute." Uriah's voice came from behind him as Rove started toward home, causing him to stop and turn. *Here it comes,* he thought, *I owe him for two now.*

"Come with me," he said, starting off toward the elder's roundhouse. Uriah had to duck beneath the door frame, the building certainly not built to accommodate a man of his size. Rove followed behind, blinking as he passed from daylight into the dark interior.

Oren was sitting in the back, holding something over the burning fire. He looked up as they entered, his glass eye seeming to pierce right through Rove, and his smile seeming almost as sinister as it was sincere. "Thought I was going to grow old enough to return to the dirt waiting on you two," he said.

Uriah didn't return the smile. Instead, he turned toward Rove. "I spoke with my wife in length this morning." *Let's get this over with.* "And after speaking with Oren, it was decided that we're not going to be able to keep you from the forest, nor should we try."

Rove's eyes widened. *What is he saying?*

Uriah answered his unspoken question. "It is time we stopped trying to limit you. One day, you will be taking my spot and it does not serve any of us to pretend otherwise."

"You mean..."

Uriah nodded. "Take off your shirt. I'm going to warn you now that the first one hurts like hell."

Rove nodded, swallowing as he removed the fur cloak he wore, followed by his woolen shirt. Uriah motioned to the bench and Rove laid down. He watched as Oren removed the object from the fire, a sharp, needle-like knife. Oren grabbed a stool and set it down beside him, placing the tool down on a table beside a small bottle of black ink.

"Here," he said, his normal demeanor suddenly gone, replaced by something that was almost kind, almost sympathetic, almost fatherly, as he placed a stick between Rove's teeth. "Bite down on this, it will help."

Uriah stood to the side as Oren picked up the tool and dipped it into the ink. "Try not to move," he said as he leaned over. "The more you cooperate, the easier this is."

Rove gripped the sides of the bench and tensed his chest, waiting. When the first prick was finally made, it hurt, but not as much as he expected. He bit down on the stick, clenching it with his teeth as Oren ran a cloth over the area and made another prick. The process continued: prick, wipe, prick, wipe. Each prick seemed to bring more pain, yet it was not as he expected, the pain almost welcome, his passage into manhood.

After a while, Oren sat back and pulled out another cloth to wipe the sweat from his forehead. "All done," he said.

Rove sat up, looking down at the same tattoo that adorned the chest of every man in the village. It was the moment that all the boys looked forward to, something he had dreamed of since he was old enough to know better.

Uriah stood before him, holding his hand out. Rove craned his neck to look up at the large man, then took it, allowing himself to be pulled up into a heavy embrace. "Welcome to manhood, son." He stepped back, his hand resting on Rove's shoulder at arm's length.

"Thank you," Rove said, all he could think to say.

"Starting tomorrow, you'll be with me at all times," he said, releasing him. "The tattoo says you're a man, but I'm going to make sure you become one."

Rove nodded and felt a different hand clap down onto his shoulder. "But for now, enjoy yourself," Oren said, about as cheerful as Rove had ever heard the man. "We'll be bringing out the kegs for you tonight."

Rove could not help the smile that crossed his face. Uriah dismissed him and he exited the hut, still topless as he walked out with his tunic and cloak draped over his arm. The Màthair was standing outside, waiting for him with Catrin by her side.

"Congratulations, Rove," she said, beaming as she kissed him on the cheek.

"Thank you," he said.

"No more getting into trouble for going into the woods, eh?" she said with a smile.

"I guess not," he said. "Uriah said I'm to train under him."

The Màthair nodded. "He is very knowledgeable. You'd do well to listen to what he has to say."

Rove nodded in agreement. "I will." Catrin smiled at him from beyond the Màthair and he smiled back.

Faye turned back to her apprentice. "Catrin, please go with the other women, there is much to prepare for tonight. After all, your future protector has become a man."

Catrin nodded and went off. "Rove, we looked into the fire again this morning," she said once Catrin was out of earshot.

"What did you see?" he asked.

"Not me, but Catrin," she replied. "She saw something that I cannot quite explain. Another man, a man riding a dragon."

Rove frowned in confusion. "A dragon?"

"A creature that has been reduced to myth. Once an army from a faraway land swept through upon the backs of dragons. They reduced the land to flames and ember, killed many people, conquered the land."

"What happened to them?"

"They were defeated by the kingdoms outside our valley, by the ancestors of the men you met in the forest." She took a glance around, ensuring they were still alone. "I don't know who this man is, but he's a part of your future."

"Is he a friend or an enemy?"

Faye shook her head. "I know not. That is for you to find out when the time comes."

Rove was unsure how to react. "How long will I have to wait?"

"As long as the gods deem it necessary. Until then, have patience. Learn from those around you and trust in the gods. In the meantime..." She ran a finger over the fresh tattoo on his chest, the pain already having begun to fade. "...earn yourself a few more of these. It would not serve our village well to send a man with only one tattoo into the world."

She walked off, leaving Rove standing in the middle of the village. His mind was racing, thinking about all she had said, about Catrin's visions, about the man on the dragon.

Just what have the gods gotten me into, he wondered.

THROUGH THE STREETS

This is the second story that serves as a prequel to an upcoming novel, this one more direct than "Before the Stake". The inspiration to this one came with one of my frequent podcasts telling a story about groups of vigilantes in Victorian England who would roam the streets in an attempt to stop crime. Like many of the previous ones, my mind seized on that idea with a supernatural twist.

Without giving too much away, I can tell you that one of these characters will appear in future works, that this ended up being a bit of an origin story. I am super excited to be able to share that novel, but that is for a later time, when I've had a chance to sit down and work through the kinks. Until then, enjoy this one, and let your imagination run wild with what the future will bring.

Everything felt right when we walked the streets at night.

There were four of us who set out every night, doing our solemn duty as citizens, as Tony always liked to say. He was our leader, Tony, and there wasn't a better man for the job. He always knew what to say, knew what to do, and he was a hell of a fighter, especially for being such a lanky guy.

Bruno was the bruiser, taller and wider than the rest of us by a good deal, the kind of guy you want on your side in any scrap. Not the brightest, but a good friend with a sterling sense of right and wrong. Tony was the brains behind the operation, but it had been Bruno's idea to start, and a good one at that.

Anders kept us supplied and came up with new contraptions for us to use. He was fond of bombs in particular, ones that confuse, that flash bright lights, that expel smoke, and that can knock huge chunks out of solid brick walls. You can see the scars on him, the nubs that used to be fingers on his left hands, and he says that he can't hear out one of his ears. I've always found him a bit crazy, but Tony says you need to be a bit crazy to do what he does.

Then there was me, Will. My job was to know everything we needed to know. I was a law clerk by trade, which was why Tony approached me, and I couldn't resist the chance to make a difference. I can't say I'm much of a fighter, never have been, but I know the laws and all the police beats, and I have connections, in case something was to happen.

It had become a nightly ritual, four men in black overcoats, scarves wrapped around our faces and hats pulled low to hide our identities, though there was no other attempt to hide. We walked the streets, our steps echoed off the cobbled stones as we made our patrol, seeking out the trouble that lurks in the shadows when the sun goes down.

Tony always said that he wished we didn't have to do this, that the city could be safe enough on its own, that the police could do their job, but that was not the case. Not when corruption ran so virulently through the ranks of the government, where a criminal who knows the right people, or the right pockets to grease, can walk free no matter how bad the crime.

The night was a cold one, the fog setting early, bathed in a blue glow from the full moon. The streetlamps were lit, some already extinguished, whether through lack of kerosene or simple negligence. A wet sheen covered the ground, reflecting the glow of the lamps, as though an upside down, mirrored world existed right beneath our feet. And all was quiet. Too quiet, as Anders was fond of saying. And he did say so.

"It's still early," Bruno said, his voice deep, somewhat nasally. "When was the last night went by that we didn't catch someone?" He slammed a meaty fist into the palm of his other hand as if to drive home the point.

"Keep alert," Tony said. He walked in the front, a baton twirling in his hand, the revolver visible from where it was shoved in the front of his belt. "It never stays quiet."

And of course, that night, it didn't.

The scream pierced through the air, long and shrill, the scream of a woman in peril. The four of us froze in place, all turning as we sought the direction it came from.

"It sounded like that way," Bruno said, pointing ahead.

"I'm certain it was behind us," Anders said, turning that direction.

"Sounded like it was coming from one of the buildings," I said.

The scream happened again, and it was Tony who pointed, his finger aimed ahead and to the left. "There," he said. "I swear on my mother."

We took off in unison, running across the wet streets in the direction in which Tony had heard the sound. Tony spotted the alley first, and he turned sharply, nearly causing the rest of us to miss it. Anders and I made the turn, while Bruno slid past it, moving too quickly to slow his bulk. He was not much further behind us, however.

We all stood at the alley's edge, gazing down the dark corridor. There was movement at the end, but no screams. Only a noise, a strange, wet sound, and something almost like a low growl. There was a spark, the sound of incineration, and a flash of light as Tony struck one of the hot burning flares that Anders had made. The alley filled with light, and we gazed upon the source of the scream.

Or rather, what was left of it.

The first thing I saw was the trail of blood, bright red in the light of the flare. It pooled, just a few feet from where we stood, and from the pool was a long trail, as though something had been dragged along the ground. Tony raised the light, slowly revealing the alley before us, slowly revealing the creature.

It was hunched over, but at first glance, it must have been eight or nine feet tall. It stood on hind legs, covered in coarse dark hair from head to toe, the former hidden behind its hunched back and the latter of which was a pair of thick claws, almost like a bear's. A pair of ragged pants clung to its waist and I could see scraps of other clothing mixed in with its fur.

It was feeding on something, and it didn't take a stretch of the imagination to figure it was the owner of the screaming voice. We were too late.

Tony stepped forward into the alley. "Stop!"

The beast turned at the sound of his voice, the movement causing me to recoil backwards, though the others gave no such reaction. It growled at us, holding a bloody claw up in front of its face, the flare reflecting off its dark eyes. I half expected something like a dog or wolf, but the face was closer to human, or perhaps ape, the jaws slightly protruding, the teeth that emerged razor sharp.

It gave one more roar, and then it bounded straight up the side of the building, sinking its claws into the brick, sending rubble showering down. Tony ran forward, standing beneath where it climbed, looking up at it, but it was only when the rest of the beast disappeared over the roof with a distant roar that the rest of us followed.

The body had been a woman, but the only way I could tell was from the ripped dress and the long blonde hair. The rest of the body was ripped to shreds and mostly eaten, no longer truly a body, but a mess of blood and guts and gnawed bones. The flies were already beginning to buzz, and all we could do was look at it.

Somehow, it was me who found my voice first, the words coming out in little more than a croak. "Well, what do we do now?"

Our hideout was once an abandoned warehouse on the river, the kind that one only has to glance upon to know it's infested with rats and roaches and all other manner of pest that thrives in the absence of humans. Tony bought it, and we cleaned it out, but we made sure that it still looked that way to any passerby. Inside, however, is a different story.

The basement had been made into something that was almost warm and welcoming. A wood furnace burned in the corner, providing heat through the pipes that lined the ceiling. We had paved the floor, and pieces of it were now covered in rugs, and with it couches and tables, a place where we would sit, discussing our routes or our marks, and sometimes even our lives outside of this, such as they were. In one corner was a wardrobe, home to our clothing when we wore when we went out on the city, and in another corner was the lab that Anders used for his gadgets. Gas powered lights bathed the space in a smooth glow, drowning out the dreariness that a basement brings with it.

We were there now, gathered together after a long night. We had come straight here, after dropping a line to the police, but the walk had taken longer than it should have, as though we were walking in a haze that clouded our senses and led us astray.

Tony was pacing the room. Anders was in his corner, tinkering with something, goggles strapped around his head. Bruno was reclined across one of the couches, his legs hanging off. Myself, I sat on another couch, gazing over the maps that lay on the table in front of me, though not really focusing on any one specific point.

Finally, Bruno spoke, his voice filling the basement space as he sat up. "Are we sure we saw what we saw?"

"Are you saying we all hallucinated the same way?" Anders asked from his workbench.

"Sure. That."

"The answer is no," Anders said. "Shared hallucinations are not something known to science."

Bruno laid back down. "So there's really a monster out there."

Anders never looked up. "That seems to be accurate."

"The real question is," Tony said, "what are we going to do about it?"

"I was afraid you'd say that," I muttered.

"We need a plan," Tony said.

"It's not exactly that simple," I said, my voice louder this time. "The bloody thing climbed up the damn wall."

Tony ignored me, turning toward our inventor. "Anders? Any ideas? Maybe something tucked away in that chest of yours for a rainy day?"

"All the days are rainy here, Anthony," Anders said without looking up.

"You know what I mean," Tony said.

Anders stood, holding a bullet in his hand. "I think this might," he said, holding it up, examining it in the light, his goggles resting atop his head.

We all looked at him. Bruno sat up, took a look, then laid back down. "A bullet, Anders? We have those already."

"Not just any bullet," Anders said. He tossed it toward us. I reached up my hand to catch it, but Tony snatched it deftly out of the air before it could reach me. Probably for the better, I would have dropped it.

Tony held it between his fingers, just as Anders had done. "Not just any bullet," Tony said, repeating Anders' words. "A silver bullet."

"Precisely," Anders said.

Tony handed the bullet to me and I examined it, the light reflecting from the polished surface of the bullet's tip. "You think this will work?"

"You're the learned one, are you not, William?" Anders said.

"On laws and charts and maps," I said. "Monsters are not my thing."

"Every legend says that a monster can only be killed by silver," Bruno said. He was sitting up now, taking the bullet when it was handed to him. "All the stories say so."

"Silver to the heart, to be precise," Tony said. "A bullet, an arrow, a sword. It's all the same. It's the purity of the metal."

"Precisely," Anders said. "I have some more ideas, a few contraptions, but it will take some time."

"I'm not sure we have time," Tony said. "Whatever that creature is, we need to kill it before it kills anyone else. God knows that poor woman suffered enough."

"Are we sure we want to?" I asked.

The room fell silent, three sets of eyes turned toward me. I tried to sink into the collar of my coat, but my head could only go so far.

Finally, Tony spoke. "If we don't, then who will?"

"I don't know," I said, my voice low, too late to backtrack. "The police? The army? Anyone better prepared than us."

Anders and Bruno both began to talk, but Tony silenced them. "No one is better prepared than us," he said. "None of them did anything about the crime, but we have. They can't react like we can, they can't innovate like we can. And they won't be able to kill this creature, not like we can."

He had walked around the couch, grabbing a bottle of whisky from the wet bar and a glass for it. He placed the glass in my hand and poured, stopping when he filled it halfway. "Drink," he said. I obeyed. The liquor burned my throat, warmed my bones.

"How many men have we put away, Will?" he asked. He didn't give me a chance to answer, instead pouring more whisky into my glass, spilling some on my hand. "Keep drinking." I did.

"How many men who if only the police were in charge would still be walking the streets?" He poured again. "Drink." I did.

"How much dangerous would this city be if it weren't for us?" He poured again. "Drink."

I did, but the burn was too much, and I coughed several times, nearly spilling the glass. "Save some for us, why don't you," Bruno said.

Tony ignored him. He was leaning forward, at eye level with me, staring at me with those dark eyes of his. "This is for us to stop. This is why we got together, why we do this. We are here to protect this city. All of us. It doesn't work without all of us."

I managed a nod, and he clapped me on the shoulder. "Glad you agree." He turned away. "Anders, we have some planning to do. I want us back out there as soon as we can."

As soon as we could ended up being three nights later.

None of us left the hideout during that time, apart from a food run Bruno and I made during one of the days. Otherwise, our time was spent waiting, fending off boredom while Anders did his work, helping on the rare occasion he called for it.

Each morning, a paper would arrive, and each morning, we would gather around to read it. Not one day passed that there wasn't another report of a mauling, a body mangled beyond recognition, partially eaten. The beast was out there, and it was killing.

Tony had a theory that the attacks being reported weren't the only ones involving the creature. He dug deeper into the papers, looking in the classifieds for missing persons, and the number seemed to climb by the day. It was why he kept insisting that we needed to hurry, why Anders and he hardly slept even as Bruno and I dozed on the couches.

Finally, on the afternoon of the third day, Tony stepped away from watching Anders work and announced that the night would be the night. "Will," he said, turning to me. "The maps."

We started by marking the places where the bodies had been found, the alleys where they'd been dragged and eaten. Looking at them all together, it seemed to form something of a circle around a few buildings, and I pointed it out.

"A hideout, maybe?" Bruno asked.

Tony rubbed his chin. "Or perhaps where the beast makes its home." He tapped at the spot. "If we can figure out where it lives, we can lay a trap for it."

"It will know we're there before we can spring any trap," I said. "Either it will flee, or it will get the jump on us and kill us all."

Bruno nodded. "Happened to my father. Waited at a cave to kill a bear that had been terrorizing a village. Bear came in behind him and ripped him to shreds."

"Do we know who lives in these buildings?" Tony asked.

"I can pull the names from the public records," I said. "But I still think it's a bad idea."

"Do it," Tony said. "We should know what kind of people are there."

"Those are in New Town, aren't they?" Bruno asked. I nodded and he shook his head. "Whoever it is that lives there, they won't talk to the likes of us."

"They will talk to Will, if it comes to that," he said. "I just want to know what we are walking into." He turned to Anders. "Tell them what we have in store."

Anders packed a few things from his desk into a box and brought them over to the table. He bent down and picked them up one at a time. First was a box of bullets. "Six rounds apiece," he said. "Enough to fill a standard revolver. I recommend not missing with the first, or you might be dead before you can fire another."

He placed the box down and picked up a small spherical object with a short fuse. "Standard bomb but laced with silver. We'll each have just one, so make them count."

"Just one?" Bruno asked, taking it from him and examining it.

"If you'd like to provide the materials, I'll be happy to make more." The next item was shaped like a star, with sharp points protruding inward from each one. "This thing sticks to the wall and is triggered by a tripwire. Just set it up in a hallway and make sure you don't trip it yourself when leading it down."

I picked one up, holding it gingerly by the tips of my fingers. "More silver, I assume?"

"Yes, but is this not the most magnificent thing you've ever seen? I'm quite proud of this one."

"Yes, yes, it's all wonderful," Tony said. "Get on with it."

Anders placed it down. "Finally, we have the best, at least in my opinion." He picked up a blade, holding it up for us to see. We all stared at it for several moments.

"I don't get it," I finally said.

"Yeah," Bruno agreed. "Looks like a normal steel blade."

"It is," Tony said.

Anders nodded. "A normal steel dagger dipped in a silver solution of my own making, a sort of liquidization process I developed. Silver blades would be much too brittle to use effectively. This will have the same effect, but with a blade that won't break off in the middle of a fight."

Bruno took the blade, turning it over and examining it. "Looks a bit shinier, I guess."

"How do you know it will work?" I asked.

"Because it's real silver," he said.

"And it'll have to work," Tony said. "Or we'll all be dead, more like than not. Now gather round, we have a plan to make, and we only have until sundown to get in place."

It was only a few hours later, as told by the pocket watch that ticked away beneath my coat. Dusk had come and gone, bathing the city in darkness and the falling fog, the streetlamps fighting a losing battle against both.

I stood alone on a corner, my coat pulled tight. Patrols were never static, never still, so the layers I wore were meant for activity, not for being stationary. So I stood there, shivering against the cold, waiting for the next steps. It wasn't my idea, being out there alone, but when all had been said, the plan laid out and our parts determined, even I could admit that no one else could break away from the job they were given. Only I had no better use.

The night was almost completely silent. At one point, a carriage passed, the sound of clopping hooves and rolling wheels comforting, the idea that someone else was out and about, but the sight did little to help. The driver hunched over, his coat pulled up such that it seemed to be just an empty shell, and no faces peered from within, the curtains drawn tight over the window. It came and went, and the silence returned.

It didn't last long, however. The cry that pierced through the night sent a shiver down my spine and goosebumps down my arms. It wasn't a scream from a victim or the terror of someone fleeing something monstrous. No, it was a howl, long and low, like a wolf calling out to its pack, or perhaps a lone wolf on the hunt. There was no response, but there didn't need to be. The creature was close.

It was hard to keep still. I tried to roll a cigarette, but my hands shook, spilling the tobacco from the paper and then dropping the paper after it. I put the pouch back; it would do no good, not if I couldn't even keep my hands still enough to roll. God, how would I be able to use a weapon?

I almost missed the sound. It was soft, like a cat dropping down from a high perch, a padding on stone. If the wind had been blowing harder or if a carriage had passed by at the right time or if there had been any other sound higher than a whisper, I would have.

But I didn't. In my paranoid state of mind, every sound, every shadow, every movement was a monster creeping up on me.

I turned at the sound and found myself staring at the beast.

Something in the past few days had made it bold, appearing on a well-lit street like this. Or perhaps the city had become too scared, the streets too empty, that this was its only choice. It creeped toward me, claws held out, jaws open so that I could see the sharp teeth and the slobber that dripped from its lips.

I wish I could say I stood there bravely, faced down the beast with a strong defiance, that I stared death in the face and dared it to take me kicking and screaming from this world. But that would be a lie. I was petrified with fear, unable to move, to even reach for one of my weapons. I didn't make a sound, didn't turn and run, somehow didn't even piss myself. I just stood there.

Luckily, I didn't have to do anything. I had backup.

The lit bomb rolled from a side alley, the fuse burning brightly, drawing the creature's gaze. Even in my stunned state, I could manage enough to close my eyes and cover my face as the bomb went off with a bang. The creature gave a yell and stumbled back, shaking its head against the flash of the bomb.

Bruno stepped out into the street, his blade drawn. He gave a roar and plunged it into the creature's back. The creature's roar blended into his own, and it flung its arm back blindly, striking Bruno and sending him flying backwards, landing hard in the street.

The creature seemed to have finally shaken off the blindness. It gave one last look toward me, roared in my direction before turning away, bounding over Bruno and taking off down the street. Anders stepped out from where he had hidden himself, aiming his pistol down the road and firing it twice. The report echoed through the buildings, but either he missed or the creature was unaffected. It didn't break stride, nor did it show any sign of pain. It just kept running, bounding onto a building and climbing over it.

The next thing I knew, I was being shaken. I looked up, and Anders was there, one hand on my shoulder, the other snapping before my eyes. "William, are you there? Come on, we need to go."

I shook my head, doing my best to rid myself of the cobwebs that infected my mind. "I'm good."

Anders looked over his shoulder, where Bruno was standing gingerly, stretching out his back. He turned back to me. "You sure? Need you at your best."

I nodded. "I'm sure."

"Then let's go, Anthony is waiting for us."

He jogged on ahead, joined by a limping Bruno. I followed in the rear, my legs feeling like lead weights hanging from my body. They gained ground on me, not stopping to wait. We all knew the route, the way to go to spring the trap. The first part was done, the beast lured out and chased back to its domain. Now for the harder part.

Tony was waiting for us at a street corner. The others reached him first, and I came jogging up a moment later.

"You saw it?" Anders asked.

Tony nodded. "The southern building. The monster climbed right up the side, up to the top floor."

I gazed up toward the top of the building, as did the others. Tony continued. "No time to waste. Everyone knows their parts."

Tony led the way into the building. The hallway was tight, a door to each side leading to an apartment and the end of the hallway taken up by stairs leading upward. There was no hesitation, Tony leading the way up toward the top floor.

I was huffing by the time we reached the third floor, and it was here that Tony stopped us. Our pace slowed, Tony motioning us to be quiet as we reached the stairs. We all paused, following his eyes up toward the ceiling, listening.

As my breathing eased, I could hear it. The creature was pacing around, stamping loudly, huffing, occasionally growling, an exasperated sound. Whatever we had done to it had done some kind of damage.

Tony led the way up the stairs, moving slowly, taking the steps one by one. He cleared the landing first, reaching the hallway at the top, the rest of us close behind. There were four doors to four apartments. Here, the sounds were louder, echoing from the end of the hallway.

Tony pointed to a spot and looked at Anders without breaking stride. "Here," he said.

Anders dropped to a knee and flipped a switch on the contraption, sticking it into the wall and drawing a string across, about knee high. Bruno and I passed quickly as Anders drew the line across the hallway, attaching it to an identical contraption on the other wall.

"Way's closed, boys," he said, coming to join us.

One of the doors opened behind Tony and a head popped out, the inquisitive look plastered upon the face of a young woman clutching a child to her breast. I quickly broke off, blocking the doorway. "Stay inside, lock the door," I said. "Find a closet and hide until it's over."

She said nothing, only giving me a wide-eyed look and closing the door, the lock clicking into place immediately. I turned and continued after the others.

Tony had stopped between the last two doors, leaning his head each way, listening to what lay behind each of them. Finally, he pointed to the one on the left and nodded.

Everyone took their places. Bruno drew his blade and exchanged his revolver for Tony's blade, leaving our leader with two pistols. Anders pulled out a trio of bombs and lit the fuse on all three. I drew my own revolver, but I could feel it shaking in my hand, nearly useless there. I could only hope that I didn't have to use it.

Nods were exchanged, and Bruno kicked in the door. He was still pulling back his leg when Anders tossed the bombs through the opening, everyone pressing against the wall to avoid the blast. They sounded off, three reports in a row, nearly deafening in the enclosed space. As soon as the third rang out, Bruno stepped into the doorway, gave a yell that I heard even over my ringing ears, and plunged through the doorway.

The ringing in my ears was fading, and I could hear the struggling from within, the growling of the beast and the grunting of Bruno. Tony waited a moment, then stepped around the corner, only to pull back immediately. Something flew through the doorway and slammed against the wall with a loud think, and it was only when it landed that I saw that it was Bruno's head.

My stomach turned, and I was certain I was about to be sick, but as it turned out, there was no time to be sick. The beast snarled as it stepped into the hallway, one of Bruno's blades still sticking from its shoulder. Tony's gun went off once, and the way the creature reacted told me it was hit, but it seemed hardly affected. It turned on a dime and backhanded Tony, sending him flying backwards.

Anders was backing up, trying to light another bomb as the creature turned toward him. The fuse caught just as the creature reached him, and it wrapped its powerful claws around his face, tearing his head clean off and spraying blood all over the hallway. The creature was already looking past him to me.

I scrambled backwards, trying to get away from it, trying to reach the stairs. I held my gun up, the barrel pointing at it, but I couldn't fire, and even if I could, it would have gone wide with the way the barrel was shaking. I was as good as dead, and I knew it.

The creature lunged at me without warning, lashing out with its claws. I felt the impact and staggered back, a hot pain flashing through my chest. Something tripped me, and I found myself flailing backwards, tumbling down the stairs.

There was a bang as my head hit the ground, and the world around me blurred, my mind losing all sense of direction, all sense of time. At some point, I landed, but I didn't know much beyond that. All I knew was that I was done for. The creature would do to me what it did to Anders, to Tony, to Bruno. I was the last one left, and I was the least of us all. There was no hope.

I resigned myself to my fate as I passed from consciousness.

There was no light at the end of a tunnel, no clouds or shining sun or angels on high. There was only darkness. Darkness and a voice.

At first, the voice was too quiet, too distorted, like trying to eavesdrop on someone through the vents in a large house. I couldn't make out the words, or even whether it was speaking to me. I did my best to block it out, to focus my attention elsewhere. To dying, I presumed. Dying shouldn't be this difficult.

The voice refused to go away, however. It grew louder, and as it did, I was becoming aware of a pain. A pain in my head and a pain in my chest. Maybe it wasn't over yet. I suppose dying wasn't supposed to be pleasant, but I'd never done it before.

The words were coming in clearer. "Mister? Mister, please."

Mister? Who was calling me?

I could feel my eyelids move, and as they did, everything became brighter. The pain was growing worse, the pounding in my head and the slow burn in my chest. Slowly, my eyes opened, even so small an act akin to lifting a carriage on my own. Slowly, the light flooded in, and I closed them again.

"Mister? Mister, you're alive!" There was a touch on my shoulder, a shaking, and suddenly, I didn't feel so fatigued. I clenched my teeth and drew in breath and heard a gasp as the touch was withdrawn. "Oh no, I'm sorry, please forgive me. You must be in agony."

I blinked my eyes, allowing the light to flood in. The scene before me was blurry, distorted, slowly coming into focus. I was at the landing, halfway between floors, laying against the wall. I tried to move, but it suddenly felt as if every muscle in my body was aching.

"Take it easy, Mister," the voice said. "You're injured. I'll fetch a doctor."

"No," I managed, the word somehow emerging from my dry throat. I managed to sit up. "No, not a doctor. My friends."

My eyes rested upon the source of the voice, the same woman from the apartment, standing now, still clutching the child to her breast. "I...I'm sorry, but they're all..."

I closed my eyes and opened them again. "No, that's impossible." My memory was coming back to me. I saw Bruno's head rolling across the hallway floor. I saw Tony flying backwards. I saw Anders ripped in two.

I tried to stand, and the woman moved to stop me. "Mister, no, you need to sit. I don't know how injured you are."

"I'm fine," I managed through clenched teeth. I stood, and when I did, I laid eyes on my chest, the front of my coat and shirt ripped open, four claw marks stretching across my chest, dried blood clinging to my clothes. I closed my eyes and thought I might throw up or faint or both, but none of it happened, and when I opened my eyes, I was still standing, the pain still very much there.

"I'm going to get a doctor," she said, starting down the stairs.

"Not a doctor," I said. "Let me see first."

She stopped, looking up at me, then continued down the stairs. I let her go. She didn't matter, no one did.

I climbed the stairs slowly, one at a time, feeling the pain rip through my body with each step. The sunlight coming through the window at the far end was nearly blinding, strengthening the throbbing in my head. I closed my eyes and pushed forward, and when I opened them, I found myself staring at a corpse.

It was a man, lying face down on the floor, naked. He was older, perhaps in his fifties, his hair silver, his body overweight. What drew my eyes, however, was the handle of the blade that stuck out from his shoulder, the ivory handle of Bruno's favorite blade. This man was the monster. Or rather, had been.

I turned him over, a much more difficult process than it should have been due to my injuries. The face that stared up at me was nearly mutilated, the man's chest and sides covered in bloody lesions. From one stuck a large shard, shining piece of metal dulled by dried blood. A piece of silver. Anders's traps had worked.

"We did it, boys," I said. "We stopped the monster."

It didn't feel like we had, though. I stood, gazing down the hallway. Anders lay a little further down, the blood between the two pieces of him still drying. Beyond him was Bruno's head, the eyes looking down the hall toward me. At the far end of the hallway sat Tony, his body partially upside down and sticking up, his head twisted all the way around.

There was only me. Somehow, out of everyone, I had survived.

Voices drifted up from downstairs. I could hear the woman speaking and a male voice responded. Was it a doctor? Or perhaps the police. Either way, I did not want to stick around, not with a scene like this.

I picked my way through the carnage that covered the floor of the hallway, reaching the window at the far end above where Tony lay. Outside the window was an iron balcony, a fire escape. I slid open the window and gingerly made my way through, stepping as quietly as I could onto the landing. I lowered the window and began the climb down to the street.

The entire time I was climbing down, I kept expecting to hear the window open above me, to have a police officer stick his head out and yell at me to stop. It was almost a complete shock when my feet touched the ground, the realization washing over me that I was alone in the alley between buildings.

I didn't wait around for someone to come looking for me. I pulled my coat over to hide the claws marks on my chest, made my way to the street, and stepped into the early morning pedestrian traffic, beginning the long walk home.

I didn't remember reaching my house or anything after, not until I awoke many hours later. The pounding in my head had been reduced to a dull ache and the claw marks itched more than burned at that point.

The light seemed little different, but the clock on the wall told me that it was now dusk instead of dawn, the sun fleeing the day instead of rising to greet it. I had stripped off all but my pants and had somehow had the presence of mind to bind my wound with gauze, wrapping it around my torso.

I sat up and rubbed my eyes. From down below, the paperboy was calling out for the evening edition of the paper, trying to sell his allotted stack to passersby on their way home from work. A paper that would likely have news of my friends, of the monster. Or was it all a bad dream? It felt like it was, but the pain said otherwise.

My body was stiff as I made my way down the stairs to the foyer and out onto the front stoop. The paperboy was in his usual spot on the corner, yelling at the top of his voice. "Get your evening edition of the Times, right here. Read about another grisly murder from the Midtown Butcher, this time with four victims. Exclusive interviews with eyewitnesses."

Eyewitnesses, huh? Only one living that I knew of, and I sure as hell didn't talk to the police. "I'll take one," I said.

He turned to me, flashing a smile of crooked teeth. "Sure thing, Mister." He handed me the paper, I handed him a coin, and I made my way back into my home.

My hand trembled as I read the paper. Their faces were there, Tony, Bruno, Anders, pictures that the paper had somehow recovered. A fourth picture was there, a man named Elias Hornsby. I skimmed through the article, reading about how he was a retired carpenter, mostly kept to himself, described by those in the building as a good neighbor.

And of course, the suspect, a skinny man in his early thirties, dressed in all black with wounds across his chest. Me. Police were compiling a sketch and would be putting out a reward for information leading to an arrest.

I burst out into laughter, a nervous, maniacal cackle right there in my foyer. Me, a killer. I hadn't even killed the monster, at least not through anything but my own clumsiness. It was a miracle I hadn't killed myself in the process. It seemed like I had tried.

My headache seemed to be returning. I tossed the paper down onto a table and made my way to the bathroom. I ran water into the sink, cold with a slight dash of hot. Once the basin was filled, I turned off the faucet and splashed the water on my face.

It didn't seem to help much. I toweled off my face and gazed at my reflection in the mirror. My skin seemed pale, paler than usual, and my eyes were bloodshot. No doubt the slash from that monster was filled with all kinds of bacteria, but a doctor seemed out of the question at the moment.

The wound was still itching beneath the stained cloth, which meant it was probably due for a change. I began to unravel it, removing it from my midsection. When I finished, I balled it up and tossed it aside, and when my eyes returned to the mirror, I found my heart caught up in my throat.

The wound was still there, but it was different. Gone were the deep gashes, the bloody trails of skin. Instead, there were only parallel scars, so faint that they seemed to almost blend in with my skin. I ran my fingers over them, feeling the slight protrusions, almost undetectable to the touch. My eyes looked down, then at the reflection, then down once more, as though my eyes were deceiving me either way. But it was real. I was healed.

"How is this possible?" I asked aloud. My head pounded and the wound itched, and my body ached and none of it felt like it was real.

A flare of pain ran through my body, as though I had been struck. I doubled over, gripping the edges of the porcelain sink. Something was happening, something terrible. The itch from the wound seemed to be spreading, coursing its way through my body, radiating out from the source, spreading like a fire through a dried forest.

When I opened my eyes, the ones that stared back in the mirror were no longer bloodshot; they were red, a deep red with dark pupils in the center. Something was pulsing through my muscles, and I could feel myself begin to change.

The porcelain cracked where I gripped it, and I fell forward, landing on my hands and knees. I could feel it now, the strength, the power, the hunger. The paper had been wrong, but that didn't mean it would always be that way. Maybe I wasn't a killer because the chance had not come. Somehow, it felt like it should be right, like I needed to make it so.

I didn't know. All I knew what that I was no longer scared, no longer timid. From the base of my throat emerged a howl, filling the room. Nothing had ever felt so right.

THE REAPER'S DUE

Long available on its own, I decided to include this as a part of this collection because I felt it really fit the theme. This is another product of /r/WritingPrompts, or at least the first part was. It was highly upvoted, probably my highest ever, and I decided to expand on it. What emerged was a novella that delves into the nature of revenge and the will of a man who refuses to allow anything to stop him from completing it. I am particularly proud of this one; though it's never been a huge seller outside of an initial run, I do feel it's one of the more poignant pieces I've ever written, which makes it a fantastic capstone to this collection.

The old man was down on a knee, one hand grasping his arm, the other clutching the hilt of a sword, the point of the blade resting on the ground. A long life this man had lived, the kind of life anyone would be proud to have. But all lives must come to an end.

The shrouded figure approached from behind, face draped in complete darkness, the cloak giving off the faintest rustle as it glided across the floor. Two pale hands gripped a long scythe, the kind a farmer would hold. But this blade was not for that kind of reaping.

The figure was within reach now, and it stopped behind the kneeling man. There were no words, no prayers, nothing spoken. There was never a reason to speak. These were the ones that came easily, because they knew that the time had come. It was the young ones, the vibrant ones, the ones still filled with life who had to be dragged kicking and screaming from the world of the living.

The blade of the scythe rose above the figure's head, the sentence to be carried out. It descended, silently cutting through the air. Silent, that is, until it struck the blade.

The old man was standing now, his eyes ablaze, the sword in his hand meeting the reaper's blade with a vibrating sound that echoed all around them. His hair was cut short, a day's growth of white whiskers clinging to his grizzled jaw, teeth clenched as the sinews in his neck strained against the force of the blow. If the shrouded figure could have shown surprise, it would have.

The words emerged from the man's throat, a growl that forced its way past his teeth and lips. "No. Not yet."

He felt the weight ease off the blade, the figure seeming to slink backwards, drawing the scythe beside it as it watched him. He watched it back, lowering his own sword, his favorite, feeling the notches on the pommel that had been made for every kill, denying the very thing that it had brought to this world for so long. It would have been fitting to accept death with the blade in his hand, but he refused to accept it.

The words came from deep within the hood, spoken as though by wind whistling through the cracks in a stone wall. "You cannot avoid your fate."

"I have delivered enough souls into your hands that I think I deserve a reprieve," he said. "And I plan on delivering at least one more before I am done."

More words, slow, quiet, spoken with a gasp. "It is your time. It cannot be changed."

"I believe I just did," he said. "I have some unfinished business to tend to." He paused, waiting for the figure to speak. "Unless, that is, you think you can take it from me."

He raised his sword and rested it on his shoulder, watching the shrouded figure. He was unsure what a fight with the reaper would be like. It might not be one that he could win, but then again, he had never lost a swordfight. He had no intentions of starting now.

Finally, the figure spoke, rasping from within the cloak. "You shall have your reprieve. How long do you need?"

"Six months." That should be enough time. Plenty of time.

"You have three."

Closer than he would like to cut it, but it would have to do. Three was more than zero. "Very well. Three."

Besides, if push came to shove, he would fight again. The reaper wouldn't be caught off guard next time, however.

"Three months." There was a gust of wind and the figure faded into darkness.

The old man sighed and lowered his sword. It was getting harder to hold, heavier by the day, but he only needed to be able to wield it for a little while longer. He meant what he had said. He had every intention of sending at least one more soul to give the reaper its due. Perhaps more. Time would tell.

He opened his free hand and gazed upon the trinket he had been holding. It was a locket, and inside was a small painting. It had cost him more than enough gold, particularly since the first few artists had gotten it completely wrong, but it was worth every shilling he had spent. The artist had managed to capture her eyes and her smile, as though she were right there with him. Perhaps she always had been.

Beneath the trinket, down along the inside of his wrist, was a tattoo. A single name. It had hurt like hell, but he wanted to make sure that he never forgot it, that he saw the name every time he looked at his arm. And when he finally plunged the sword into the sorry bastard, he would draw a blade across the name, and the reaper would have what was rightfully his.

He closed his hand over the trinket and put it safely into the pouch on his belt. He hoisted the sword onto his shoulder and began to walk. He still had a long way to go and only three months to get there.

The cold of winter seeped into the room. Even with the fire burning in the hearth just behind him, he was still shivering. His wife, however, was sweating, and had even insisted on opening a window. And who was he to refuse?

The room looked upon the garden, painted a pristine white in the dead of winter. The trees were stripped bare, the bushes devoid of their color, the ground appearing as smooth as ice, covered in a white sheet of snow.

He shivered once more as he stood by her bedside, keeping his hands clasped around hers. The midwife was urging her to push, telling her that the child was almost there. She let out a loud cry, and it was met with a louder cry, one that persisted for a moment before fading into the wailing of a newborn child.

"There you are," the midwife said. "All done."

He could only smile, a big goofy grin crossing his face as the midwife snipped the umbilical cord and wrapped the girl, his baby girl, into swaddling clothes. He felt a squeeze on his hand, and he squeezed back. The mother pressed her forehead against his hand, and he smiled down at her.

The midwife finished wrapping the child and gently placed her in her waiting mother's arms. "Do you have a name for her yet?"

"We have not," the mother replied. She stared into the child's dark blue eyes, pulling at the edge of the swaddling with her finger. "We wanted to see her before we tried to name her."

"And she is perfect," he said.

The mother gave the child a light kiss on the forehead and handed her up to him. He held her, so tiny, so delicate in his thick, calloused hands. A tiny child who would one day grow into a woman.

"I'm happy you were able to meet her before you went on campaign," the mother said. "I was afraid that if you went without seeing her, she would never have a chance to know you."

"I would desert before allowing her to grow up without a father." He gave her a kiss on his own and handed her back to her mother. "However, I do think our lord may think I have deserted if I do not come soon."

The mother held the daughter close and began to sing softly. It was a song she sang often, usually when she was alone, when she was cleaning or brushing her hair or just sitting in the gardens. He closed his eyes and listened for a moment, hearing the words and the melody and the soft tune, just as his daughter heard it for the first time.

He started to turn away, but felt a soft hand grasp his. The grip was nowhere as strong as it had been during the labor, but it was still firm. He turned and saw her looking at him with her blue eyes, the same blue eyes that the child had.

"Make sure you come back to us," she said. "To me." She looked down at the child. "To her."

"I always will," he said.

There was nothing left in his body that didn't hurt. All the years of training, of fighting, old injuries that never quite healed before they were injured once more. There were lines on his body from age and lines from scars, and most days, it was impossible to tell the two apart.

The land was at least flat here, easier to traverse, but already he could see the shapes on the mountains in the distance, the mountains where his destination lay. From the jagged peaks descended the cold winds of autumn, awakening the ghosts of broken bones and bruised muscles. Somewhere within those peaks was a grand castle, a castle he once called home. Within that castle was a lord, a lord whose name rested upon the inside of his wrist.

As he walked, he found himself glancing back over his shoulder. Each time, there was nothing there but empty road, but that did not mean he could lower his guard. His old master had always told him that there was no bargaining with Death, and despite his success, those words still rang in his mind. Every time he turned, he expected to see the dark cloak, the blade of the scythe descending to claim his soul, leaving his mission unfulfilled. Perhaps he would have seen it in his dreams as well, but those were already claimed. In his long life, his own death was far down the list of horrors he had experienced.

The road was muddy from recent rains, the slog slowing him down, causing him to tire more easily. A horse would have been ideal, but horses were hard to come by this far north. But even on foot, he had enough time. More than enough time. He just needed to make the most of it.

There were sounds from ahead of him, the plopping of hooves in the mud. He couldn't see the source, but he could hear the approach. There were at least two, the way the cadence overlapped, possibly more. He kept his head down as he walked, hoping that whoever it was would pass right on by. There were few good things that could come from a rider meeting a traveler like himself on the road.

He saw their heads first, appearing over the rise as they approached him. There was a knight, sitting tall and proud atop a massive warhorse. His face and body were hidden behind thick plated armor, his sword hung from his side and a shield bearing his sigil hanging from his saddle. Beside him was his squire, dressed in leathers instead of steel, perched upon an ass instead of a horse, carrying the knight's extra gear in addition to his own.

The knight pulled on the reins of his horse, drawing it to a stop as they drew near. "Hail, traveler," he said, raising a gauntleted hand.

"Hail," the old man said. He did not look up and did not stop as he passed the knight.

He could hear the stamping of hooves behind him as the beasts were brought around. "Do I know you, traveler?" the knight called out. "I don't believe I've seen you on my lands, but your face seems familiar."

The old man elicited a grunt. He knew the type, had heard it in the knight's tone, in the way he mentioned his lands. The words were new, his piece of the kingdom no doubt won in some illustrious conquest for his liege lord. It was those with new power who were always the quickest to exert it.

He continued walking, and from behind, he could hear the footsteps approaching, the thick plopping of the warhorse as the knight caught up to him. "Are you just going to ignore me?"

Another grunt. He may have been playing with fire with this young knight, but he owed this man nothing.

The knight was silent for a moment. "I know where I've seen your face before."

"I think you're confusing me with someone else."

"That sword says differently, old man. It is a rare man who carries a blade so boldly."

"Wherever you think you know me from, you're wrong. I am not from these parts."

The knight still paced him, and by now, the squire had caught up atop the ass. He heard the clanking of armor as the knight turned toward the boy. "William, tell me, do you recognize this man?"

"I do not, Sir Everett."

"Have you ever been to Lord Carbold's castle?"

"Only the courtyard, Sir."

"Ah, of course. You see, there's a tapestry in Lord Carbold's solar, one of a famous battle from many years ago. What was it, old man? Twenty years? Thirty?"

It had been thirty-seven, but the old man didn't respond.

"Something like that. Definitely before either of us were born. The Battle of Breakneck Ford, it was, a terrible bloody battle. Fewer people know the war than the battle. It's a bit of a misnomer, though, for the battle didn't take place in the ford, but in the marshes formed by a bend in the river nearby."

"Aye, I've heard of the battle," William said.

The old man only grunted.

The knight continued. He spoke loudly from the chest, projecting his voice before him like he was a town herald. "A mighty battle it was. It's said that thousands died on both sides, that the waters ran red with blood. It was a deadly stalemate. Until, that is, a famous knight, a legendary swordsman led a sortie into the fray. This was a man who had trained all his life, a master in all manner of blade and technique."

"I had never heard that," William said.

The old man shifted, moving the heavy blade from one shoulder to the other. He still refused to look at them, continuing to trudge through the muddy road.

"It was said that he killed three dozen men on his own that day," the knight said. "All by himself. He ensured the victory for his side, the legendary swordsman who killed so many, both in that battle and throughout his life, who is said to have never lost a duel. The incredible, invincible…"

"Enough," the old man said.

The knight drew his horse around, blocking the old man's path. The old man looked up at him for the first time, gazing upon the towering knight in the shining armor, his face still hidden. The knight looked the old man up and down.

"The artist who made the tapestry was good. You're older, yes, but it still appears to be you."

"You may believe what you want," the old man said. "I am merely passing through."

The knight once more moved in front of him and leaped down with surprising nimbleness. "Yes, you traverse my land, yet you have not paid the toll that the law calls for. Will you pay?"

The old man examined the knight. Even on the ground, he stood a head taller, broader, stronger. "I have no money."

The knight drew his blade from the sheath, the polished steel reflecting the grey light of the day. He pointed it at the old man. "Then will you duel for it?"

The old man lowered his sword, resting the point of the blade on the ground. "I am not the man you think I am. That man has already been given over to death."

The knight twirled his sword. "Then you will prove that you are not him. That will be the price of your passage through my lands."

"Sir," the squire said. "If he cannot afford the tithe, are we not to show charity? That is what the good bishop preaches."

"He can afford the price," the knight said. "The price is a duel. A duel to the first blood."

"I am not here to duel you," the old man said.

"Then I will cut you down."

The squire had gone pale atop his mount. "Sir, that's murder."

"You should walk away, boy," the old man said.

The knight took a violent step forward, the blade extended out. "Boy? How dare you? I am a knight, christened by and sworn to Lord Carbold himself. You will show me the proper respect that I am due."

"A boy can still be made a knight. Do not force me to fight you."

"You will fight me." The knight was practically screaming behind his closed helm. The squire had taken the reins of the warhorse and moved it a safe distance away, watching with a blank look on his face. The knight stepped closer. He moved slowly, each step squelching loudly in the muddy road. "I killed half a dozen men in the king's name, and I will not hesitate to kill another."

The old man leaned on the sword, his hands resting on the pommel. "If you must brag about killing, then it shows that you are not ready to take a life."

The knight attacked. His movements were slowed by the armor, but the old man could hardly claim to have the quickness he did as a youth. When the battle in the marsh had happened, he had heard afterward that he had moved like a gale, hardly seen as his sword had sliced through the men. The three dozen the knight had quoted was an exaggeration, but not the greatest he had ever heard. At the end of the day, he had just wanted to make sure that he made it home.

Now, his movements were more like a whisp, a light breeze on a summer day, but the knight moved like a boulder, lumbering whichever way his momentum carried him.

The old man dodged the knight's blows easily, one way, then the other. He used the movements, swinging the blade with his body instead of his arms, using his momentum and his opponent's. Each strike was planned, strategic, designed to place the knight further off balance while avoiding the sharpened edge of the shimmering blade.

It was a bold thrust that was the knight's doom, a lunge at a target that was already moving, already out of the way. The old man spun and struck the knight in the back with the flat of his blade, sending the armored man sprawling face first into the mud.

The knight began to rise, and the old man placed a boot on his back, driving him back down into the mud. He shoved the point of his blade into the ground, then removed a small dagger from his belt. Two quick slices severed the straps that held the knight's helm in place, and the old man ripped it off, tossing it aside.

The face beneath truly belonged to a boy, likely not yet twenty, and certainly not much older than the squire who accompanied him. He had sandy blonde hair, blue eyes, a smooth face adorned with fuzz that longed to be a beard.

The cut was quick, precise. Only the slightest bit of blood leaked from the wound, but it was blood. The first that either of them had bled. "Our duel is over," the old man said.

The knight spat mud from his mouth and clenched his teeth. He struggled, but the armor restricted his movements, preventing him from fighting off the old man's foot. "Let me up."

"Do you recognize that you have lost the duel?"

"I said let me up!"

The old man eased his foot off, and the knight scrambled to his feet. The armor no longer shined, covered in mud and grime, the knight's handsome face dirtied, marred by the scratch left by the dagger.

The knight reached for his sword, but the old man kicked it away and pushed the knight back down. "I had hoped to leave it at that, but you seem to suffer from a hubris that one sees in many young knights."

The knight was crawling away, moving awkwardly in his armor. The old man drew his blade from the dirt and walked toward the knight. He could still see the anger in the knight's eyes, the arrogance, the defiance, and beneath it, perhaps a bit of fear. It was a look that the old man had seen all too many times.

A shadow passed over the dreary day and there was a whisper in his ear, silent, raspy, almost a trick of the wind. "Give him to me."

The old man balked, the knight managing to extend the distance between them. The whisper came again. "Your promise."

"This is not him," the old man said. "This is not your due."

"All men meet me eventually."

"Not this one. He is not ready."

"The agreement can change."

"The agreement remains," the old man said.

The knight's look had changed slightly, his expression betraying confusion. The old man closed the distance and delivered swift kick to the face. The knight fell backwards, his eyes staring up at the sky. With his free hand, the old man pulled on the right gauntlet, and it came off easily, revealing the pale hand beneath.

"Sir?" He had almost forgotten about the squire. He turned and saw the boy still standing by the mounts, watching everything unfold. "What are you planning to do?"

"What needs to be done," he said. He brought the sword down, the sharp, heavy edge slicing through skin and bone, severing the hand at the wrist.

The knight drew the severed arm to his chest, holding it close as blood poured from the end. He screamed, his cries echoing across the empty road as he writhed in pain.

"Let it be a reminder," the old man said. He placed the sword on his shoulder and turned away. "Lord Carbold will soon receive a lesson of his own."

He walked past the mounts and the stunned squire. He paused as he passed them, and noticed that the squire was shaking, his eyes pointed downward. "Wrap his arm tightly enough that the blood stops flowing," the old man said. "Then get him to someone who knows how to cauterize it and treat it. If you don't, either he will bleed out, or the wound will become infected, and he will lose it."

The old man began to walk again, and he did not look back.

The blooms were always thickest at the height of spring, the trees erupting in a sea of light pink blossoms, contrasted by the deep red of the rose bushes that grew beneath them.

Even from a young age, she loved the garden during the spring, especially the fallen blooms, a sea of pink covering the ground. When she was little, she would sprint through them, scattering them to either side as birds took off from the trees at the sound of her laughter.

Today, she was joined by another, a boy her age, dressed in finery, though he had no qualms about sullying his clothing. Nor did he seem to mind that the girl wore ragged clothes, the kind that belonged to a peasant on a farm rather than a girl in a lord's castle. It was a remarkable thing about the young, the way they often saw beyond class or station.

He stood to the side and watched the children, and beside him stood a man older than himself, a man dressed in similar finery to the boy, though he was nowhere near as active, leaning on a cane to support himself. Lord Carbold, lord of the castle and his liege. And his friend.

"Do you remember being young?" he asked the lord. "Being so spry?"

"I remember," the lord said with a smirk. "You certainly still are."

"I am hardly spry. Half of your knights can match my speed, a few exceed it."

"But none of them can match your skill. You may grow slower, yet you have still never lost." The lord turned to him. "I have news. Will you accompany me to my solar?"

He turned his eyes to the garden, where the lordling was gathering up blooms in his hands and throwing them at his daughter while she squealed with laughter and ran away.

There was a hand on his arm, and he turned to find the smirk turned to something much warmer, much friendlier. "They will be fine. My son knows that it is his duty to protect her, even in the safety of our halls."

He took one last look at the children at play, then nodded and followed the lord.

The solar overlooked the garden, the colored glass doors open onto a small balcony covered in the same pink petals, allowing the crisp cool breeze into the solar. Below, he could hear the children, still laughing.

"It is such a gift to us as parents that they get along as they do," the lord said, easing into the cushioned chair behind his desk.

"There is no reason to think they wouldn't. We did when we were children, did we not?"

"Children are not their parents," the lord said. He sighed deeply. "Just as my brothers are not me."

"What troubles you, my lord?"

"You know that I am not well, have not been well for some time."

"We all have periods of being unwell. You will overcome it."

The lord coughed, and smeared blood remained when he wiped his lips. "Not this time. My doctors fear the worst. They feel that I will not make it to the winter."

"I...am sorry."

"I have enough sympathy from my retainers," the lord snapped. "I will not have it

from you as well.”

He gave a slight bow, hiding the smile on his face. “What will you have from me, then?”

“To not be so damn stiff. I am not in the ground yet, and I need you to be a friend as much as a knight. But more importantly, I need to be sure that you are there for my son.”

He gazed out the window, listening to the sounds of shouting and laughter below. “Whether you are here or not, I am still sworn to your family. I will treat him as my own.”

“It is easy to say standing across from me now. Once I am dead, my son becomes lord, something he will not be ready for.”

“No one is ever truly ready to face the pressures life throws at us.”

The lord nodded. “True, but he will be even less ready. My brothers will no doubt be chomping at the bit to take advantage of a young lord, if not seize the seat for themselves. They made power plays when I was young…”

“I remember.”

“…and my son will not have the fortitude to keep them in line as I did. Not yet.”

“His is a bright boy. I have no doubt he will succeed.”

“Bright, yes,” the lord said. “He is intelligent, no doubt. Strong, loyal, already a good fighter. And he knows his duty, knows what is right. But there are other things I see in him, traits that may make him difficult to serve under. He is stubborn, headstrong, unwilling to budge when he feels a certain way. He is kind enough, you see that with your daughter, but a temper lurks beneath, one that at its worst frightens even me.”

“Still, I take my vows to heart. Your son may as well be my own.”

“I know you do, but I want to ensure that you have more reason than a vow. We have been friends all these years, but it is time we become family. I hope you will accept a betrothal between my son and your daughter.”

He found himself speechless, choking on his words. “My lord, I…”

“You what?”

“This is…beyond gracious. I do not know what to say.”

“Say yes.”

The word was on the tip of his tongue. “What of alliances? Of other lords in the kingdom? Surely your son should be used to ensure your family’s future.”

“Alliances matter not to me. And your daughter can provide for my family’s future as well as any lady in the realm. My family matters to me. And you are family.”

“Yes, of course. I accept.”

A warm, almost sad smile crossed the lord’s face. “Good. There is paperwork to draw up, signatures to be placed, and announcements to be made, but I have people to handle that. For now, let us return to our children. I am sure they would like to hear the good news.”

They both stood. He noticed as they departed the solar that the laughter and shouting had started. Instead, there was a soft song being sung by a young girl, the notes drifting through the window with the spring breeze and following him into the hallway.

The snows began to fall as he made his way into the foothills. By the time he started his ascent into the mountains on the High Road, the snowfall was knee deep, hindering each step he took. It was common knowledge to avoid the northern reaches during the cold months, which was the reason the court had always either departed in autumn or wintered in the keep. Even the hardiest travelers could be laid low by the frigid temperatures.

He was here now, however, the first time he had braved this path during this time of year, and he could feel why, the cold seeping through to his very bones.

The sun descended early in this part of the world, or rather, what sun there was behind the grey clouds and swirling flurries. The light dipped behind the jagged peaks, casting the land into shadow in the late afternoon and drawing forth a cold that even the hardest of men would find overbearing.

The thought of stopping crossed his mind, but his heart fought harder, and his legs followed his heart. So he continued trudging through the snows, even as the temperature dropped with the coming darkness.

The light had almost completely faded, the relative warmth of the day but a fleeting memory, replaced by freezing wind and driving snow. At this point, it was no longer pride that kept him going but sheer will, and will would only take him so far before anatomy gave out. The time had come to find shelter.

Not far off the path, the snow piled up beneath an overhang, the area behind it dark. The old man pushed his way through the snow and nearly stumbled as he stepped into the dry area beneath the overhang. It was still cold, but at least it was out of the wind.

He found his way to the back wall in the near darkness and began to lay out his blanket. He was laying down when a sound caught his ear.

At first it was low, nearly lost in the wailing winds that cut through the mountains. He listened closely, straining his ears to hear, one hand gripping the handle of the blade. It came and went, like an audible mirage, but it was definitely there, almost like an echo as the words came to him in an indiscernible timbre.

He was on his feet, his legs carrying him in the direction of the sound. He left his blanket behind, but he carried his sword, holding it before him with every intention of using it.

The voice led him deeper into the mountain, the overhang revealing itself as the entrance to a cave. The air warmed around him as he walked through curved tunnel walls, worn away by years of dripping water. The voice was no longer an echo, growing louder with each step he took, manifesting itself in a song, a familiar song sung in a rugged male voice. He could see a light up ahead, a light that grew in intensity alongside the sound of the voice. Even more tantalizing, however, was the scent of roasting meat that he could now smell.

The old man turned a corner, and the fire was there. He was no longer in a cave, but once more under an overhang, the snow continuing to fall beyond the reach of the fire's warmth. The fire itself was tended by a middle-aged man, clad in ragged unwashed layers. His hair was long and stringy, his beard thick and uneven. In a gloved hand, he held one end of a spit, turning a large hunk of greasy meat over the flames.

He stood back in the shadow of the cave, observing the scene and considering his options. The man did not seem dangerous, but not all dangerous men appeared that way. The question was whether he would need to kill this man or not. Perhaps there was no quarrel here, or perhaps the reaper would have another soul to add to its docket.

It was the other man's voice that filled the space, breaking him from his thoughts. "There is no need for that sword, traveler. We're all friends around this fire."

The old man hesitated, and the man at the fire looked up at him, revealing milky white eyes. "I am no threat to you, I assure you. Put the blade down and come warm your bones."

"My apologies," the old man said, lowering his blade as he approached the fire. "It is not often I meet friendly travelers."

"Then perhaps you are traveling the wrong roads," the blind man said.

"Perhaps." He settled down on the other side of the fire, feeling the warmth seep into his bones. The scent of the roasting meat was strongest here, and he could feel his belly start to rumble. "Or perhaps they are rarer than you think."

"The way I see it, a stranger is just a friend you haven't met before."

"And how many times have you been robbed, stranger?"

The blind man gave a sly grin. "It's hard to rob a man who has nothing." The spit continued to turn in his hand as he took a drag form a dark colored bottle. He handed the bottle across the fire. "What's your name, stranger?"

The old man took the bottle and drank from it. It was mead, strong mead, sweet to the taste and warm to the veins. "I'd prefer not to say."

"Ah, I see. A mysterious traveler. No shortage of those on these roads."

"Just like yourself."

"There is nothing mysterious about me. I am just a traveler, getting by on my instincts and the kindness of others."

"Seems you have more than enough kindness to give yourself." He took another sip, the burn less on this one. He could already feel his body begin to numb. He made to offer it back, but the blind man refused."

"I've had enough. The rest is yours."

"My thanks." He took another sip, a longer one. "I find it surprising a traveler such as yourself would choose these mountains, especially this time of year."

"This time of year, no place is pleasant. The days are short, the nights long, the winds cold." The blind man shook his head. "But of course, I have no home but the roads. You, sir, I can smell it on you. The smell of home, of family, of love."

The old man clenched his teeth, fighting against looking down at the name on his wrist, against reaching into the pouch and drawing out the locket. "I have none of that. Not anymore."

The blind man only nodded. "Anger. Yes, I feel it now. You do well at masking it, and I am sorry for drawing it out. What is it that angers you, sir?"

A wind blew through the space, sending shadows from the flames dancing across the walls. "A promise," was all he said.

"I won't pry then. All I'll say is that it's no good to hold onto anger. It can eat away at you, destroy you from the inside out. It did that to me, at least until I learned to let it go."

The old man clenched his fist and felt the metal within. He looked down and realized that he was clenching the locket tightly in the palm of his hand, the string attached to it falling across the tattoo on his inner wrist.

Carbold. The name etched in ink, forever marked on his skin. A man deserving of every ounce of his hate.

"What do you know about anger?" he asked.

The blind man ran his fingers gently over his eyes. "That it cost me these. That it cost me so much more."

"Sometimes, anger is all that keeps a man alive."

The blind man was silent for a moment. "Then I will pray for your soul."

"You won't have to pray for long."

"I hope that one as hale as yourself is not so quick to cross to the other side. The world needs people like you."

"You don't know what kind of person I am."

The blind man nodded. "I do, more than you may think. But I am not one to come between a man and his wishes. Some causes are beyond the help of a wandering stranger."

"I accept your advice, though I refuse to take it."

"Very well, but I hope you take this advice. I know you make for the castle in the Hardwind Pass. They've holed up for the winter, so entry may be difficult to come by."

The old man closed his fist around the locket. "They will open the doors for me. I can guarantee that."

"Even so, the path ahead is still dangerous, even for a seasoned warrior.

The upper reaches of the pass grow even colder, and there is word that a troll has been sighted. They normally avoid the more frequented roads, but when the winter is colder than usual, like this one, it drives them from their territory, makes them bolder."

"A troll. I cannot say I've ever seen one in person. I have seen the destruction they can bring, however."

"They are big, and they are aggressive. Few men can stand against one alone. If you see it, I recommend trying to make sure it doesn't see you."

"And if it does?"

"Then I suggest you run, and make sure you pray to your god. Even with that sword of yours, your chances of killing it are not good."

"I am not meant to die at the hands of a troll," the old man said. "I will find a way if I run across it. Still, I appreciate your advice."

"I am always willing to help one in need. The roast is almost ready. Eat your fill and sleep in the warmth of the fire. It may be the last you ever experience."

"A pleasant way to think of it." But the blind stranger was right. The old man used a knife to slice off a steaming piece of meat and bit into it. Grease dripped from his chin, and it was hot enough that it burned his tongue, but he savored in the flavor, the first true meal he eaten in days. He finished the piece in a couple of bites and was reaching to cut off another chunk before he even finished swallowing.

The hunk of meat looked like it could have fed several grown men, but between the two of them, even with the blind man eating sparingly, it was soon down to the bone.

The blind man removed the remains from the spit and tossed them out into the night. "Something for the wolves to fight over," he said. "They won't come near us as long as the fire burns."

As if on cue, a long howl echoed in the distance, and another answered from a place not far away. The old man gazed out into the night in the direction of the sound. "We've seen instances where they become desperate in cold like this, just like the trolls. I remember having to post sentries to ensure our camps were not attacked when winter was at its worst."

"There is still game enough for them in these mountains, though perhaps not for long. Even the elk have begun to move to warmer lands."

The old man laid his head back. The movement of game was not something that concerned him, not like it once would have. He could feel his eyes growing heavy, his now full stomach and the day he had spent on the road both weighing on him. The locket was in his fingers, but he didn't open it, only turning it in his fingers, feeling the weight of it.

The blind man had begun to sing again, an unfamiliar song in a haunting baritone. As the old man drifted off to sleep, the song began to change, morphing itself into something much more familiar.

The young lord had given his solar to the bride, and the aging knight stood in the room as she brushed her hair, singing the song her mother had taught her so long ago.

She had grown, just as all children do. Tall and beautiful like her mother, athletic and tough like her father. Brown locks fell upon the shoulders of her cream-colored dress, and one of the maids had applied powder and paint to enhance the curves of her cheeks and the blue of her eyes.

The song stopped, and she gently placed the brush down, standing and smoothing out the dress as she examined herself in a full-length mirror. "I am not sure how I feel about this," she said.

"Your mother would be proud to see you in a dress like this," he said.

She turned in place, looking at how the dress fit her from the side. "She put me in plenty of fine dresses. They never lasted, though."

"Because you always soiled them within minutes of wearing them. She got tired of trying to keep them clean." He smiled and shook his head. "I wish she could be here to see you now."

She turned and smiled back at him, taking his hands. "I do too, Father."

There was a knocked at the door, and it opened without waiting for an answer. One of her ladies in waiting, the eldest, a large, boisterous woman who was never afraid to make her presence know. She was dressed in finery of her own, a rare sight for the woman. "My lady, your groom awaits. Are you ready?"

"Almost," she said over her shoulder. She turned back to him. "Truly, how do I look?"

"Beautiful," he said. "Just as she did."

She nodded and wiped away the wetness that had begun to form in her eyes. "Alright, before I lose my nerve."

He offered his arm, and she took it, allowing him to lead her to the door.

It was the height of summer. The colorful blooms of the spring had given way to a luscious green that spread across the garden, from the leaves of the trees to the grass below. The sides were flanked by bushes, roses red as blood and white as clouds blooming from the ends of thorny stalks, casting their fragrance upon the space.

An arch crafted from flowers stood at the far end, and there beneath it stood the young lord with the priest. The son had grown tall and broad as he had aged, a handsome lord to wed the beautiful daughter of his sworn knight.

He felt his daughter shift her grip on his arm as they walked between the rows of standing attendees. When he looked down at her, he found her unable to contain the widening smile that crossed her face. Up ahead, the lord tried to remain stoic, but even the lordly face he tried to hold could not resist the infectious grin.

They reached the end of the aisle. His daughter kissed him on the cheek, then glided across the grass to stand with her groom.

"I will take the best care of her," the young lord said.

"I know," came the response. "I will be here to be sure of it."

The lord turned to face her, and the old man stepped away, watching as the daughter and the lord said their vows.

The blind man was gone when he awoke.

The pit where the fire had been built was still giving off warmth, though the fire had been reduced to embers and ashes. The light of the sun had begun to poke through, not yet atop the eastern peaks and still mostly hidden behind the grey skies and falling snow.

The old man shook off the cold and the echo of the dream in his mind. The vision was still fresh, fading with the rising sun, but still present with stunning clarity every time he closed his eyes.

He glanced at the dying fire but decided against reviving it. Bringing warmth back to the nook would only make it more difficult to leave, would only make it harder on himself when he decided to brave the cold once more. No, it would be better to get moving now, to get the blood flowing.

His bones creaked and his muscles ached as he pushed himself to his feet. He could see the spot where the blind man had been, now vacated, but there were no footsteps. Few footsteps survived for long when the snows were this heavy. He picked up his sword and turned away from the fire's remains, stepping out into the snow.

The snow had grown deeper overnight, but he could see the path ahead. It wound upward, into the mountains, into the pass, toward the castle. Toward Lord Carbold.

The day grew brighter, and with it, the snows grew thicker. Soon, he was trudging upward, the snow accumulated on the path up to his chest in some places. The fatigue was setting in, and with it, the cold, but he continued on, sword in hand, occasionally using it to dig in, using it to support himself like a staff.

His mind was still on the dream. It was so vivid, as though he was reliving it, the sight imprinted on his mind like a painting on canvas. The blue of her eyes, the blush of her cheek, the silk of her voice. The way she had smiled when she had stood with the lord beneath the arch and the way she had laughed when they had danced.

He sighed. Remembering how happy the day had been only made it worse. Was it a punishment, perhaps a price for what he had done in denying the reaper his due?

The thoughts swirled around him like the flurries, so thick that he didn't notice the beast until he was nearly upon it. When he finally did, the entire image faded from his mind, and he froze, staring upon what lay ahead of him on the path.

It stood facing a cliff wall on the side of the road, perhaps twice his height. Thick white fur covered its body, stiff and dirty, and long arms hung down at its sides, ending in gargantuan hands. There was a definitive stench, the kind that fills the nostrils and offends the brain, nearly enough to make him gag, though he managed to hold it in. Nothing to draw attention, nothing to make it notice him.

The troll was digging at something on the side of the path, grunting loudly as it worked. The old man waited for a moment, watching, making sure it hadn't seen him. The creature never took its eyes from its work, so he started to edge his way forward, moving slowly to avoid making any noise.

The path continued sloping upwards, and it wasn't much further before he would be out of sight of the troll. He had already passed it, and it had still not budged from its spot, continuing to dig at the side of the path. He fought the urge to hurry, to increase his pace, looking between the creature and the path ahead.

From as close as he was, he could see the side of its face, the pinkish skin, the protruding snout, the razor teeth, the beady black eyes. A true monster, one that the stranger had been right to warn him of. He wanted no part of it.

He didn't feel the loose rocks beneath the snow until he stepped on them, and by then, it was too late. He could feel the ground shift, and with it, the snow. It wasn't quite an avalanche, but it was enough to create a rumble, and more than enough force to send him tumbling back down the slope, landing in a patch of icy powder right behind the creature.

The troll stopped, grunting as it glanced over its shoulder. Its beady eyes saw the disturbed snow and followed it to where the old man now lay. It bent over, examining him. He could see his reflection in the dark eyes, smell the stench of its last meal on its breath, could feel the wind as it sniffed him. Its eyes narrowed and it let out a roar, its fists rising high in the air and slamming into the ground to either side.

The fists were rising again as the old man moved. He was on his feet, sword swinging, but it only glanced off the thick fur of the beast's side, the sharp blade not even penetrating deep enough to draw blood. He leaped out of the way before the fists came down again but didn't get far. A backhand swipe sent him sprawling several meters away.

He could see the troll lumbering toward him as he picked himself back up. It moved with surprising speed and was on him before he could fully stand. It was all he could do to roll to the side to avoid another blow. He brought his blade up again, this time in the direction of one of the arms, where the fur was less thick. The blade bit into it, a splash of blood falling upon the white snow. The troll gave a roar of pain and lashed out with its other arm. It struck him in the chest, driving the air from his lungs, and he fell to the ground, pain radiating through his body.

Another blow struck him, and he felt ribs crack. Movement was hard, the snow piled around him on both sides. The troll had its hands to either side of him, supporting itself as it brought its face in close, its jaws open wide, ready to close around him.

The sword was jammed up against his body, the quarters too close to use it. His hand grasped at his belt, feeling for his dagger, finding the hilt and wrapping his fingers around it. He pulled it from its sheath as the troll bit into him, razor teeth piercing both leather and skin to dig into his shoulder. He gritted his teeth against the pain as he drove the blade into the nearest eye.

Blood ran over his hand as it seeped from the wound. The troll released his bite and let out a deafening roar. Its head jerked away, pulling the dagger from his hand. The creature staggered away, stomping around in the snow, hands clutched over its face as its roars filled the mountains.

The old man shoved the point of the sword into the snow and used it to pull himself up, holding his side. The troll was still holding its bleeding face with one hand, using its other hand to swing blindly, as though trying to hit him without seeing him. He began to move, stepping quietly as he strafed it, keeping his distance, sword in one hand while the other clutched to his side. He was limping now, his steps slow, but it was clear from the troll's movements, that it had no idea where he was.

As the creature moved, the old man's eyes were drawn to a spot on the ridge beyond, no longer obscured by the troll's body. It was all too familiar, the flowing black robe, the obscured face, the shining blade of the scythe.

I see you're keeping a close eye, he thought. *Well, I'm still not ready yet.*

There was no response, not that he expected one. The figure stood still as a statue; maybe it could have been one had it not been for the robes fluttering in the cold wind.

The old man forced his focus back to the troll. It was still swinging its arm, though its motions seemed to have slowed. He remained cautious, however; his training was in fighting men his own size, not in creatures that could crush him with a single blow. He could not afford to make another mistake, not when the next blow might shatter his bones and innards.

Blood was leaking down his arm where the creature had bitten him, leaving a bright trail of red dots that followed him as he circled the troll. He saw the creature come to a stop where the dripping had started, sniffing the air. It turned and began to follow the trail.

The old man flung his arm, gritting his teeth against the pain as he tried to scatter the blood across the area, but it was a futile effort. The troll was gaining speed, the scent guiding it in a way its sight could not.

It closed on him, swinging wildly, its hand sweeping the area before it. The old man timed it, then leaped past the swinging arm. His landing made a padding sound in the snow, and the roll gave a roar and turned toward him. He tried to jump aside but was too slow. This time, however, the troll did not strike him, but grabbed him, wrapping its long fingers around one of his legs and lifting him off the ground.

He nearly lost his sword as the troll pulled him up, holding him upside down in the air. It was looking at him through its remaining eye, its teeth bared and a low growl coming from its throat. He wasn't sure what it was waiting for, but he knew he wouldn't have another chance.

The sword in his hand lashed out, and he felt resistance as it connected with the creature's mouth. There was a roar of pain, and he felt himself flying as he was tossed aside like a ragdoll. Its hands were back to it face, and it was stumbling around, this time not even bothering to search for him. The old man picked himself up and staggered after it, holding the sword in both hands.

He moved behind the screaming beast, as fast as his own injuries and the thick snow would allow. He drew the blade up, swinging it as hard as his injured body could muster as the back of the creature's knee. The fur was still thick here, resisting the cut of the blade, but he could feel it pierce, feel it go into the skin. Blood stained the white fur, and the creature roared in pain again.

The old man was already moving, trudging through the snow as the creature fell to the ground. It was in pain, but it was still dangerous. He needed to deal with it swiftly.

It spotted him with its good eye as he came around, and he saw it squirming, making a futile attempt to reach out and grab him, to take him with it. The old man drove the sword through the troll's other eye as deep as it would go, piercing the creature's brain. It stopped in place, its mouth hanging open, the last bit of life fading from its body. Beyond, the hooded figure stood, watching.

"Not yet." This time the words came out loud, hanging in the air with the frost of his breath. He drew the bloody sword from the troll.

As he stepped away, he caught a waft of the troll's stench. He suddenly felt lightheaded, as though he was going to faint. He stuck the point of the sword into the ground, leaning on it to steady himself, fighting against losing consciousness. His shoulder felt as though it were on fire, and he looked down at the nearly forgotten bite, the blood still trickling where the sharp teeth had pierced through his leathers.

He was now sitting in the snow, though he didn't remember doing so. The sky seemed darker, as though night were coming on in the middle of the afternoon. The cloaked figure was still there, still standing silently on the ridge, watching.

"Not yet," the old man repeated, but the words came out as barely a whisper, a breeze on the still lips of a man fading into darkness.

She was already dead by the time he arrived. There was nothing that could have changed that, no way it could have been helped. Word traveled slow at all times of the year, and the journey back from the front lines was even slower.

Her body lay in the garden, as it always should have. The leaves of the trees had turned a deep red and had begun to fall, carpeting the ground in a way that was too near to spilled blood. The chill in the air ached his bones, reminding him of his age, but it was not the pain that slowed him. When he had received the news, he had begun to run and had hardly stopped until he stood where he stood now. It was only when he saw her lying there that he slowed, as though taking his time would make it any less real.

She wore a fine white dress, the kind befitting of a lady, though even in death it was out of place on her. It seemed to hang loosely on her, as though death had stripped her of part of her body. It had certainly stripped her of her radiance, the light that had seemed to surround her at all times, replaced with a pallor that nearly matched her dress, made more evident by the bright rose bouquet clutched in her hands.

The leaves crunched beneath his boots as he walked, approaching the bier. He took up her hand, her cold, lifeless hand. He fought against the tears, closing his eyes tightly, but when he opened them, they came anyway. It was not fair; someone like her did not deserve a death like this, not so young, not while someone like him was still allowed to live.

He was not sure how long he stood there. The sun was lower, nearly gone, and the temperature had dropped. The only thing that made him look up was the steward approaching, an aging man with a large belly, holding his robes tightly against the wind and carrying a torch.

"Sir, I know you are in grief, but you will catch a chill if you remain out here much longer."

"I do not fear a chill," he said. "Nor do I fear death."

A gust of wind caused the torch to flicker, sending dark shadows dancing across the garden's walls and trees and ground. The leaves glowed a richer red in the torchlight.

"How did it happen?"

"Illness," the steward said. "As the letter mentioned."

"Were there any others?"

The steward shook his head. "No. We identified it quickly and were able to keep it contained."

"I know the illness you mentioned. I have seen it at work in camps. It spreads quickly and is never contained to one person."

"Yes, that is true. We were extraordinarily blessed."

"I am also familiar with corpses of those who died from it. They develop rashes in the later stages that they scratch at, sometimes clawing straight through their skin." He pulled up the sleeve of her dress, looking down at the smooth, pale, unblemished skin of her arm. "But I'm sure you already knew that."

He could hear the crunching of leaves as the steward shifted. "Your daughter's constitution had been...weakened recently. It took hold of her quickly and killed her before it could grow so advanced."

The old man balled his hands into fists and clenched his teeth. "Where is Lord Carbold?"

"He...he was driven with grief and could not stand to be here. I am afraid he departed before you arrived because he could not...could not stand to see her like this."

"Tell me," the old man said. "Tell me what happened."

"It is as I said..."

Even with his aching bones, even with his aging muscles, his draw was quicker than any in the kingdom. The blade was out, the edge against the steward's neck. The man gave a sound akin to a squeak, the torch falling from his hand and landing on the damp ground between them, sputtering, but remaining lit, throwing their shadows across the garden.

"The truth."

"Please no, don't hurt me."

"I won't if I hear the truth."

The words came out like vomit. "It was for the good of the house. It had to be done."

"The good of the house?"

"It was a mercy. She was suffering."

He stepped forward, the blade drawing the slightest bit of blood. He could hear the anger in his own voice. "Which is it? A mercy or the good of the house?"

"It..."

"Quit stuttering and spit it out."

The dark spot on the steward's robes said that the man had lost his bladder. He wept as he spoke. "It had to be done. The lord made the call and did the deed himself."

"Where is the lord now?"

"I told you, he left."

"Where?"

"The...the..."

"Where?"

"The Lakelands. To the southeast."

He drew the sword back and sheathed it, the movement as quick and practiced as the draw. The steward collapsed to his knees and wept in the fading firelight. The old man stepped past him, pausing for a moment.

"Make sure she receives a proper burial. One that someone like her deserves."

He made it a few more steps before the steward called out after him in a shaky voice. "Wait, where are you going?"

He paused at the edge of the garden. It was all silent; even the wind had faded. A place that all his life had been filled with song, with laughter, with happiness.

"I have a promise to fulfill."

He sat straight up, awakened in complete darkness. He breathed in quickly, deeply, ignoring the pain that shot through his side with each breath.

"Where am I?" he asked, and he could feel the words nearly get trapped in a parched mouth. "What happened?"

His senses were slow to come around. The first thing he noticed besides the pain was the warmth. He was no longer enveloped by the cold of the mountain, but instead surrounded with a steady heat from the blanket that covered him and the air around him.

The pain reminded him of his wounds, and he reached up to touch them. When his fingers brushed the spot where the pain was the worst, he felt cloth. Someone had bandaged his wounds. But who?"

"Oh, you're awake."

The voice was quiet, the voice of a woman, not far away. He jerked his head in the direction of the sound. "Who are you? Where am I?"

There was a sound of metal scraping on metal, and a light appeared, slowly growing as the lamp came to life. She set it on a table next to the bed, then took a seat in a chair right by it. She seemed young, though everyone seemed young to him these days. Her face was marred with pockmarks, a piece of cloth wrapped around her thick blonde hair to hide one of her eyes. She had a slight build, as though she had spent most of her life underfed.

"You should hold off on any questions for now," she said, reaching out and adjusting the bandage on his side. "You've been through a lot, and I don't want to do anything that may put more shock on your system."

He grunted and pushed aside the blanket, moving away from her touch and putting his feet over the side of the bed. He had been stripped of most of his clothing, though she had at least left him his undergarments. It seemed like his entire chest was black and blue beneath the bandages, but he was still in one piece, so there was that at least.

The room was small, the walls carved from stone, the ground earthen. There was no window, just a bed, a chair, and the table that held his clothes and the lantern. Almost like a prison, though the door did not appear to have a lock. At least not one he could see.

"I have survived much worse as far as shocks go," he said as he grabbed his clothes and began to put them on. "Or injuries for that matter."

"You were near death when we found you, sir."

"When who found me?"

"One of our patrols."

The old man paused in putting on his leathers, then resumed as he spoke. "Only keep maintains patrols in the area I was in. Especially in this time of year."

"Yes, sir."

"Do you know who I am?"

There was a pause as she swallowed. "I do. Everyone here knows who you are. That was why you were brought here to recover instead of left to die."

The old man nodded. "Here...Hardwind Pass. The thermal caves beneath Mount Starward." He could feel it now, the way the stone walls were warmed by the geothermal activity of the mountain, how a place like this could remain so warm in the coldest of climates. More importantly were the warm springs where he had spent many a day, easing life back into tired and injured muscles.

"Yes," she said. "We've been treating you with the waters. Please, sir, you should rest more. You're not fully recovered from your wounds."

That confirmed it. He was here. He was home.

And Lord Carbold was within these walls.

"Where is my sword?"

The woman did not say anything, her eyes staring at the dirt floor beneath her feet. He slammed his hand on the table, a fresh jolt of pain running through his palm to his arm as the sound filled the room.

"Where is my sword?"

The woman jumped, wincing as though in pain. "They...they took it. Sir Galad said he would take care of it for you."

Galad. He didn't recognize the name. Of course, most of the people he had known had likely been gone for years. Just as he should have been. But he was alive, for now at least. Until the time was right.

He moved toward the door, and the girl moved to block his way. "Please, sir, you mustn't move. You are still injured."

"I have rested enough," he said. "I want to see the lord."

"Lord Carbold said he would come see you when you are well."

"Is this room guarded?"

Once more, she didn't respond. The old man grabbed her chin and turned her gaze toward him. He would have liked to say he did it gently, but the grimace she gave told him otherwise. It had been a long time since those gnarled hands had been capable of a gentle touch.

"Tell me."

"No."

"I am no prisoner here?"

She shook her head. "You are not a prisoner here."

"Then I am leaving."

The girl stepped up to him, holding her holding her clasped hands before her, looking up at him with her pockmarked face and lone eye. "Sir, you cannot leave. I was supposed to look after you, lord's orders it was. If they see that I didn't, they may take everything away from me. If the lord orders, it's as good as God's word."

He pushed past her, once more trying to be gentle, but only succeeding in sending her to the ground. "I don't intend on any innocents suffering on my behalf. You will not have to worry about the lord's wrath when I am finished."

The girl yelled out after him, and he could hear her sobs as he made his way from the room. He walked down a long hallway, carved from the same stone as the room, the same dirt floor beneath his feet. There were more rooms to either side, hidden behind thick wooden doors.

He could feel the warmth emanating off the walls around him as he walked. He didn't recognize this area in particular, but he could feel the uphill slope, taking him from the mountain's depths up toward the keep. The source for the springs was somewhere up ahead, and beyond that, the entrance to the castle. Lord Carbold's castle.

The hallway opened up into a wider cavern, a haze hanging in the air from the steam that drifted from the pools. The ground turned to stone beneath his feet, stone that was wet from moisture in the air. The room was mostly empty; he could see a couple more women tending to the few who occupied the springs, resting in their healing waters.

He strode down the path in the middle, drawing looks from the occupants, though none said a word. He made no eye contact as he walked, picking up the pace as he held to the far end. It was like the woman had said, they all knew who he was, but he didn't care. He was only here for one reason.

There was a notable temperature change as he entered the keep, despite the roaring fire in the hearth. He remembered this room well, the barracks, the guard room that all passed through on the way to the caves. It was the same as it had always been the weapons lining the walls, the armor on the racks, men sleeping on the bunked beds or playing cards at one of the tables.

The old man paused just past the doorway, looking at the guards. None had turned his way, not until one of the card players noticed him, that was. The guard stood quickly, knocking the table with his knee and nearly sending it toppling over. One of the others cursed at him before turning and reacting in a similar way.

The other guards were now taking notice. All were standing, but none drew their weapons, though a few held their hands close to the blades they wore. No doubt they knew how dangerous he was. The old man made no move.

The one who had first noticed him had gathered himself and was now approaching. The old man could see the markings of a captain on his breast, the man in charge. "Sir, we, uh, did not expect to see you."

"My sword," the old man said. "I understand you have it."

"There are…" The captain coughed and cleared his throat, then stood up straight, puffing his chest out. "Blades are not allowed in the keep other than those of the guard."

"I wasn't asking."

The captain drew his blade, but the old man could see the way that his hand shook, even standing before an unarmed foe. "I must ask you to turn around and return to your chamber. The lord will come to you when the time is right."

"I think I'd rather see him now."

The captain swallowed, still holding his blade up. Finally, he said, "Bind his hands. We will bring him to the lord."

The guards all stood where they were for a moment, before finally a pair stepped forward. The old man allowed his hands to be bound behind his back, and the guards quickly backed away. The captain nodded and turned, leading him from the barracks. Others walked beside him, but none touched him. None dared to.

It had been years since he had walked the halls of the keep, but everything seemed just as he remembered, as though frozen in time. The arched ceilings, the suits of armor, the tapestries, the rugs, the way the cold seeped through the stones despite the torches and braziers lining every wall. These walls held a familiarity, bordering on comfort, though they could never again be his home. Not with what had happened here.

The old man had no concept of time in the room but was greeted to a raucous sight as they entered the main hall. The occupants of the keep were settling to dinner, the lords and retainers seated to a feast at the long wooden tables. The smell of roasted meat and mead filled the air, the sounds of conversation rendering anything said lost on deaf ears.

He did not have to look very far to find the lord. The head table sat upon a small dais, and it was there that Lord Carbold sat, his food spread before him. He was not alone, however. Seated next to him was a younger woman, a glowing smile on her face, her fingers interlocked with the lord's.

As the old man watched the lord, his teeth grinding and his fists clenched, a man broke away from one of the tables, rushing over to where they stood. He was dressed nicely, in the kind of finery that a newly minted knight would waste his money on. He was tall, broad, and bearded, like a bull stuffed into colorful silks. He was also frowning, the expression forming a crease in his wide forehead.

The captain saluted as the man approached. "Sir Galad."

Galad had to practically shout to be heard. "What is this man doing here? He was not to be allowed from the healing room, by Lord Carbold's orders."

"He just appeared. I have not heard why they let him leave."

"Did you think to find out? Or take him back?"

The captain stole a look back at the old man. "He...insisted on coming before the lord."

"Insisted? Did he hold you at knifepoint? With his arms tied behind his back?"

"He was not bound. We did that."

"Brilliant. Did anyone think to put a guard at the door as well?"

"It was insisted that he was not a prisoner."

Throughout the entire exchange, the old man never took his eyes off of the lord. Gradually, the conversations in the room had died off as the knight and the guard captain went back and forth, until they were the only ones speaking, and all eyes were turned toward them. It was as the last bit of talk vanished that the lord finally met his gaze.

"Sir Galad." The younger lord had always had a commanding voice and it could still fill the room, though it had grown deep and worn with age.

The knight turned away. "Yes, my lord."

"Bring him here."

Sir Galad turned and motioned with his head. The captain stepped aside, and the old man stepped forward.

All eyes were turned on him, and he could feel them as he walked toward the front of the room. It was nothing he wasn't used to, nothing that unnerved him. His eyes, however, never left the lord as he walked past the quiet whispers.

Finally, he stood before the dais, looking at the lord and his new wife over plates of uneaten food. Up close, he could see the youth and beauty of the girl, the girl who had replaced his daughter. He could also see the age on the lord, the weight he had put on, visible even beneath the thick furs he wore, and the hair cut short over the receding hairline.

"Untie him," the lord said. "I will not have him in this castle as a prisoner. Not a hero like this."

The captain stepped forward and quickly undid the bindings before stepping back. The old man said nothing. He could feel his teeth clenching together as he fought back the urge to kill the man right there.

"I did not expect to see you today," the lord said. "They said you were still recovering. I would have prepared a place of honor for you."

"To patronize me?" the old man asked. "To rub it in my face as you sit there with that girl in her seat?"

"To honor you. You know as well as I that your tapestry still holds a place of honor in these halls."

"I would never break bread with you," the old man said. "Not unless it was over your corpse.

The lady gasped, but the lord only frowned, his lips pressed tightly together. All eyes were on them, and the whispers were growing, though none dared speak out. "Do old grudges truly die so hard? Can you not accept that she grew ill, that her passing was the work of God?"

"Your own steward told me the truth."

"A man will tell any truth you wish to hear when a sword is at his throat."

"'For the good of the house,' he said. Hardly the ravings of a man thinking only of his life."

"Do you truly think I killed her? That I did not spend years mourning her the same as you? That even as I accepted a new betrothal, I wasn't thinking only of her?"

The lord's young wife was looking at him, a look that could have been sympathy or sorrow at his words, but she remained silent.

The old man shook his head. "No, I don't." He slowly pulled up the sleeve, revealing the tattooed name on his wrist. "And no, this is a grudge that will not die."

The expression remained the same as the lord nodded. "You were always a wild card. Father knew that too. I tried to keep up with the news from the south, of the tales that always followed you wherever you went. They said you had died, not long ago."

"Not yet."

The slightest of smiles. "I see that. Sir Holland always said that the reaper himself would have to drag you kicking and screaming from this life."

The old man shifted in place. "I didn't come here to talk of the old times. I came here for you. I owe the reaper a soul."

The lord's wife gasped once more, and the lord patted her on the arm to calm her. "Sir Everett's squire brought us news of what you did to the knight on the roads. When I heard, at first I couldn't believe it was you, not after the news of your supposed death. I was hopeful, hopeful that you were coming to forgive, to bridge the gap between us. I did call you father once, because once he died, you were the closest I had. When they told me they had found you half-dead in the mountains, I told them that they must bring you here, that they must nurse you back to health, because I just knew that you were here to talk."

The lord shook his head. "It seems I was wrong."

"You were wrong," the old man said. "A million times wrong."

Another sigh from the lord. He patted his wife's arm once more, then stood. "Come, then, we will settle this. Sir Galad, fetch his blade."

"My lord, is this wise…"

"His sword." The words were curt, the tone final. "Bring it to the garden."

The old man did not need to be led; he knew the way, but he followed the lord and his guards nonetheless. Through the door behind the dais, past the Eagle Tower stairs, out the thick wooden doors that held out the worst of the cold. He reached the threshold, took a deep breath, and stepped into the garden.

It seemed a shell of the garden from his dreams, and yet so much more brilliant at the same time. The winter winds had stripped the trees of their leaves, yet the snow and sleet had fallen and frozen on the branches, leaving behind crystal leaves that caught the fading light of the day. The walls of the castle rose around them, balconies and sealed windows and the Eagle Tower stretching above it all, ending in the pointed spire where the golden birds made their roost in the warmer months. All around them, even higher than the tower, were the snowcapped peaks, a reminder of the heights in which the castle was built and the power of the nature around them.

The ground was covered in snow, smooth from a fresh dusting, the flurries still falling in the fleeting light. Beneath the trees, he saw the bushes, the roses normally so brilliantly colored and fragrant in the summer months now buried in powder. At the far end, there was something new, something he did not remember from before, that had never been there in his dreams.

There was a slab of stone, rising above the ground. Winter roses grew from beneath the snow on either side, their dark violet petals blooming amidst the white of the garden. On the slab rested a lone sarcophagus, carved from marble and sealed with a matching lid.

Beyond the sarcophagus was her.

She may as well have been frozen in stone for how skilled the sculptor had been. The soft eyes, the small hands clasping the rosary at her waist, the way her hair fell in ringlets upon her shoulders, her mother's cheeks and his own athletic build. His baby girl, cast in white marble.

"She loved this garden," the lord said. "I could never bury her in a dark place, even if her rightful place was in the crypt."

"I don't need you to tell me that she loved this place," the old man said. He stepped forward, his feet sinking into the freshly fallen snow, leaving a trail of footprints as he approached the grave. "And she deserved to be far away from you."

"She was a Carbold," the lord said. "Whether you agree or not, it matters not to me."

The old man reached the grave and stopped. The stone was mostly cleared of snow, the fresh fall leaving only a mild dusting. He gazed over it, ran his hand over the smooth stone. They kept it clean, but none of them deserved to touch it. Not the lord's attendants. Certainly not the lord himself.

The garden was silent. Even the snow seemed to be paying heed to the dead woman in the grave, the flakes seeming to fall around it without landing. For a moment, there was no lord, no lady, no guards, no knights, no retainers. Just the old man and his daughter.

He pulled the locket out of his pocket and looked at it once more. The painting was still there, a bit faded from travel, but it was still her. The artist may not have been as renown at his craft as the sculptor, but looking at the two, there was no comparison. The statue was bigger, more prominent, would last for centuries before fading to dust, but the painting was a truer depiction. It was colorful, vibrant, full of life, just as she had been. Not cold, empty, still.

The old man brought the locket up to his face and pressed his lips against it. He closed it, making sure it was latched, and put it on top of the sarcophagus. He then turned away.

There were no retainers, not that he could see. No doubt they had sprinted away to the upper rooms, peering through the closed windows in a hope to get a glimpse of the battle to come. Even the knight had departed, leaving the lord alone with his wife. He held his sword in one hand, while she grasped his other, looking up at him.

"Don't do this," she said. "He will kill you."

"There is no other way," he said. "I know him. He will never stop."

"What of our family? What of your brothers?"

"They will do what they will do. It will not matter, because I will win."

The wife glanced toward the old man, then back to her husband. "You are the lord, put an end to this nonsense."

He kissed her on the forehead. "Go tuck yourself into bed. I will join you soon."

"I will be praying for you," she said. One last glance toward the old man, and she was gone.

"Did you show such tenderness to my daughter before you killed her?" the old man asked.

The lord held his sword in his hand, as though weighing it, testing the balance. "I had hoped that visiting her would grant you solace. Has it not?"

"It has only strengthened my resolve."

"Very well."

There was a thump, and the old man turned to see his sword lying in the grass. Above, the doors to the lord's solar closed, once more leaving them in solitude.

"Go on, pick it up," the lord said. "Let us be done with this charade."

The old man picked up the sword and tested the weight of the blade. It felt as though it weighed several more pounds more than it had when he had last held it, yet the feeling of it in his hand gave him comfort.

"Let it be said that I did all I could to avoid this."

"There was only one way this could have been avoided." The old man leveled his blade at the lord, fighting against the shaking in his arm and the pain in his side. "Now quit talking and fight."

Neither made an immediate move. They circled each other in the snow, each of them testing their footing, watching their opponent's movements.

The lord was the one who struck first, a feint to the left that the old man easily blocked. Not a serious attack but a test on his injured side.

The lord pulled back after the feint, frowning as they continued to circle. "You are in no condition to be dueling. The troll nearly killed you. Should have killed you."

"Quiet," the old man growled.

"Was it not you who taught me to always respect your opponent? An unfair fight is no victory."

The old man gritted his teeth. "Was it a fair fight when you drove the blade through her chest?"

There was the slightest stutter in the lord's step. "She died of an illness."

"She died to your blade. Speak the truth."

"I do."

"Your own actions betray you."

The lord lowered his sword. He looked away and shook his head. "I...you're right. She asked for it. She was begging me to end her suffering."

The old man gave a cry and rushed at the lord, casting a flurry of blows at him. The movements felt different, though, slower, as though he was moving through water. There had been few fighters in his experience who could match him blow for blow, and Lord Carbold, even in his younger days, had never been one of them. Yet the lord deflected each one, as easily as if they came from a green squire.

It was only when the lord dodged away instead of parrying that the old man took a step back to catch his breath. The lord's breathing had increased as well, but he hardly seemed as fatigued.

"Your anger betrays you," the lord said, raising his voice so that it filled the garden. "You know what I say to be true. I did her a service. I was her angel of mercy when the pain was too great, and I honored her here, in her favorite place. Would a murderer do such a thing?"

The old man's head swam from the pain. He staggered, then took another step in an attempt to hide it. Not yet, it couldn't happen yet. "Only a murderer who wishes to convince even himself of his innocence."

"There are many in this castle who saw here on her final days. They saw what happened to her."

"People who would lie for you."

Another rush. Another series of blows. More easy parries and easier dodges. The lord stepped away, but the old man pushed the attack, following him through the snow. The move seemed to catch the lord off guard, enough that the old man was able to lock blades with him.

They stood there for a moment, each pushing against the other's strength, faces inches from each other as their feet grasped for purchase in the snow.

The lord was stronger, younger, healthier. He managed to push the old man backwards, knocking him to the snow. The old man attempted to roll, seeing the blade flash as it lashed at him and feeling the bite in his left arm as the steel cut through cloth and skin to draw blood.

He regained his feet from the end of his roll, holding out the sword with his good arm while trying to examine the wound on the other. The cut had taken him on the back of his arm, out of his sight, but he could see the trail of blood he had left on the white snow. Too much. He needed to end this. Quickly.

"Don't make me kill you," the lord said. "You are a hero, and you were like a father to me. I do not want your blood on my hands."

"Your hands are already stained with the blood of my daughter. They will not be stained with mine."

Their blades met again, the lord pushing the advantage. The old man held his own, but he could feel himself moving slower, struggling to keep up. The ache in his ribs and the burning in his left arm were felt with each movement, the pain steadily growing worse.

More blood was drawn; a cut on the lord's forehead, a gash in the old man's leg, a chopped little finger on the lord's off hand, a piercing cut in the old man's lower belly. Blood stained their clothes and their blades and the snow around them, painting the garden in deep red splotches.

"Give up," the lord said as they once more stood apart. "You have bled me, and I have bled you. Let us bind our wounds and speak as the friends we once were."

The old man was hunched now, breathing hard, feeling the lightness in his head. "I will not until I have seen you bleed out."

"You will bleed out long before me."

There was movement by the sarcophagus, a rustling of wind perhaps, the winter roses shaking as a dark figure glided past the statue. The old man blinked his eyes and shook his head, and it was gone.

The lord followed his gaze toward the grave, then turned back. "What, are you seeing things now? You are dying, old man."

He shook his head again, but his legs didn't want to hold him up, his eyes didn't want to see straight. "Not. Yet."

"You will die unless you accept my help. We saved you from the brink of death from the troll, and we can do it again. Lay down your sword."

The old man breathed in deeply and summoned what strength he had, forcing himself to stand up straight. He couldn't bring the sword all the way up, the tip resting in the bloody snow, but he tightened his grip on the hilt.

"No."

The lord wiped a hand over the cut on his face, smearing blood across his forehead. "She certainly got her stubbornness from you. Even as she was sick, when she knew she was dying, she held on for so long, until the pain was too unbearable."

The old man tried to lean against the sword, but the tip slipped in the snow. The sword fell out from beneath him, and he fell to a knee, his free hand planted into the ground. It was all he could do to stay upright, the wounds continuing to leak blood onto the snow. His energy had fled him, any strength lost to the wounds he bore.

The lord was approaching, his boots crunching in the snow. The old man forced himself to look up, to look beyond the approaching man, to the grave. The shrouded figure stood beside it, but it did not look at him. Its hooded head was turned toward the winter roses, one pale hand holding the scythe while the other cradled one of the blooms. At its touch, the bloom seemed to darken, growing a shade of maroon that was almost black in the light of the garden.

The voice came as a whisper, as though the wind was rustling the leaves of ice that hung from the trees. "You promised."

"I…" He looked down to the red stained snow beneath him, the pristine white surface soiled by their bout. "I am too weak."

"The flesh is weak, but the spirit is strong." The figure stepped down from the grave, the base of its tattered robe only faintly brushing the white below. "If the spirit was weak, you never would have been able to stave off your fate."

"How can I if the flesh is weak?"

The lord stopped before him and crouched down. He stole a look back toward the grave. "What are you seeing there, old man? Is it her? Is she telling you the truth as you die?"

The old man said nothing. He only listened to the whisper that floated through the garden with the falling snowflakes. "You promised."

The lord's voice was lower now. "All these people, they were listening to the truth, the truth that you refused to accept."

The old man felt his own voice in his throat, the sound as weak as his body felt. "Your steward said for the good of the house."

"Everything I do is for the good of the house," the lord said. "I wish you could see that."

The old man shook his head. "Not that. Not her."

"No, you're wrong." The lord stole another glance over his shoulder. Beyond, the old man could see the young wife watching from a balcony, the only one brave enough to come outside to watch. "What they heard is the truth because it is how it was written, how those who come after us will know it. But it had to be done. For the good of the house."

"Liar."

"You have only known violence in your life. The only good of the house you know is that which can be dispatched with a blade. You don't consider what happens when someone grows ill, when an illness can spread through closed quarters, the way it can decimate an entire castle."

"No different than a camp," the old man said. "But we never kill our own."

"It is when your brother means to take your keep from you and destroy what your ancestors have built to sate his blood lust," the lord said. "Or when you know that an illness will destroy a womb, and that you know that you must find a way to continue the line for the sake of your people? What choice does a man have?"

"He accepts that which God gives him."

The lord was speaking through clenched teeth. "That is not good enough. Did you ever have to look into the eyes of your men and tell them that they must serve under a sadistic man who would send them to their deaths? Or that you have sentenced them to death because you chose to save one who was already dead? Tell me."

The old man remained silent.

"No, you never did. You never had to. But some of us, some of us have to make impossible decisions." He shook his head. "She had more than your stubbornness. She had a violent streak too. It was rare, but it came out. Just like yours did in battle. You were like an animal, you know, unleashed on those who never had a chance. They can speak of your heroics all they want, of the duels you won, but they never knew the blood lust you had. But that changes today. They see the real you now, the man driven mad by grief who turned on the lord he once served so loyally, who will stop at nothing to kill."

The old man gritted his teeth and tried to get up, but his knee lifted little more than an inch before falling down.

The lord shuddered. "Perhaps it was a blessing that she never bore me a child. I do miss her, but the world is better off without your brethren walking it."

The old man was gritting his teeth as he tried to move. But it felt different now. The fatigue was still there, but the pain seemed to be fading. The whisper came once more, so close it may have been in his ear itself. "You promised."

The lord stood, raising his blade to deliver the final blow. "I hope you look forward to the hell that awaits you."

The blade descended, and the garden rang with the sound of steel on steel.

The lord couldn't mask the surprise on his face as the old man rose, pushing back against the blade. The lord broke it off and stepped back, allowing a smile to cross his face. "Let it not be said that you allowed yourself an easy death."

The old man lunged toward him, and their blades met once more.

Moving was like watching someone else in his body. He no longer felt anything, no pain, no fatigue, no coldness. His entire body had gone numb, his movements as quick as he could ever remember them being.

The lord was the one on the retreat, taking cuts as the old man delivered them. First to his leg, then to the shoulder, then another to his side. The last came on a desperate counterattack, where the lord left himself exposed. It worked, at least partially. The lord's blade caught the old man in the side, but the old man did not feel a thing as he drove his own blade through the lord's belly.

Lord Carbold gasped as the sword entered him. He staggered back, ripping the hilt from the old man's hands. The lord dropped his own sword and attempted to pull the other blade from his belly, but only managed a few inches before he fell forward. He stopped himself before hitting the ground, holding himself up with what strength remained.

The old man said nothing as he stepped toward the dying lord. He grabbed the sword by the hilt and pulled it out of the lord's chest in a single motion. The lord somehow remained up, but his breathing was heavy, the arm supporting him shaking as he held his other hand to the bleeding wound.

"For you, my little girl."

A single swing, and it was done. The lord's head tumbled from his neck, rolling along the bloody snow before coming to a stop. A scream pierced through the garden as the body collapsed to the ground, and Lord Carbold's reign officially ended.

The old man stood there in the snow, staring at the lord's body. All around him was the sound of hushed conversation, and that of quiet weeping. He drew his eyes upward and saw that the retainers had made their way to the balconies and windows, talking quietly, their faces painted with wonder and fear. On the balcony of the lord's solar, his widow had collapsed to a sitting position, her face covered as she sobbed.

Perhaps the lord had been right on one thing; the world did not deserve someone like him.

The lord turned his gaze away from them, tossing his sword to the ground. The lord had a blade on his belt, a small dagger, and the old man bent over and drew it. With the blade in hand, he limped his way to the grave.

The shrouded figure had returned, his appearance clear as crystal. He stood next to the sarcophagus, watching the old man from behind the dark hood. The old man ignored the figure, stepping up to the grave and putting his hand on the cold stone.

The figure seemed to lean in toward him, casting a shadow across the grave. "You promised."

"And I am a man of my word."

"Now."

"In a moment."

Feeling was returning to his body, the fatigue, the pain, the cold. It was time, time to end this. Everything he had come here for was accomplished.

He kissed his fingers and touched them to the sarcophagus, then leaned against it and eased himself into a sitting position. He slowly rolled up the sleeve on his left arm, revealing the tattoo. Part of it was covered in drying blood, and the skin around it was growing pale, but the writing was as clear as ever.

He hardly felt the blade as it pierced the skin of his wrist. Even with a shaking hand, the cut was straight, slicing through the skin across the letters of the lord's name. Blood poured out over the ink, dripping down his arm to the marble below.

The cold began to fade, and with it, the pain. He felt a shadow pass over him as the figure stepped forward. He closed his eyes, took a deep breath, and willingly gave his soul over to the reaper.

Somewhere in the distance, he could hear a soft voice singing a familiar song.

I hope you enjoyed these stories. If you did, I would greatly appreciate it if you took a moment to rate it on Amazon or Goodreads.

If you'd like to receive updates on future works and other news, please subscribe to my mailing list on www.drewmontgomerywrites.com. I promise not to spam, plus you'll get a free short story for signing up!

ABOUT THE AUTHOR

Drew Montgomery is a graduate of Texas A&M and the author of books such as <u>The Last Dragonkeeper</u>, <u>The Burial</u>, <u>Taika Town</u>, and <u>The Elder Gods</u>. He currently lives in Houston, TX, where he moonlights as a product manager. When not writing, you can often find him reading, playing video games, drinking craft beer, and occasionally watching and complaining about the local sports teams.

You can find him in many places on the web:

Website: https://www.drewmontgomerywrites.com/
Patreon: https://www.patreon.com/drewmontgomery
Twitter: https://twitter.com/dmontgomery008
Reddit: https://www.reddit.com/r/drewmontgomery/
Facebook: https://www.facebook.com/drewmontgomerywrites

www.ingramcontent.com/pod-product-compliance
Lightning Source LLC
Chambersburg PA
CBHW071927150726
47999CB00001B/134